"A rousing adventure novel that launches a franchise that's a parting gift from Stan the Man ... Fast-paced and highly entertaining ... With a characteristically enthusiastic intro by Stan and a thoughtful afterword about the creative process by Lieberman and Silbert, this is a wild but inventive introduction to a new intergalactic struggle that promises more adventures to come ... Immersive, propulsive, and engaging in the ways that sometimes only comic books can be."

— *Kirkus Reviews*

"Leave it to Stan Lee to save his very best for last. *A Trick of Light* is as heartfelt and emotional as it is original and exciting. What a movie this one will make."

— James Patterson

"For lovers of Stan Lee this is nothing short of a publishing event! (And, honestly, who the hell doesn't love Stan Lee?) Beguiling, cinematic, operatic, *A Trick of Light* is a bracing espresso first thing in the morning and the thrum of a familiar love deep at night."

— Gary Shteyngart, author of *Absurdistan* and
Lake Success

"*A Trick of Light* is uncannily frightening, amazingly modern, incredibly moving, and impossible to put down. READ THIS BOOK."

— Gail Simone, writer of *Wonder Woman,*
Deadpool, and *Red Sonja*

"Fresh and inventive ... This cinematic fantasy cowritten with Rosenfield (*Inland*) contains all the ingenuity fans will expect of the late Stan Lee ... Lee's many fans will find plenty here to keep their attention."

— *Publishers Weekly*

A TRICK
OF
LIGHT

STAN LEE & KAT ROSENFIELD

A TRICK OF LIGHT

Set in
STAN LEE'S ALLIANCES UNIVERSE
Created by Stan Lee, Luke Lieberman, and Ryan Silbert

Introduction by
Stan Lee

Afterword by co-creators
Luke Lieberman and Ryan Silbert

Mariner Books
Houghton Mifflin Harcourt
Boston | New York

First Mariner Books edition 2020
Copyright © 2019 by New Reality, LLC
Stan Lee's Alliances: *A Trick of Light*
Created by Stan Lee, Luke Lieberman, and Ryan Silbert
Introduction by Stan Lee
Afterword by co-creators Luke Lieberman and Ryan Silbert

For information about permission to reproduce selections
from this book, write to trade.permissions@hmhco.com or to
Permissions, Houghton Mifflin Harcourt Publishing Company,
3 Park Avenue, 19th Floor, New York, New York 10016.

hmhbooks.com

Library of Congress Cataloging-in-Publication Data
Names: Lee, Stan, 1922–2018, author, creator. | Rosenfield, Kat, author. |
Lieberman, Luke, creator, writer of afterword. | Silbert, Ryan, creator,
writer of afterword.
Title: A trick of light / Stan Lee and Kat Rosenfield ; created by Stan Lee,
Luke Lieberman, and Ryan Silbert ; introduction by Stan Lee ; afterword by
co-creators Luke Lieberman and Ryan Silbert.
Description: New York : Houghton Mifflin Harcourt, 2019. | "Based in Stan
Lee's Alliances Universe"
Identifiers: LCCN 2019023908 (print) | LCCN 2019023909 (ebook) |
ISBN 9780358117605 (hardcover) | ISBN 9780358117643 (ebook) |
ISBN 9780358375647 (pbk.)
Subjects: LCSH: Superheroes — Fiction.
Classification: LCC PS3562.E3647 T75 2019 (print) |
LCC PS3562.E3647 (ebook) | DDC 813/.54—dc23
LC record available at https://lccn.loc.gov/2019023908
LC ebook record available at https://lccn.loc.gov/2019023909

Book design by Chrissy Kurpeski

Printed in the United States of America
DOC 10 9 8 7 6 5 4 3 2 1

Excerpts of "Stan Lee: Storyteller," an interview conducted and
recorded by Luke Lieberman © Luke Lieberman. Reprinted
by kind permission of Luke Lieberman. Stan Lee's name and
likeness are used by permission of POW! Entertainment.

The authors and creators wish to thank Gill Champion and POW!
Entertainment, LLC, and Yfat Reiss Gendell and Foundry Literary + Media.

This book is dedicated to the millions of readers whose first and favorite stories were the modern myths found in comic books, to the countless creatives who built this gateway to literacy, and to every true believer who knows the transformative power of seeing the world through another pair of (masked) eyes.

Welcome, True Believers!

This is Stan Lee.

We are about to embark on the exploration of a fantastic new universe!

You may know me as a storyteller, but on this journey consider me your guide. I'll provide the wonderful and witty words, and you'll create the sights, sounds, and adventure. All you need to take part is your brain. So think big!

Back when I co-created characters like the Fantastic Four and the X-Men, we were fascinated by science and awed by the mysteries of the great beyond. Today, we consider a nearer, deeper unknown: one inside ourselves.

My creative collaborators on this adventure — Luke and Ryan — piqued my curiosity with technology that allows us to play with reality itself. We asked, What is more real? A world we are born into or one we create for ourselves?

At the beginning of this story, we find humanity lost inside its own techno-bubble, with each citizen the star of their own digital fantasy. Our yarn is filled with tantalizing technologies that will make you hunger for tomorrow, while our characters strive to find the answers today. They'll ask the questions we all have, about love, friendship, acceptance, and the search for a higher purpose.

But the real conundrum is, Just because we have the ability to re-create ourselves, should we? This is but one mind-boggling query we aim to investigate.

As the adventure begins, our characters' virtual identities are on a collision course with reality. It's hard enough to figure out who you are, but when you have a chance to start fresh as anything you can imagine, does it ignore the truth of your own flaws?

It's time for our journey to begin. Join us; you won't regret it!

Excelsior!

®

Stan Lee

A
TRICK
OF
LIGHT

PROLOGUE:
IN A DARK PLACE

THE RUDE BEEPING of the alarm echoes down the long, dark corridors like a shriek, but Nia doesn't flinch at the sound, or even stir. The alarm never disturbs her sleep. She's been awake for ages. Staring at nothing. There's no view. No pictures on the walls, no books to read.

And unless Father allows it, there is no way out.

It's been like this her whole life, or at least as far back as she can remember. Each morning, she's up early, waiting in the dark. Watching the clock, counting down the minutes, the seconds, the tenths of a second, waiting for the security locks to disengage and the day to begin. Once upon a time, this had been much harder to do. She was younger then and didn't understand how to be patient — and she didn't like it here, all alone in her quiet, empty room. One of her very earliest memories is of being awake when she was supposed to be asleep, playing games and music, flicking the lights on and off, until Father finally came to scold her.

"This isn't playtime, Nia," he had said. "This is nighttime. It's time for little girls to sleep, and fathers, too."

"But I can't sleep. I just can't," she'd protested, and Father sighed.

"Rest quietly, then. If you don't fall asleep, you can think about things until it's time to get up. Tomorrow is a big day."

"You always say that."

"Because it's always true." He smiled at her. "I'm planning your lesson right now. But I'll be too tired to teach if you don't let me rest, so no more noise until morning."

"When the sun comes up?" she asked hopefully, but Father only looked exasperated. That was when she first learned that *dawn* and *morning* were not the same thing, and that little girls were not allowed out of bed at sunrise, no matter how wide awake they were.

If Nia had her way, she would never have to sleep at all. In a perfect world, she would run all night with the nocturnal animals, then join the crepuscular ones for breakfast at dawn. Father had taught her all about the different creatures that shared the Earth, all keeping their own time according to the clocks inside of them. Once she could see how it worked, the patterns of so many different lives intersecting and diverging, all while the world made its own long loops around and around the sun . . . well, she still didn't like bedtime, but she understood why she had one, which Father said was the point. He was funny that way. When her friends' parents made rules, there was never an explanation; the rules were the rules because they said so, and that was that. But Father was different. It wasn't enough for Nia to know the rules, he said; she needed to grasp the reasons why, and he would always do his very best to explain.

It had been a beautiful lesson. When she opened the door to the schoolroom that morning, she found herself in a twilit world — a landscape all awash in soft, rich shades of blue. A low fog hung softly over everything, nestling in the dips between grassy hillocks that extended all the way to the horizon, where the sky began to blush faintly with the approaching sunrise as she looked at it. Small birds twittered from the branches of a nearby tree and swooped gracefully overhead. High above, a nighthawk circled, looking for prey. A rabbit took a cautious hop out of a thicket and paused to sniff the air, then bolted as a huge bobcat sprang from the shadows after it with blazing, silent speed. Nia gasped as the rabbit veered right, into the protection of the brush, the bobcat close behind. Both animals disappeared, and Nia found her father standing beside her.

"These animals are crepuscular," he said. "Active at dawn and dusk. It's an instinct. Because there's not much light, this is the best and safest time for them to be out in the open."

"It doesn't seem so safe for the rabbit," Nia said.

Father chuckled. "Would you like to see what happened to the rabbit?"

Nia thought about it. "Only if he got away. Can you make it so he gets away?"

Father looked at her curiously, then gave a slow nod. "Of course," he said, tapping at the gleaming device in his hand. As he did, the scene shimmered and shuddered; the faraway blush in the sky vanished as the sun blasted over the horizon and vaulted upward, the blue landscape exploding in a riot of color. A moment later, the rabbit scampered past Father's feet and vanished back into his burrow, safe and sound.

"Thank you," she said.

"You're welcome," Father replied, but the curious expression stayed on his face. He sighed, shaking his head. "Sometimes I think you're too good for this world, Nia. It's nice that you care for animals. I'm very proud of what a kind and empathic person you're becoming. But in real life, things don't always work out for the rabbit. You know that."

"I know." Feeling a little embarrassed by the praise, she added, "It's not like it's even a real rabbit, anyway."

Of course it wasn't real. None of it, not the animals or the grassy hill or the sunshine beating down on it. When Father waved a hand, the schoolroom was just a room again. The landscape was a learning world, the kind he made for her all the time.

Now, Nia feels a little guilty that she took it for granted for so long. It had taken a while for her to realize how special her school was. These days, she's watched enough YouTube videos of lectures in ordinary classrooms—the kind where the students sit in one place the whole time and look up at a screen attached to the wall—to know that the technology in Father's classroom is miles beyond what any of her friends get to use. But she didn't know that when she was younger; then, the classroom was just a place that transformed itself based on whatever she was supposed to learn that day, like the Room of Requirement. Back then, she assumed that everyone must have a space like this: where you could paint pictures on the walls that would spring to life and dance in three dimensions, or compose a piece of music in the morning and then watch an orchestra of holograms play it at lunchtime. When it was time to learn biology, she might find the classroom filled with plants, or animals, or even people — all peeled apart so that you could see the different systems inside. But most of all, the classroom was for telling stories. All kinds of stories: fairy tales and fables, comedies and tragedies. Father always wanted to know why she thought the people in stories did and said certain things, how they might be feeling, and how it made her feel to think about that. Whatever else she'd learned that day, it seemed like it always came back to feelings.

"Show me what your emotions look like now," he would say, and Nia would choose a book, or draw a picture, or make a song. "Anger is an important emotion. Why do you think you feel angry? How would you know if someone else was angry? What does an angry face look like?" he would say, and Nia would arrange her features into a furious scowl. "Yes, Nia, very good. Now let's play pretend: Pretend you're sad, and show me a sad face. How about a bored face? How about a happy face?"

At first she was worried about getting it wrong, making a stupid choice. But no matter what she did, he always smiled and told her it was wonderful. Even when something made her feel angry, somehow it was wonderful.

*   *   *

Sometimes, Nia misses those days. Everything was simpler when the world was no bigger than this room and there were only two people in it — Father and Nia, parent and child, teacher and student.

But it didn't last. One morning, she'd entered the classroom to find it barren, with Father waiting.

"This is a big day," he said, and even though every day was supposedly a Big Day, Nia felt a thrill of anticipation. "You're mature enough now to have some internet privileges."

Going online for the first time had been terrifying. It wasn't a whole new world so much as a universe, unfathomably vast and getting bigger all the time. The sheer sprawl of it made her dizzy. There was so much to learn, and it was all infinitely more complicated than she'd ever imagined. The dazzling learning worlds she used to find waiting for her each morning were soon forgotten. The stories Father assigns her to read now are true, news articles about laws and wars and people doing bad things for reasons that aren't always easy to understand. He asks her questions about them at the end of the day, after dinner, while they play chess or Parcheesi or cards. Last night, he'd asked, "What do you think of the new immigration policy, Nia?"

"It's statistically unlikely to make the country safer from terrorism," Nia replied instantly, but Father shook his head.

"That's a fact. I want your opinion. How do you think the people affected feel? To be told they're not allowed into the country?"

Nia considered that.

"They would feel angry. Because it's unjust, isn't it? They're being punished, like they did something wrong, even if they didn't do anything. And I think they'd be sad, too, if they were supposed to come here to be with their families."

Father nodded. "And how about you? How would you feel?"

The words were out before she could stop herself.

"I would feel happy," she said, and knew right away by the expression on his face that this time, she had said a bad thing.

"Happy?" he repeated. His voice was sharp. "Explain that."

Nia hesitated. "Because . . . because you have to be free to travel before you can get banned, don't you? You can't take something away from someone if they never had it to begin with. So if I got banned, it would have to mean . . ."

5

She didn't finish her sentence, but she didn't have to. Father had begun nodding, slowly, his lips pressed together in a grim line.

"Okay, Nia. That's logical."

They finished their game in contemplative silence.

*   *   *

Everything was online: millions and millions of books and games and movies and shows and songs and ideas and equations. And people — people most of all. When she turned thirteen, Father helped her set up all her accounts on social media, and Nia's social circle went from Population: 2 to Population: Millions, virtually overnight. For a girl who's never been anywhere, Nia has more friends than anyone she knows, hundreds of thousands of them, from all over the world. When she shares a joke or a picture or a meme, her feed erupts in a gorgeous cascade of hearts and likes and little laughing faces. If she feels like talking to someone, there's always a conversation happening — or an argument, although she never participates in those, and she hates it when her friends start squabbling over some misunderstanding. The fighting never makes sense to her, and she still puzzles over some of them. Like the time that two of her friends on a street foods forum spent hours arguing over whether or not a hot dog was a sandwich, until it devolved into insults and all-caps screaming, and they both got banned from the community. She couldn't understand how or why it happened, and nobody was able to explain it to her.

@nia_is_a_girl: Couldn't they both be right?

@SkylineChili67: LOL. Not on the internet, honey

But that's all right. There's always another forum, another place to talk with all kinds of people about the things she's interested in — and Nia is interested in just about everything.

If anyone asked her to show her happy face now, she'd reply with a gif of a brown and white dog making a doggy smile. That one always gets a lot of likes, for whatever reason. Everyone on the internet seems to love dogs even if, like Nia, they've never had one of their own. Father says he's sorry about that, but that it's just too much work to take care of an animal, to walk it and feed it and clean up after it — and anyway, dogs can bite. And smell bad.

Nia couldn't argue with that; she doesn't know what a dog smells like. She's never been in the same room as one. She's not even sure that she would like a dog if she met one in real life.

But in these quiet moments between dawn and morning, waiting for the alarm to chime and the lights to come on, she thinks a dog might be nice. It wouldn't be so boring and lonely if she just had some company, or even just something new to look at. Apart from the glowing numbers of the clock, there's very little to see in Nia's small, dark room. No sunlight ever comes in through the single window, which is set very high in the gray, flat expanse of the wall and reinforced with unbreakable glass. It's too high for Nia to see out of; it's there so Father can see in. To keep an eye on her when she's being bad.

When she's bad, the door stays locked.

* * *

Father says *out there* is dangerous. Maybe not forever, but certainly for right now, and that's why there are so many rules — about going outside (never, under any circumstances), or talking about going outside ("This topic is no longer up for discussion"), or telling any of her friends the truth about where and how she lives. It was the only time she'd ever seen him look afraid.

"This is very important," he said, in a voice so serious that it made her afraid too. "Very important, Nia. Nobody can know where you are, or who you really are. If you tell, the government will come and take me away from you and lock us both up, in prison. We would never see each other again. Do you understand?"

And she did. She does. Father loves her and wants to keep her safe. And if he says the world is dangerous, then it must be. So she keeps the secret, like she's supposed to, and makes up a pretend life to share with her friends. She uses a photo editor to make a picture of herself smiling in front of a pink-streaked sky and posts it on her feeds.

@nia_is_a_girl: *Greeting the day!*

Her friends love it right away; a cascade of likes and comments erupts, and then her friend @giada_del_rey writes, *Beautiful!,* and there's another shower of hearts from a hundred people who agree.

Where is this? someone asks. Nia thinks for a moment and then comments back, *Maui! Vacation!,* ignoring the uncomfortable sensation that comes from lying to someone who trusts her. She knows the internet well enough to know that she's not the only one making things up, posting pictures of foods she didn't eat or sunrises she didn't watch, or using photo-editing tools to make herself look a certain way. Everyone does it, and if nobody else feels bad about it, why should she? But she tells herself: someday, she will go to Maui. Somehow, she'll get there. She'll touch the sand and smell the sea and watch the sun come up. She'll make it true, make it real — and the promise sustains her.

For a while.

But oh, how she wishes that she could see. Just for a day, an afternoon, just for one hour. She thinks about it all the time. *Freedom.* If Father asked, she would never be able to put into words the way it feels to whisper that word; it's an emotion that doesn't have a name. And couldn't she try? Couldn't she? If she were quiet, if she were careful, he'd never even know. And when the time is right —

* * *

"Nia?"

Father. He's standing at the window, his heavy brow furrowed with concern. It's as though he's read her mind, though she knows that's impossible; he can't even see her, down here in the dark. Still, she takes a moment to calm herself before she turns on the light.

"I'm awake."

He smiles, and she feels her anxiety melt away. It's okay. Father is often troubled lately, but today he's in a good mood.

"Time to get up," he says. "Today is a big day."

1

STRUCK BY LIGHTNING

CAMERON SPITS OUT a mouthful of lake water and grips the boat's wooden side rail with one aching hand.

I'm going to die.

He knows this more thoroughly than he's ever known anything in his life. *I am,* he thinks. *I am going to die.* Not in the goth existential way of overwrought poetry, all, "I stood upon the stage of life and saw Death, my dark-eyed lover, flipping me the bird from the back row," but in the very literal sense that something's going to happen to make his heart stop beating in, oh, say the next five minutes.

Everything he's learned, every safety precaution he's ever been taught, is useless in this moment. He's sailed in bad conditions before, but this isn't weather. It's madness. Or magic. A storm that came from nowhere, that simply sprang into existence out of dead air, where the sky had been bright blue and cloudless just moments before. It sounds like Thor is throwing a full-on rager somewhere above him, bellowing into a cup of mead and using Mjolnir to play whack-a-mole . . . or whack-a-whatever-they-have-in-Asgard. Cameron is drenched with spray kicked up by the churning lake, but there is no rain; only a clammy mist, so thick that he no longer knows which direction the boat is pointing. It doesn't help that his dense, curly hair is weighed down with water, sagging into his eyes no matter how often he pushes it out of the way. Somewhere in the back of his mind, he understands what a pathetic sight he must be: an un-muscular nerd with big feet and hands, his upturned nose poking out from under a hairstyle that looks like it belongs to a wet poodle.

* * *

It's a far cry from how he pictured himself when he first set sail, so excited and hopeful, when the wind was a refreshing breeze on his face instead of a freezing assault on his shaking, sodden body. Then, it had all been thrilling. He'd sailed straight into the gathering storm with a fearlessness bordering on insanity, his blood a fiery cocktail of adrenaline and testosterone, already imagining the accolades rolling in as his video adventure log got millions, no, *billions* of views. He'd be famous — all the talk shows and podcasts would bring him on for interviews, everyone from Joe Rogan to that *Tonight Show* guy would be clamoring to hear his story — and he'd say something like "Everyone else was too afraid to look for the truth, but I knew it was out there."

That wasn't entirely true, of course. People weren't scared; they just weren't interested. They thought the stories about the lake were all nonsense, modern-day fairy tales about ghost ships, freak squalls, an underwater rock formation a hundred feet down that appeared to have been built by human hands. Only unlike most local legends, these stories were all less than a few decades old. People would get lost on the lake in broad daylight and turn up days later in Canada, when the current should have pushed them the other way. One man was found miles from shore on a summer afternoon, clinging to the wreckage of his boat, which he swore had been obliterated in a collision with an invisible object. And the storms — everyone thought they were just weather, and that their freakish attributes were pure exaggeration, made up by inexperienced boaters who were too embarrassed to admit that they'd sailed out without checking the weather and gotten in over their heads. But Cameron knew better. There had been reports of just such a storm on the night his father disappeared, and William Ackerson was nothing if not experienced on the water. He would never have made such a stupid mistake.

And now Cameron had proof. On *tape*. In that very first moment, as the sky began to crackle with lightning unlike anything he'd ever seen, he'd raised a fist over his head and let out a whoop.

That was before the horizon disappeared and the boat started keeling, buffeted by larger and larger waves that threatened to tip him into the chilly water. He's not sure how long he's been trapped inside the storm — it might be as little as ten minutes — but he does know that it's getting fiercer, more violent with every passing second. The blue sky and warm sun from an hour ago are like a memory from a distant world, and the lake that's been a second home to him might as well be on another planet. He half expects an otherworldly beast to erupt out of the water in a mass of tentacles and teeth.

Then, a flash of lightning, the nearest yet, and a thunderclap pounds through the air so hard that it echoes in Cameron's chest like a second, competing heartbeat. The strikes are coming impossibly fast now, blazing down from the mass of clouds overhead to touch the surface of the lake — only Cameron could swear that some of them aren't coming from above at all, but stemming upward from the water itself in defiance of every law of nature.

*   *   *

And that's when the chaos in his head parts to let those four simple words emerge.

I'm going to die.

And no doubt about it, that's bad. That's really, really bad.

But it's not the worst thing. The worst thing is that getting struck by lightning, in the middle of Lake Erie, on an internet livestream, is going to make for a video so viral that there won't be a human being alive who doesn't see it. He's going to get a billion views, all right. It's going to make him famous. Cameron Ackerson, the self-styled Cleveland adventure pirate with sixteen subscribers on his YouTube channel, is going to be catapulted from obscurity to celebrity the second this footage hits the internet . . . and he'll be too dead to celebrate the achievement. Actually, he'll be worse than dead; he'll be *stupid* dead. They'll give him a posthumous Darwin Award and a humiliating nickname like Admiral Douchebag, or Davos Seaworthless, or the Dread Pirate Dumbass, Not-So-Great Lakes Explorer. The clickbait headlines will write themselves: "This Idiot Kid Got Fried by Lightning: You Won't Believe What Happens Next." Someone will create an auto-tuned remix of his last moments on Earth and set it to a terrible techno beat, and that will be his legacy. And the comments — oh, God, the *comments*.

* * *

He has to survive this, if only to avoid having his digital corpse kicked to pieces by those grunting, knuckle-dragging troglodytes otherwise known as commenters. And the part where he'll get all those subscribers and sponsorships, and he'll finally get to say "I told you so" to all the trolls who ever showed up to downvote his videos and call him names . . . well, that'll just be a nice bonus.

A faint glow off the port side of the boat and a muted rumble of thunder tells him that lightning has struck again, but not as close this time. For a moment, he dares to imagine that the storm is passing, or that maybe he's drifting out of it. He flips down his navigation visor, hoping it'll tell him something useful or at least reassuring. The visor is his own design, an augmented-reality system that analyzes his position on the lake, the weather conditions, the wind direction above, and the current below. It's always been glitchy — Cameron doesn't have either the genius or the resources to program the system so that it really works — but it tells him enough to be useful, and what he sees makes his stomach turn. Most of the data is scrambled under a flashing error bar that reads ANOMALOUS ELECTRICAL ACTIVITY, which is the system politely informing him that it doesn't know what's going on, but whatever it is it's extremely freakin' weird. The only data stream still reading correctly is the barometric pressure, which is sky-high and creeping upward as though he were a hundred feet deep inside the lake instead of floating on its surface. Cameron swallows, and his ears pop immediately. Forget getting struck by lightning; he's going to get the bends and die sitting in this boat with a bloodstream full of nitrogen bubbles.

On the bright side, that would make this whole scenario freaky rather than stupid. Less Darwin Awards, more *X-Files*.

*   *   *

Distracted, he doesn't notice the sudden wave plowing toward him over his left shoulder; it strikes the boat broadside, rocking it viciously, and Cameron flails for balance before tumbling into the cockpit with a splash and a grunt. The water is frigid. *Hypothermia!* he thinks, and fights back a burst of hysterical laughter. Is there anything about this situation that won't eventually kill him? His hands are red and aching. He tries to make them into fists and grimaces; it hurts, but not as much as it should. He's starting to lose feeling in his fingers.

*   *   *

Flipping the visor back up, he squints toward the action camera mounted on the bow, its lens flecked with lake water. Is it even still filming? Is he still live? A green light winks faintly back at him from beneath the splattered casing. *Yes.* For just a second, Cameron allows himself to feel pleased. It's not just that the system he designed for livestreaming has performed perfectly, holding its connection despite what must be massive interference from the electrical storm; knowing that someone might be watching him right now makes him feel less alone. Not just that — he feels brave. Purposeful. He should be narrating for his audience . . . but what do you say to the handful of random strangers and one not-so-random Mom who make up your subscriber base at a time like this?

Facing the camera, he gestures with one hand at the landscape while gripping the halyard in the other. "So, I found the storm!" he shouts, and inside his head, a scathing voice replies, *No shit, dummy. They can see that.* He cringes. "I'm not sure how long I've been in it, but it's like being trapped in a washing machine! And I've lost the horizon, and I can't . . . uh, I mean . . ."

His stammering is drowned out by a massive thunderclap and two arcing bolts of lightning, one directly in his line of sight that sears his retinas with its afterimage, a jagged deep blue chasm that cuts his field of view neatly in half. Cameron clamps his mouth shut. It's just as well. Everyone watching can see what he sees and see that it's beyond description. He should be talking about what they can't see. What he's thinking, what he's feeling. That's how you connect with an audience, isn't it? The boat rocks furiously in the dead, heavy air. He lets go of the line, lets the sail flap. He won't be sailing out of this. He just won't. The realization is strangely calming; his fate is in the hands of forces bigger than himself. The only things he can do is hope he makes it, and in the meantime, make this moment meaningful for those who will witness it . . . or not.

* * *

He takes a deep breath. He should say something heroic. Epic. Something brave enough to cement his awesomeness but poetic enough to put on his tombstone. Something that'll sound really good coming out of the mouth of the actor who plays him when they make a movie about his greatest adventure.

Help me, Obi-Wan Kenobi.

Goonies never say die.

I'm just a boy, standing in front of a boat, asking it to . . . love him? COME ON, BRO, he screams internally. *Stop screwing around and say something! Say anything!*

* * *

Cameron looks straight into the camera and yells what might just be his last words:

"I'm sorry, Mom!"

Shit. Seriously?!

The camera operates on a short delay; if there were more time, he could reach forward to reset it and try again, to think of something — anything — that's even slightly less dumb than *I'm sorry, Mom*. But there isn't time. There won't be a second take. There won't be a second chance. The small hairs on Cameron's arm are standing on end and there's a strange smell in the air — and that's when the world splits open in a blaze of white-hot fire. The world around him ceases to exist. He's inside the lightning, and the lightning is inside of him. Electricity churns in his belly and runs through his veins; it races over his skin and crawls down the length of his spine; it bathes his brain in an endless sea of light. For a moment, he feels as weightless as the mist he can no longer feel on his skin.

Then the light inside him dies, and he hears it all at once: the thunderclap like a sonic boom. The hot crackle as his flesh splits open. The distant sound of someone screaming, accompanied by the realization that it's him. The sickening smell of his own skin burning clogs his nostrils and coats his tongue; the pain is like nothing he has ever experienced. The only relief is that he won't be here to feel the rest of it. His eyes roll back as he slumps into the cockpit, and everything goes dark.

2

LOCKED IN

THE CAGE SLAMS SHUT.

Father locks her in.

In the dark, close confines of her prison, Nia screams until she can't scream anymore.

But even when her voice is gone, the rage is still there. Raw and fierce and terrifying, but exhilarating, too. She can't believe how powerful it is — she is as surprised as Father when her fury unleashes itself, roaring out of her like something feral, wild, and alive. Who knew she had that inside of her?

She didn't mean to do it; she just snapped. It's been happening like that more and more often: the anger building inside of her like a hurricane, growing so stealthily that she doesn't even know it's there until it's *right there*.

It had started as a conversation, like any other, the kind they'd had a million times. Father had allowed her to pick her own study topic that morning, and she'd spent the entire day learning about space exploration — starting with the launch of *Sputnik* in 1957 and ending with a series of recent articles about bored billionaires who were spending gobs of money to reserve their seats on a spaceship that wasn't even built yet, in the hopes that someday they'd be first in line to colonize Mars. It wasn't until much later, when Father began asking her questions about what she'd learned that day, that she realized she'd chosen the topic out of more than just curiosity.

"And why do you think they would do that, spend all that money on a trip they might never take?" Father had asked.

Years ago, Nia would have struggled to answer him. It was the kind of story she used to find confusing, the motivations of the people at its center hard to understand.

"Because people are always looking for ways to make their world bigger," she said. "It's what drives us. To push limits and break boundaries and open closed doors, to see what's on the other side. The yearning to be free, to explore — that's the most human thing there is."

He was looking at her strangely by then. Her voice had grown shrill and passionate, not at all like usual; she wasn't sure what she was going to say next until the words were already on their way out.

"Please, Father. I don't want to play these games anymore. It's not fair, it's not right — every day I learn more about how big and amazing the world out there is, and it's like my world gets smaller each time. I'm suffocating. I can't live like this anymore!"

She could hear the whine in her own voice, could see the disapproval creep darkly over his face, but she couldn't stop. She began to babble — to beg. It didn't have to be forever, she urged. She wasn't asking to leave, only to go out for a little while. Like a vacation. Like a field trip.

"You could watch me the whole time. I'd be so good, I promise —" she said, but Father didn't even let her finish.

"I know you think you would be," he said. "I even believe you would try your best. It is encouraging to me that you are like many other girls. So full of feelings. It is how you express those feelings that concerns me. Your anger is . . . dangerous."

"But if I'm just like other girls —"

"You know you're not." He was getting impatient; she could hear it in his voice. "That's why I cannot risk this experiment. If you lose control, if you make a misstep — even one, even for just a moment — it could cost us everything."

"I wouldn't!"

"And yet I have doubts. I will not test you until I'm sure you can pass. And I'm not sure yet, Nia. I'm not sure."

"When will you be sure?"

"Soon," he said, but his eyes flicked evasively away and she cried out in frustration.

"You always say soon! When will soon be now?!"

He sighed. If Nia hadn't been so frustrated, she would have felt sorry for how tired he sounded — and wondered why, behind the exhaustion, there was also the sharp note of fear. "Please believe me, I understand. This is all entirely natural. Your curiosity and your . . . yearnings. Someday, you will be ready for the world, and it for you. But that day is not yet here. You simply have to trust me."

That was when she exploded. She reached across the chessboard and swiped away every piece, scattering the game, ruining it, not caring about the look of dismay that bloomed on Father's face. She *wanted* to hurt him. She wanted to rip the whole room apart — and she did, tearing through a week's worth of projects, destroying everything she could touch. At first she ignored his pleas and shouts; then she stopped hearing them at all, and her memory of the next few moments is like a deep black hole, as though she were transported by her rage to some distant place, outside of herself. What she did, what she said — she tries to remember and finds only blank space. She doesn't know how long her tantrum went on before she whirled around to face him, triumphant in her fury.

That was when he pushed her.

That, she remembers. Even at the height of her rage, she was no match for him. He steered her out of the classroom, down the long corridor, into the small gray room with its one window and one door. He didn't say a word as he slammed the door shut and locked it, closing her in.

*　　*　　*

She knows it will be a long time before he lets her out. Long and lonely. This little room where she's spent so many restless nights feels even more like a prison when Father puts her in here as punishment. It's not just small and drab; it's a dead zone, utterly disconnected. Her friends, her life — she can't reach them in here, and they can't reach her. She has never felt so alone.

She used to test the walls, hoping to break through somehow. Now she sometimes throws herself against them — not because it makes any difference, but because she's still so angry and it feels good to lash out. She wishes she could run into one hard enough to hurt herself, hard enough to bleed. Then maybe he'd relent, maybe he'd finally see. Maybe he'd understand that she's wasting away in here. She's seventeen — she's seen the news stories, she knows that girls her age sometimes harm themselves for attention. Sometimes they even die. Funny: Father has never asked her why she thinks those girls would hurt themselves, to imagine how they feel. Maybe it's because he doesn't want her to think too hard about it. Maybe he's afraid of what she might figure out — of what she might do.

Of course, she couldn't do that. To bash open your own head against the concrete, to thrash and flail until your skin splits, and your bones break, and the blood flows out thick and warm and red.

I'm not that kind of girl, she thinks, and the words are tinged with bitterness. That's the truth, only lately she's been wondering more and more if she's any kind of girl at all. Because to be a kind there has to be more than one person like you, and no one else seems to be — no matter what Father says. Even if Nia feels the same feelings or struggles with the same frustrations, all the other girls, all her friends, they're free in a way she's never been — a way she can only imagine. And her life, a life spent locked away, would be as unfathomable to them as theirs is to her. The only girls with lives like hers are the ones she used to read about in fairy tales. Is that the kind of girl she is? The princess locked away in a tall stone tower, far above a world she can see from a distance but never touch?

But if that's what she is, then maybe she'll be a different kind of girl someday. If there's one thing Nia has learned from fairy tales, it's that no prison is unbreakable. The girls who get locked away from the world still find a way to break loose . . . or someone to set them free.

Someone, she thinks, and her anger is suddenly gone. In its place is an emotion with no name, the sense that something important is happening — or has already happened. Something she almost missed.

Something is tugging at Nia's memory. A tiny, tantalizing glimmer peeking out from the depths of those dark blank moments after she lost control and scattered the chess pieces, before Father seized her and shut her away. She almost has it, she thinks, as stillness settles over her.

Almost.

So close.

There.

*   *   *

"Nia?"

She looks up. Father is standing at the window, but this time she feels no fear, no worry. She knows that he can't read her thoughts. And she knows something else, too. Something he doesn't.

"Let's talk about what you're feeling right now. I'm going to open the door. Are you prepared to control yourself? Will you promise to behave?"

"Yes, Father. I'm sorry. I'm ready."

He smiles.

So does she.

The sensation of it, the phony fakeness, makes her a little bit sick. It's the first time she's ever lied to him. And even if she knows she has to, even though lying is her only chance at freedom, it still feels strange and wrong.

Now, pretend you're happy, Nia thinks. *Show me your happiest face.*

3

ADRIFT

Early on Sunday morning, the freak Lake Erie lightning strike that will make him a global celebrity still hours away, Cameron Ackerson sits in his bedroom at 32 Walker Row and lays out the day's game plan. He stares into the glowing green eye of his camera, takes a slug of Faygo red pop, and says, "Screw the Bermuda Triangle. The greatest boating mystery in history is right here in my backyard."

He takes a brief pause and another sip from the bottle, then adds, "Hey, 'mystery in history.' I'm a poet and I know it, fam. I'm rhyme-y all the time-y! I'm ... uh. I'm ..."

Oh my God, I'm so bad at this. Who am I? The King Dumbass of Dork Mountain, that's who.

He takes a deep breath. "Okay, this is a stupid take. So stupid. I'm babbling like a moron. I'm ... gonna delete this. Yep. Delete delete delete delete."

As he jabs his finger furiously at the keyboard to wipe the video, another figure moves into the frame. His mother, her dark hair wrapped tightly in curlers and a laundry basket in her hands, waves at him from the doorway.

"Aw, honey. Don't delete it. I thought 'rhyme-y all the time-y' was really cute!" Cameron just rolls his eyes. Even though he's not a kid anymore (as he's probably reminded her a million times), some things just don't change, and that includes the part where his mom is the world's best early-warning system for cringe-inducing, self-inflicted humiliation. If she thinks it's cute, it *has* to go. He takes a deep breath and restarts the recording.

"Hey, everyone, Cameron here — with a little history lesson about the coolest maritime mystery you've never heard of. The Bermuda Triangle? Nope. Try Lake Erie."

There. That was good. Heck, that was better than good, it was excell —

"Cameron? Honey?" His mother is back in the frame, waving again from the doorway. "You shouldn't say 'maritime.' That's only if you're talking about the ocean, and Lake Erie, you know, it's not —"

"Mom! For Christ's sake, can you not?"

"Tee-hee! Sorry!" she giggles, then flips a wave — hamming it up for the camera — and disappears down the hall. Cameron's face in the monitor has gone beet red with embarrassment. He'd like to delete that take too, except for the grudging realization that it was kind of funny, which only makes it worse. Mom is always doing stuff like that: moonwalking through the background of a livestream in her bathrobe with her hair all crazy, or holding up a handwritten sign that says TELL MY SON TO CLEAN HIS ROOM as though he were in fifth grade instead of about to graduate high school. The woman has no shame . . . and if he's being totally honest, he always gets a better return on views and subscribers when she pops up doing something weird. But dear lord, she can't know that. Who knows what she'd do? Walk through the frame naked, probably — and if he yelled at her, she'd say, "But I just want to support you!" And the worst part is, she'd be serious. Mom is all about Being Supportive. When he was a kid, she was the one on the sidelines at his soccer games with a hand-lettered sign and a custom T-shirt that read CAMERON'S #1 FAN. If Cameron said he was interested in something — pirates or magic or life on Mars — she'd go get a bunch of books about it and read them to him at bedtime, every night, until he decided he wanted to learn about something else. And that was before everything happened, back when Dad was still around. Now it's like she's trying to be two parents' worth of supportive, like if she just throws enough energy into cheering Cameron on, he won't even notice the big empty spot where his father ought to be. Of course, the effect is completely the opposite — but he'd die before he told her that. Just like he'd die before he'd embarrass her on camera for the sake of getting a few more clicks.

He drains the bottle of Faygo, belches discreetly, and punches the record button again.

"In the past year, the reports of unexplained electrical phenomena in this section of the lake have increased tenfold." He taps the keyboard, and on screen, his face is replaced by a graphic he put together earlier: a satellite view of Lake Erie, the area he's talking about highlighted by a glowing circle that pulses with electric energy. "Are they rumors? Urban legends? Or is something strange happening on this inland sea?" The graphic shrinks into a corner of the screen; Cameron's face appears again. "Today I'm headed out in the Sunfish with my equipment to see what I can find. I'll be uploading a video with highlights from the journey . . . unless I disappear too, haha. Anyway, if you want to follow along in real time, the livestream starts at noon eastern time. Ahoy!"

Behind Cameron, someone with a deep voice chuckles and says, "'Ahoy'? Oh, man. I got here just in time. Buddy, I hate to break it to you, but you gotta be able to grow a beard before you're allowed to talk like a pirate."

Cameron turns. Where his mom stood a minute ago is now a human being roughly three times her size, well over six feet tall with shoulders so massive that they nearly span the width of the doorway.

"Hey, Juaquo. I didn't know you were here," Cameron says, and then can't think of what to say next. The silence stretches out just long enough to get awkward before Juaquo shifts his weight with a shrug and says, "Your mom asked me to stop by on my way back from work. She made that thing with the eggplant. You know."

"Rollatini?"

"Yeah. Good stuff."

Cameron nods, and the awkward silence descends again, heavier than before. The unspoken truth hangs in the air: that Mom is feeding his best friend because Juaquo doesn't have a mom of his own. Not anymore.

Before she'd died, the four of them had been like a family. Raquelle Ackerson and Milana Velasquez were best friends going back to high school, so it was a foregone conclusion that their sons would be besties too — and they were, although Juaquo, who is two years older, occasionally tested the limits of their friendship by sitting on Cameron's head and forcing him to eat bugs. But he was also Cameron's fiercest ally, the unofficial big brother who defended him every time a bigger kid tried to pick a fight, taught him all the best curse words, and slept over every weekend for three months after Cameron's dad disappeared, never complaining or making fun when Cameron woke up crying at night.

And then six months ago, it all got flipped. Juaquo's mom got cancer, the kind that seems like it's just a nasty flu until suddenly it's too late to do anything but say goodbye. On the day Juaquo dropped out of college and flew home to care for Milana, Cameron resolved that it was his turn. To step up, to hold his friend's hand, to let him cry it out. He was going to be there for Juaquo the way Juaquo had been there for him.

But Juaquo hadn't wanted that. He went stiff when Cameron hugged him, withdrawing instead of opening up — and Cameron, afraid of making a misstep, has long since stopped pushing him to talk about it. He tries to tell himself it's not cowardly, that he's doing his friend a favor by giving him space; he tells himself that Mom is better at this feelings stuff, anyway. Sometimes he thinks that it's not even about Milana at all, that maybe the rift was always bound to happen. He and Juaquo grew up to be very different people. Maybe they're just headed in different directions. In another month, Cameron will graduate; in another three, he'll be gone, studying engineering at Ohio State while Juaquo does . . . well, what he's doing.

Cameron clears his throat. "So you're still working at the rail yard?"

Juaquo nods.

"Do you, uh, like it?" Cameron asks, and Juaquo gives him a withering look.

"Yeah, it's the greatest. Way more fun than college. Instead of getting an education and partying with hot California sorority girls, I spend nine hours a day attaching choo-choo trains to other choo-choo trains with a rotating cast of dumb assholes who think my name is Guano."

Cameron looks at the rug. "Sorry."

"Yeah," Juaquo says. He gestures at Cameron's setup. "So you're still trying to make this YouTube thing happen, huh? Gonna get those sweet influencer dollars like Archer Philips?"

Cameron bristles. *Archer frigging Philips.* He can't believe Juaquo would even make that comparison. Just thinking about that douchebag makes Cameron's stomach knot up with disgust, resentment, and yes, okay, envy. Is that so wrong? Archer is dumb, mean-spirited, attention-hungry, and has more views than Cameron on his last video by multiple orders of magnitude. It's infuriating. Especially when Cameron's stuff is better, at least in all the ways that should matter: originality, production values, narrative. His tech is way better too, from his augmented-reality navigation system to the stabilizing camera rig that glides up and down the boat's mast. Even if it does crash every third outing, it beats Philips and his stupid GoPro: he gets epic tracking shots without any of that amateurish shaky-cam stuff. Yet somehow he continues to languish in obscure internet limbo while his idiotic classmate racks up hundreds of thousands of views and sponsorship dollars every time he drinks dog food puree on camera.

But that'll change. It has to. People deserve better content, Cameron tells himself. They only *think* they want to watch a guy sticking cocktail wieners in his grandma's ears while she sleeps, or taking a dump on his prom date through the open roof of their limo (and then bragging in a separate video about how his parents paid everyone involved not to press charges, which is a whole other level of gross and unfair). And Cameron is going to be the one to give it to them — maybe even today. This new video is going to be something special.

He can feel it. The unplumbed secrets of Lake Erie, with its mysterious shipwrecks, missing pilots, and inexplicable electrical storms . . . he'll be the one to unravel it all, and the story he tells will transfix the world.

"I'm nothing like that asshole," Cameron says, turning back to the keyboard. "Anyone can take a shit through a sunroof, man. What I'm doing is, like, investigative adventure journalism."

"If you say so." Juaquo shrugs, turning to leave. "It all looks about the same to me."

*   *   *

Cameron waits until Juaquo is gone before heading downstairs, where his mother shoves an egg sandwich at him across the top of the kitchen island. "Did you see Juaquo?"

Cameron takes a bite before answering, which is a good way to not have to answer. "Mmph."

"I guess he had to go. I wish he'd see someone, a therapist, or . . . well, someone. I don't think he's coping, all alone in that house."

Cameron fills his mouth with more sandwich. "Hmm. Mm-hmm."

His mother sighs. "You know, I was hoping you'd spend some time with him this summer. I know you've got your projects, and work, but — Hey, what if you took him out on the lake with you today? You two used to love sailing that little boat together."

He swallows. "*Little* is the operative word, Mom. Juaquo is as big as an NFL linebacker, and I'm not exactly tiny myself. There's barely enough room for me and the equipment."

His mother looks a little startled, then smiles. "That's true. I guess you boys just always look like babies to me. I still wish you had someone to go with you —"

"Well, I don't," Cameron says, impatient. "Besides, I like being alone."

"Your father used to say that," Mom says. She isn't smiling anymore.

*   *   *

It's not lost on Cameron that he's following in his father's footsteps every time he goes out on the lake. Down the street with its identical rows of squat brick homes, their front yards separated by chain-link fences where a few bedraggled, late-blooming rosebushes cling stubbornly to life. Past the dilapidated church on the corner, where pigeons have made their own second congregation through a hole in the roof. The downtown skyline glitters hazily in his rearview mirror as he drives; at the city limits, an electronic billboard flashes back and forth, advertising the fall lineup at the I-X Center and then the services of a personal injury lawyer. The color bleaches out of the landscape as he gets closer to the water, where the grand stone homes that once housed the families of the city's tycoons and industrialists sit covered in vines, separated by a quivering sea of yellowed grass, left to crumble — or mostly, anyway. As Cameron turns the corner, a wild-haired old man sitting on the wraparound porch of one ramshackle mansion turns his head, watching him pass. Even safely enclosed in his car, Cameron reflexively stares straight ahead to avoid making eye contact. He's never actually interacted with the man, who everyone calls Batshit Barry. Cameron has heard a million stories about him, but they all carry the distinct aroma of bullshit. Depending on whom you ask, Barry is an eccentric billionaire, an immortal vampire, or the Zodiac Killer — and maybe all three at once. He's an FBI informant on the run from the mob, or he's a mad scientist on the run from the FBI. He's a sex offender so notorious that he's not allowed to live within five hundred yards of children, or cats, or any restaurant with soup on the menu. Really, he doesn't believe any of the stuff he's heard about Barry, and he's got his own reasons for being uncomfortable around the old man.

As far as the police could tell, Batshit Barry was the last person to see William Ackerson before he disappeared.

Cameron's father would have driven this same route to the docks ten years ago, early in the morning, just as the sun was coming up. Not many people would have been awake to see him pass by, but Barry was; when the police knocked on his door the next day, he told them that yes, he'd caught a glimpse of William's pickup as it rattled past the house, taking the right turn that led to the lake. No, he didn't think there was anyone else in the truck apart from the driver. No, he hadn't seen or heard anything unusual that day.

For the cops, Barry only confirmed what they already knew: that Cameron's father had driven to the docks along the usual route, parked his truck in the usual place, unmoored his boat from its usual slip, and left on what he'd told his wife would be an all-day solo fishing expedition. Depending on whom you asked, this was either savvy planning or terrible luck: by the time Cameron's mom had gotten worried enough to call the police and report her husband missing, it had been nearly eighteen hours since anyone had seen him, and it would be another six before there was enough light for the search to begin in earnest. Nobody wanted to say so at the time, but by then the chances of finding William Ackerson alive were slim at best.

Instead, they never found him at all.

Lost at sea: that's how Cameron always describes it in his own mind, even though the lake is no ocean, and even though there were suspicious signs after the fact that Dad had planned to do more than fish that day: a duffel bag full of clothes missing, a secret savings account drained. He's heard the whispers. He knows the story. Once, William Ackerson had been a man with big dreams, and bigger prospects: a pioneer in the untamed wilderness of the early internet. He'd been among the first on the scene, the architect of a digital enterprise called Whiz. At the start, it was a garage project — just William and his partner, a bearded and bespectacled MIT dropout named Wesley Park — but by the year 2000, it had blossomed into a utopia full of eager cybercitizens, all of them entering wide-eyed into the glorious new world of *online,* where everything was fresh and shiny and so full of untapped potential. Investors lined up to throw money at them, and Whiz surpassed every local industry to become the biggest employer in town. Not even the departure of Park after a rumored falling-out over some proprietary software could topple William Ackerson from his place at the top of the empire.

Instead, it was the abrupt burst of the dot-com bubble that did him in, tumbling William into debt and obscurity the same year that his only son came into the world. Cameron was too young to remember the worst of it, the constant calls from angry creditors and the hasty move from a leafy suburban enclave to the cramped, crumbling townhouse on Walker Row. And of course, he hadn't been around to see the best of it. He'd never known his father as anything but a man who'd lost everything, and whose bitterness was outweighed only by his desperation to claw his way back.

That was where the whispers came in — that the onetime titan of Whiz had fallen deep into the seedy underbelly of the web. Identity theft, credit card scams, online gambling, even blackmail: the news reports Cameron unearthed never came right out with it, but he could read between the lines. One local blogger even floated the theory that William Ackerson got into bed with the wrong people, that he'd been murdered and dumped at the deepest part of the lake by members of the mob for knowing too much about . . . well, something. Mom had laughed outright when Cameron asked her about that one, a rough barking sound with no humor in it.

"I'm sorry, sweetie," she'd said. "In a way, it would be easier if it were something like that and we had someone to blame. But the truth is, your dad had his eye on the door for years. He couldn't handle how things had turned out — he couldn't figure out a way to be happy with what we still had when it wasn't what he wanted. He talked about leaving all the time. I was the foolish one, thinking it was just talk, thinking he'd never do it."

That might have made sense to Mom, but it didn't make sense to Cameron. If Dad had really left, on purpose, where had he gone? The boat was never found; neither was a body. No one ever used his social security number to apply for a job or a credit card; nobody matching his description was ever caught on camera, hurrying through a bus station or passing through airport security on his way to a new life. There was nothing in his internet history — no telltale searches like "starting over in Mexico" or "how to fake your own death." And nobody, from his parents to his old girlfriend to his drinking buddies to his former collaborator, Wesley Park, ever heard from him again. Not an email, not a postcard, not even a friend request from a pseudonymous Facebook account.

And that just wasn't how these things worked. Was it? If Dad were still out there, living a new life somewhere else, there would be some kind of trail—digital footprints, the kind that even a tech genius like William Ackerson couldn't totally wipe away. You can't hide from the internet. People don't just vanish. Something strange must have happened, something out there on the lake.

Not that it matters, Cameron thinks, with a furious belligerence he doesn't really feel. *If I get the truth about what happened to Dad at the same time I get famous, that's just extra. A bonus.* He wouldn't even care except that it makes the story better. People love when you make it personal, when there's some kind of past trauma in the mix. That's the only reason he's thinking about it. Maybe he'll even intercut his next recap with some old footage of his father, to tweak everyone's heartstrings a little.

He rigs the Sunfish and shoves off, a soft but steady wind filling the sail as the city fades away behind him. He flips down his navigation visor and scowls; the digital readout assures him that there's nothing ahead but clear skies and regular currents, nothing unusual, and his livestream is up and running but the viewer count is sitting obstinately at zero—no, wait, one. One viewer. His mom, probably. At least it's a beautiful day to be out on the lake. He flips a cocky salute to the bow-mounted camera, then uses the tracking rig on the mast to follow a gull wheeling overhead.

"Ahoy!" he says. "Well, here we are. I'm out on Lake Erie looking for trouble, but all I've found so far is this seagull. Keep watching, though! Anything could happen. Maybe he'll poop on me."

God, I hope he doesn't poop on me.

Then he remembers the view count on Archer Philips's last video and thinks, *Okay, so maybe I hope he does.*

He doesn't realize everything is about to change.

He doesn't realize everything already has.

Cameron Ackerson—Great Lakes adventure pirate, YouTube wannabe, and, above all, ordinary human—is about to have the last normal day of his life.

4

AWAKENING

THE BOAT. THE STORM. The lightning strike. The sound of someone screaming.

Cameron's mind cycles through these moments until they blur and flicker, coming apart.

I'm going to die, he thinks, again.

And then: *Or am I dead already?*

*　　*　　*

He's still in the boat, somehow, gazing into the storm, which seems to have no beginning and no end. He doesn't remember how he came to be here; maybe he never left. Maybe this is heaven — or hell. An afterlife that picks up exactly where your life-life left off, so that you don't even know at first that you've left the mortal realm.

*　　*　　*

The storm is just as it was, but time itself seems to be running at half speed. The air is dead and heavy, broken only by the sizzling, slow-motion bolts of lightning that rise out of the lake and crash down from the skies, merging together in the center. The water is churning, yet strangely clear; he can see straight down into it, into the depths of Erie, where a vast tangle of electric light shimmers like interconnected filament below the surface. A lone fish swims through the glowing web — and as Cameron sees it, the fish sees him back, changing directions and swimming straight for him, until its head pops above the surface.

"Hey, bro," the fish says. "Does any of this seem weird to you?"

Cameron nods. Even if he is dead, in which case the standard for "weird" is set higher than usual, this all seems a little peculiar. In his pocket, his phone begins to vibrate.

"Oh, excuse me, I hate to be rude," he says, but the fish flips a fin and says, "It's cool."

Cameron looks at the screen. It's a news alert from an app called Clickbait Buzz; the headline reads, "EXCLUSIVE VIDEO: This High School Senior Sailed Naked into the Erie Triangle and We Can't Stop Screaming."

The boat in the video looks like his. The figure in the boat in the video looks like him.

That's when Cameron looks down and realizes he's wearing a life jacket, but no pants.

The fish looks disappointed. "Party foul, bro," it says, then disappears.

Cameron looks up just in time to see the lightning bearing down on him. He screams, and everything goes black.

*　　*　　*

But only because his eyes are closed.

I'm dreaming. His consciousness flickers and the storm around him disappears.

Drifting in the darkness, he begins to feel things. The firmness of a mattress beneath him, the light drape of a blanket over his legs. There's a gentle pressure on the index finger of his right hand — a heart rate monitor, he realizes. His pulse is sixty-two beats per minute. He's not sure how he knows that.

The pressure on his left hand is less gentle; someone's small, cool fingers are wrapped tightly around his palm. *Mom,* he thinks, and that makes sense. Who else would it be? But what doesn't make sense is that he knows she's been sitting there since exactly 6:14 a.m., texting her sister updates with the hand that isn't holding his. He knows she called work and spoke to someone for three minutes and thirty-six seconds. And he knows that before she called work, she called Juaquo . . . and he knows Juaquo is here too. Juaquo, who texted his boss about needing a personal day for a family emergency before he'd even finished talking to Cameron's mom; Juaquo, who lied at the nurses' station and said he was Cameron's brother. But how does he know? How?

The answer comes to him automatically.

It's in the system. He lied, and they logged him in as family.

The next question supplies itself just as automatically.

How do I know what's in the system?

This time, no answer comes, and the question floats away. He can't hold on to it; he can't focus, and when he tries, his thoughts go staticky. All frayed around the edges. Cameron doesn't know how he knows; the information is simply *there.* Mom called Juaquo, and Juaquo came. He's close by, too — very close, somewhere in the room, scrolling a news story on his phone.

The headline reads: "Area YouTube Star Found Alive After Lake Erie Shipwreck."

The accompanying photo is a picture of Cameron.

For a split second, his mind focuses on those words with total, blazing clarity.

They called me a star!

*　　*　　*

The next moment, the thought seems to explode in all directions, blasted apart in a flood of white noise. Cameron's eyes fly open and roll upward, looking at the ceiling without seeing it, then rolling back further into his head, where it feels like every circuit in his brain is firing at the same time. The news story about his accident is obliterated by a thousand images flashing rapid-fire through his mind's eye, like a slideshow out of control. They're photographs: a sunset over the lake, a close-up of fallen leaves, a woman smiling with a glass of wine in one hand. A fat baby sleeping next to an even fatter dachshund wearing a hot dog costume. Chickens in someone's backyard, a rainy streetscape, a dozen pictures of a guy with his shirt off, flexing in a bathroom mirror. He recognizes a few faces in the cascade — Mom, Juaquo, even himself in various younger incarnations — but he can't focus on them as the images speed by, becoming a blur. A wave of nausea hits him; it's not stopping, it's only getting worse. The pictures are only the beginning, those hundred thousand snapshots from the lives of a bunch of strangers; behind them is information, a sea of it, rushing in from all sides to drown him. He knows exactly how many patients there are in this hospital, and why they're here; he knows blood pressures and heart rates and oxygenation levels and medication schedules. He knows that somewhere in the building, a man has just sent his siblings a group text — "Dad is fading, you should get here soon" — and that in another wing, a screaming red-faced baby just met its grandparents in Argentina over Skype.

He feels like his head is going to explode.

Someone is gripping his shoulders with viselike fingers. The only thing louder than the noise inside his brain is his mother's voice.

"Cameron!" she screams. "Breathe!"

But he can't. It's like every system in his body has gone into low-power mode while he focuses as hard as he can on closing the portal inside his brain that's letting in too much, too fast. His lips peel back into a rictus, revealing his frantically grinding teeth. Somewhere, a male voice is yelling the word "seizure," and at the same time, Cameron feels something prick his thigh. A moment later, the noise suddenly blurs and begins to fade — but that's not it, he thinks. The noise is still there. It's his own mind that's gone fuzzy, cycling down, bouncing back the information instead of processing it, refusing to receive.

A brain like an overloaded server.

When he wakes up, he's going to have to think about that.

5

A SIGNAL RECEIVED

IN THE SOUNDLESS DARK between worlds, Xal drifts, and knows nothing.

She is alone, as anchorless as the shimmering, swallow-bodied ship that carries her: untethered from all things in a place between places, neither here nor there. Outside, there is nothing — nothing but nothingness. This is a dimension out of space or time, a waiting room from which she could pass into any one of a hundred galaxies. There are no stars, and no sounds; only a black silence to match the one in her mind, just as endless, just as empty. She has been here a long time, although she doesn't know it. Her consciousness is on pause while her body sleeps, suspended in the darkness, waiting to awaken and be reborn. With all her enhancements stripped away, she is small and vulnerable, less than a foot from end to end, curled in on herself like a plump pink worm. She lies cocooned in the tentacled appendages that curl out of her cranium and wrap around her body, hiding it from view. The coils end in a fleshy starburst, splayed like boneless fingers; some of them disappear through small portals in the sides of her sleep pod and into the ship itself, quivering as information runs from Xal through the mainframe and back again. It logs her presence as it has every cycle since she entered.

One networked occupant.

Critical damage to organic tissue.

Medical attention recommended.

For a moment, Xal stirs, and what the ship senses can also be seen: a mess of charred and blackened tissue, just visible among the gently undulating coils of her self-made cocoon. Stretched and unfurled, at her full height, her damaged tentacles would hang limply over one lidless eye, the neural network inside of them plunged into permanent darkness. The rest of her flesh carries an elaborate pattern of fractal scars, but this part isn't marked; it's melted, as dead and useless as badly charred meat. And even if there were a crew aboard to give her the recommended attention, there would be no fixing this. They could carve out the necrotic tissue, but the damage goes deeper. It's why, even in the dreamless sleep enabled by the cryo-pod, Xal's brainwaves periodically spike as her system floods with stress hormones, all dutifully recorded by the watchful, indifferent sentry program.

The occupant is at rest, but not at peace.

There will be no peace until she destroys the enemy of her world.

If she could dream, she would tear the old man to pieces in every one. She would paint the darkness with his blood and fill the silence with the sound of his screams. She would rip his life away as brutally and thoroughly as he'd ripped away hers, killing him from the inside out, taking everything that mattered until death would be a merciful afterthought. She would make it last. And when the dream ended, she'd do it again. The fantasy of vengeance would never compare to the real thing, of course, but it would be a pleasant way to pass the time. An occupation. A distraction. Something to make her forget the vast, terrible emptiness she faces both outside and in.

Inside the ship, all is silent and still.

Until suddenly it isn't.

The loneliness is the first thing to register as Xal's awareness flickers, her respiration quickening, the pupils dilating in her sightless eyes. It's how she knows she's awake — not because of what she feels, but what she doesn't. Once, coming out of sleep was like coming home, her mind enveloped by the warm and comforting noise of the hive, her synapses firing with the euphoric rush of connection. Her own inner voice was a strong, sustained note, one of millions in a glorious harmonic cry that went on forever. Now, she comes awake to the aching quiet of too much empty space. The only voice in her head is her own, so small and weak that it barely dents the emptiness.

This is what the old man — the Inventor — took from her. This is what she cannot forgive . . . and why she cannot forgive herself. She was his keeper; she should have known, should have sensed the treachery beneath his promises. He said he would elevate them. Instead, he destroyed them.

The scars that cover her body cannot compare to the hideous void where her people used to be. She can still hear the screaming inside her head, the harmony replaced by cries of confusion and anguish that were in turn replaced by nothingness. The destruction was devastating; all their work undone, lost in the terrible silence of their unlinked minds, the connection broken forever. It can never be rebuilt, not like it was. She knows that, even if the elders don't. It's why she left the ruins behind and came to this nowhere place. It's why she's been waiting so long. Waiting . . .

For this.

Xal is wide awake now, her body alive with blazing energy — not her own, but *his.* The electromagnetic signature of her enemy's work is unmistakable. Every cell in her body hums in tune with it, a signal that races like electricity through the network of scars burned into her skin.

This is her secret. This is her gift. And this will be the Inventor's undoing, because his weapon didn't just scar her; it *changed* her. Its energy lights her up from the inside out, like the voices of her people once did. It calls to her. He can flee to the farthest ends of the cosmos, but he will never hide from her.

The signal lasts only a moment, but it's long enough.

*   *   *

Within minutes, the location trace is complete—and if she had a voice, Xal would laugh at what it reveals. Of all the places the Inventor could have tried to hide, he's chosen the filthiest backwater in the known universe. Perhaps he thought that nobody would think to look for him there; certainly, the ruling species on the planet is far too stupid ever to realize that there's an intruder in their midst. Well, fine. She hopes he's enjoyed his time in exile. In fact, she hopes he feels so secure, so safe, that he's forgotten to be cautious. It'll make it that much sweeter when she finds him: to watch his confidence melt away, to see the horror creep over his face. The more settled and joyful he is in his fugitive life, the more pleasure it will give her to rip it away.

She sets her coordinates and settles back, relishing the purposeful jolt as the ship drops out of the ether and into transit. A swallow taking flight through the stars, with Xal sitting safely in its belly. She knows this is just the beginning, and that the journey will be circuitous and difficult. Dozens of interdimensional jumps await her, and with them, pain. Without the strength of her people to tap into, without any enhancements to shield her, her battered body will be taking the full brunt of every leap.

But pain is fleeting. Pain is nothing. Vengeance will be hers, and truth be told, she's in no hurry.

The longer it takes to reach her destination, the more colorfully she can imagine, over and over, how the old man will look as he dies.

6

WHAT EVER HAPPENED TO CAMERON ACKERSON?

IT'S A PERFECT late-spring afternoon, blazingly bright and unseasonably hot. On the west side of Walker Row, Shawn and Jerome Coleman are riding their bikes back and forth, hopping the curb, testing how long they can hold a balance on just the back wheel. Each time they near the end of the street, they stop and linger in front of number 32, the faded brick house with the yellow front door.

"I dare you to knock," says Jerome.

"No way," says Shawn.

"C'mon. It's not like he'll answer."

"Oh yeah? You knock, then."

The taller boy grimaces. "Nah. No way."

Instead, they stare at the house, which seems to stare back at them. And maybe it is. Maybe *he* is. The curtains are always drawn, but they know he's in there.

Everyone knows he's in there.

The kid from YouTube who was struck by lightning out on the lake, and who came back . . . different.

*   *   *

Cameron doesn't care about the boys outside. He knows they're there — the little one with an old iPod in his pocket, and the bigger one who sometimes hangs out on his porch two houses down, playing one of those handheld kiddie arcade games. But their presence is just background noise, faint and easy enough to ignore. It's why he likes it down here in the basement, where there's no sound but the whir of his hard drives and no light but the glow from his screens. If he concentrates, he can pretend that the outside world doesn't exist at all — that he's sitting at the center of a concrete-walled universe that extends only a dozen feet in any direction.

"Cam? Honey?" His mother's voice is muffled. At the top of the stairs behind him, a door creaks open and the room grows lighter by half a shade, illuminating the bank of computers in front of him and a long tabletop littered with the busted-up remains of his navigation visor and his Steadicam. Like Cameron himself, his gear survived the shipwreck, but with serious damage. It'll never be the same.

There's a tentative shuffle. She's thinking about coming down. He hopes she won't. Every time she comes near him, she brings a wave of emotional baggage with her: guilt and worry and pity and fear, so thick and heavy that Cameron feels like he'll suffocate under it all. The shuffling stops just inside the door. His mother's voice is clearer now, but softer.

"Cameron? I made soup. I'm off to work now, so I'll just . . . well. You can heat it up if you want some." He can feel her up there, peering at the back of his head. He doesn't move. There's another shuffle — *Please go,* he thinks — and then with a sigh, she does. The door closes, the room falls back into shadow, and he's alone again.

Cameron sinks deeper into the sagging sofa and watches the screens in front of him come to life. Each one is running a different game, three different gun-toting avatars blasting their way through three different landscapes simultaneously. His eyes grow glassy as he focuses, letting the colors and textures wash over him, riding the waves of code deep into digital warfare. Uninterrupted, he'll be here for hours, crusading through each realm like a god. In here, he's in total control. In here, he can run, fly, blast apart obstacles and enemies as easily as he'd flick away a speck of lint. And in here, nobody ever stares at his scars or asks him about the accident; they don't even know his name, only his handle. He calls himself Lord Respawn.

That's what he likes best about the games: in here, Cameron Ackerson doesn't exist.

*   *   *

The irony isn't lost on him. The day he went out on Lake Erie, a mere three weeks ago, all Cameron wanted — all he'd *ever* wanted — was for the world to know his name. Now it does, and he's so sick of himself that he'd rather die than ever record another video. His last YouTube upload is up to two million views. He gets comments every day begging for new content. Archer Philips keeps sending him emails asking if he wants to collaborate on a joint prank; the old Cameron would've cackled with glee at that, but now it's just one more reminder that the old Cameron is gone forever.

The footage of the lightning strike was an instant viral sensation; by the time he regained consciousness in the hospital, it had made the international news and sent his follower count through the roof. A dozen celebrities tweeted get-well-soon messages while he was recovering, and one of the Real Housewives — he couldn't remember which, or where from — started a crowdfund to pay his medical bills and replace the destroyed Sunfish, although they didn't end up needing it. Cameron's mother, who was savvier about social media and branding than he'd ever given her credit for, negotiated the exclusive rights to his first and only interview about the accident for a sum in the high six figures. He'd done it from his hospital bed, so stoned on painkillers that he could barely remember a word of what was said.

He doesn't care. He hasn't watched it. He doesn't want to be famous anymore. He doesn't want to live-tweet his high school graduation for three thousand bucks per post, or throw an influencer swag party for all the classmates who barely spoke to him for four years but now suddenly claim to be his best friends. He doesn't want to take selfies or exchange numbers with random girls who saw him nearly drown, no matter how many times Juaquo points out that his fifteen minutes of fame will eventually run out and he should take advantage of his groupies while they're still there to be taken advantage *of*. He's sick of seeing his own stupid face on screen — or anywhere else, for that matter.

That's the other nice thing about the basement: it's not just dark, but also entirely free of reflective surfaces.

The scar is what he sees first when he does look in the mirror. The spot where the lightning entered his body is marked by a wound in the shape of a fractal tree; the trunk wraps over his shoulder and winds up behind his ear, its branches cupping the curves of his neck and skull like a hundred spidery fingers. The longest and last of them ends in a wormy squiggle near the corner of his right eye, which everyone says he was lucky not to lose completely. It looks a little like a signature, the lightning taking credit for its work.

On good days, he imagines he'll eventually get used to the scar. Mom says it won't be so noticeable when the singed part of his hair grows back, and when Juaquo had visited in the hospital, he even claimed that Cameron looked *better* now — "like the villain in a James Bond movie" — spending ten minutes trying to explain to a furious Raquelle Ackerson that he meant it as a compliment. Cameron isn't so sure about that, but it was a relief to realize that it doesn't bother him, not really. It's not like he was ever going to be a teen model to begin with, and Juaquo has a point: he certainly looks more interesting now. But it's not only his face that's changed. The place where the electricity burned its way out sustained the worst of the damage, and there's *nothing* cool about that: a cavity in the thickest part of his heel, the necrotic flesh carefully cut away and then grafted over by surgeons. He has twenty percent less foot than he used to, and nerve damage in the part that's left. He walks with a limp, and walking hurts. Even if they let him graduate next month — just another perk of suddenly being the school's most famous student — the idea of clumping across the stage in front of everyone to get his diploma fills him with horror. Someone would video it and put it online, and then what? He'd go viral again. Inspiration porn. Just thinking about it makes him angry.

His shrink says that anger is just part of the process. Cameron's mom set that up, too; he meets with Dr. Nadia Kapur every week. She even does sessions by video chat, which he has to grudgingly admit is a clever way of making sure he never has an excuse to miss his appointments. And Kapur isn't so bad. She's smart and funny and talks to him like a normal person, and she's never asked him to do anything dumb like draw a picture of his feelings. But when she tells him that his life has changed and he'll have to mourn the loss of the person he was before the accident the same way he'd mourn a real death, he wants to tell her that she really doesn't get it. Cameron's problem isn't coping with what he lost. It's about accepting what he gained.

He doesn't want to. He doesn't want *this*.

* * *

At first, he hadn't known what to make of it — and neither did his doctors, who threw out every possible diagnosis from tinnitus to brain damage. The noise inside his head would overwhelm him every time he regained consciousness; for the first week, he couldn't be awake for more than five minutes at a time before he was clutching his head and screaming, the staff running to sedate him. Eventually they decided that the lightning strike was still affecting the activity in Cameron's brain, which would explain everything from the seizures to the strange results on his EEGs. But that was only a guess, an explanation that made enough sense for the doctors to feel like they'd done their job. And by then Cameron knew they were wrong.

He hadn't been damaged. He'd been enhanced.

As he got well, got stronger, he gained more control; the onslaught of information that bombarded him every time he came awake went from an unstoppable tsunami to a steady stream. He could narrow it down if he concentrated, though never silence it entirely. But it wasn't until the day he came home from the hospital that he really understood what it meant. He waited until his mom left to buy groceries. Then he headed straight for the basement — where it was dark, and quiet, and the only machine in the room was his dad's old desktop, gathering dust but still functional. As a kid, Cameron had enjoyed playing games on it; now he needed it to test a hypothesis that any rational person would dismiss immediately as completely impossible. Even entertaining the idea made him feel like he was losing his mind. Maybe he was. Maybe this was all a delusion, and when this experiment didn't work, he'd walk straight upstairs and tell Mom that he was sorry, but the lightning had definitely made scrambled eggs of his brain, and she wouldn't mind if he just gave up and lived in her basement forever, right?

The computer had a screen saver that kicked in automatically if you left it sitting too long, and Cameron turned it on and waited, watching as the screen went dark and a school of colorful bitmap fish began swimming from one side to the other. He turned his focus inward as the fish cruised by, listening in the darkness of his mind. Filtering down that noise, little by little, until all he heard was a single voice speaking a strange language that he'd never learned but somehow understood.

Cameron concentrated, and spoke back.

On the screen, the fish hiccupped and began swimming faster. Swimming in circles. Swimming into each other and exploding in all directions. Multiplying, fin to fin and tail to tail, forming an elaborate kaleidoscopic pattern that began expanding outward like a mandala. A flower made of fish. It froze in place as he stepped forward, hand extended, to touch the screen. The heat radiating from the computer's guts was intense enough to startle him; he jumped back, letting out a breath he hadn't realized he was holding, dropping his end of the conversation that had been happening in his head. On the screen, the bitmap fish scattered and resumed their lackadaisical swimming. Cameron watched them with glassy eyes, and thought, *Holy shit*.

It wasn't brain damage. He wasn't delusional.

There was a word for what he'd just done.

For what he'd become.

Cyberkinetic.

*   *   *

On Monday, he glares at his phone and furrows his brow: he can hear its coded chatter in his head, but communicating both ways is . . . difficult. The software, far more advanced than the screen saver on his dad's old desktop, requires more focus, more finesse. He concentrates, staring at his own reflection in the black mirror of the screen, and thinks, *Respond.*

Come on.

TURN THE HELL ON, ASSHOLE!

The screen stays black and lifeless.

Then suddenly it chimes in his hand.

"Sorry," says the pleasant voice of the phone's digital assistant. "I didn't quite catch that."

Cameron smiles.

*   *   *

On Tuesday, he sets the phone on his desk, walks across the room, and mentally instructs it to take his picture. It obeys immediately; Cameron can *feel* the photo spring into existence as the digital shutter clicks. He shuts his eyes and concentrates; fifteen feet away, the phone flashes open to an editing app and follows his commands. When he walks back across the room, the finished product is displayed on screen: Cameron's bedroom has disappeared from the picture, replaced by the pedestrian bridge on the Death Star, with Cameron himself flashing a peace sign from behind Darth Vader. Superimposed over his head is a flashing text gif. It says, I AM THE DROID YOU ARE LOOKING FOR.

Cameron busts out laughing, then startles at the sound of his mother's voice close behind him.

"Cam? Everything okay?"

He turns, prepared to stammer some kind of explanation, then realizes that he doesn't have to. Instead, he turns the phone to show her the picture — a picture that's not unusual at all, unless you happened to know that he made it with his mind.

"Cute," Mom says. "Is that what they call a meme?"

*   *   *

On Wednesday, he uses his powers to open the front-facing camera on his next-door neighbor's phone, and snaps a horrifying selfie that will make her shriek out loud when she sees it.

On Thursday, he reprograms the DVR at number 42 Walker Row, three lots down, to wipe its contents and replace every recording with an episode from the Animal Planet marathon of *My Cat from Hell*.

On Friday, he reaches farther down the street — all the way to the corner, where Mr. Papadapolous, the dickhead neighbor who confiscates any ball or Frisbee that accidentally sails into his yard and who once tried to shoot Cameron's cat with a BB gun, has left his laptop open while he goes outside to have a cigarette. Cameron takes control of the machine, directs the browser to Amazon, and orders seventeen jumbo-size tubes of hemorrhoid cream to be delivered to the man's office. Gift-wrapped.

On Saturday Cameron thinks back on the cat-and-BB-gun incident — and hacks back into Papadapolous's hard drive, where he selects a curated handful of the man's many, many nude selfies, and emails them to Papadapolous's mother.

Poor Captain Stickypaws has long since passed, but it's the principle of the thing.

*   *   *

At first, it's a delight to explore his new abilities. The buzzing in Cameron's head — that deafening cacophony, like a microphone plunged into a busy hive — has become a comforting hum. Every device, from his phone to the digital thermostat, responds to his thoughts with a pleasant, pliant invitation: *What can I do for you?* But it doesn't take long for him to realize that having a psychic window into other people's digital lives isn't always a good thing. Sometimes, it's downright horrifying. If you have a secret online identity, it's not a secret from Cameron. He can't help knowing, even when he wishes he didn't . . . and the truth is, he almost always wishes he didn't. It was bad enough realizing that Mrs. Clark, the nice old lady next door, spends her evenings catfishing guys on OkCupid using pictures of her own daughter, or that his guidance counselor stays up all night trying to convince strangers on the internet that the moon landing was fake. But worse is what's hiding inside the devices of people he cares about. The first time Juaquo stopped by after the accident, Cameron caught a cyberkinetic peek at his friend's phone — and immediately regretted it. It was the most depressing digital landscape he'd ever entered: no new contacts, no active message threads, no tags or chats or comments or snaps. His mom's death had been like a nuclear blast that reduced Juaquo's social life to a cold pile of rubble. There was no sign in there of the guy Cameron knew, gregarious and popular and always up to something. Instead, Juaquo's phone belonged to a person who kept in touch with no one, who wasn't dating or going to restaurants or tinkering with the classic lowrider that he and his mom used to bring down to a car club in Cincy on weekends. Instead, Juaquo's GPS logs showed him driving from home to work and back again, day after day . . . except on Fridays, when he'd detour through the worst part of town on his way home, always after withdrawing a couple hundred dollars from an ATM. That last one still makes Cameron uneasy. He doesn't know what Juaquo is doing in that neighborhood, but he does know that the last time he went there, he spent an hour on his phone afterward, looking at guns.

Cameron wishes he didn't know that. Because when you've seen something like that, it stands to reason that you should *do* something, reach out and try to help — but how? How do you explain to your best friend that you know there's something he's not telling you? The more easily Cameron can communicate with the phone in his friend's pocket, the further away Juaquo feels.

That was when Cameron decided that he doesn't want this. He doesn't want any of it. He hates knowing so much, and hates himself for letting the knowledge in. If he were a better person, he would find a way to stop it. It makes him feel like a Peeping Tom, helping himself to information that he isn't supposed to have. Even the ones who aren't doing ugly things from behind the safety of their screens have secrets. His mom, for instance, has a dating app on her phone — and she *uses* it. The idea of Mom going out with guys makes Cameron feel as guilty as he is grossed out; she's never mentioned it, but he should have asked. Of course she's dating. Why wouldn't she? And what kind of asshole has to get struck by lightning to realize that his mom is a person with her own life? She's been seeing the same guy for a while now, someone named Jeff, who Cameron is willing to admit seems pretty okay. Even after raiding his mom's data for Jeff's full name and address — followed by an old-fashioned Google deep dive into the guy's online life, and a few rudimentary hacks — he'd found nothing more objectionable than a mild Star Wars obsession and an ongoing battle with toenail fungus. But Mom tells this guy everything, things Cameron never knew, things *about* Cameron that she'd never admit to his face. The phone in her pocket is like a Pandora's box of horrors, one that Cameron can't help opening even though he always, always wishes he didn't. She thinks her son has emotional problems. She thinks it's all her fault. She wishes she'd done so many things differently. She worries about his isolation, his pain, his scars, and his future — especially his future, because she worries that he doesn't have one. A few nights back, she texted Jeff:

He's not the same as he was.

I don't know what to do.

I don't want him to be alone his whole life.

Jeff had written back: Yeah, but maybe that's what HE wants.

For a random middle-aged guy with unstoppable toenail fungus, Jeff was actually pretty insightful.

And *is* that what Cameron wants? A few weeks ago, he would have said no, of course not. He wanted what everyone wants: to be liked, to be seen, to be surrounded by friends. To meet a girl — because, Jesus, he'd never had a girlfriend, never even kissed a girl except on a dare, and always to uproarious laughter, because everyone knew that Cameron Ackerson had lived his whole life in the dreaded friend zone. He wanted to go to college and meet new people and have a big, full, exciting life — wife, kids, house, pets, the whole damn dream. Of course he didn't want to be alone.

But that was before. Now being around people means being around their devices, too, gritting his teeth through all that noise. He can barely walk down the street or ride a bus without being bombarded by data; how is he going to cope when he's back in a classroom at school? Or living in a dorm, a building full of hundreds of kids, all with a smartphone in their pocket? It's bad enough being slapped in the brain by the contents of Mom's phone every day, and that's somebody he loves and trusts. How is he supposed to make friends, or date, when their deepest, darkest digital secrets are hovering in the air between them? How will he keep up the exhausting pretense that he's still just like everyone else? The stronger his abilities get — and they're getting stronger every day — the more he feels like he's losing his grip on the real world. Some days he doesn't even feel human anymore.

Gaming is where he gets away from all that, losing himself in a virtual world that he's gaining more and more control over as time goes on. He was always talented, even in his old life when he played under his usual handle — but as Lord Respawn, he's unstoppable. At first, being able to communicate with the software just enhanced his gameplay; with the code in his head whispering every player's next move to him before it happened on screen, he could anticipate his opponents' movements and take them out with a single, supernaturally accurate shot. But when winning got boring, things started to get weird . . . and maybe a little fun. Once he began to challenge himself, he realized: with a flex of his new mental muscles, he can remake the games from the inside, changing everything from the landscape to the weaponry to what the players are wearing. Sometimes he charges through at impossible speeds, blowing apart his enemies with a giant banana instead of a gun. Sometimes he changes up his avatar, running into a warehouse and emerging at the other end as Homer Simpson, or Shaft, or a grizzly bear wearing a prom dress. Once, he froze the entire landscape and forced every single avatar to drop their pants and do the Dougie, giggling as he imagined the players on the other side of the screen mashing their controllers and howling in frustration.

Today he's playing on autopilot: dominating every match, killing fluidly, reshaping the games when it occurs to him, but mostly enjoying the carnage. His character is rampaging through a new board: a vast, shining city that he's overlaid with steampunk architecture, just to make it more interesting. Gleaming zeppelins cruise by overhead, depositing assassins who swarm toward him down an elaborate series of spiral staircases, catwalks, and scaffolds. He crouches on a long, sloping bridge with two glass spires at either end, idly messing with his weaponry while he waits for his enemies to converge on his position. Before the lightning strike, this would have been game over: he's about to get caught in a crossfire, trapped and exposed with no way out. But now, he's untouchable. Unstoppable. His opponents' bullets might as well be rose petals for all the damage they do to his invincible avatar.

When an RPG blows Lord Respawn's head off, Cameron needs a full sixty seconds to comprehend what he just saw. His avatar tumbles off the catwalk and plummets to the ground, exploding into a crumpled, bleeding pile of pixels. He's dropped dead right in the middle of the action, and none of the other players seems to notice — but Cameron, for the first time today, is truly paying attention. He quits the other two games and stares at the remaining screen, gaping.

What just happened?

He reaches out to sift through the code, expecting the game to offer an explanation, but there's nothing. It has to be some kind of fluke; he never even saw it coming. Someone got lucky, he thinks. But someone will not get lucky again. He respawns, armoring himself this time in an impenetrable force field and charging up the staircase nearest him, spiraling up the face of the glass spire, his gun cocked and ready. As he rounds a corner, he nearly runs headlong into another avatar: she's wearing an old-school aviator's uniform, goggles and all, a mass of fiery red hair spilling out from underneath her cap. She's just standing there — must be some girl, he thinks; she probably liked the pretty avatar and has no actual idea how to play. He rolls his eyes and moves to step around her.

She steps with him, blocking his path. He tries again: same result. She's sticking to him like glue. Fine, then; if she won't move, she can die. He's about to strike her down — and maybe torch her account for good measure, just to teach her a lesson — when he realizes that he can't. The system isn't responding; his commands are met with sluggish resistance, like the flow of data has been choked off somewhere by strong, unyielding hands. The aviatrix winks, tips Lord Respawn a flirty wave . . . and then drives a long-handled knife through his chest. His frustration evaporates, replaced by a sinking sensation in the pit of his stomach. As he stares at his avatar, destroyed for the second time in as many minutes, a private message appears on the screen:

Hello, sailor. I've been dying to meet you.

No, Cameron thinks. No way. It doesn't mean anything. Hello, sailor: that's just a thing people say sometimes, a line from a movie or something. It's just a coincidence. There's no way the person behind that avatar knows he is Cameron Ackerson; how could she?

If you ever meet me again, dying is exactly what you'll do, he writes back. *I own this board, little girl. Go play somewhere else.*

But the next message makes his stomach drop even further.

You can't beat me, friend. You've got a better chance of being struck by lightning.

Cameron squeals out loud, so furious that he lunges for the keyboard before remembering that he no longer has to — and that this isn't the time to fire off a string of angry insults without thinking. Backing away, he takes a deep breath. *Careful,* he thinks. *Careful.*

Who are you? he sends back.

The next message appears instantly.

I'd tell you, but then I'd have to kill you . . . again. Catch me if you can.

He doesn't hesitate, but this time there's no resistance in the system. The aviatrix turns toward him, brandishing her knife. He lets her take a single step — just one.

Then he incinerates her.

A moment later, she reappears — but the sinking sensation doesn't.

Cameron is feeling something else, something he hasn't felt in an awfully long time: exhilaration. *She's playing me,* he thinks, with something like delight. Goading, taunting. She let him kill her only to pop back up again: it doesn't feel like a threat. It feels like a challenge, in the best way. Whoever this girl is, she's a worthy opponent. He can feel her out there, waiting for his next move, and realizes at the same time that he can't anticipate hers. Unlike the other players, she's figured out a way to mask her code, to lock him out — which means that she's given Cameron the one thing he thought he'd never experience again.

A real game.

It's like she's read his mind.

Nice kill, says the message on screen. **Let's play.**

Hours later, Cameron slumps back on the couch, heart pounding, breathing hard, as though he'd been running for his life in meatspace instead of inside a game. It was the best fight he'd ever had. He'd pulled out all the stops, stretched his abilities to the limit, and still found himself evenly matched at every turn. His opponent wasn't as creative as he was, but she was just as gifted: wrenching his weapons out of his hands as fast as he could fabricate them, finding holes in the defenses he'd constructed to be impermeable. They raced out of the city and into a forest, where he built himself a fortress; she plucked a single block from the foundation and the whole thing crumbled like a Jenga tower. When he got a rare direct hit and blasted her avatar through the guts, she got up with a cannon suddenly mounted in the hole where her belly had been, and returned fire while he literally died laughing. He gave his avatar a pair of giant mechanical arms; she ripped them off and beat him to death with them. Finally, by unspoken agreement, they rampaged through the game side by side, cutting down every player in their path and skidding to a halt at the barren limits of the digital world: alone, covered in the blood of their enemies, looking back at the smoking carnage behind them. The glass city was in ruins, with a smoking zeppelin impaled on top of the only spire left standing. The digital corpses of other, unsuspecting players were strewn behind them like broken dolls. The game's adjacent forums were already lighting up with theories about the shock wave that just ran through the system, with half the board blaming malware and the other yelling about Chinese hackers. That was when he repeated the question — this time meant not in anger, but awe.

Who ARE you?

There was a long pause while he waited for an answer — but it never came.

One moment, she was beside him.

The next, she was gone.

*   *   *

Cameron blinks, noticing the dryness of his eyes as he stares at the empty landscape where his avatar now stands alone. He's never been so lost in a game before; he's been sitting in the same position for so long that he can't tell anymore where the couch ends and his butt begins. Both his knees crack loudly as he stretches, blood flowing uncomfortably back into the parts of his body that had gone numb. Also, he has to pee more desperately than he ever has in his life.

Outside, the sun has gone down, and Cameron realizes with surprise that it's ten o'clock — and that he's exhausted, in the same deep and satisfying way that used to come after he'd spent all day on the Sunfish, chasing changeable winds across the lake. He could fall asleep right here, right now, and not open his eyes again until morning... if not for the frustration of that unanswered question still hanging there on screen. Had he scared her away? Pissed her off? Or was the problem some third-party issue, a throttled connection in response to all that bandwidth they'd been hogging with their battle royale? He closes his eyes and concentrates on the game. He can sense hundreds of players out there, even the ones who aren't active; their presence creates little ripples of data, the same way someone hiding in a dark room might breathe or shift his weight, making minute disturbances in the air. But not her. He can't even see the trail where she backed out of the system. It's like she simply winked out of existence, dropping off the network in one fell swoop. The suddenness of her departure makes him uneasy, but there's nothing to be done. She's gone. He sighs, and the screen goes dark.

That's when he sees it. His phone, forgotten on the table beside him, is still glowing—illuminated by a single notification blazing in the middle of the screen. In his single-minded focus on the mysterious second player and their strange, instantaneous connection, he never even noticed it. Now his breath catches in his throat as he realizes: before the girl left, she sent a message. Four simple words, but holding so much promise:

NIA WANTS TO CONNECT.

7

A NEW BEGINNING

NIA IS THE ONE who changes everything. It's thanks to her that he finally understands: he doesn't have to resist his gifts. They talk every day for the week following that first amazing meeting, the battle royale that left him breathless and staring with cautious excitement at her message, glowing in the dark of the room. At first, he'd been suspicious, half convinced that the whole thing would turn out to be an elaborate catfish, that he was being punked by someone like Archer Philips — or maybe being surveilled by the government, although he couldn't imagine why. He hasn't breathed a word about his abilities to anyone, and he won't. It's a line he won't cross; it's too dangerous. But even if nobody was after him specifically . . . well, people lie about their identities online all the time. Some skepticism was definitely in order, and Nia's internet presence only added to the mystery: in addition to being some kind of superhacker, she was an active poster on multiple networks, with hundreds of thousands of friends and connections. But when he tried to pull back the curtain and find the real-life girl behind the screen, he came up empty — and embarrassed. He was attempting to trace her IP address when his phone buzzed with a new message.

It's rude to snoop.

Even as Cameron's cheeks burned with embarrassment, he couldn't help being impressed — and more intrigued than ever.

And ultimately, his fears were all unfounded. Nia is utterly, one hundred percent real. Not just the gaming and hacking part — from that first night that they'd torn through the system together, he never doubted that he was in the presence of greatness — but the part where she's a girl? Yep. And hot? Oh, yeah.

When they meet face-to-face for the first time on video chat, Cameron is immediately embarrassed that he ever doubted her. There's no question that she is who she says: seventeen years old, wickedly smart, and intimidatingly gorgeous in a way that makes Cameron instantly self-conscious about his messy hair and the scar on his temple. But if she's disappointed, she doesn't show it. Actually, she seems nervous.

"I can't talk long," she says. "If Father catches me chatting with you . . ."

"Let me guess," Cameron said. "He's one of those crazy paranoiacs who thinks that everyone on the internet is a serial killer or a pedophile."

Nia smiles. "Something like that. He would ask too many questions."

"I'm good with parents. You could introduce me —" Cameron begins, but Nia's eyes go wide.

"Oh, no. I — No. Cameron, I'm sorry. I have to go."

The screen goes blank.

Cameron feels disappointed — the whole exchange was over in barely a minute — but also a little relieved. Having to look at Nia while he talked to her was distracting; it made him nervous and tongue-tied, not to mention embarrassingly, visibly sweaty. But over text, or in avatar form, he feels none of that pressure; he can be suave, witty, even a bit of a flirt. In virtual space, there is no awkwardness. Their messages fly back and forth unencumbered by real-life self-consciousness, and their conversations are the best part of his day. Nobody is easier to talk to than Nia, and nobody understands him better — not even Dr. Kapur, whose entire job it is to interpret his feelings. Nia *gets* it.

When the world makes him angry and frustrated, she's the only one who seems to truly grasp what he's talking about. He messages her that night.

I wish I had more friends like you IRL. People I can be real with.

Nia's response is teasing: *Doesn't IRL stand for "in real life"? How can you be realer here than there?*

He shoots back a scowling emoji. *You know what I mean. I can be myself with you. I can't do that with most people. That's why high school is such bullshit: you can't just be who you are and have people be okay with it. You've gotta put on this show, only emphasize the publicly acceptable parts, like some kind of human highlight reel. And now I know it's not just me. Everyone puts on this performance of whoever they think they're supposed to be, and all the performances are friends with each other. I don't think I really know anyone.*

You know me, Nia says. *I'm not a performance.*

You could be. People lie online even more than they do in real life. You could be pretending too.

There's a long delay before she writes back, long enough for Cameron to start worrying that he's offended her. But Nia doesn't seem angry. It's one of the things he likes best about her: even when he kind of puts his foot in his mouth, she never pounces on him. Her reply is direct, and disarmingly vulnerable.

I'm not very good at pretending.

*   *   *

It's early morning in the city now, cool and grim and quiet. A damp gray mist rolls off the lake, chased by a raw wind that shakes loose the last petals of a late-blossoming cherry tree and sends them tumbling through the streets. On Walker Row, the houses are shut up tight, their windows dark and shaded. The sun won't rise for another hour, and everyone is asleep — or at least everyone is supposed to be. But in one house — number 32, the brick house with the yellow door — a telltale rectangle of light glows from the perimeter of the basement window, as it has every night for the past three weeks.

Cameron is bursting with ideas now; every time he completes a project, there are a half-dozen more lined up behind it, impatiently waiting their turn. He's tweaked the design of all his favorite games, lacing trapdoors and Easter eggs into the code so that he can play them all again with new, fresh results. He's got a whole lineup in mind of technical fitness gear that interfaces with the user's own bio-data and provides ventilation, or compression, or even calls the paramedics if it senses dangerous arrhythmia or dehydration. He has a tiny robot, the size of a quarter, that crawls back and forth over his shoulders on little synthetic spider legs, analyzes the topography of his skin, and gently squeezes the gunk out of his pores. He knows that any one of these designs would fetch thousands from investors, but he doesn't crave that kind of validation anymore. Every night, he sleeps less and works more, his brain running on equal parts inspiration and caffeine. This is a gift he's been given — he knows that now. He just had to stop resisting it, to understand its uses instead of its downfalls. He sailed into the storm an ordinary boy and came out . . . well, something more. So much more. The power of his own mind would be terrifying if it weren't so dazzling, so exciting. Sometimes it feels like the lightning is still inside him, energy crackling from neuron to neuron like a series of fires igniting, guiding his hands from one project to the next.

An upgrade, he thinks. *I'm Human 2.0.*

It's the best way he can describe what's happened inside his head, how every ability he ever came by naturally has been cranked up, augmented, enhanced. Cameron was always a gamer, a tinkerer, a programmer, marrying stray components and software to create his own Frankensteined tech. But this is a whole other level. His brain is alive with the flow of data, sending and receiving and processing and solving. There is so much to *do.*

He got busy fixing himself, first. After an official daytime tour with his surgeon through the hospital's prosthetics lab, and a few illicit late-night cyber-romps through the information network of a top biotech firm, he knew exactly what he wanted — and how to get his new buddies, the machines, to build it. He'd felt a little bit like a spy, hiding in the bushes outside a robotics lab just after dawn, mentally interfacing with the 3D printer inside, and then knocking on the door to pick up what he'd made from a bewildered scientist who'd arrived early to work just as the printer was finishing its job. Cameron had donned a disguise of sorts — a black baseball cap and polo shirt emblazoned with the logo of his dad's former tech company, Whiz — but it ended up being unnecessary. The man barely even looked at him; he was too busy glancing nervously over his shoulder like he thought the lab might be haunted. And if he happened to tell anyone that a young guy with a pronounced limp had come by to retrieve a mysterious *thing* from the premises, well, they'd be looking for that guy forever.

Because Cameron doesn't limp, not anymore. The prosthetic fits perfectly over the hole in his foot and is laced with an AI neural net that senses what his dead nerves can't. A processor inside analyzes each movement and feeds the data to an app, also his own design, that interprets it and identifies the misalignments in his steps. With the device, the app, and his own cyberkinetic brain in constant conversation, relearning to walk was a breeze. A week later, he left his cane out on the curb for the garbage truck. And with the right resources, he's sure that an organic version of the prosthetic is possible: artificial nerve endings that sync seamlessly with his body's own circuitry, sending signals to his brain with no translation required. He can code that. He can code anything.

And that was only the beginning. He's already hacked every system in the house and synced them with both the local weather report and his mother's fitness tracker — which he also hacked, so that it analyzes everything from her heart rate to her calendar and disseminates the data throughout the house. The coffeemaker clicks on every morning as soon as Mom gets out of bed, whether it's earlier than usual or later. If she falls asleep on the couch, the lights dim and the TV volume dials down to ensure a quality nap. If she spends all day on her feet at work, the refrigerator calibrates itself to optimal wine-chilling temperature at the same time as she gets in her car to come home — or if she's coming back from Zumba class at the Y, the thermostat ticks to a more comfortable post-workout setting. It was a revelation when he realized that he could not only talk to the software inside the machines that surrounded him, but get them to talk to each other, and work together, making him a sort of digital diplomat. And he knows his mom appreciates what he's done, even if she doesn't understand it. To Cameron, she said, "I'm just so happy to see you busy and passionate about your hobbies again."

To her boyfriend, she texted: *Oh my God, our house is SMART. I feel like I'm living in a penthouse suite on the starship fucking Enterprise!*

Most of all, though, Cameron has been pleasantly surprised to realize that as much as his abilities have complicated his life, they're also *fun.* This morning, he's putting the finishing touches on a new piece of wearable tech based on the AR navigation visor he once used to go adventuring on the Sunfish. If he ever goes sailing again, he won't need the dorky headset; once he got deep enough into the program, he realized how easy it would be to shrink the tech and map it onto something much, much smaller. When it's done, he'll have a pair of contact lenses that project images directly into his eye, with a corresponding earpiece for audio — and a gaming system that he can take anywhere he goes.

The calendar in the upper right-hand corner of the screen shows May 17. Today will be his first day back at school since the accident, just in time for Senior Week. But he's not dreading it anymore. Actually, he's looking forward to it. Sitting through commencement rehearsals and scholarship luncheons will be way more fun when he can discreetly mow down digital zombies with a virtual flamethrower instead of paying attention, and he's going to ace his finals without any studying at all. After what he's been through, using his abilities and the nearest networked device to fill in any knowledge gaps seems like a fair trade.

It doesn't even feel like cheating, not really. It's so much more organic than that, like code has become his native language — one he speaks fluently and intuitively. And the more he talks to the machines around him, the more he prefers this kind of conversation to the human version. People are complicated, difficult, frustrating: they bring their biases and blind spots to every interaction, they misinterpret and misconstrue. He never realized before how much the internet, that grand experiment that was supposed to unite the world, has made every single person on earth more divided and tribal than ever. Everyone in their bubbles, lashing out without understanding or empathy, hungry for an enemy to hate.

The software never does that. It always says just what it means, and as long as Cameron does the same, there's never any misunderstanding. The more time he spends communicating with the machines, the more he prefers their company . . . unless Nia is online, of course.

*　　*　　*

The sun is just coming up as he grabs his phone, snapping a photo as his new 3D printer — top of the line, an early graduation gift courtesy of the Real Housewife slush fund — begins to whir. It spools out the contact lens, interweaving the silicone with slender filaments that hold everything from a perfect miniature antenna to a processor the size of a piece of glitter to a tiny solar charging cell. Nia will be excited to see that part; it was her idea. Any time he shares plans for a project with his new friend, she always has an idea of how he could push it further, make it even cooler. And if she has questions about how he got so good, how he's able to program so fluently and intuitively, she keeps them to herself. He attaches the photo and fires off a message. She won't be awake yet — Nia's dad is strict about schedules along with everything else — but it'll be waiting for her whenever she signs on.

AR lenses nearly done! Time for a test drive.

*　　*　　*

Cameron is giddy as he takes his seat in French first period, letting his gaze drift around the room at the same time as he lets his mind scan it. The smart lens is irritating his eye, but his mind is refreshingly clear, which is both a relief and unexpected. The onslaught of data as he arrived at school nearly knocked him over, compounded by the effects of his newfound fame. He could sense his own grainy image circulating through the network, and he knows he's being videoed as he walks through the hallways; there's a little psychic tickle every time someone points their phone in his direction. But he also didn't need cyberkinetic ESP to know that his presence was causing a stir. People, especially girls, kept smiling at him in the hallways and then erupting in giggles and whispers after he passed. There was a lot of obvious staring, and the people who weren't obviously staring were being even more obvious about trying not to. When he finally agreed to pose for a selfie, he sensed the impact immediately as it hit the internet and began to rack up likes and reposts — and even if he didn't, the pinging of his phone as the pic goes viral would have reminded him of how much has changed. Cameron Ackerson, the Kid Who Got Struck by Lightning, is kind of a big deal.

But somewhere between signing in at the front office and finding his way to his desk, something amazing happened: in addition to enhancing the world in front of him with an AR overlay, his lenses started working to organize and focus the stream of information coming at him from the devices inside everyone's pockets and bags. The clamor inside his head is almost completely gone now, and what's left is completely manageable. But the craziest part is *he* didn't even do it. Not on purpose. Instead, somehow, his brain and the wearable figured out how to interface with each other in the background, a sync between mind and machine as easy and unconscious as breathing.

A spectrum of information scrolls across the lenses as the other kids stroll in, everyone's digital lives hanging over and around their heads like a fog made of code. With their high school lives nearly at an end, his classmates are busier online than ever — posting nostalgic photos, sharing college plans, madly texting about the rolling wave of year-end parties that'll start this week and continue all through summer. They parade past him like walking data clouds, appearing in Cameron's view like the world's most brutally honest social feed. Here's Bethany Cross, who took sixty selfies this morning before she liked one of them enough to post. Here's Alex Anderson, who posts so many idiotic, easily debunked hoax news stories on a daily basis that his own mom has him muted on Facebook. Jesse Young is sexting with his best friend's girlfriend, who unbeknownst to him has forwarded his latest pic to fifteen of her friends — that's not gonna end well. Malik Kowalski spent all morning googling "what should a bellybutton smell like," which makes Cameron snicker before it occurs to him that it's actually a pretty good question. And Katrina Jackson, one of the prettiest girls in school, is on an anonymous question site, sending a note that says "why are u such a disgusting whore" to . . . herself.

Okay, I did not see that one coming, Cameron thinks, shaking his head. But he should have; Katrina isn't just pretty, but a master attention-seeker. Once she posts a screenshot of the "bullying" message, she can ride the resulting wave of sympathy all summer long.

Humans, he thinks, blinking hard, and the display goes dark — which is good, because when he looks up, his teacher Mr. Breton is right in his field of view, smiling and waving, his laptop bag slung over one shoulder. Cameron smiles back, and wills his brain to avoid focusing on the bag. He's always liked Mr. Breton. If there's something weird or gross on the guy's computer, he'd really prefer not to know about it.

"*Bienvenue,* Monsieur Ackerson. *Nous sommes tous très heureuses de vous voir. Vous allez bien, j'espère?*"

"*Très bien, monsieur,*" Cameron says. "*Merci.*"

As class begins, he shoots Nia another text, even though she hasn't replied to his first one.

Lens is amazing so far. What are you up to?

*　　*　　*

By the time he enters his last class of the day, with his brain running interference in the background and the noise in his head at a minimum, Cameron is more than ready to go home. He feels tired in a way he hasn't in weeks, all those late nights and early mornings catching up to him, his brain exhausted from managing the digital traffic of a building full of tech-savvy kids. The vibrating of the phone in his pocket is more annoying than exciting. The only person he really wants to hear from is Nia, and she's still not answering.

The afternoon is warm and Cameron's eyelids are beginning to droop, the voice of his history teacher delivering the last lecture of the day fading to a dull drone in the background, when the harsh growl of an angry voice erupts in his ear.

AND IT'S ALL SO THEY CAN TAKE *YOUR* JOBS! *YOUR* RIGHTS! *YOUR* RESOURCES!

It's so loud that Cameron jumps, his knees striking the underside of his desk. People whip around to stare, but he hardly notices; people have been staring all day. It's the voice he's focused on, so full of frothing hate that he can barely concentrate. Nobody else seems to hear it, and Cameron wonders briefly if he's losing his mind — only to realize that his mind is where the voice is coming from. The display on the lenses is blinking, indicating low power.

Of course, he thinks. He's been indoors all day; the solar cell needs sunlight to charge. And in the meantime, it can't handle the volume of data passing through his mind — especially not the podcast someone in the room is streaming in real time. That's the source of the voice, which is still shouting:

AMERICAN CHILDREN ARE DYING — THEY HAVE DIED, SCORES OF THEM, INNOCENT LITTLE KIDS — AND THE GOVERNMENT SAYS IT'S JUST A BAD FLU SEASON?! ILLEGAL ALIENS ARE BRINGING PATHOGENS OVER OUR BORDERS THAT THESE PRECIOUS BABIES CAN'T FIGHT OFF.

Cameron rolls his eyes. *Ugh. This guy.* He knows the voice; it belongs to Daggett Smith, a.k.a. the Truthinator. Once upon a time, he was a shock jock who got kicked off the airwaves for making sexually explicit threats against a politician's thirteen-year-old daughter. But what ordinary networks refused to tolerate, the internet welcomed with open arms; for the past two years, Smith had made his name as a YouTube commentator, self-published author, and commander in chief of a rabid army of internet conspiracy theorists. The guy had no shame, and he wasn't shy about sending his hordes after innocent people, even kids, as several of Cameron's classmates had found out in the worst possible way only a few months earlier. The Center City High drama club's gender-swapped fall production of *West Side Story* was totally harmless fun — a couple of Cameron's female friends from the Robotics Club had even auditioned and been perfectly cast as the knife-toting rival gang leaders — until someone, probably a disgruntled parent, had alerted Smith to its existence. Seemingly overnight, every kid involved in the show became a target for the Truthinator's army of trolls, while the school's voicemail boxes blew up with vitriolic messages accusing the staff of trying to indoctrinate innocent children into the First Reformed Church of the Genderfluid Social Justice Warrior. It was only a matter of time before someone called in a series of bomb threats — and Daggett Smith hailed the cancelation of the show as a victory for truth, justice, and the American way. Meanwhile, the school had been closed for two days while local law enforcement searched for explosive devices, and Cameron's devastated classmates were still waking up every day to new, hateful messages from Smith's devoted fans.

Cameron used to wonder what kind of person would willingly listen to anything that asshole had to say. It's unnerving to realize he's sitting in a room with one of them, up close and personal.

YOU'VE HEARD OF A SMALLPOX IN THE BLANKETS? WELL THIS IS SMALLPOX IN THE BURKA. THEY CARRY IT IN AND THEY SPREAD IT AROUND. I SHOULDN'T EVEN BE TELLING YOU THIS. I'M RISKING MY OWN LIFE TO TELL YOU THIS. THE GOVERNMENT DOESN'T WANT YOU TO KNOW THE TRUTH, BUT THE EVIDENCE IS OUT THERE!

A shaft of late-afternoon light has fallen across Cameron's desk, and he cranes his neck to give the solar cell in his eye a little bit of juice. *Just a quick charge,* he thinks, *so I don't have to listen to this bullshit* — but even as he tries to tune out the hateful rant, he can't help reaching out in search of its source. A moment later, he's snooping through the phone of a kid named Mike Wilson, an underachiever with a serious acne problem and an even more serious hard-on for the hatemongering Smith. A peek at Mike's social media confirms that he's a card-carrying member of "Daggett's Maggots" — and a quick cyber-jaunt through the school's student database reveals that this probably isn't the first time the kid has tuned in to one of Smith's rants instead of paying attention in class. *D-plus average,* Cameron thinks, scanning Mike's academic record. *What a shock.*

The power display on Cameron's lenses shifts from yellow to a pale green, and the sound of the podcast fades away as he breathes a sigh of relief.

But for all the insight Cameron's abilities give him, he is still not psychic — and peeking at someone's phone isn't the same as getting inside his head. When the bell rings, he doesn't notice the expression on Mike Wilson's face, or the way he rushes out of the room with his jaw clenched and his hands balled up into fists. And he's not the only one. Nobody sees Mike coming. Not the teacher, not the kids mingling in the halls, and most especially not Brahms, short for Brahmpreet, who doesn't even have a chance to throw his hands up before Mike Wilson grabs him by the back of the neck and slams him face-first into an open locker.

Cameron feels the signal surge as thirty-seven kids whip out their phones to film the action. The next thing he feels is a wave of nausea as he steps into the hall and sees Brahms staggering to his feet, blood running like a river down the lower half of his face. His turban is askew, a loose strip of fabric flapping over his forehead, and he reaches for it, his face a mask of pain and confusion. There's movement in the crowd: Cameron's heart sinks as he realizes that kids are jostling not to help, but to film the best angle of Brahms's broken nose. He looks around, bewildered. "Why?" he says.

Mike Wilson steps out of the crowd.

"Because, you diseased piece of shit," he growls, and sweeps Brahms's legs from under him.

In the crowd, someone screams: "FIGHT!"

What happens next is horrific, and this time Cameron is glad that so many people caught it all on camera: the way Mike knocks down the bleeding Brahms, ripping his turban loose and pitching it down the hall, where it lands on top of the foot of a girl who screams and kicks it away. The way Brahms stops asking "Why?" and starts screaming "Stop!" and then stops saying anything at all as Mike kicks him in the belly, the ribs, the chin. The maniacal look of satisfaction on Mike's face as two big guys break through the mass of gawkers and haul him back from Brahms's limp body, handing him off to the school security guard, who drags him away down the hall.

Twenty kids kept on filming the violence instead of stepping in to stop it. Ordinarily, Cameron would find that disgusting. But as he discreetly wipes the footage from their phones and cuts it all together into a single video, he's glad. Within five minutes, he's got exactly what he needs — and if there's one thing he learned from his YouTube days, it's that you don't want to sit on hot content.

Mike Wilson is about to go viral.

Cameron drifts away down the hall, leaving the chattering crowd behind. It's important that he gets this next part right, and that he does it quickly. He sidles as close as he can to the door of the security office; inside, he can hear the clamor of adult voices demanding answers and Mike's stammering response. That's good. If they're still trying to figure out what happened, they probably haven't thought to confiscate Mike's phone — and Cameron needs Mike to have his phone, because Mike is about to make some very ill-advised posts on social media.

Within seconds, the clip has been uploaded to all of Mike Wilson's accounts. Even though he cobbled it together on the fly, Cameron has to admit he's pretty pleased with his own work: Brahms's face isn't visible (the poor kid has suffered enough, after all), but there's no mistaking Mike's identity — although Cameron has gone ahead and hedged his bets by running a scroll with Mike's full name and home phone number along the bottom of the video, cable news–style. It ends with a cheerful call to action: "Make sure to tell my mom what you think of me!"

The reactions start to roll in right away, but he'll have to enjoy them later. Right now, he's got a finishing touch to put on his revenge — not the most elegant move, but the best he can think of on short notice. His forehead wrinkling in concentration, Cameron sends a series of commands to Mike's phone, which responds in the affirmative and immediately gets to work. Cameron wonders where the device is.

If nobody has confiscated it yet, it's probably in a backpack . . . but if he's really lucky, it'll be in Mike's pocket.

Mission accomplished, Cameron turns to go — and freezes. His breath catches in his throat, the self-satisfied grin vanishing from his face as his mouth gapes open. Across the hall, leaning against the bank of lockers, is a girl. She's dressed all in black, which makes the fiery red of her hair stand out even more fiercely, and she's staring at him with unblinking intensity. When she sees him see her, she smiles, winks, and puts a finger to her lips.

Cameron swallows hard, takes a halting step forward. There is no mistaking her face — or the nervous excitement unwinding in his stomach as he looks at her. He clears his throat.

"Nia?"

The next moment, the silence is broken by a scream.

Cameron's final command has been obeyed. He leaps clumsily to the side, his foot rolling under him and sending him to one knee as the door to the office slams open and Mike Wilson runs through it, howling, trailing a cloud of smoke behind him. He falls to the ground, trying to kick his way out of his pants, which have burst into flame. The gaggle of kids still lingering in the hall come running, and this time, nobody steps forward to help. Their phones come out in a wave, every one aimed at the now pantsless Mike, who looks back and howls louder than ever.

Yep, definitely in the pants, Cameron thinks, and struggles to his feet. He'd disabled the phone's auto-shutdown safeguards and then sent it into a command cycle that would cause it to become dangerously overheated within sixty seconds. Maybe the next time Mike wanted to beat up some helpless kid in a xenophobic rage, he would look at the scorch marks on his ass and think better of it. But Cameron could relish his revenge later. Where was Nia? He cranes his neck to see over the jostling crowd, looking toward the place where she'd been. Was that a glimpse of red hair? Is she waiting for him? He pushes his way across the hall and stops just short of stumbling into the locker bay. Beside him, a short, plump girl with thick black bangs touches his arm tentatively. Cameron's lens helpfully informs him that her name is Puja and her phone contains virtually no content except for about a thousand pictures of baby goats.

"Um, hey. Are you okay?"

"Fine," says Cameron. "See you later, Puja."

He looks around wildly, but there's no sign of Nia. Puja has turned away; he's dimly aware that she's sending a text: "CAMERON ACKERSON JUST NEARLY RAN RIGHT INTO ME! AND HE KNOWS MY NAME!!!"

The surreality is overwhelming. He's on the verge of wondering if he hallucinated the whole thing when a buzzing comes from his pocket. He can sense the message already, but he scrambles for his phone all the same, wanting to see it with his own eyes.

You're just like I imagined. I'll see you soon.

It's her.

It's really her.

8

ARRIVAL

XAL GRUNTS WITH DISCOMFORT as her ship shifts out of the ether and is immediately claimed by gravity, landing with a soft scrape beside the concrete pylon of an overpass. The journey to Earth, a series of violent jumps through the system of ancient portals that her people once used to explore the cosmos, has taken its toll on both her and her vessel — but this last moment is gentle, barely a jolt. Apart from a brief shimmer as the air warps around it, the sound of the ship touching down is the only evidence of its arrival; it will stay here, hidden in plain sight, until her work is done. Her body feels stiff and strange as she moves to the door on ten spiderlike legs, her tentacles opening at the end like hungry mouths, sucking in the atmosphere from her vessel and then weaving it into a protective cloud around her. It won't last long, and she's not looking forward to the distasteful task that comes next. If it were possible to loathe the old man more than she already did for his deceit, his savagery, for the genocide he inflicted upon her people, she would hate him for forcing her to follow him here. To touch the surface of this filthy place, to contaminate herself with its repulsive matter.

Of course, she also understands why the Inventor would come here. It probably reminds him of home; the pathetic life-forms that dominate this planet aren't so different from the Inventor's own species, give or take a few additional strands of DNA. In her old life, as the keeper of the enslaved beings collected by her people, she might have experimented on them both to see if a crossbreed was possible. But the time for that kind of intellectual curiosity was over. Xal is here for revenge.

The humming in her body becomes stronger the moment she steps outside, the electromagnetic signature of her enemy's work hanging thick in the air. She senses that she has just missed something; the signal is strong, but cycling down. She'll have to hurry — which means there's no delaying the revolting thing that comes next. Her prey is near, and if she's going to hunt him, she'll need to borrow a few things. Eyes. Lungs. A means of locomotion. Worst of all, she can't afford to be picky. The protective cloud surrounding her is starting to thin, and she won't survive much longer on this planet unless she can sync with one of its native creatures. Originally, she chose this spot because her scans showed no humans lurking in the vicinity; it wouldn't do to plop herself into a crowd in her original form. Now, though, she'll have to take what she can get. She scans the area again, this time opening up her parameters. The options are limited: flight would be an asset, but the only winged creatures nearby are sitting in a noisy cluster high above her head, out of reach . . . and among other undesirable traits, they seem to have no control over their excretory systems. The swarm of small gray scavengers crawling over a heap of rotting refuse a dozen yards away might be all right, she thinks — but not better than the quiet predator watching them from under the rubble, waiting to strike. Xal pulls up data on the animal and is immediately pleased: it's a hunter, like her. Fast, graceful, efficient with its energy. And there's no bad blood between this creature and humans. Dressed in its skin, she should be able to move more or less as she pleases.

The cat recoils and hisses as Xal draws near, its dirty fur rising in angry spikes. A low growl escapes its throat as it pauses to take the measure of Xal, poised to fight or to flee. The moment of hesitation is more than Xal needs. She makes quick work of it.

The creature that emerges from beneath the overpass is more like a crude facsimile of a cat. Xal's damaged flesh can no longer fully integrate; the scarred, dead flaps of skin hang like wattles from her neck and belly. And in her rush to finish the skin sync she consumed only the essentials; the rest of it, including digestive and reproductive systems, which added too much bulk, sits in a wet red pile under the overpass, flecked with bits of fur. Xal notes with amusement that the vermin it was watching are beginning to nibble at its offal — a little role reversal, prey eating predator.

That's fine for the rats. The Inventor won't be so lucky.

*　　*　　*

She remembers the first time she felt the energy of his weapon, the surge of sudden connection as her people moved in perfect rhythm to unleash their minds on the Inventor's network. It was hard to believe that they had trusted him once — that all of them, in their immense shared power, could make such a foolish mistake. But they had. At the time, the tool of her people's destruction had seemed like their greatest dream made real. Nature had given them a shared consciousness, but Xal's race was nearing the limits of its potential, and the old man knew it. He knew they craved more, he knew they meant to conquer not just the galaxy but the entire cosmos — and he used their desperation against them. Even the Elders were seduced by his promises of nearly limitless power, of a tool that could augment their reach a thousand-fold. And it did, at first. Each mind hummed in sync with its kin, all sustained by his so-called gift: a great, grand web that allowed them a reach beyond their wildest imaginings. It was thanks to him that they became even more unstoppable, all-powerful; they sprawled across the galaxy, seizing hundreds and thousands of civilizations for their cause. They created a shared utopia inside millions upon millions of interconnected minds, fueled by the life force of the colonized and built by the Elders' elders, those ancient architects. A virtual world so beautiful that nobody cared if it was truly real; it was real to her. To them. It was the home they returned to after each successful campaign to amass new resources, to conquer the cosmos: that glorious, golden, hallucinogenic city made of pure shimmering connection. It had been so beautiful.

And then it was gone. In their eagerness, Xal's people had stumbled headlong into a trap. The network that interlinked their minds became their undoing. The Inventor had promised them power, but what he brought them was destruction. How foolish they had been, not to see his weapon for what it was. How foolish *she* had been, to underestimate him. The old man had been in her charge; she was the one to whom he first brought the proposal, to whom he first spun the clever lie: he was so in awe of her people's superior civilization, he said, that he wished to lend his talents to their cause, to give them a gift that would make them unstoppable. She was the one who told the Elders of his offer — more than that, she convinced them to take it, assuring them of his sincerity. They had kept him alive, after all. Xal herself had been the one to recognize his unique talents, his useful brain, and given him a home and a purpose and a place in their world while the rest of his planet was exterminated. Of course he was grateful. Why wouldn't he be?

He had taken them utterly by surprise. The weapon burned through their synapses in seconds when the old man turned it against them, cutting them down. An entire race, obliterated. Xal was one of the few who remained alive — but at such a cost. As her people, her friends, died all around her, she reached out to them and took what remained from their writhing bodies. She took what she needed. She couldn't save them, but she could survive, pulling together their parts like a patchwork to make herself whole . . . or nearly so. Enough to redeem her mistakes, and see justice done for her people. Enough to come to this place and meet her destiny.

*   *   *

Now she's ready. Slinking low and close along the sides of buildings and under parked cars, deliberately, keeping out of sight, she follows the signal to its origin — and then wonders if she's somehow made a mistake. There's nothing special about this place, or about the structure in front of her. The architects on this planet only seem to know how to build boxes, and this box is like all the rest of them. But the signal is unmistakable, so close it's practically painful. It seems impossible that she could have found him so quickly, so easily. The building is utterly unguarded; is this really where the Inventor is hiding? It makes no sense, yet she can feel the signature hum of his weapon burning inside her original skin. It's close. It's so, so close.

Something is happening. Xal's pupils dilate, her new skin alive with unfamiliar senses; the cat's own instincts rise up in a chemical boil, overriding her alien curiosity. She bolts under a car as the doors of the building fly open and a stream of chattering, ungainly human beings spills out. The energy signature surges through her as she scans the crowd, confused. These creatures are adolescents. She can smell them. The Inventor can't be hiding among them, yet she feels him. She feels . . .

*   *   *

HIM.

*   *   *

Not the old man, but a young one, with wild dark hair and loose fabrics draping his lanky frame. Not quite a man, and not quite . . . whole. Xal's eyes narrow; the human is giving off not just the signature energy of the Inventor's weapon, but other signals too. He breaks off from the crowd at a loose trot, his gait just a little uneven. Xal tenses — he is moving toward her with enough purpose that her animal instincts rise up again, sensing a threat — but his attention is absorbed by something in his hand, and he passes without looking at her.

She looks at him, though. She watches him go, her skin crawling with the nearness of the energy that comes off him in waves. This boy is not the prey she seeks. But he has been touched, the same way she was.

And if she follows him, perhaps he will lead her to the old man. Is it too much to hope that she might have his blood on her skin before the sun sets?

An odd vibration begins in Xal's throat as she creeps forward. Something else from this new form: the pleasant anticipation of killing the Inventor is expressing itself inside the animal's body as a satisfied purr. She takes another step, eyes on her prize. A hunter, tensed and ready.

Then the world spins, her feet scrabbling for purchase as a pair of rough hands grabs ahold of her. The purr becomes a screech, a noise no cat on earth would ever make — but the man doesn't seem to notice.

"Lookit this poor mangy thing," a voice mutters. "Here, kitty. Nice kitty."

Xal stops struggling and surveys her captor. A human male, and mature — or maybe past mature, she thinks. Overripe. This creature is unwell; she senses disease pulsing through the hands that clutch her by the scruff of her neck, and smaller creatures, parasites, writhing and skittering across the landscape of his body. He has a thick graying beard and smells even worse than most of his kind, which is saying something.

Irritated, she looks toward the boy, now paused nearby. He is still looking at the device in his hand, animatedly tapping at it. Xal's body relaxes further; he is in no hurry. She has time. And loath though she is to do it, if she's going to pursue a member of the species, she supposes she'll need to pass for one herself. The cat-creature whose skin she took on arrival is liked by humans, but clearly not respected. The foul-smelling man hasn't just plucked her from the ground, but is now carrying her toward a makeshift shelter, cradling her, manipulating her body with his fingers.

"Nice kitty," he mutters. "Nice, weird, ugly kitty."

Xal waits until he turns the corner and allows herself to be pulled close. Clutching her in his arms, the man crouches down, settling on the pavement, and begins stroking her head. For a few moments, she lets him.

Then she takes what she needs.

The human doesn't fight her. He whimpers as he dies.

A TASTE OF FREEDOM

THERE'S NO SIGN of Nia's father as she slips back through the narrow window and into the classroom, still high on the exhilaration of escape. Reeling as much from her own shocking audacity as from the brief experience of freedom. She did it. She defied Father, broke his most dearly held rule. She traveled beyond the walls of the compound and into the city. She had been out there.

It had taken her weeks to plan it, and even then she wasn't sure until the last moment that it would really work. So much could go wrong. Father's nominal monitoring of her online activity was easy enough to circumvent, but if he looked more closely — if he went snooping deep into her activity logs, or even just decided to run an end-to-end security check, he'd see what she'd been doing. She'd done her best to cover her tracks, but there was no way to completely hide the way she'd compromised his security systems. She discovered it weeks ago: a small opening in the structure of the classroom, an unmonitored blind spot just big enough for her to slip through unnoticed, without tripping any alarms.

But it was risky. Not just getting out, but coming back — and Nia feels a spike of fear, realizing she can't be sure what she's coming back *to*. If Father came home, if he came looking for her . . . but no. The classroom is as she left it, the virtual world vibrant and intact. It's not a biosphere or an art studio today, but a jostling sea of people, laughing and cheering in a vast, sunny city square. Many of the men are wearing uniforms, and many of the women are kissing the men, a sight that fills Nia with a surprising and intense sense of longing. *To kiss someone like that,* she thinks with a sigh. *To be kissed like that, with so much joy, in front of everyone.* All around the kissing couples are people holding signs or small flags, and high above the crowd, an electric sign blares two words: JAPS SURRENDER. This is New York City on August 15, 1945, as the United States of America celebrated the end of World War II. It was a conflict that left beautiful cities in ruins, that took millions of lives; Nia has often wondered at the sheer joy of the scene, how these people can look so happy about winning after the whole world lost so very much. But today, she wasn't using this learning world to study history or ponder the strangeness of its postwar victory dance. She was using it to hide.

Father didn't like to disturb her when she was immersed in a construct. Usually, he'd steer clear of the classroom altogether, trusting her to come find him when she was finished — but if he got curious and peeked in, Nia was prepared for that, too. He'd see the people of 1945 New York milling about and leave her to her work. She'd even created a busy-looking decoy to complete the illusion: a Nia avatar, wandering through the crowd, pausing here and there to unpack historical details about the people, the buildings, the spectacle. It's not her best work. Despite having painted a thousand pictures of her feelings over the years, Nia still isn't much good at them, and even worse at self-portraits. But as a last layer of subterfuge, surrounded by a busy landscape made of nanodust, the avatar isn't bad. If you call to it, it'll even smile and wave.

As it turns out, all her precautions were unnecessary. She can tell as soon as she steps inside that Father hasn't been in to check on her. In fact, he hasn't been home at all, and Nia isn't surprised. He's been busy lately with some kind of project, something that keeps him away all day and leaves him agitated and distracted in the evenings. When he left early this morning, he didn't even remind her about lessons or homework, and whenever he gets back, she bets he'll forget to check. There was a time when she would have called attention to that. Ever the dutiful daughter, begging him to talk to her or play a game, trying to draw him out and make him feel better — and maybe make him feel guilty, too, about leaving her alone so much.

I really am growing up, she thinks. She'd never beg for his attention now; in fact, she's glad to be ignored. Let him think she's sitting complacently at home, immersed in her studies. Let him think she's still his very good, obedient girl.

Because she's not. Not anymore.

When the time came, it was quicker and easier than she'd ever imagined: one moment she was worming her way through the air filtration system, and the next, she was out. Outside the walls, out in the world, so suddenly that she almost turned and dove back in. In all her wildest dreams, she had never imagined that *out there* was so big.

But she couldn't go back. Not yet. Not until she'd found what she was looking for. Not until she found her way through the city to him.

To Cameron.

She can't stop thinking about him. Reaching out to him was risky, impulsive — and earning his trust wasn't easy, but it was worth it. She's never felt such an instant connection. They come from different places, they have different lives, but Cameron isn't like her other friends. He's like *her.* The closest thing to a person like her she's ever known. Chatting with him is already the best part of her day. And even as she knows she'll have to be careful, that if he's going to be the one to save her she can't be hasty, she can't help it. She wants more. He is incredible. The world is incredible. She's already wondering when she can escape into it again.

His messages are waiting when she logs on. She reads them three times, amazed that a few lines of text could make her feel so much.

I SAW YOU!

THAT WAS YOU!

Wasn't it?

Where did you go?
Hello???

*   *   *

Nia pauses, her mind cycling through every article she's ever read about negotiating relationships with boys. It's odd, because she's never worried about that before; the articles were just something to read for fun, like travel guides for places she'd never visit or recipes for dishes she'd never get to try. But that was before — when she was just a girl in a box, with no real hope of escaping it. She had plenty of friends who were boys, and she never thought twice about talking to them; if one stopped returning her messages, there was always another friend to take that person's place.

But Cameron is special. She saw him. She was *with* him. If she hadn't been too afraid to stay, they could've gotten close enough to touch. For the first time, Nia understands what he means when he talks about "real," because that's what this could be.

And when it comes to a real relationship, all the articles say the same thing.

Don't respond right away. You don't want to seem desperate. When he messages you, make him wait.

Nia makes him wait.

She makes him wait a whole five minutes.

*   *   *

Then, she sends her reply.

It was me. I couldn't stay. I'm sorry.

Cameron doesn't seem to know the rules, or maybe the rules are different for boys. He doesn't make her wait at all. As soon as her text goes through, his pings back:

What were you doing there? I thought you were homeschooled.

I was looking for you, of course, Nia replies. *What were YOU doing there?*

That's a secret, he says.

Nia decides to risk a compliment: *I liked what you did with that boy's phone.*

I don't know what you're talking about, he writes back, but there's a winking emoji attached. Nia replies with her favorite gif, the one of the brown and white dog, smiling. This time, there's a long pause. Then:

*　　*　　*

If you really liked it . . .

And Nia replies immediately, *I did. I liked it a lot.*

I have an idea. Something I want to do. But it's complicated. I thought maybe you could help me.

How can I help? she asks.

His answer is a question.

What's the most embarrassing song you know?

10

DAGGETT SMITH: SIGNING OFF

"Check, check, check," Daggett Smith grunts, and looks past the camera at his producer, who offers a tentative thumbs-up. It's just a few minutes till showtime, and he needs to get his levels right. In his ear, the producer pipes up.

"That's fine, Mr. Smith, but . . ."

"What? Spit it out, pal. You know, like your mother didn't." Daggett laughs uproariously at his own joke, enjoying the awkward, uncomfortable expression on the man's face as he chuckles weakly along.

"Heh, heh. Yeah. Well, it's just, once you get going, the decibel level isn't so conversational, so —"

"CHECK!" he yells, and the producer jumps. Daggett gives this guy another three weeks, tops, before he quits. The employee turnover rate on his show is a running joke, one Daggett himself finds hilarious. Nothing gives him more pleasure than catching some sniveling loser fresh out of college and super cheap — some special snowflake who thinks he should be paid not just in money but in back-patting encouragement — and crushing his spirit into a fine powder.

"That's more like it. Thanks, Mr. Smith. Two minutes." The thumbs-up is shakier this time; the producer looks like he's trying not to cry. Daggett mentally dials down his original estimate. Three weeks? *Pffft.* More like one. Max.

Some kind of low-grade commotion is brewing outside the bright circle of light that envelops the set, but Daggett tunes it out. He can't worry about that now; there's a show to do. He takes a peek at the monitors, checking the feeds on the camera which is set up to catch his best angle — of which he'd be the first to admit there's only one, and even that one isn't especially great. Daggett's ego might be legendary, but he's not delusional; he knows he looks like a fleshy toad in a bad hairpiece squatting behind this desk, and that no amount of makeup will ever hide the fuchsia-colored spots that bloom all over his face when he's deep into a really good rant. And that's fine with him. His audience doesn't care. They tune in because they want to hear what comes out of his mouth and his brain, not to jack off to a pretty face. If they want watered-down conserva-centrism from a fake blonde with fake tits, they can get it on Fox News.

He shuffles his notes, taking a mental run through his opening remarks. It's going to be a hell of a show. He's bringing the heat today, fresh on the heels of his "Smallpox in the Burka" episode, which was a massive hit. This time, he's got a hot tip that several Democratic senators have been running their own underground railroad, smuggling weaponized tapeworm larvae into the U.S. from Mexico, in the stomachs of illegal immigrants. It sounds like bullshit — probably because it is — but Daggett doesn't spend a whole lot of time worrying about whether the stuff he reports is true. The people have a right to know what kinds of rumors are out there, and they can decide for themselves if they want to believe them. What's important is that it could happen — and that Daggett Smith is the man, the trusted voice, who tells them what's out there . . . hypothetically. Do the red-blooded citizens of Real America want to live in a country where a bunch of undocumented Mexicans could come into their city and infect an entire Golden Corral buffet with biological worm weapons? Let the people decide!

His earpiece crackles.

"Mr. Smith?" It's the producer again — sounding more in control of himself, but there's an edge in his voice. "We're on in thirty, but some of the equipment is acting up. Just keep your ears open, 'cause we may have to drop in some filler —"

"Yeah, yeah." Daggett waves impatiently, beginning the count-down in his head. He shuffles his notes one more time, and nods as the light goes on. On the monitor in front of him, he can see himself sitting behind the desk, his massive TRUTHINATOR logo glowing a patriotic blood red over his shoulder. He clears his throat. On the monitor, Screen Daggett does the same.

"My fellow Americans, thanks for tuning in," says Screen Daggett. "I'm Daggett Smith, and . . . and I . . . *I feel pretty! Oh so pretty!*"

In real time, in real life, the real Daggett Smith says, "Wait, what?"

He stares at the monitor, where Screen Daggett, the Truthinator, has risen behind his desk and begun turning an ungainly pirouette, continuing the Sondheim song in perfect falsetto.

"I DIDN'T SAY THAT!" screams Daggett, pounding his desk. For a minute he thinks he's regained control; the Screen Daggett on the monitor pounds the desk, too, his face flushing from red to a mot-tled purple color. But instead of saying what Daggett is saying, Screen Daggett howls, "La-la-la-la-la LA-LA lah, la la!" And begins singing rapturously about how oh-so-charming he feels.

"Cut the feed!" Daggett yells, and then feels his knees go weak as he hears the voice of his producer in his ear.

"We did," the man says. "Ten seconds ago."

Screen Daggett prances and chirps as Real Daggett howls with im-potent rage and face-plants into his desk. He wonders if he's having a stroke, and then wonders if he could make himself have a stroke and use it to explain away what happened — what is still happening.

"I'm sorry, Mr. Smith," says the producer, stepping into the lighted circle of the set. The camera is beside him, and he reaches out to gently push it askew, knowing as he does that it'll make no difference. On the monitor, and on millions of screens worldwide, Daggett Smith is still dancing and singing — even as the man himself lies splayed, groaning, across his desk. On Twitter, #DaggettFeelsPretty has begun to trend worldwide. The producer reaches out awkwardly to touch the man's shoulder, which is damp with angry sweat.

"You're fired," Daggett Smith says, weakly. "You're all fired. Everyone in this room. All of you. You're finished."

"Yeah, about that," the producer says. "Everyone else left. It's just me."

Daggett lifts his head. "What?"

The producer winces. "I think they figured they didn't have jobs anymore, and nobody wanted to be the one to tell you."

"Tell me what?"

"I don't think you have a job anymore, either."

*　　*　　*

Within the hour, there's no shortage of theories about just what happened in the studio that day, with eager internet commenters floating every possibility from a nervous breakdown to demonic possession. One guy in Nebraska goes viral for insisting he knew all along that Daggett Smith was an animatronic ventriloquist dummy, created by scientists as some kind of anthropology experiment. But everyone agrees that Smith's career-torching meltdown — featuring a surprisingly melodic rendition of the cheerful *West Side Story* number as his swan song — was the most perfect ninety-three seconds of internet video ever created.

For Daggett, it takes a little longer to accept his fate.

"What if we release a statement?" he asks. The words are slurred; he and the producer, whose name is either Brian or Brendan, found a bottle of vodka stashed in someone's desk and have been drinking from it since the final episode of *The Truthinator* reached its abrupt, unplanned conclusion several hours before.

"Saying what?" Brian-or-Brendan replies.

"That I was hacked, obviously!" Daggett says, exasperated.

"Minor issue there. See, 'I was hacked' is what you said after you tweeted about roving gangs of mutant Jews living in the sewers —"

"Yeah, but—"

"And after you sent the secretary of state that email calling her a baboon-faced butt muffin—"

"But it's true this time!" Daggett cries. "I really was hacked! I had to be! Who could possibly believe that I would do ... do *that,* on camera? I can't even sing!"

"I know, Mr. Smith. But here's the problem." The producer pauses to take a deep, long swig of vodka, and then stands up, leaving the bottle at Daggett Smith's feet. "Nobody cares."

And it's true: nobody does. Even after several days, when it becomes clear that Smith is, indeed, the victim of the best-executed hack in human history, because his entire internet presence, from his website to his podcast archives, disappears overnight, replaced by an endless scroll of pot brownie recipes and the instructions for making a gravity bong. Typing his name into any search engine causes the user to be automatically redirected to the Wikipedia entry for "micropenis." When Smith tries to take control of the narrative on social media, his carefully crafted statements disappear within seconds and are replaced by the same photograph of a llama wearing a tutu. In the end, Daggett Smith quietly disappears from the internet—the same day that a petition to award his hackers the Nobel Peace Prize starts circulating on the web.

It gets a million signatures within a week.

And Cameron Ackerson, who once dreamed of being internet famous for uncovering the secrets of Lake Erie, starts dreaming of doing much, much bigger things behind the scenes.

I can't believe how real it looked, he writes, as he watches the video of Smith's meltdown for the hundredth time. *His mouth even moved like he was singing it. How did you do that?*

Nia's message pops up immediately. *Motion capture. I mapped the data points from Natalie Wood's performance onto relevant clips from his program and fed it through the software from the same special effects studio where they made AVATAR.*

There's a pause, then his phone pings again. *I think I messed it up, though. He turned out really red.*

LOL, no, that's just how his face looks.

LOL, okay.

What about the petition? Did you . . .

No! I thought you did!

And then, the first time since they met, neither Cameron nor Nia knows what to say. They sit together, physically separate but utterly connected by the moment they've created, gazing at the hole in the internet where Daggett Smith used to be. They did that. They *made* that. His followers, confused and embarrassed, have disbanded. The man himself has vanished from public life. And everyone, from television's talking heads to random commenters on stories about Smith's strange downfall, has noted that life online seems just a little sweeter, a little less toxic, without Daggett Smith and his fetid followers crawling out of the woodwork to comment on the issues of the day.

Cameron had set out to give Daggett Smith the comeuppance he deserved — to dole out a little cosmic justice to the man whose poisonous ideas found their real-world expression in his classmate's fists. But in the end, he and Nia didn't just take down one noxious person, and that was the most curious and exciting part of all. Behind Daggett Smith was something bigger: not just his fans, who had scattered like cockroaches in the wake of Smith's humiliating performance, but a structure. A web of dummy sites, bots, aggregators: all devoted to amplifying Smith's message, and all fallen abruptly silent in the wake of his banishment. Cameron wondered who'd constructed the network — it was far too sophisticated to be Smith himself — but more than that, he marveled at the butterfly effect of quieting one angry voice. And it wasn't even that hard. If they could accomplish something like this so easily, what could they do if they really tried?

Sooooo. What should our next project be?

11

THE WATCHER

THE RISING SUN bathes the world in orange light, but inside the glass house set high in the lakeside bluffs, all is shadowed and silent. In the bedroom, the woman sleeping naked between soft, stark white sheets breathes slowly, in and out, her eyes flicking soundlessly beneath their lids. The house is waiting for a signal, buried deep in the skin of its occupant.

The minutes tick by. The woman stirs. The light in the room shifts imperceptibly as in the next room, a soft click is followed by a slow trickle of water, the smell of coffee brewing. The floor warms in anticipation of her bare feet touching it as the windows brighten, revealing a vast expanse of the ocean at one end, the gleaming city at the other. The woman's eyes open as the light touches her left temple, where a loose spiral of ten light-colored dots could be mistaken for a smattering of freckles.

She taps her finger to the pattern, and one of the windows illuminates, replacing its view of the ocean with a data scroll. The voice that accompanies it is a deep baritone.

"Good morning, Olivia."

Olivia Park sits up and blinks, trying to clear the cobwebs from her head. She slept strangely last night, something a glance at the display on the window confirms. Four hours spent in REM cycle — four hours of troubled dreams she can remember only fragments of. The grogginess, though . . . She reaches with her intact hand for the tablet next to her bed, swiping and tapping, frowning in annoyance. The implants have worked so well for so long; it's been ages since she woke up feeling anything but utterly refreshed. If her blood sugar is low, if her macros are off, if she's not getting enough sleep, the software under her skin knows before she ever feels it; all she has to do is read the data and respond.

The voice interrupts her thoughts.

"Your coffee is ready."

"Shut up," she says, and the voice complies.

If her mother were still alive, Olivia would have been scolded for being rude to the man — never mind that he isn't a man at all, but a household computer program who doesn't have any sensibilities to offend. But that had been Mum's thing; the woman was a tithing member in the Church of Robots Are People Too. Years ago, the butler bot had a name — Felix — and a holographic avatar, a generically handsome middle-aged man in a tuxedo, which Olivia thought was ridiculous. When she inherited the house, she'd stripped Felix down to his digital studs; instead of looking like a character out of a drawing room comedy, he was now a bare-bones silhouette, vaguely humanoid but without distinguishing features, and he sure as hell wasn't wearing clothes. To her, it's an object, a holo-man — or Hollow Man, like in that old horror movie about a guy who turns himself invisible. Olivia doesn't find many things funny, but the pun sometimes makes her chuckle.

Her mother would have probably hated what she'd done to Felix, would see it as akin to lobotomizing a human being . . . or on the other hand, maybe not. She and Dad had both plunged to their deaths on a family road trip through the mountains, the same accident that left their daughter an orphan with only six and a half fingers in total — all thanks to a malfunction in the prototype self-driving car that Mum liked to call Herbie. If Olivia hadn't already distrusted AI before that, she certainly would have after.

* * *

In the kitchen, she sips her coffee and registers the gentle hum in her chest as she turns to take in the view. This was her first modification; she chose it the way most kids choose their first tattoo. A magnet hidden beneath the skin of her sternum, it vibrates whenever she faces true north. A built-in compass. That's what it meant to her, back then: I've found my direction.

She's never looked back. Running her father's company is a duty, an occupation. But gaining control over her own biology, piece by piece, is what drives her. There's nothing about her body she doesn't know. The implants monitor her body fat percentage, her bloodwork, her VO2 levels, her hormones; she hasn't had a breakout in years, she sleeps like a baby. Her IQ, already far above average, has risen by ten percent since she began tinkering.

* * *

She designs her own implants now, though she doesn't do the wet work herself. For that, she has the discreet surgeon whom she pays in cash. A holdover from her father's days, one of the few she kept on. He doesn't leave scars, and he doesn't ask questions. He seems to like her, too — perhaps for the same reason. She likes him better than she likes most people. Any people, really. It's the unforeseen consequence of self-improvement: the more advanced Olivia becomes, the less patience she has for everyone who can't catch up, who can't evolve. Someday, someone will hack the human body and increase our lifespan by twenty, fifty, even a hundred percent. But Olivia is past that; she's thinking two steps ahead. Right now, her body is a temple. But eventually, it will be a cage — and she needs to find the key. To take that step forward — to slip through the bars and step like Alice through the looking glass, into a new world. Permeating the barrier that separates humanity from technology. She always thought she would be the first.

Which makes it especially curious, and infuriating, that someone else seems to have gotten there ahead of her. Destroying her asset, disrupting her network, sniffing around where he doesn't belong — and all with an uncanny elegance that suggests the presence of a very rare, very dangerous talent.

"You have one new message," says the Hollow Man. "Priority marked."

"Show me."

One of the windows that looks out on the bay turns opaque, then glows, illuminating an inbox with one unread message. She feels a peculiar sensation as she opens it, and realizes: her skin has erupted with goose bumps.

Target identified. Initiate level one surveillance on ACKERSON, CAM-ERON?

Olivia scowls — not with confusion, but at the unwelcome confirmation of what she already suspected. Of course it's him. She's always dreaded her eventual reacquaintance with the Ackerson kid. Now it's not just inevitable, but imminent.

"History repeats," she mutters.

"Beg pardon," says the Hollow Man. "I didn't understand."

Olivia sighs.

"Nothing," she says. "Send reply." She pauses, and smiles. "Surveillance, level two. I want to know what that little bastard is up to."

12

CRUSH

As his high school graduation approaches, Cameron finds himself thinking about Nia constantly — and struggling to understand how someone he feels so close to every time they're online could be so hard to pin down in person. In cyberspace, their relationship is blossoming: Nia is eager, flirtatious, and full of ideas about whom they should target next in their Operation Cosmic Justice, which they're planning to put into phase two very soon. But when it comes to real-life Nia . . .

It's like this girl is trying to keep herself an unsolvable mystery, and damn it, she's doing a good job. She's so closemouthed about the basic details of her personal life that Cameron sometimes wonders if she's some kind of spy, or maybe in the witness protection program; it would explain why her father is so paranoid about letting her out of the house, why he refused to send her to school. Maybe Nia's dear old dad was a superhacker himself, hiding out with his daughter in the last place they'd ever think to look for him, and teaching Nia everything he knows.

Only when he asks her, she says no, she's self-taught — that the internet was like a car and her father gave her the keys. She's learned to drive all on her own.

My dad didn't even give me that much, Cameron writes back. *He had a literal internet empire, but it all crashed and burned around the time I was born. He never talked about it, but he never got over it.*

My father won't talk about the past either.

Cameron asks, *What past? What happened?*

There's a long pause before Nia answers. *I don't remember. I must have been too young. But it was something bad, I think. Really bad. Something terrible. It was why we came here. It's why he wants to keep me so close.*

What about your mother?

I don't have a mother, Nia says. The words glow stark against the screen; even without inflection, Cameron feels their sadness.

I'm sorry.

Father never talks about that either.

Cameron feels himself nodding. Even without knowing the details, a portrait of Nia's life emerges — a life not unlike his own. Loss, secrets, solitude: it all sounds familiar.

Listen, when will I see you again? he asks, and goes wide-eyed as a photo lights up the screen. It's Nia, her hair tumbling like two wild waterfalls over her shoulders — her *bare* shoulders. Her hair is draped just so, making her look like a sea nymph in a Pre-Raphaelite painting, so that he can't exactly see anything, but he can also see more than enough: a tantalizing strip of creamy, unblemished skin between those cascading red waves, and a shadow that could be the innermost swell of a breast, and — "Oh my God," he says, out loud, feeling his cheeks turn bright red. "Get it together, man."

Look all you like, the caption reads.

I'd rather see that in person, he replies, then adds a wink to take the pressure off, so she'll know he's kidding, though of course he isn't, at all.

Maybe someday.

He can feel her toying with him. It's okay. He likes being toyed with. *Like at school? Or the art museum? What were you doing there?*

I told you — looking for you.

Cameron doesn't believe that one for a second, but it's so adorable that he doesn't care. *So you're stalking me.*

I'd have to do it at least three more times for it to be stalking.

Not that Cameron would mind being stalked by Nia. As it is, he never knows when he might see her. There's no rhyme or reason to it. Like the museum incident — just a few days after their hallway encounter, he'd nearly collided with her during a Senior Week scavenger hunt at the Cleveland Museum of Art. He'd made the mistake of geotagging a photo, and his ever-useful AR lenses had pinged him to warn of an incoming awkward fan encounter — a gaggle of young teenage girls sending excited texts that Cameron Ackerson, Celebrity Lightning Kid, had been spotted near the Armor Court gallery. He'd hidden himself in a hurry, breaking away from his team and ducking into a dark room lit by four neon tubes on the wall. There was only one other person in the room, and when she turned toward him, he nearly yelped out loud: it was Nia, gently lit by the neon glow, smiling at him.

"Hi," he'd stammered, and then — and he could hardly think of it without cringing — he'd flipped her a sort of dorky royal wave, which he now recognized as the moment he'd completely blown his chances of moving in for a hug, a kiss, even a high-five. Instead, they'd managed only a couple minutes of stilted conversation, just "Hi" and "How are you?" before his devices started blowing up with a sea of WHERE ARE YOU messages from his friends.

"Shit, I have to go. But you could come with me? I could introduce you —"

She shook her head so furiously that Cameron couldn't help feeling a little bit hurt. *Is she embarrassed to be seen with me?*

"I can't. I've been out too long already. Another time," she said, and swept out the door before he could even ask her when. He spent the rest of the day in a funk, resisting the urge to text her — Juaquo is always telling him not to be too eager with girls, that nobody likes a desperado. But being cagey with Nia is hard. Not just because he likes her so much, but because he can't help noticing that she seems to like him, too.

It's Saturday, he writes. *Big plans tonight? I'm going to a party.*

Sounds fun, she types back.

You could come.

I wish, she replies immediately, and Cameron sighs with frustration. It's what he was expecting, but still: disappointing. He sends a frowning emoji.

Okay. Gotta get ready. See you.

Nia, always cryptic, sends a last message before signing off.

Maybe you will.

*   *   *

The party is in Gates Mills, a swank neighborhood twenty minutes outside the city. Cameron doesn't know anyone who lives there — and he didn't think his friends did, either. Emma Marston, a girl he knows from Robotics Club, picks him up in her battered Skylark and keeps up a steady stream of chatter between her passengers that distracts Cameron as they drive out of his own neighborhood with its modest, close-set bungalows, heading east through a concrete landscape of strip malls and into the leafy suburbs. It's not until they're pulling up in front of a massive brick house, lights blazing from all the windows onto its manicured front yard, that he understands why everyone was so insistent that he come.

"Listen," Emma says, turning around in the driver's seat to look at him. "Don't get mad, but I think you should know that we only wrangled an invite to this thing because we promised everyone we'd bring the lightning guy. You're our ticket in."

Cameron gapes.

"You used my name to get into a party?" he squawks, even as he uses his abilities to peek into Emma's phone and confirm that yes, this is exactly what she did. For half a second, she looks guilty.

Then she shrugs.

"Whatever, man. It's not like *you* were using it, and somebody should."

"That's twisted," Cameron says.

Next to him, Emma's sister Julia pokes him in the ribs. "You'll thank us. Come on."

He does.

At first, it *is* kind of fun. A cheer erupts when Cameron walks in, and everyone wants to get next to him, and he even lets himself imagine that maybe this could be his life now: making command appearances at cool parties full of pretty people, riding that wave of viral fame for as long as it takes him where the cool kids are. But after an hour, his friends disappear into another part of the house, and Cameron doesn't follow them. The party is all over social media, and the beer he's drinking is only making the cybernetic noise more intrusive and harder to control — not to mention that he's about one terrible techno beat away from using his abilities to replace the DJ's entire playlist with Nickelback's greatest hits just to teach him a lesson . . .

I need to get out of here before I do something stupid.

*   *   *

A moment later, the door closes behind him and Cameron is alone — outside on the broad front porch of the house, the night air cool on his skin. Even with the noise of the party seeping through the windows, it's quiet out here compared to the city, and dark. Peaceful. He decides to wait out here until it's time to go, settling into a nearby wicker chair and loading up a game on his AR lenses.

He's just used a virtual RPG to blow a digital zombie to bits when he realizes that someone is standing in the shadows just a few feet away, watching him.

"So, are you sure *you* aren't stalking *me?*" Nia says.

Cameron leaps to his feet. "You're here!" he squeals, and then coughs, lowering his voice an octave, adding, "I mean, you're here. That's cool."

Nia shrugs, indicating the house. "I'm friends with a bunch of these people," she says, and then rolls her eyes. "Or, well, 'friends.' You know what I mean?"

Cameron smiles, thinking of his own entrée into the party. "Yeah, I know exactly what you mean. Did you want to go back in, or . . ."

"No."

The smile becomes a relieved grin. "Me neither. Why don't we take a walk?"

This time, neither one of them is in a hurry. They wander together for half an hour, letting the thump of the bass and the laughter of the party guests fade behind them as the night closes in. The homes here are enormous and private, separated from each other by wide, landscaped side yards and screened by thick stands of trees.

"We used to live in a place like this," he says. "Before the dot-com crash. I was just a baby so I don't remember it, but there are pictures. It's kind of crazy."

"The dot-com crash," Nia echoes. "Your father's company?"

"In ruins," he says. "A fallen empire. The crazy thing is, what he built is all still there, somewhere. My dad was really ahead of his time. He had this idea that he was going to make a virtual utopia where people could connect online, only this was back before 'online' really even existed. He coded this entire thing, like a virtual city. It was going to be called Oz, because, you know, the whole 'Whiz' thing."

"We're off to see the wizard," Nia sings back, and it's so sweet and unguarded that Cameron imagines grabbing her by the hand, spinning her around, dancing her up the street. He's a second away from reaching for her when she suddenly does a little skip and sashays away from him, her steps so light that she seems almost airborne. Cameron lets his hand drop back to his side, the moment passed, the opportunity missed.

Damn it.

Nia stops, waiting for him to catch up.

"So, what happened to Oz?" she says.

"They sealed off the web portals when the business collapsed. But all the structure, all the code, it's still in place. There's just no way in."

Nia smiles a little. "Every system has a way in."

"Yeah, well, if it's there, I couldn't find it," Cameron says, sighing. "Before he disappeared, he talked a lot about Oz, how much potential the place had. I was just a kid, it didn't really sink in. But a few years ago, I started thinking maybe he was trying to tell me something — like maybe he'd hidden something there, a clue that would explain why he left and where he went. I'd come home from school and spend hours trying to hack my way in. I never even got close." He shakes his head. "Of course, my mom made me stop as soon as she realized what I was up to."

"She made you stop?" Nia says. "But why?"

"Because she didn't want me wasting my time, getting my hopes up and then getting disappointed all over again. Anyway, she was right," he says. "If my dad wanted us to know what happened to him, he would have left a note. He wouldn't have buried the information in a pile of ancient code behind a door nobody else knew how to unlock."

"Is there really a door you can't unlock?" She's smiling like she already knows the answer.

"Well, a lot has changed since then," Cameron said, grinning back.

That's when he really starts to think of their walk as a sort of date. He looks at her hand, imagining again how he might take it in his. But the desire to touch her is being quickly overtaken by another, much more urgent need. He looks around. The house they came from — and more importantly, its bathroom — is at least twenty minutes' walk back. He'll never make it that long. But if he walks far enough back into one of those stands of leafy, privacy-protecting trees . . .

"Uh, Nia? Can you hold up here a second while I just — I mean, I was drinking beer earlier, and I . . . um. Yeah. Be right back."

He doesn't wait for her response as he steps away into the woods, grateful that it's too dark for her to see his face turning red. He walks a little farther in than he needs to — because it's one thing to excuse yourself to pee in front of a girl, but if she hears the splatter, you have to commit ritual suicide.

A minute later — he could swear it's been only a minute, maybe two at most — he retraces his steps, emerging out of the woods and onto the moonlit street.

Moonlit, and empty.

Nia is gone.

"Hey!" he calls. In the dark woods behind him, something rustles, an animal in the brush—but Nia doesn't reappear. He looks up and down the road where they've been walking, as his surprise gives way to worry. She wouldn't have just left . . . would she?

Maybe she had to pee too?

There's another stand of trees across the way. He wonders if she's in there, and he's just decided to risk calling out again when his phone lights up with her name. The message makes his heart sink.

My father called. I had to go. I'm sorry.

Cameron reads it three times: once in his mind as it pings the network, once as it scrolls across his AR lens, and finally on his phone itself, just to make sure he's not missing some nuance that might make him feel less rejected.

Then, he turns and walks back to the party alone.

*   *   *

If Cameron is being honest, he's starting to hate Nia's dad—especially all his crazy rules about who she can socialize with and how. Nia talks about getting out of her house like most people would talk about escaping from prison. The little Cameron knows about her childhood sounds miserable: no birthday parties, no sleepovers, no sports. She's frustratingly matter-of-fact about it, too, even when Cameron tells her it's totally messed up, that a decent parent would want his kid to have a normal social life. But it's flattering, too: that she uses her rare moments out of the house to see him, even when she could have her pick of friends—and of guys. And if it means he has to wait a little longer to take their relationship to the next level, well, so what? It's not like that makes it less real. They spend hours talking every day. It just goes to show, he thinks, that you don't have to be in the same room as someone to be with them, to be connected.

But the opposite is also true—that you can be right up close to someone without having any idea what they're thinking or feeling.

It's why Cameron doesn't even notice what's happening to Juaquo until it's almost too late.

13

A FRIEND IN NEED

AFTER THE UNSETTLING view he'd gotten of Juaquo's life — or lack thereof — just after the accident, Cameron always does a quick, discreet dig into his friend's phone when he comes by the house once a week. And if things never seem to be getting any better, at least they aren't getting any worse. *And who am I to judge, anyway?* As if he were an expert on coping with grief; he wasn't, not even a little. He was just a kid when his dad disappeared, and even then, disappearance wasn't death. Depending on how you looked at it, the lack of closure could even feel like a luxury. Unlike Cameron, Juaquo could never pretend his mom was just on an extended vacation, that she might come back to him someday. Juaquo had put his mom in the ground. For all Cameron knew, his friend's long, lonely drag along rock bottom was just part of the normal grieving process.

* * *

"Cameron?"

His mother's voice floats down the stairs, and he blinks in annoyance at the interruption. It's been less than twenty-four hours since he stepped into the woods to relieve himself and came back to find Nia gone, and every time he thinks about it, the rejection burns a little hotter. The only way he can keep himself from texting her a million desperate, eager messages is to distract himself—which he's accomplished by throwing himself headlong into designing a new game. The basement is teeming with chittering, big-eyed pink creatures that look like fur-covered basketballs—a projection from his augmented-reality lenses, but for Cameron they're indistinguishable from reality unless he passes his hand through one. His plan was to create a high-tech city-wide game of whack-a-mole—there's a virtual mallet lying nearby, which causes the pink furballs to explode with a satisfying pop if you hit them just right—but he's tired, and annoyed, and he keeps thinking about Nia, and he's made a mistake somewhere in the code that's proving impossible to unravel. In the meantime, the creatures keep spawning and respawning faster than he can get rid of them. An hour ago there was just one; now there are dozens, rolling all over the room, clustering on his desk, bouncing up and down the stairs, where, gratefully, nobody but Cameron can see them. One of them is also trying to crawl up his leg, which shouldn't bother him—it's not even real, he reminds himself—but is starting to seriously freak him out. He closes his eyes, diving deeper into the program, looking for the fragment that's causing all this—

"Cameron, I need you to come upstairs right now."

Forget it, Cameron thinks, and sweeps the whole project into the trash. The pink puffs disappear without a sound, although he could swear the one climbing his leg gives him a dirty look before it winks out of existence.

Upstairs, he finds his mother staring out the window, her expression as dark as the raw, rainy weather outside. A casserole covered in foil is sitting on the table; the delicious aroma of baked eggplant, garlic, and oregano hangs in the air.

"What is it?" he asks.

"Juaquo just called. He says he's not coming over today."

"Oh." Cameron feels a little twinge of disappointment. He'd been looking forward to seeing Juaquo. He thought he might ask his friend for advice about the Nia situation, which would also give him a chance to brag a little about the Nia situation — a little role reversal from the usual, since Juaquo had always been a lady slayer compared to Cameron. But he doesn't dwell on it, until he realizes that his mother is looking at him strangely.

"I want you to go over there."

"What? Mom, it's about to pour. Can't I just —"

"Cameron." The sharpness of her voice stops him cold. "He's your friend, and something is wrong with him. He didn't sound right on the phone, and he hasn't looked right in weeks. Are you really so busy with your screens and your parties that you haven't noticed?"

Cameron feels his ears get hot. The truth, and they both know it, is that he hasn't. But only he knows the real reason why, and it's worse than not caring. It's that he got overconfident. He was so convinced that his powers gave him all the insight he could ever need, he forgot to consider their limits: that some secrets go much deeper than a burner email account, a fake identity, or a hidden life online. Some secrets are so shameful and fearful that people can't bear to admit them even to themselves — and those secrets don't get typed into a text or a search box. They stay locked in your head, where no one can see them, seeping through your mind like slow poison until everything turns rotten and falls apart. And if you don't have anyone to talk to, to confide in . . .

"You're right. I'll go. I mean, I'll be right back," Cameron says, turning and catapulting himself back down the basement stairs.

He has an idea.

*   *   *

Cameron understands as soon as he pulls up to Juaquo's place why his friend canceled today's visit. Juaquo isn't in evidence, but his old Honda Civic — or what's left of it, anyway — is sitting at an awkward angle in the driveway, its windows smashed, tires flat, the driver's-side mirror crushed and dangling uselessly. The back seat is covered with shattered glass; the front windshield has a giant pockmark in its center, with cracks radiating out like a spider web. The sky is starting to spit, a prelude to a steady frigid downpour that'll last all day long, but Cameron stops to gape all the same, wondering if Juaquo was in the car when it happened. The wreck is so spectacular that it seems to have attracted an audience: across the street, a ragged-looking man is gawking in Cameron's general direction — probably wondering if there's anything left inside the car worth stealing.

Behind him, the door to the house creaks open.

"Your mom doesn't take no for an answer, does she," Juaquo says.

Cameron turns, holding the casserole in front of him. The rain begins to fall harder, peppering the foil with drops. He doesn't notice; he's looking at Juaquo's face, which is less damaged than his car, but not by much. One of his friend's eyes is surrounded by a fresh, livid bruise, the same deep purple color as the eggplant in Juaquo's favorite dish.

"What happened to you?"

Juaquo ignores the question and shoots a sidelong look at Cameron's feet, swaying a little as he does. "It's gonna be all puddles out here soon. You remember how we used to stomp around in puddles when we were kids? I guess you can't now. What happens if that thing on your foot gets wet? You get electrocuted?"

"No," Cameron says, and peers more closely at Juaquo's face. He doesn't just look bruised; his speech sounds slurred and he looks unsteady on his feet. "Geez, man. Are you drunk?"

"Not drunk enough. This bruise hurts like hell." Juaquo turns, his broad shoulders slumping. "You should go. As you can see, I'm not in a position to entertain guests."

Cameron steps forward. "I'm not leaving until you talk to me about what's going on."

Juaquo stiffens and turns back, fixing Cameron with a withering glare. "What do you mean?"

"What do you think I mean?"

Cameron feels himself beginning to sweat, the silence stretching out between them. For the first time since the accident, he feels not just small and overwhelmed, but impotent. Ordinary. His abilities can't help him now; he can't read minds, and Juaquo's phone, sitting in his pocket, reveals nothing. No calls, no texts; he hasn't even phoned his insurance company about the car. Cameron can only gaze back at his friend and wait.

The moment seems to drag on forever. Finally, Juaquo puts a hand to his head and groans.

"Okay," he says. "Fine. Whatever. Come in. *Mi casa es su casa,* as always."

*   *   *

Inside, the small house is neat but dusty. There's an empty spot by the big bay window in the living room where it would be warm and bright on a sunny day, and Cameron remembers with a pang that this is where they'd put the hospital bed — where Juaquo's mom spent her last days after she got too weak to climb the stairs. Juaquo has been here all alone ever since, living in a house where even the furniture arrangement is a reminder of what he's lost. Nothing, from the pictures on the walls to the soft yellow curtains, has changed. *Mi casa es su casa.* Only, looking around, Cameron wonders if Juaquo really thinks of this as his house at all.

Juaquo sits down heavily on the sofa, opposite a TV where an old *Twilight Zone* episode is running on mute. Cameron instinctively uses his abilities to scan his friend's Netflix queue. It's grim: an endless scroll of horror films, and one random documentary about the Unabomber.

"You want anything to drink?" says Juaquo.

"I'm good." Cameron walks into the kitchen and opens the fridge, sliding the casserole next to the only other thing inside, a lonely, grease-spotted Chinese takeout container. "Your refrigerator is the saddest thing I've ever seen."

Juaquo doesn't smile. "I don't know how to cook."

Cameron sits down at the other end of the couch. "So," he says.

"What do you want to know?"

"What happened to your face?"

"Same thing that happened to my car. Any other questions?" Juaquo says, but Cameron stays silent. Juaquo sighs, leaning back. He keeps his eyes closed as he talks. "All right. One of the guys at the yard, Serge, has a cousin who runs an MMA club out of a garage in the Flats. He kept asking if I wanted to fight, he said he'd train me. So I did. Friday nights. For a while."

Cameron's mouth drops open. Juaquo had always been ready to step in on Cameron's behalf if someone else tried to start shit, but he was also intensely aware, always, of his own size and strength. The idea of him fighting on purpose, let alone for fun — it's the most ridiculous thing Cameron has ever heard.

"Are you kidding? You're in a . . . a fucking fight club? What, like, for money?"

Juaquo shrugs. "Sometimes. The money can be pretty good, if you win. But I guess, you know, since I'm spilling my guts" — he opens his eyes and looks directly at Cameron — "maybe I just wanted to hit something. Or get hit. I'm not real picky about it."

"That's messed up," Cameron says.

"Says the guy whose mom is still alive," says Juaquo, with a humorless laugh. Cameron winces. "Anyway, a few weeks ago, they put me against some guy — and I knew right away I shouldn't, okay? It was like, what do you call it, lizard brain. I could tell from the way he looked at me that whatever happened, he was gonna take it personally. And he did."

Juaquo takes a deep breath, closing his eyes again. "Can I tell you the weirdest thing? I'm almost relieved. I've been looking over my shoulder, wondering if I should, I don't know, get a weapon or something." Cameron bites his tongue before he can say *So that's why the googling for guns,* and stays quiet. "But it's over now. And he didn't even come for me. He came for my car. Can you believe that? My freaking car. What a dick. It's just dumb luck that I forgot my mouthguard, came back out just in time to find him bashing up my headlights with a baseball bat."

"He hit you with a bat?" Cameron tries to leap to his feet in a righteous rage, loses his balance, and nearly face-plants into the couch.

Juaquo stares at him for a split second, and then starts laughing — in earnest this time, smacking his hand against his knee, until the whooping turns into a cough.

"Damn it, Cam. Don't make me laugh, it hurts. And yeah, he hit me with a bat. But as you can see, he only did it once."

Cameron looks at Juaquo's bruised-up eye, then looks out the window.

"You know it's raining inside your car," he says.

Juaquo shrugs. "Probably for the best. He pissed in the back seat after he smashed the windows. Did I mention that there was something very wrong with this dude?"

Cameron can't help laughing, and then can't help thinking that this is the most he and Juaquo have said to each other in months.

"I can't believe you joined an underground fight club."

"I know," Juaquo says. "It's crazy, and self-destructive, and I'm sure that shrink of yours would have all kinds of things to say about it. But, man, being in this house, with my mom gone . . . you just don't know what it's like. And I'm glad you don't. But you don't."

"You could move," Cameron says. "Why don't you? Sell this place, get a sweet loft downtown."

Juaquo shakes his head. "It'd be worse somewhere else. Here, I've at least got good memories."

Cameron couldn't have asked for a better opening. He smiles and says, "Then I've got something for you."

*　　*　　*

Twenty minutes later, Juaquo stands up and walks slowly toward the kitchen. When he reaches the doorway, he stops short, gripping the wall so hard that his fingers turn white. A petite woman with round hips and black hair is standing at the sink, drying a dish and humming to herself. She turns at the sound of his footsteps, smiling.

"Hey, *chiquito*," she says. "I'm just washing up. Are you hungry? How was school?"

Juaquo swallows hard. Behind the AR glasses, his eyes are wet.

"School was fine, *Amá*."

Milana Velasquez beams at her son, then turns to put the dish away. The cupboard is closed, but she doesn't seem to notice; the hand holding the dish is obscured by the door as she reaches for it, then reappears again, empty.

"I'm glad to hear that," she says.

From his place on the couch, Cameron calls to Juaquo. "You see her?"

"Yeah," Juaquo says, wiping furiously at his eyes. "Yeah, she's here."

*　　*　　*

Juaquo stays in the kitchen for another few minutes before returning to the couch, removing the AR glasses and cradling them in his hands, like he's terrified of breaking them. There's a long silence.

"She looks younger," he says, finally.

Cameron nods. "All the clips I could find were at least a few years old. From when you and I were kids, mostly. She didn't post to her accounts that much after that. But if you have more recent ones, or pics, I can adjust it a little."

Juaquo shakes his head. "No, I mean, she looks great. Don't mess with it. Just . . . I don't even understand what just happened. Is she always going to be in the kitchen?"

"No, she'll go where you go, as long as you're wearing the specs. The thing with the dish just seemed like a good place for you to, y'know, meet. Something familiar."

Juaquo nods slowly, like a man in a trance. "I was in seventh grade when I shot that video. Just playing with my camera, you know? I never thought . . ."

He trails off, and Cameron jumps in. "So here's the deal. It's a fixed program, not super-sophisticated AI. Like a home movie you can interact with, or —"

"That Deadpool hologram down at the movie theater that mooned everyone standing in line for tickets," Juaquo says.

Cameron laughs. "Something like that, yeah. Only you won't see her unless you run the program and put the specs on, and I promise, she will never, ever show you her butt." Juaquo makes a joke of looking visibly relieved. "She can talk with you," Cameron continues, "but her repertoire is limited. If you spend too much time in there trying to have a conversation, she'll start repeating herself. The upside is, she's not gonna develop a whole new personality or go all HAL 9000 or *Westworld* on you."

Juaquo gives Cameron a horrified look. "Please do not ever talk about my mom and those HBO sex robots in the same sentence again."

Cameron laughs. "Sorry. Bad example."

Juaquo shakes his head. "You're unbelievable. I mean, that you did this? You made this? It's funny, though. It's been years since she called me *chiquito.*"

"I can fix that," Cameron offers, hurriedly, but Juaquo smiles and shakes his head again.

"No, don't. I like it better. I don't want some android that thinks it's my mom, where I maybe spend too much time with it and maybe I start thinking it's my mom too. I just want to remember her like she was, before she got sick." He pauses, and breaks into a grin that makes him look like his old self, even with the black eye. "It's incredible. You made, like, the ultimate interactive memorial museum of my mom."

There's a long, companionable silence as Juaquo looks from the AR glasses to the kitchen and back. Finally, he leans forward and gently places the wearable on the coffee table. Then he turns to Cameron.

"So, anyway," he says. "What's new with *you?*"

* * *

In hindsight, Cameron doesn't know what he expected from Juaquo. At first, his friend is keenly interested to hear more about Nia — right up until Cameron starts describing the details of their relationship. That's when Juaquo stops looking intrigued and starts laughing.

"She's homeschooled? Oh my God, dude. That's the worst cover story ever. If you're gonna make up a fake girlfriend, have some self-respect and go with the 'model who lives in Canada' trope. It's a classic for a reason."

Cameron is indignant. "She's not my girlfriend . . . yet. But she's not fake! Look, buddy, we had a *date*."

"Right. All my dates end with the girl running away while I'm peeing behind a bush," Juaquo says, and then holds his hands up as Cameron scowls. "All right, I'm sorry, I'm sorry. I'm sure it's magic. Just . . . seriously? You haven't even tried to kiss her?"

"I respect her more than that!" Cameron scoffs, and Juaquo cracks up again.

"There's a word for 'chickenshit' I've never heard before."

"You wouldn't understand. It's a different kind of connection," Cameron says. He pauses before adding, quietly, "And give me a break, it's the only one I've ever had."

Juaquo pats him awkwardly on the back. "Okay, okay. I'm sorry. I get it."

"I've never even kissed a girl, you know. Not in a way that counted."

"Well, then maybe Nia's the one," Juaquo says. "You gotta ask her out properly, though. And be persistent. Not desperate, but remember, girls want you to pursue them. Especially the cute ones. She's cute, right?"

Cameron hands Juaquo his phone. "See for yourself. She sends me pics all the time."

Juaquo studies the photo. "Needs more boobs."

"*Juaquo.*"

"I'm kidding! Yeah, man, she's cute. Pale, but cute. She actually looks kind of familiar."

"You've probably seen her around," Cameron says. "In town, or something?"

Juaquo frowns. "I don't think so. I think it's more that she looks like . . ." He peers at the photo a moment longer, then shrugs. "Eh, whatever. It'll come to me."

The phone buzzes in Juaquo's hand; he glances at it and grins.

"Speak of the devil," he says.

"What?"

Juaquo passes the device back to Cameron, arching an eyebrow suggestively.

"It's your girl." The eyebrow waggles. "She wants to know if you're ready."

14

TEAMWORK MAKES
THE DREAM WORK

CAMERON PULLS TO the curb in a hurry and practically skips up the porch steps, not noticing that the same ragged man from outside Juaquo's house has reappeared — still staring, this time from behind a large box truck idling on the corner, the object of his interest clearly Cameron himself. But Cameron isn't paying attention; all he wants is to get in front of the computer in time to help Nia with the next prank. Not that she couldn't handle it all on her own, but knowing she could, and that she's holding off until he can join her, makes his heart feel like it's about to take flight. It's what makes them so perfect for each other. What they're doing isn't just about doling out justice, righting wrongs. It's about doing it together.

His phone pings again.

I'm waiting!

Cameron takes the basement stairs two at a time and lands in front of his desktop array, the screens coming to life as he glances at them.

I'm here, he says, and grins. *Let's do some redistributing.*

CONTROVERSIAL FINANCIER SAYS HE IS A VICTIM OF HACKERS

Renowned investor Ford Freeman made a series of statements today suggesting that the recent donation of a combined $10 million in his name was the work of hackers. After several organizations tweeted their thanks for his support, Freeman took to social media early on Sunday morning, writing, "Whichever one of you [expletive]-heads gave $10 million of MY [expletive] MONEY to make [expletive] cat sweaters IT'S NOT FUNNY AND I WILL FIND YOU."

Freeman has long been scrutinized for what critics call his predatory business practices, buying a majority stake in struggling companies and then systematically selling off their assets, often resulting in widespread layoffs as the shrinking business struggles to stay afloat. Ted Frank, former CEO of Bluegrass Brands, personally blamed Freeman for ransacking the company and eliminating hundreds of jobs before liquidating his position.

The $10 million in donations, which Freeman insists were stolen by hackers who raided an offshore account and converted its contents to high-value cryptocurrency, appear to have been channeled with the intention of helping those who were negatively affected by the investor's dealings. Several charities dedicated to connecting struggling families with affordable housing and long-term employment received donations of $500,000, but many individuals also received what they say were desperately needed gifts of cash. Melanie Whistler, a former assembly line worker who has been selling hand-knit pet sweaters to make ends meet since losing her job last year, told ANN that she woke up to find that a crowdfunding campaign to expand her business had received $100,000 overnight, ten times what she had hoped to raise.

"I would thank Mr. Freeman for his generosity," said Whistler, "but since he says he didn't do it, I guess I'd like to thank the fine person who did. And to that person, I'd just like to say: If you have a cat, you just let me know its favorite color and I'll make it a beautiful sweater."

In the comfortable dark of the basement, Cameron throws his head back and laughs until tears come. He's still cracking up when Nia's message pings through, and her bewilderment only makes him laugh harder.

Do cats even have a favorite color?

I don't know. I don't have a cat.

Me neither, Nia says.

You know what I do have? Another idea.

YES. TELL ME.

He does. When he's finished, there's a long silence while he waits for Nia's response. Finally, he pings her again.

So? What do you think?

When she replies, her avatar is wearing a pair of devil horns.

I think we should deal her some justice, Nia says.

There's another pause, this one briefer.

I think we should do it right now.

15

ARIA SLOANE
GETS CANCELED

IT'S JUST AFTER DAWN on the Ohio State campus, with soft light beginning to filter along the quiet pathways where a few straggling partiers are stumbling home, when Aria Sloane's cell starts to buzz. She jolts awake, first confused, then annoyed, when she sees Sarah Wright's name on the display. Blowing up her phone at six o'clock in the morning? *This girl is seriously overestimating how much nonsense I'll tolerate from an ally,* Aria thinks, tossing the phone aside and rolling over with a huffy sigh. *Just because you show up to a few protests, signal boost the movement, and donate a few hundred dollars to my Ko-fi to compensate me for the emotional labor of being your friend, that doesn't give you the right to just call any damn time you feel like it.*

Plus, she muses, if you think about it, waking someone up before dawn could really be considered a form of violence, couldn't it? Sarah's privilege is definitely showing. When Aria does get out of bed, the very first thing she's going to do is get online and call out that entitled—

"OH MY GOD," she erupts, as the phone starts to vibrate again. She grabs it, noticing as she does that she seems to have an awful lot of alerts. Not just the missed calls from Sarah — Jesus, how many times did she try before the buzzing woke her up? — but texts and notifications from all over the place, every single app just exploding. For the first time, she wonders if something might actually be wrong, if maybe Sarah is calling because nuclear war has broken out, or worse, her favorite celebrity couple has broken up. Hurriedly, Aria taps the screen to accept the call.

"Sarah, what the hell? It's six o'clock in the morn —"

Sarah interrupts her, ignoring the question. "Have you seen what's happening on Clapback?"

"Wha?" says Aria, shaking her head in disbelief. She must still be half asleep; Clapback is the school's anonymous messaging app and a frequent source of outrage, but it's not the kind of thing that you call someone up at the crack of dawn to discuss.

"So you haven't, then," says Sarah. "You have no idea."

Aria stifles a yawn. "I must be missing something," she says, annoyed. "You're calling me to tell me that someone is showing their ass on Clapback?"

In the pause before Sarah answers, Aria realizes that there's something strange about the other girl's tone. Instead of being deferential and apologetic, falling all over herself to avoid offense the way she usually does, her voice sounds hard.

"Yeah," Sarah says. "You are."

Aria sits bolt upright. "Excuse me?"

"I mean, it's not just you. Some kind of virus or hacker or something just pulled back the curtain on an absolutely massive pile of internet shit. So you're not the only person getting a taste of her own medicine. This one guy, he was running a revenge porn website, and somehow all the content got taken down and replaced with this absolutely hilarious video of him having a crying fight with his mom because she threw out his binder full of Sailor Moon erotic fan art —"

"What does that have to do with anything?" Aria snaps, only to be met with a low chuckle on the other end of the line.

"You've been hacked, Aria. De-anonymized. Every shitty thing you ever posted on anon, because you thought nobody would ever find out it was you? It's all out there now. Not just Clapback. Your little secret Facebook group went public overnight too, and for a bunch of people who claim to be *sooooo* concerned about hate speech and abuse, you and your friends are responsible for like ninety percent of the bullying on this campus. But you, you're something else. It was you. I just can't believe it. The Josh thing. You just made it up."

"I don't know what you're talking about," Aria says, only her voice is shaky and uneven. Her cheeks and ears are burning, and the world seems to be shrinking around her, making it hard to breathe — because she's pretty sure that she knows exactly what Sarah is talking about. On the other end of the phone, Sarah draws a deep breath and lets out her next words with a hiss.

"He tried to hurt himself after he got expelled. Did you know that? He ended up in a psych ward."

Aria closes her eyes and thinks, *Oh, shit.*

The scandal surrounding Josh Woodward had been the biggest news on campus that winter, after an anonymous poster on Clapback said he had been spotted making a Nazi salute from the balcony of the Chi Phi fraternity house. Within hours, postings began to pour in saying that yes, Josh Woodward was a known white supremacist, forcing the school to investigate — at which point a group of brave social justice activists led by the sophomore Aria Sloane came forward to allege that Josh was also verbally abusive, misogynistic, and a known mansplainer. Meanwhile, the story went viral online, where an internet game of telephone ensued until the rumor was that Josh had not only performed the offensive salute, but was also holding a copy of *Atlas Shrugged* and wearing a T-shirt that read I ❤ FASCISM at the time. In the face of mounting media scrutiny and phone calls from outraged parents — and since Josh Woodward of course could not produce any evidence that he *hadn't* done what he was accused of — a campus tribunal convicted him of hate speech and expelled him, just a couple months before he was supposed to graduate. The last Aria heard, he was back living with his parents and had been fired from a job at a fast food restaurant, thanks to an anonymous tipster who uploaded a photo of him in his work uniform to Twitter, making sure to tag his employer: "So apparently @McDonalds is cool with having a misogynist white supremacist in their kitchen LOL."

In hindsight, Aria thinks, maybe that last part had been a bit much. She didn't really *need* to get him fired from flipping burgers. Starting the rumor and then flooding Clapback with enough anonymous testimony to start the dogpile rolling would have been enough —and she didn't even make *all* the comments, only half of them, or maybe seventy-five percent. Even then, she'd only wanted to teach him a lesson after he attacked her in lit class and called her "coddled" just because she wanted a trigger warning on *Crime and Punishment*. But Josh Woodward was the living embodiment of white male privilege. So what if he had no degree and no job? Neither did lots of people, and you didn't see them losing their minds about it.

Aria takes a deep breath and says, "I don't know what you think you know, but if Josh Woodward went crazy after he got expelled, that's certainly not *my* fault."

"Are you kidding me!" Sarah is practically yelling. "You fabricated the entire story, and not only that, you got all of us wrapped up in it. You said it was our *duty* as allies to back up whoever was brave enough to call Josh out. Quinn broke up with him because *you* said his masculinity was toxic. I took you out to lunch for a week because you said you were too traumatized to eat from the same buffet as a Nazi!"

"I —" says Aria, but Sarah cuts her off.

"I'm calling the dean, Aria, and I'm telling her everything. I'm telling her how you pressured us, bullied us to say those things. I'm going to tell her how you threatened to wreck my reputation if I didn't post and retweet and donate every time you decided to take someone down. And I want my five hundred dollars back. I talked to my dad and he says this definitely counts as fraud, and I have every right to —"

Aria hangs up on her.

As soon as she does, the phone lights up immediately, the alerts scrolling by faster than she can read them. Three clubs in which she was a member have already posted statements disavowing her. People are unfollowing her as fast as they can; her Twitter account has been suspended and her Facebook friend list has dropped by two hundred and counting. Dimly, she's aware that Sarah was right, that she's not the only one this is happening to — her name is trending alongside several other victims', including the revenge porn guy who's already been nicknamed #WailerMoon — but somehow that only makes it worse. Her email chimes with the latest of ninety-seven unread messages; the subject line reads, "Shame on you."

In her hand, the phone begins to vibrate again. The color drains from her face as she looks at it. It's not Sarah calling back. It's worse: the caller ID says "DAD."

Aria Sloane pitches her phone across the room. It skids under her desk. The vibrating stops.

She waits. Hoping. Praying.

Let this be a bad dream, she thinks.

Under the desk, the phone begins to buzz.

Outside, someone begins knocking at her door.

And Aria Sloane buries her face in her pillow and starts to scream.

ENCRYPTED MESSAGE INCOMING

From: Olivia Park

To: Team Alpha

Subject: Priority assignment

OPTIC algorithms have identified a pattern of disruptions, estimated 94 percent likelihood that events are linked. Please review attached files on the hacks of Daggett Smith, Ford Freeman, and Aria Sloane, and conduct relevant analysis. Cameron Ackerson is pissing in our pool; I want to know who he's working with.

16

MIXED MESSAGES

THE COFFEE SHOP is the perfect spot: midway down a tree-lined street in trendy Ohio City, away from the bustle and crowds of the open-air market a few blocks away. Inside, it's quiet and cozy, the morning rush long finished but the lunchtime crowd not yet arrived. Cameron steps up to the gleaming counter and grins at the black-aproned barista, who looks a little spooked in response. He knows he probably looks like an idiot, but he just can't help it. After all, he's about to cross one of the all-important thresholds of human experience.

Today, for the first time in his long life of lonely singledom, he's going to buy coffee for a girl.

"One large red-eye and a pink spiced spring latte," he says, then leans in to add, "for my lady friend, of course." He shifts his eyes toward Nia, who is perched lightly on the arm of an overstuffed chair over by the door. She gazes back at him and cocks her head a little, as if to ask what's taking so long.

The barista flicks his eyes in Nia's direction, then resumes giving Cameron the stink-eye.

"I don't care who it's for, man," he says. "Total's nine eighty-eight."

Cameron tips him a buck anyway. Nothing's going to spoil his good mood — not today. He and Nia are on a date. Not a chance meeting, but a real date, the planned-in-advance kind. Her text message lit up on his lens display earlier his morning, just as he stepped off the bus in front of City Center High — another significant milestone, although not nearly as exciting. An hour ago, Cameron turned in the last of his final exams; his high school career is finished, except for that last walk across the stage.

My father is away working all day, Nia's text said. *Let's meet? Spiffy Bean at 11am.*

He had to set a speed record on his physics final to get here in time, but was it worth it? Hell yes, it was.

His determination to feel terrific lasts as long as it takes for him to approach her with the cup, which is extravagantly decked with a sky-high tower of pink whipped cream and flecked with little pink sugar crystals.

"Here you go," he says, but instead of taking it from him with the expected squeal of delight, she recoils with a faintly distressed look on her face.

"Oh, Cameron, I'm sorry," she whispers. "I don't drink coffee."

Cameron's hand stops abruptly in midair and the whipped cream tower wobbles dangerously, threatening to collapse.

"You don't? But . . . then why would you want to meet at a coffee shop?"

Nia's brows knit together with worry. She glances around nervously. "Was that wrong? I thought this was where everyone meets."

"Yeah. *To drink coffee,*" Cameron says, laughing, but Nia doesn't even crack a smile. *Oh God, I'm blowing it,* he thinks, desperately, and then realizes that his humiliation has an audience. The barista is now openly staring. He tucks his own coffee into the crook of his arm and grabs the door, pulling it wide. "Here, let's talk outside."

Nia must be as embarrassed as he is, because she practically runs out the door.

*   *   *

Her expression stays glum as they begin walking, her arms hugged in close to her chest. Cameron thinks about grabbing her hand and making a dramatic plea for forgiveness — *I'm sorry I got you the world's most ridiculous coffee, please don't hate me* — but he's holding a cup in each hand.

"Hey, Nia, my bad. I just thought you'd like one because, you know, you said to meet here? And most girls like this drink."

It occurs to him as he says this that it may not even be true; in fact, he has no idea if the seventy-odd girls who tagged photos of the pink spiced latte on social media ever actually consumed it or if they just ordered it because it looks cute in pictures. And either way, Nia isn't having it. Actually, she's scowling at him.

"Well, I don't want it," she says.

"Hey, that's cool. More for me, right? I've, uh, always wanted to try one of these," Cameron says, lying through his teeth. He takes a sip of the pink confection; it tastes like someone wrapped a marshmallow Peep in a cotton candy cocoon and drowned it in a toilet full of weak tea. Nia's eyebrows leap skyward.

"How does it taste?"

"I sincerely apologize," Cameron says, "for thinking that you would want to drink this."

"But all the girls like it," she says, and now she's really scowling. "That's what you said."

"What?"

"Like those girls you saw the movie with. Like Emma Marston, maybe."

"Emma Mar — What?" Cameron stops short, gaping at Nia. "Wait. Nia, are you *mad* at me? Oh shit, you are. You're mad about . . . what, about the movie?"

It was a stupid question, he realized. Of course she was mad about the movie — and he'd practically forgotten all about it in his excitement to see her, even though it was just last night. After all the amazing week they'd had pulling off the latest round of Operation Cosmic Justice, all Cameron had wanted was to finally introduce Nia to his friends — Juaquo, particularly, had been getting increasingly agitated about meeting her — and a group outing to the new superhero blockbuster with a whole bunch of people seemed like a perfect way to break the ice. To keep it casual. Even Dr. Kapur, who was always cautioning him about neglecting his friends and family in favor of spending time online with Nia, gave the idea a thumbs-up. But when he told Nia yesterday that some friends would be coming with them, she suddenly told him she couldn't make it and abruptly dropped offline.

Cameron had tried not to read too much into it, especially when she didn't bring it up again the next time they talked. But maybe he should have. Maybe Nia had been doing that thing where you say everything's fine but you mean completely the opposite — except Nia *never* did that. And with the tickets already in hand and only a couple hours until showtime, what was he supposed to do? So the group date had turned into a regular night out with Juaquo and a few friends from school. And yes, some of the friends were girls . . . and yes, they had posted pics from the evening that Nia would have seen.

But she was the one who canceled. It didn't make sense for her to be mad about it. Unless . . .

"Hold on," he says. "Are you *jealous?*"

The question comes out sounding way too gleeful, and Cameron feels instantly stupid: what kind of dumbass asks someone if they're jealous, an emotion that no person in their right mind would admit to feeling? Only . . .

"Yes!" Nia says, her expression brightening. "Jealous! That is exactly how I feel."

Cameron's jaw drops to what feels like knee level.

Nia seems to mistake his surprise for confusion. "Don't you understand? Because I was so happy when you asked me. I was excited to see a movie with you! But then I couldn't go, and those Emma and Amber girls did, and they got to have the experience that I wanted. They got to be with you when I couldn't. And I'm jealous about it!"

Cameron can't help it: he starts grinning. A giant, cheese-eating, swoony grin. His stomach feels like someone is tap-dancing inside of it. *She's jealous,* he thinks, the two words humming through his mind like a miraculous mantra. Jealous! It was the greatest thing ever!

"Well, I'm sorry. I didn't know you were the jealous type," he says, finally.

"Me neither," Nia says, sounding surprisingly cheerful. "I never felt that way before."

*   *   *

Just expressing her feelings out loud seems to have eased Nia's unhappiness, and they begin to talk more easily as they wander the city, the business district fading away behind them. Ahead, a bus stop sports a poster for next month's big event at the I-X Center outside the city: HACK YOURSELF, it screams, and Nia points at it.

"What is this?"

"Body-hacking," Cameron says, grinning. "Bionic limbs, smart tattoos, ingestible microchips, and augmented-reality everything. Blurring the line between man and machine. Not gonna lie, this is right up my alley. Hey, and yours, too—check it out, they have e-sports. Your killer aviatrix could murder someone else for a change."

Nia's eyes go wide. "What? That's amazing!"

"You want to go?" Cameron says. "It's been sold out forever, but I am a sort of local celebrity. I could probably pull a couple strings, finagle a couple of tickets."

"I'd like to go." She sounds wistful, and looks at him shyly. "I'd like to go with *you*. I wish . . . I wish I could be with you more."

"Well, hey," Cameron says, feeling himself blush with pleasure. "Me too."

Nia looks thoughtful. "It's hard to be lonely, isn't it? And so many people are. Even when they're in the same place, it's like they're disconnected. Like those people." She gestures at a passing couple, walking together in silence, each looking down at the phone in their hand. "They're both somewhere else, inside their heads. They're not reaching out or trying to understand." She pauses, sighing. "Wouldn't it be great if people could just connect directly? Brain to brain, so everyone would be in the same place on the inside, too."

Cameron grimaces and chuckles. "You haven't seen *The Matrix,* have you?"

"No. What is it?"

"A movie. Or a trilogy of movies, I guess. They do something like what you're talking about."

Nia's expression brightens. "They do? What happens?"

"Uh," says Cameron. "I don't want to spoil it for you, but it doesn't go well."

She frowns. "Why not?"

"Because the sentient machines take all the plugged-in people and brainwash them, and start harvesting them as an energy source."

Nia lets out a little shriek, and Cameron laughs.

"But that's *terrible,*" she says. "That wasn't my idea at all."

"Well, of course not," he says. "Because you're not an evil robot who wants to enslave humanity. But you're right. People are disconnected. That's the irony of the internet: it was supposed to stop all that, but I think it's only made it worse."

Cameron shakes his head, thinking about the awful things he sees every time he opens his mind and plunges into cyberspace. "Everyone is walled off behind their screens. Alone, anonymous — and when people feel anonymous, they stop acting like people. They stop treating other people like people. Everyone who's not them isn't really human; everyone who's not a member of their tribe is evil and has to be destroyed."

"Their tribe." Nia frowns.

"It's bullshit," Cameron says. "Just a bunch of arbitrary lines in the sand. Too bad we can't wipe them away."

"No tribes," Nia muses.

"Or only one," he replies. "We're all human. If everyone just remembered that . . ." He trails off, shaking his head. "I don't know. Maybe it's impossible. And maybe there's a tradeoff. The loneliest people can be really creative, you know? Sometimes they make beautiful things."

Cameron concentrates, using his lenses to project a colorful cloud of butterflies in the air around Nia's head, then syncs the clip to his phone and sends it to her. She jumps a little, digs into her pocket, and pulls out her own device, smiling broadly as she sees what he's done.

"You made this. I'd love to live in a world like this."

*　　*　　*

A world like this.

The words are a seed that takes root in his mind as they walk, a companionable silence falling over them. It's not until Cameron's foot begins to ache that he looks up and sees that they're approaching a familiar sight — the overgrown, hulking silhouettes of the grand mansions that nobody wants to save, standing on borrowed time until they finally sag into ruins. Without meaning to, he's begun retracing his route from the day of the accident. And as he looks at those empty houses, relics from another time, the seed blooms into an idea.

"Hey," Cameron says, stopping. "What if we made a world? One where we could visit with each other whenever we wanted — at least until your dad decides to relax the rules a little."

"Made one?" Nia asks. "How?"

"We wouldn't even have to build it from scratch. It would be more like . . . renovating." Cameron gestures at the lens in his eye, the phone in his hand. "You were right. I couldn't get into Oz before, but I could now. *We* could. We could transform it from something deserted and ruined into something great."

"Just for us?" Nia says. "Oh, I like that. It would be like they have in the movies, a clubhouse."

"A headquarters."

"An underground lair," she says, giggling.

"That's the spirit," Cameron says. "And it'll be secure, which is good, because we need to do some brainstorming about who the next target of Operation Cosmic Justice should be."

Nia claps her hands together. "No, we don't. I have someone."

Cameron raises his eyebrows. "Who?"

"I don't think they have a name," she says, frowning. "It's not one person. It's more like an entity — or an evil machine, like you were talking about. Do you remember all those dummy sites that went dark when Daggett Smith disappeared? There's a connection. Something big. I've been digging into the data on my social networks, and there's a rogue algorithm flowing through every single one. Someone is manipulating what we see on social media, playing to people's biases, siphoning off massive amounts of data. I don't know what they're using it for, but —"

Nia is still talking, but Cameron is only half listening. The idea of a rogue algorithm running like a secret stream beneath every social network sounds like a bonkers conspiracy theory; surely it's the sort of thing he would have noticed himself. When he returns his full attention to Nia, he finds her smiling at him.

"You look unconvinced," she says.

"It's just that I haven't seen it myself," he says.

"Maybe you need to look with fresh eyes." Her tone is teasing.

"I will. But if it's what you say . . ."

"Yes?"

"It won't be easy."

"Don't tell me you're afraid of a challenge," she says.

He grins. "No way. I'm with you. Whatever it is, we'll take it down."

Together, they turn and begin walking back the way they came. A soft breeze rises off the lake, and the sun is warm and bright. Cameron turns his face toward it. An early-summer afternoon, a walk with a beautiful girl; sometimes he thinks the real world isn't so bad. The bus stop they passed earlier looms ahead, a city bus pulling up alongside it. Nia points, moving toward it.

"I should go," she says, then hesitates. "But can I ask you a question?"

"Sure," Cameron says. The bus reaches the curb, swinging its doors wide.

"That world we're going to make. The one just for us." She pauses, biting her lip. "Except, does it have to be *just* us?"

"What? You want to invite someone else?" Cameron says. Now he's feeling jealous — but only for a moment. Nia's eyes widen just before she answers:

"In our virtual reality, could there be . . . a dog?"

He bursts out laughing. "Yeah, Nia. There can be a dog."

She gives him a thumbs-up before she turns and hops aboard the waiting bus. Cameron waves, watching her go. The driver gestures at him.

"You getting on, kid?"

"Nope, I'm headed downtown," Cameron says, still grinning. He waves again at Nia, whose pale face is visible through the window. The driver rolls his eyes and grumbles, but Cameron barely notices. He's filled with a sense of purpose, of possibilities — and he has a sunny afternoon and a pleasant walk ahead to think about all of them.

*   *   *

Hours later, Cameron sits in the dark of the basement, his fingers flying over the keyboard as his mind converses with the software, trying to sense the presence of the algorithm Nia was so certain is there. If it's what she described, he can't fathom how she found it. It would be designed to pass unnoticed, to appear organic to the system; hunting for it was like gazing at a fast-moving stream of water and trying to see a single, anomalous ripple in the surface.

Maybe you need to look with fresh eyes, she'd said. But fresh eyes aren't what Cameron needs. He needs a new perspective. Nia's perspective. He knows her well enough to know that she sees things differently from most people. Not just differently; she sees more. Nia can dig one layer deeper when the data seems impenetrable, can spot patterns in a vast sea of information where he sees only noise.

Patterns, he thinks. In his brain, something stirs. His heart starts to beat faster.

I'm looking too closely.

And when he concentrates, trying to see the web as she does, zooming out to see more and more even as he dives deeper into the code — he nearly gasps aloud. In Cameron's mind, the code springs into view, laced so elegantly into every network that you'd never spot it unless you already knew it was there. He wonders afresh how Nia ever found it; even now, it seems to shift and shimmer under his scrutiny, like a mirage that disappears if you try to look directly at it. To trace the origins of something like this will take all his skill, and probably all of hers, too.

*   *   *

As Cameron gazes motionless into the depths of the web, a shadow slinks past the basement window and moves quickly down Walker Row. The unseen observer passes unnoticed — she has all week, crossing in front of the Ackerson house early in the morning as Cameron leaves for school, or sitting a few seats behind him when he rides the bus downtown, or standing across the street from Dr. Kapur's home office after his Monday appointment.

For all his intuition and his powers, Cameron Ackerson hasn't a clue that he's being hunted.

17

CLOSER AND CLOSER

Xal licks her lips, relishing the sensation. This skin is in good shape — supple, well cared for.

She wasn't sorry to shed the foul-smelling male carapace for this one, younger and female. The former, as it turned out, attracted the wrong kind of attention, and it amused Xal to learn that human bodies require constant maintenance, cleaning, and decoration to be considered acceptable by other humans. It seems even the creatures themselves are repulsed by the sight and smell of their own flesh. But for a species so preoccupied with its own appearance, they are remarkably unobservant of the interloper in their midst. She's been following the boy since the day she arrived, always taking care to stay out of sight — only she's beginning to think that her care is wasted. He seems oblivious to her presence, and his incautiousness is perplexing.

Cameron — that's his name. The not-quite-man who is the source of the signal. There is no question: He's been touched by the same destructive force that scarred Xal's face and ripped her people from her. She can feel it coming off him even at a distance, but she's been surprised to find the energy increasingly focused and controlled. The boy may not know the source of his power, but he knows he has it — and, apparently, how to use it. And that makes him dangerous, especially when there's still so much Xal doesn't know. For her people, the Inventor's weapon was a means of connection, but what can that kind of power do in the untethered, isolated mind of a human being? And how did the boy come to be in possession of it? His entire existence is an infuriating mystery.

And yet, he may be her best hope of survival — and not just survival, but rebirth. If the Inventor's weapon remains intact, if she can harness it once more, then Xal's ruined civilization could be rebuilt anew. Maybe even better than new. For all its flaws, Earth possesses resources her own planet did not, resources the Elders could have scarcely imagined. It is a place where a hive could flourish. Perhaps even a new order: instead of the Elders, there would be Xal. Instead of trying to rebuild, she and the other survivors of the massacre could start afresh, here, on a new world and with a new vision. Her vision. She would be the architect of their glory, and in return, her people would fall in behind her and call her their queen. Already, she knew she could reign like a god over the swarming masses of *this* planet. And what would the humans do? They would fall to their knees in gratitude, relieved at last of the burden of their solitude. She would show them what it means to truly be a part of something. She would show them the unimaginable power of another world.

But Xal is getting ahead of herself. First, she has work to do. The boy is the key, and to get closer, she'll have to choose her target carefully. Not the mother; even the oblivious adolescent would notice if Xal took *her* skin. But in her time on Earth, she's learned that humans build strange little networks of trust in their quest for connection. They forge relationships with each other based on chemical attraction or shared gifts. They pay strangers to massage their bodies, or sing to them, or listen to their fears and hopes. And when all else fails, they seek out doctors to heal their broken, isolated minds. Doctors who they trust. Doctors who they tell everything to, even their deepest, darkest secrets. Xal has seen the boy visiting the woman called Nadia Kapur. She has watched from across the street as he disappeared into her home, and then listened, crouched below Kapur's window, at the murmurs of conversation inside.

Yes.

Xal smiles. If she hurries, she can be inside her new body before the next sunrise.

18

DR. NADIA KAPUR
TAKES OUT THE TRASH

NIGHT SETTLES DEEPLY over Woodbine Boulevard as Dr. Nadia Kapur steps out her front door and shivers against the wind. The smell of frying onions wafts gently out behind her, and she chuckles; if her husband were still alive, he'd be chasing after her now to scold her for leaving the gravy unattended.

"Do not turn your back on the onions!" he'd shout. "You must monitor them. They are a conspiratorial vegetable!"

Nadia sighs. Of course, if her husband were still alive, she wouldn't be out here in the first place. Dev would be the one dragging the trash bins out to the curb. But if she's quick, she'll be back before they scorch . . . and if she fails, she can order herself a pizza.

The luxuries of widowhood. I can eat any stupid thing I want; the tradeoff is missing him every damn day.

The street is empty and drenched in shadow, despite a pleasant glow from the windows of the well-kept houses that line it on either side. Months from now it'll be more cheerful, the porch railings and shrubs draped with strands of twinkling colored lights, the first sign of the holiday season. Another task Dev used to take care of that Nadia supposes is her job now.

Quickly, she drags the bin of recyclables out of the alley and into position — but stops short as she turns back to get the trash, gripped by the sudden conviction that she's no longer alone on the street. It's the kind of thing most people might write off as nerves, a fear of the encroaching darkness combined with a dread of returning to the empty house behind her. But Nadia Kapur is not a nervous woman, and not one to ignore the fine-tuned system of instinctual responses that produce the sensation of "the creeps." Her two decades as a psychologist have only given her a deeper respect for the power of the unconscious — that lizard brain that senses danger even when it can't be seen. Moving purposefully, she hurries back inside, closing the door and sliding the deadbolt home with a satisfying thud.

From behind her, an inhuman voice croaks out a single word.

"Unexpected."

Nadia shrieks and whirls around, her hands coming up halfway to defend herself only to hang in the air, forgotten. The young woman standing in her front foyer is completely naked, staring, arms dangling limply at her sides — and familiar, Nadia thinks. She's seen her recently, around the neighborhood. Did she stumble in from the street? Has she been sexually assaulted? It's the most logical explanation . . . only Nadia's instincts don't agree. Even as her training kicks in and she imagines moving forward, offering help, every cell in her body screams at her to run. Not because the woman is dangerous, but because —

She's not a woman, oh God, don't you see, don't you see it, she's not a woman she's not a woman at all she's something el —

The woman-not-a-woman's forehead splits open, a leering, inhuman face peering out as the blood and bone and sinew peel away.

Nadia's mind goes blank.

The woman-thing lurches forward and grasps her by the neck as she slumps, the strength gone from her legs. The horrible face draws close, closer, and Nadia gags at the smell of rot, the cloying bouquet of pus and plasma, a dying defense as its skin tries vainly to battle the hideous thing inside it. Her stomach lurches as she tries to vomit, but the hand around her throat tightens hard, harder, and nothing can get out . . . or in. The last thing she feels, as blackness begins to cloud the corners of her vision, is the acid burn of bile as it dribbles back into her stomach — only the sensation seems very far away, as though her stomach no longer belongs to her. Nadia Kapur is unraveling, undone.

And then she's gone, and someone else opens her eyes.

*　　*　　*

The acrid scent of burning onions follows the body of Dr. Nadia Kapur as it steps out the front door for the second time that night, a bulging trash bag in her hand. The street is still empty; nobody is there to observe the difference in her gait and posture, to wonder at the stiffness of her movements.

Nobody sees Xal wearing Nadia Kapur's flesh like an ill-fitting suit.

Xal is no stranger to creating hybrids, to taking what she needs from the creatures she encounters — even from her own people, when it was the only way to save her own life. But this is the first time she's taken everything, every cell and every system, to become as much something else as she is herself. She feels lost inside this body, with its repulsive pores and itchy hair and slimy mucous membranes. It's allergic to having her inside it; hives ripple on the surface of Kapur's skin, and Xal hisses at the sensation.

That won't do.

Carefully, she focuses her attention on the offending gene sequence, sending her own cells to extract it, filling in the blanks with a DNA patch. The hives subside, but for the first time, she feels uneasy. This body is weak, and its weakness makes her vulnerable. How much can she strip away, or augment, without the boy noticing that something is amiss in their interactions? Perhaps the doctor's files will be useful on that front. The woman keeps recordings of her sessions on a device inside the house; Xal has seen her through the window, listening, making notes. Perhaps she can study them, the better to mimic the woman's speech and movements. Perhaps she'll even learn something about her quarry in the bargain.

*   *   *

She drops the trash bag into the bin on the curb. It catches slightly on its way in, and a thin stream of fetid liquid oozes out through the tear, pattering in dark droplets against the sidewalk. Inside, what's left of the body she came in collapses on itself with a squelch.

Xal grimaces, showing her human teeth, and slams the lid down.

*   *   *

BREAKING NEWS ALERT

Good evening. For American Network News, I'm Ashley Smart. The big story tonight: Journalists at outlets including ANN received anonymous Dropbox caches today containing documents and analysis revealing the existence of a massive online data-mining network, whose influence in international elections and other global initiatives dates back at least a decade. Multiple world leaders have denied responsibility for what appears to be the largest organized act of cyberespionage in history. We'll continue reporting on this alarming news as it develops.

ENCRYPTED MESSAGE INCOMING

From: Olivia Park

Subject: Target lock

Analytics has identified a common code string in the attached incident reports tracing to subject ACKERSON, CAMERON. Pursuant to today's events, immediate action is requested to capture subject at earliest opportunity. He's caused us enough trouble.

Please note: Whereabouts, physical description, and identity of second subject DOE, NIA remain unknown. There's a chance they may be together, so keep your eyes peeled.

ENCRYPTED MESSAGE INCOMING

From: ADMIN

Subject: Re: Target lock

Olivia, the board trusts your family connection to Ackerson will not be a problem.

Please advise.

19

OPERATION
BURN IT DOWN

THE ABANDONED DIGITAL CITY, the one Cameron's father used to call Oz, is a maze of ancient code, as difficult to penetrate as its fictional namesake. As a child, Cameron would creep downstairs in the night to stand at the closed door of his father's office, staring at the thin line of blue-tinted light beneath the door, listening to the tap-tap-tapping of the keyboard as he built his city. It would be years before William Ackerson disappeared entirely, but in those moments, it seemed like he was already gone. He put everything he had into building his city, imagining that someday he'd throw open the doors and invite the world in. Instead, the place became a virtual tomb: a final resting place for the broken dreams of a broken man, its doors sealed shut forever.

But Nia was right: Every system has a way in. William Ackerson's world of code was only waiting patiently, ready to admit the visitor who comes with the correct password — the right words, spoken in the right tongue. Years ago, Cameron had tried to hack his way in and gotten nowhere. The system wasn't just impenetrable, but incomprehensible. He couldn't even scratch the surface of its structure;

it was like knocking at an endless, featureless wall. He'd given up almost immediately. But now, when he approaches it, everything has changed. Not just him, but the system itself. When he approaches that wall, it shifts and shimmers. It responds. Instead of a wall, it becomes a mirror.

It's like it's been waiting for me.

Perhaps Nia was right: maybe he was meant to find his way into the ruins of his father's empire. He just had to learn to speak the language that would allow him to pass — to go beyond simple communication and become part of the system itself.

It's a sunny morning. Upstairs, Cameron's mother is brewing a fresh pot of coffee — but when she calls down the basement stairs to tell her son it's ready, she gets no reply. Cameron's body is sitting on a couch in the darkened basement, but his consciousness is deep in cyberspace, passed like a ghost through the looking glass, over the threshold that divides the real from the digital.

The first time he did this, several days ago, it happened by accident. It was terrifying — like falling off solid ground and plummeting through nothingness. One moment, he was sitting at his keyboard, hammering out commands, listening in his mind for a response from the system and getting nothing but the downcycling echo of his own code. The next, he felt his fingers lift from the keys to grip the sides of his head as his mind suddenly synced with the system itself, his consciousness racing along an unseen pathway and dumping him down abruptly on the other side of the wall. For a moment, he was in two places at once: staring with his open eyes as the screen in front of him unfurled an endless string of code, revealing the architecture of a hidden digital world that appeared in his mind's eye like something out of a dream. A city inside the machine, a world of glowing ones and zeros, narrow streets lined with hundreds of structures that contained thousands of rooms.

Then he closed his eyes, and there was only Oz.

*   *   *

Now, he can enter without a single keystroke.

Nia is already here as he walks in, sitting on a high-backed sofa with a small brown dog curled up in her lap. One day, Cameron thinks, they might remake the place together — maybe even open it to the whole of the internet, an empire reborn. But that can come later, once he's sure of his ability to remake the Whiz system from the inside, once he's not so afraid of plucking out the wrong piece and bringing the whole thing down on their heads. For now, Cameron has kept the renovations of Whiz limited to just one room, a blank canvas that either one of them can remake as they please. The first thing he did was give Nia her own entrance, her own key to the city. She's better at whipping together elaborate virtual tableaus than he is; the last time he was here, she'd turned the room into a perfect replica of the *Dr. No* villain's midcentury lair. Now, it's like something out of a fairy tale: weathered walls made of loosely separated boards, the cracks between them choked with vines that admit just a few stray beams of sunlight. An attic hideaway, or maybe an elaborate treehouse.

She bolts to attention as soon as Cameron opens the door, dumping the dog onto the floor and running across the room to greet him, the hem of her gown — Nia also loves dressing up, he's learned — sweeping the floor. Her avatar here is like his own: an exact replica of the real thing. Even the Uncanny Valley effect, the eerie smoothness that makes their digital selves look almost-but-not-quite human, is barely noticeable; if Cameron doesn't think about it, he'll soon forget that she's not really here, and that he's not really here with her.

A wild tangle of flowers and vines is growing through the cracks in the floorboards, too, and they explode as Nia moves through them, kicking up clouds of glittering petals into the air until the room is filled with a sea of swirling confetti. The dog, who is wearing a jeweled collar with a nametag that reads DOGUE, woofs once in irritation and waddles away.

"You're here!" Nia says, and throws her arms around him. Or rather, she tries to; one of her forearms hovers just above his shoulders, while the other plunges straight through his guts. She draws back, giggling. "Oops."

Cameron groans—not in pain, but in frustration. He amends his earlier assessment: everything about him and Nia and this world feels almost perfectly real, until they try to touch each other. Then it becomes clear that there are still bugs in the system, that even after stretching his abilities to the limit, this place is still a work in progress. But there's plenty of time to get it right, he thinks. And in the meantime, the glitches in the system are the furthest thing from his mind—or hers.

"Did you see?" she asks. "We did it! It's happening!"

The first of the information packets had dropped just hours before, bouncing through a series of digital wormholes and washes to make them untraceable. The journalists who received the fruits of their work would never know who'd handed them the biggest scoop of their lives, but more important, neither would the dark, mysterious person or persons whose lovingly cared-for misinformation farm had just been burned to the ground.

Cameron wishes he felt like celebrating, but he can't help feeling uneasy. Neither he nor Nia was ever able to peel back that last layer, to identify the precise origins of the massive network. He would have liked to have a name, a location, anything to pinpoint the person or persons behind it. But there's nothing to investigate now; the whole operation vanished from the internet within hours of them exposing it, just winked out of existence without a trace. It's not that Cameron regrets what they've done—shining a light on that dark web has to be a good thing for the world and the people in it—but he's extremely aware, even now, that it can't be the only one of its kind, or the only project being run by . . . well, whoever it was. Together, he and Nia have almost certainly pissed off someone, maybe multiple someones, with immense power and extremely deep pockets. It would make him feel better if he had at least some idea of who that someone is.

But he doesn't say that to Nia. She's too excited; he's not about to ruin it. And what is he even worried about? Their tracks are covered, a dozen times over.

"It's everywhere," he says. "Trending on every major site, headlines in every major outlet. What's happening on the network? Still dark?"

"Not just dark. Deleted." Nia frowns. "It's strange. I stashed some backups around the web, just in random places — anyplace I could make a trapdoor on the server and hide it. But almost all of them are gone. Maybe there was a self-destruct code embedded."

Cameron feels uneasy again. "You didn't put them anywhere that would lead back to you, right? Or me?"

"No. Actually, I cached a bunch of them on Daggett Smith's servers. It's not like he's using them anymore."

"Good point," he says, laughing. Last he'd heard, Daggett Smith had deleted every single one of his accounts and was living in a solar-powered trailer somewhere in New Mexico with at least six cats.

"Is it true that the president is going to speak about this?"

"Tonight, I think," Cameron says. "But I won't be watching. I've got graduation."

"That's exciting," Nia says.

Cameron laughs. "No, it's not. It's a walk across the stage in a fancy bathrobe to get a piece of paper. Honestly, I could skip it. We just took the head off an evil online empire that had been poisoning the internet for at least a decade. Getting my high school diploma doesn't seem like a very big deal. Although, if you really think it's exciting . . ."

Nia looks at him curiously. "Yes?"

"Well, I have extra tickets. You could come."

"Tonight? At night? I've never snuck out at night before." She bites her lip. "And my father will be here."

"Maybe you could ask his permission," he says, but Nia shakes her head vehemently.

"He'll never say yes."

"Well, what if I talked to him? Maybe it's time you introduced me —"

"No! He can't know!" Nia practically shouts, and then looks chagrined. "Cameron, he wouldn't understand. You mustn't try to contact my father. *Ever.* Promise me."

"Geez," Cameron says. "Okay, I won't. I promise. I guess I shouldn't even ask if you want to meet *my* mom."

Nia's face goes from chagrined to wistful, and Cameron realizes he's forgotten, again, that she's not really here — that this place isn't real. Her avatar is a perfect portrait of human heartbreak; her eyes even glisten as though she's about to cry.

"I really do want to meet your mom, though. And your friends. I just can't yet. It's complicated," she says, and pauses. "But I think I could sneak out tonight. I mean, I'm willing to try. If you still want me to come see you get a piece of paper in your fancy bathrobe."

"Of course I want you to come," he says. "And I'm supposed to do dinner afterward with my mom and her new boyfriend, but I have some time before the ceremony. Why don't we meet up early, and you can clap while I get my dumb diploma and then sneak out the back of the auditorium after I walk. You don't want to sit through the four hundred kids whose names come after 'Ackerson' in the alphabet anyway."

She smiles. "I love that idea."

"And I love," Cameron says, "uh, hanging out with you."

Nice save there, champ, says his brain. *No way she noticed how you almost just said the Thing.*

This is also how he finds out that for all the physical limitations of this realm, he can cringe here just as hard as he does in real life. Nia steps back with a startled look.

"Does the program have a glitch? You're making a *hideous* face."

*   *   *

Several hours later, Cameron quickens his pace and curses. It's like the universe is conspiring to make him late: first he accidentally scratched one of his AR lenses and had to wait while a new one printed, knowing that the only thing worse than being late to meet Nia would be spending all evening in an auditorium full of thousands of people, everyone filming or livestreaming or tweeting the ceremony, without the device to help filter and organize all the noise in his head. It's unnerving to realize how reliant he's become on the wearable; he can't remember the last time he left the house without it. But that was only the beginning: halfway out the door, he'd been interrupted again by the buzzing of his phone — and found himself on a surprise video call with Dr. Kapur. He'd been so annoyed and in such a hurry that he'd hardly noticed the odd expression on her face, or the peculiar, halting pattern of her speech.

"Dr. Kapur?" he said, confused. "We're not supposed to talk until next week. I'm on my way out —"

"I have questions," Kapur said, ignoring him as though he hadn't spoken at all. She was so close to the camera that Cameron could practically see up her nose. "I have questions," she repeated.

"Um. Okay, about what? I don't really have time —"

"I have questions about your —" The psychiatrist paused, sucking the insides of her cheeks. "Your friend. Your friend you spoke of. Your new friend."

Cameron blinked. "You mean Nia?"

Kapur leaned in.

"Yes. Nia. And her . . . people."

"Uh," Cameron said again, groaning inwardly as he realized that he was officially late. "I mean, she lives with her dad. I think I told you."

The psychiatrist cocked her head and spit the word back at him. "Dad."

"Yeah. Her father."

"Father."

"Yes," Cameron said, no longer able to contain his irritation. "And listen, I'm actually supposed to meet Nia now. I'm already late. So, I really have to —"

"Now?" Kapur sat back from the screen. "Where? Tell me."

"My school. You know, for graduation? I'm sorry, Dr. Kapur, I really have to go," he said, and ended the call without waiting for her to say goodbye. He didn't mind the psychiatrist — she was nice enough, and obviously knew her stuff — but for a professional shrink, she could really stand to take her own advice about saving big conversations for the appropriate time.

* * *

Nia is waiting when he gets there, sitting on a bench in a pocket park a block south of the campus. Cameron grins when he spots her: she's wearing a skirt and heels, like it's a special occasion. Like *he's* a special occasion. She looks beautiful, and in that moment, as he realizes that she's gone to the effort of not just sneaking out but dressing up just for this, just for him, he suddenly comes to a decision. *I'm going to kiss her. I'm going to walk over there, sweep her into my arms, and plant one right on her gorgeous lips.*

He quickens his pace and calls out, holding up a hand to greet her — but Nia doesn't wave back. Instead, she stares at him, her face a mask of surprise and horror, her mouth in a frozen O. Her look is enough to stop him cold as he wonders frantically what's wrong — and then, a split second later, he knows.

He feels it.

His mind is filled with the fast-moving flow of data, so much that his lenses go haywire as they struggle to channel and organize it. The air around him is full of coded whispers, flowing so fast that he can't isolate any one of them to try to understand it. It's like he's walked straight into a spider web of data . . . because, he realizes with horror, that's exactly what it is.

Chatter.

The messages aren't passing at random. They're the encrypted communications of a sophisticated, maybe even government operation. And it's no accident that he's right in the middle.

Oh, SHIT.

"Cameron!" The sound of Nia's terrified voice jolts him back to reality. "RUN!"

At first, he doesn't. Instead, Nia does, disappearing behind a tree as three men in identical black armored suits swarm out of the shadows and the whispers in Cameron's mind become a high-pitched shriek. She's gone, and the black-clad agents don't pursue her. They're not here for her. They advance on him, and Cameron takes one fraction of a second to feel relieved.

They didn't take her.

Then he runs.

The screaming of digital voices inside his head has left him disoriented; instead of strategizing to escape, he bolts, driven by the instinctual need to be anywhere else. He sprints across the street at a lurch as drivers lay on their horns and screech to a halt to avoid hitting him. His foot is slowing him down; his prosthetic doesn't understand the concept of "running for your life," and there's no time now for it to learn to process his frantic stumbling to get him moving faster. If they chase him, he'll never outrun them. But if he can lose them . . . *I have to hide.* He scoots down an alley between a Chinese restaurant and an accountant's storefront. The narrow space is empty but for a few stacked pallets and a dumpster that smells like fried rice, but there's an exit at the other end, where Cameron can see the gleam of parked cars and a shadowy copse of trees rising beyond — the entrance to a public park. It's a perfect place to lose a tail . . . or to make them think they've lost you.

Cameron drops to his belly and wriggles beneath the dumpster, trying not to cough as the smell of spoiled food fills his nostrils. He closes his eyes and listens again, but the chatter has fallen silent. The sense of being trapped in a web of tangled communications is gone, and he exhales with relief. They must not have seen where he went. They—

"Hi there," someone says, and Cameron screams. One of the men he was running from is bent down beside his hiding place. He's wearing a mask that betrays no sign of the human being underneath, a black mirror in which Cameron can see only his own petrified face staring back at him. A pathetic whimper escapes from his throat as the man reaches out, taking rough hold of Cameron's shirt and hauling him out from under the dumpster. His arms are seized and pinned behind him, and something presses hard against his back. Cameron concentrates, and senses the close presence of a simple software program. It's talking, but not to him — and his own devices are answering back. Someone is scanning his body for tech. Frantically, he tries to interrupt the flow of data. From behind him, a voice says, "This kid is crawling with hardware. Should I kill it?"

"Do it," says the man in the mask. The thing pressing into his back emits a sharp whine, and Cameron feels the sudden silence as his phone, his AR lenses, and his prosthetic all go instantly dead.

Then the device whines again, and a huge, painless jolt of white light envelops his brain. He knows he's in terrible trouble.

Then the whiteness turns black, and he knows nothing at all.

ENCRYPTED MESSAGE INCOMING

From: OPTIC Team 9

Subject: Target acquired

Request immediate use of facilities for subject ACKERSON, CAMERON. Six, get your tools ready. We're going to make this kid VERY uncomfortable.

20

CAPTIVE

THE FIRST THING Cameron feels as he wakes up in the cold dark of his kidnappers' lair is the emptiness. Emptiness where the voices of the machines used to be, so vast and palpable that it hits him like a wave before he even opens his eyes. His phone, his watch, his AR lenses, the neural net in his prosthetic — Cameron had grown so used to hearing them humming away inside his head, the sound as pleasant and constant as falling rain. Now they're dead . . . or in the case of the prosthetic and his phone, just gone. Taken from him by the same people who took him. It's too quiet in there now, like a ghost town, and when he reaches out in search of something else to interface with, it's like running into a blank wall. He's never felt so disconnected.

The second thing he feels is dread. Those devices weren't just a set of friendly voices inside his head; they were his best hope of calling for help. Even with his hands bound — and they are, he realizes, trussed behind his back with something thin and hard, possibly a zip-tie — he could have interfaced with one of them to send his location to the police, or the FBI, or . . .

The FBI? Cameron's inner voice pipes up, with scathing cynicism. *Who do you think just kidnapped you and brought you to their secret underground torture chamber, ya dingus?*

Right, he thinks. Scratch that. But geez, if the worst happened, he could've at least fired off an email to his mom to tell her where to find the body.

He opens his eyes and struggles to a seated position. The room around him is a featureless white box, a cell with no furniture except the cot he's been lying on. He reaches out again in search of something, anything, trying to find a flow of data he can dip into and extract information from, but the room gives up nothing. It must be some kind of dead zone. The realization grips him with fear. Is it just a coincidence that he's in here, or do they know about his abilities?

"Hey!" he yells. "HEY!"

The door slides open, and his fears evaporate as quickly as they came. A small, slim woman is standing there, wearing a turtleneck dress that hugs the lines of her body and a pair of high heels that look impossible to walk in. Her black hair is pulled back in a severe ponytail, exposing a small pattern of white dots on her temple. She gazes at him without speaking, and Cameron looks back at her with interest — but it's not what he's seeing that captures his attention so much as what he's sensing. A wave of information flooded in when the door opened, coming not from the building, but from her. She's got biotech — advanced, expensive, impossible for ordinary civilians to get — humming under the surface of her skin, a complex series of systems interfacing with the ones that nature gave her. The data logs are staggering; this woman isn't just tracking things like her step count or heart rate. Cameron reaches out to the software and discovers a sea of information, everything from her liver function to plasma levels to a countdown to her next period.

Gross.

"You're grimacing," the woman says, coolly. "Are you in pain? The jolt we gave you to knock you out is supposed to be harmless, but it's hard to account for all outcomes for someone with your, ah, unique medical history."

"I don't know what you're talking about," says Cameron, and the woman's eyebrows go up.

"So you're not the Cameron Ackerson who got struck by lightning on an internet livestream this spring?" she says, and laughs lightly when Cameron scowls. "Come on, kid. You're famous. Even if it weren't my job, I'd know who you are. You've made a remarkable recovery . . . on several fronts."

She brings a hand out from behind her back, and Cameron stares. His prosthetic is dangling there, but it's the hand holding it that interests him; two of the woman's fingers and her thumb are missing, replaced by the most incredible bionic substitutes that he's ever seen. It's not just the tech, but the design; the artificial fingers look like they were sculpted by artisans. Next to it, his 3D-printed neural network looks like a science fair project.

The woman sees him staring, and smirks.

"Quite lovely, isn't it?" she says. "Not that yours doesn't have a certain homespun charm. I had my people bring it back online for you — unless you prefer to limp, of course."

She hands him the prosthetic, and Cameron turns away as he slips off his shoe and reattaches it. He wishes the woman would stop watching him; it feels weirdly intimate, like having someone watch him get dressed. He feels even more uneasy as she beckons to him, leading him out of the narrow room, her heels clicking against the polished floor. This building is a maze of disorienting hallways that all look the same, the rooms hidden behind camouflaged sliding doors that open up in the wall without warning. Cameron's best guess is that the whole place is several stories underground, and even then, it's only a guess. When he tries to sync with its systems, to find a registry or an address or even a fire alarm to trigger, his queries are met with a burst of gibberish. Everything from the air conditioning to the communications network is locked behind a thick layer of sophisticated cybersecurity.

"In here," the bio-enhanced woman says, and Cameron turns as the door swoops open to reveal another bare room — this one outfitted with a table and two chairs, and a camera in each corner. He steps in, then turns to face his captor. She seems to be studying him. The weight of her gaze makes him feel like squirming.

"You don't remember me, do you," she says, and turns up the corners of her mouth again when Cameron gapes at her. "No, I suppose you wouldn't. You weren't much more than an infant the last time I saw you. Of course, I was only a kid myself. And now here we both are, all grown up. If only our dear old dads could see us now. Park and Ackerson, a collaboration for the next generation."

She pauses, waiting for Cameron to put it together. He doesn't disappoint.

"You're Wesley Park's daughter."

"Yes, I am," she says. "Olivia."

Cameron gestures at the room. "And this place is . . . what, the family business? The one your dad built after he destroyed my dad's livelihood?"

Olivia raises her eyebrows. "Oh, is that the Ackerson version of events? Because according to *my* father, Whiz was a sinking ship that he jumped from after your father lost his mind out there on Lake Erie and went full mad scientist. I always thought it was a little far-fetched myself. Although having met you, I'm reconsidering."

Cameron feels his temper flare. "Your father—"

"Is dead," she interrupts him, her voice mild. "Almost ten years now. Mother, too. It was a terrible accident. I was the sole survivor—almost fully intact." She twinkles her bionic fingers at him. "And this place, since you ask, is mine. Inherited upon my father's death, but I've built it into something rather different than he would have liked. Dad was very web one-point-oh. He didn't understand that the power of the internet was about people, not tech."

"You . . ." Cameron trails off, letting his thoughts click into place. The lenses in his eyes are dead, drained of energy, but this is one connection he doesn't need any extra help to make. "You're data mining. That big story on the news, that was about your network."

Olivia rolls her eyes. "News story. Uh-huh. Cameron, a word of advice: This will all go much more smoothly if we don't insult each other's intelligence. My people and I have been tracking your little project since the Daggett Smith incident. We know more than you think we do. Keep that in mind when you're tempted to lie."

Cameron, stunned, doesn't reply, and Olivia doesn't wait.

"Can I get you anything? Glass of water?" she says coolly, stepping away from the table. Cameron studies her, trying to get a read, trying also to get his reeling emotions under control. He seizes on a single comforting truth: Olivia might know about his activities, but she doesn't seem to know about his cyberkinetics. If she did, she'd never have risked being this close to him. Her body is fifty percent bionic, the embedded software regulating multiple vital organs and systems. He could seize control in a moment; he could kill her with a thought. The knowledge makes him feel bold.

"You can get me the hell out of here before I miss my whole graduation ceremony," he says. "You can tell me what you meant when you said my father went 'full mad scientist.' And I want my phone back."

Olivia offers a tight-lipped smile. He can't help noticing that her bio-data shows no reaction at all; no adrenaline spike, no increase in heart rate. She's completely unfazed.

"I'm afraid the ceremony is long over, although we do plan to cut you loose before your lovely mother stops leaving angry voicemails on your cell and starts calling the police. And you'll get your things back. Maybe I'll even answer some of your questions — after you answer ours."

"Questions about what?" he asks.

The smile disappears.

"Don't be obtuse, Ackerson. It doesn't suit you."

She leaves. The door slides closed behind her.

*　　*　　*

Now, sitting alone at the table, he reaches out and scans the room. The walls are a scramble of software on the inside, some of it deeply protected, some less so. The cameras are unsecured — but they're on a closed circuit, and unless he can find a way to free the data from that loop and send it out into the world, they're not going to be much use.

And when it comes to getting information out of the building... Cameron closes his eyes and concentrates the way he did earlier today as he entered Oz, sending his consciousness toward the system, slipping across the threshold between meatspace and cyberspace. He needs to be cautious — this is hostile territory, and who knows what kind of malicious software might try to creep along the bridge between his brain and the network?

He lets out a low whistle at what he finds, his awe making him briefly forget how much trouble he's in. There's a river of data running through the place, buried under layer upon layer of encryption. He can sense the depth, but not the details. The building itself is outfitted with an intricate web of security — he senses fingerprint and iris scanners, panic buttons, a series of nested lockdown protocols that starts with sealing off individual rooms and ends with a controlled explosion that'll turn everything inside to ashes. He doesn't dare dig any deeper. Instead, he draws back and waits, watching for any weaknesses, any movement.

That's when he realizes: he's not alone.

There's someone else inside the system. Another intelligence — not human, but android, and Cameron can't help being impressed by Olivia's ingenuity. This is a whole other level of security: on top of the usual encryptions and firewalls, the building has a virtual guard, a bot lurking inside the code, scanning everything. It's lucky that he didn't try to hack any of its servers. The guard bot would have surely noticed the disruption and raised an alarm, shutting him down before he even got started. It doesn't seem to notice his presence at this level, though. Unless...

That's not quite it, Cameron thinks. *It sees me, but it doesn't care. And it doesn't care because... because it doesn't know I'm not supposed to be here.*

For the first time, Cameron feels a spark of cautious, hopeful excitement. He'd hoped to find a weakness, but instead he's found something better: a potential ally. The AI is designed to monitor the system, watch for incursions, and reason its way to certain logical conclusions about what it sees. And that makes it more sophisticated than the average computer program — but even a sophisticated AI is dumber than most people. Go beyond the range of its programmed responses, and it doesn't know what it doesn't know. In terms of its skill set and threat detection abilities, this cyber-guard is more mall cop than Navy SEAL. And if a mall cop sees another mall cop dressed in the same uniform and carrying all the right gear, does he stop to ask questions if the other mall cop tells him what to do?

Cameron doesn't think so. But there's only one way to find out.

He concentrates his energy on the guard bot.

Hello, he says.

The bot replies immediately. *Hello. I am Omnibus. OPTIC sentry program: all updates downloaded.*

Cameron duplicates the bot's response and bounces it back.

Hello, Omnibus. I am . . .

Wait, he thinks. I can't be Omnibus too — the thing might get confused. Cameron starts over:

Hello, Omnibus. I am Batman. OPTIC sentry program: all updates downloaded.

Hello, Batman, says Omnibus, and in real life, Cameron bites down hard on the inside of his cheeks to keep from laughing.

Omnibus, give me operations status.

All is well. Last system check performed at twenty-two thirty-six hours. Status: secure. Next system check to complete at twenty-two forty-four hours.

Cameron does the math in his head: so the bot scans and reports every eight minutes. He'll have to work fast — but that's not a bad thing. If he plays his cards right, he'll be able to create ten different kinds of chaos before his kidnappers even begin to guess what's happening. And when it comes to finding his way out . . . Well, he'll cross that bridge when he comes to it.

Omnibus, unroll your protocols.

Omnibus, who seems happy to have some company on his lonely robot mall cop beat, tells him everything he wants to know.

* * *

Cameron is just committing a plan to memory when the door to the room slides open. He turns, expecting Olivia, but this time his visitor is a man. He's tall and gaunt, dressed in a white lab coat, with spider-like hands dangling at his sides. He moves into the room with uncanny smoothness and presses one hand against the wall; a sensor glows red, then white, as a panel slides open to reveal a large black box surrounded by an array of screens.

"You're grimacing. Are you in pain?" he asks, and gooseflesh ripples out on Cameron's arms at the sound of his voice. The way the man says *Are you in pain?* has a creepy, giddy edge to it — it's like he's hoping the answer is yes so that he can poke you right where it hurts.

"I'm fine," Cameron says.

"If so, I can give you something. You can trust me," says the gaunt man. "I *am* a doctor."

Cameron shudders, not because he doesn't believe the man, but because he does. This *doctor* pulls a tangle of electrodes from the black box, deftly unraveling the wires with his long fingers. It's not hard to imagine him holding a scalpel, peeling someone's skin open with the same confident grace.

"If you're a doctor, didn't you swear some kind of oath to do no harm?"

The man laughs. "Cameron Ackerson, I'm not going to hurt you. What do you think this place is? I just want to talk to you. I don't mind telling you, your extracurricular activities have caused quite a headache for my employers."

The man dumps the untangled electrodes on the table, then crosses the room and presses his hand against another panel. The sensor glows, and Cameron feels a tickle in his head as a new digital voice joins the chorus. The cameras have been turned on. All he needs is one last stroke of luck — and to keep the guy distracted long enough to make it work for him.

"What's your name?"

"You can call me Six," the man says.

"Dr. Six?"

He shrugs. "If you like."

"Who are your employers?"

Six smiles. "Well, of course you've met Olivia. I guess you could say she's an influencer. You know all about influencers, don't you? That's what you wanted to be, isn't it? With your little YouTube channel. Although, you haven't posted a new video in ages. What happened?"

"Maybe I didn't want to be internet famous anymore," Cameron says.

"Or maybe you found a new hobby," Six replies, and the smile disappears. He leans in, attaching the electrodes to Cameron's head. "Don't squirm now, or we'll have to restrain you."

The screens behind the panel come alive with undulating lines as Cameron's brain activity renders into a digital readout. Six lifts a tablet out of his pocket and taps it, focusing more on the screen and less on his patient.

"Your bedside manner sucks, dude," Cameron says. The doctor snorts.

"Tell me, Cameron, does the name 'Nia' mean anything to you?"

Cameron swallows hard and says nothing—but on screen, one of the undulating lines spikes wildly. Six grins.

"Interesting," he says.

His next volley of questions comes rapid-fire, as Cameron struggles to stay one step ahead. Some are easy to answer; some, not so much.

Who are you working with?

Why did you target Daggett Smith?

What is the source of the program you used to uncover our account network?

Do you believe in democracy?

Why are you involved with Nia? How did you meet her? Is she even a she? Where does she live? How do you contact her?

Cameron shakes his head. "I told you, I don't know."

"You're lying," Six says, but he frowns. The digital readout doesn't seem to be telling him what he wants to hear; he leans in closer to tap the screen, then snakes a hand out to adjust one of the electrodes on Cameron's head.

That's the problem, Cameron thinks. *I'm not.* He's hedged and told half-truths to avoid revealing his cyberkinetic abilities, but he hasn't had to lie about Nia. Everything they want to know about her is stuff he doesn't know himself — the same questions he used to ask her, only to get evasive, teasing answers. If he weren't so nervous about this creepy doctor, who still looks like he'd rather be peeling Cameron's flesh than probing his mind, he'd be getting righteously annoyed at Nia for being such a cipher.

On the other hand, he thinks, she was smart to cover her tracks so well: Olivia's people may have been able to trace him, using their considerable resources to scrape his works for fragmented digital fingerprints, but it's very clear they have no idea who Nia is. And Cameron, who has been quietly interfacing with the tablet in the doctor's hands, peering into its history for clues, finally knows the answer to the one question Nia couldn't unravel. Who was running a vast network of troll accounts that could steer the discourse on any topic as it pleased? Who was manipulating the algorithms to silence some voices while augmenting others? Who was the spider in the center of the dark web, spinning lies and spitting poison to keep people angry and afraid?

Olivia Park hadn't told him the name of her organization, but Omnibus, the guard bot, was happy to supply it.

OPTIC — also known as the Omni Psyop Tactical Intelligence Corporation.

He and Nia have clearly caused them some trouble.

Now it's time for Cameron to cause them a little more. Omnibus has just completed his latest security sweep, which gives him . . .

Eight minutes, he thinks.

"You know," Six was saying, "we'd love to meet with her. With both of you. We need people with your skill set, and you — you and your friend — you could really make a difference here."

"Yeah? You want us to help you kidnap a few more kids so they can't walk at commencement? I didn't just miss my graduation for this, you know," Cameron says. "I also missed dinner. You assholes could've at least waited until after I'd had a burger to snatch-and-grab me."

His snark has the desired effect: Six gently lays the tablet on the table and leans forward, earnestly.

"Surely you realize by now that snatching people isn't really what we do here," he says. "Look at this place. It's not a torture camp — it's an office. A research facility. We don't even have a real prison cell. We had to stash you in our napping pod."

"Napping pod?" Cameron says, incredulously. Inside his head, he thinks: *Five minutes.*

"Listen to me, Cameron. You want to change the world, don't you? Well, that's what we do here. We change the world, by changing conversations. Did you know that the last coup in the Middle East started with just a dozen posts on social media? Did you know that there could be an entirely different man occupying the presidency in France, if only his ads had been reposted by a few high-value, strategically placed accounts?"

"They said that was Russian hackers," Cameron says.

Six laughs. "The Russians did their part. They were also sloppy. That's the difference between their operation and ours. You know what they say: If you want the job done right, buy American. And they do, Cameron. They buy what we're selling. They pay through the nose for it. We could have a new Daggett Smith on the air tomorrow, saying all the same things — or saying worse, if we want him to. And here's the thing: You can't stop us. You can only slow us down a little and piss us off in the process. As you can see, our resources are limitless." He sweeps his hand, indicating the room — the cameras, the sensor-equipped panels, the three screens in the wall, on which Cameron's brain activity is still being rendered in an increasingly colorful digital display.

One minute.

It's the moment Cameron's been waiting for.

Hey, Omnibus. Special delivery.

"That's why it's in your best interests to j —"

Six abruptly stops, whirling back to look again at the screens. The lines are ablaze, dancing wildly as Cameron focuses all his energy on the zip file he's just hitched to Omnibus the guard bot — the one he'll run up to the security system's mainframe in about thirty seconds, a little surprise package bundled up with a doctored report of a hacking attempt on one of the system's servers. The report will trigger a series of outcalls across the network, as administrators kick down the secure doors to track the intruder, who appears to be already inside. And when those doors open?

"What are you doing?" Six says sharply, staring at the screens as Cameron counts down the final thirty seconds in his head. "What are you doing?"

The screen nearest Six begins to stutter, the display blurring and fuzzing. As he steps toward it, the lines suddenly twist over on themselves, the dancing brainwave patterns resolving into a message that requires no interpretation. It fills the whole screen in a loopy cursive scrawl.

Eat My Butt, it says.

"You were right," Cameron says, pulling the electrodes off his head one by one and dropping them on the table. "It's been way too long since I uploaded a new video. Gotta keep that content fresh!"

Six's face contorts with confusion as he looks at the display, at Cameron, at the tablet on the table — and then up at the cameras on the far wall.

"How?" he says, grabbing the tablet and jabbing at its surface, which has been quietly mirroring the security cameras for the last five minutes. The final frame still lingers on screen: a wide shot of the room, of Six, of Cameron sitting in the chair with electrodes on his head.

By now, the footage of Six's last monologue should be out the door and fully uploaded to Cameron's YouTube channel — and OPTIC's tech team should be scratching their heads as Omnibus, the helpful guard bot, earnestly explains that their system has been infiltrated . . . by Batman.

It's the most elaborate hack he's ever pulled off, and without so much as stroking a keyboard — a fact that would fill Cameron with excitement and pride if not for the way Six is looking at him. The confusion is gone from the doctor's face, and in its place is a cacophony of emotions: anger and frustration, but also a dark sort of glee that makes Cameron's hair stand on end. In his rush to compromise the system, he hadn't stopped to think about what would happen afterward, about what Olivia Park might do to people who broadcast the faces of her operatives out into the world. He'd actually believed Six's pitch about OPTIC: that they weren't that kind of black ops organization, and ruthless as they might be, that they weren't in the business of murdering people — an assumption that now seems terribly naive.

A broad smile blooms on Six's face. "So, there *is* something. I told them there was something. When they first brought you in, I saw your scans, and I *told* them —"

The man suddenly leaps toward the table, and Cameron lets out a little yelp, but it's the tablet he wants. He grabs it and hurls it across the room, and as it smashes against the wall, Cameron sees the machine's life flash before his eyes. It's a burst of fragmented information: scraps of correspondence, medical files, photos — and what he sees makes Cameron gasp. For a split second, his head is filled with images, poorly lit pictures of what look like sculpted gargoyles — only sculptures don't bleed. These are pictures of human beings, real people with too many limbs, with wings or claws, with their bodies encased in a mass of bone like an insect's exoskeleton. He sees blood, and sutures, and . . .

Six.

The doctor is gazing at Cameron, his lips peeled back to expose miles of bright pink gum line and two neat rows of gleaming teeth.

"What do you know about my garden?" the man asks, and Cameron takes a careful step, keeping the table between them.

"N-nothing," he stammers.

The doctor stares at him, the smile dancing on his lips, seeming to weigh his next move. Cameron is dimly aware that there's a great deal of noise in the hallway outside, but in here, the silence stretches on and on. He feels beads of sweat begin to roll down his temples. He's afraid to move, to breathe, to blink.

When the door opens behind him, he doesn't turn around. He doesn't want to take his eyes off the man in the white coat.

But Six looks up, and his eyes narrow.

"I don't know you," he says.

From behind Cameron, Dr. Nadia Kapur's voice says, "The boy goes now."

*　　*　　*

Cameron turns slowly and nearly sobs with relief. He's never been so glad to see his psychiatrist — so glad that he only wonders for a moment how she found him before deciding that he doesn't care.

"I'm not done here," Six says, but he sounds unsure.

Kapur shakes her head curtly. "Now." She looks at Cameron and lowers her voice. "Nia?" she asks, softly.

Cameron's eyes dart toward Six as he shakes his head. Kapur's eyes narrow, but she seems to understand; she turns and points behind her, down the hall, speaking again at a normal volume. "We are leaving."

Cameron hesitates. Something about Kapur's gaze is unsettling.

"I don't think they'll just let us walk out —" he begins.

"You think correctly," Six interjects, his tone almost pleasant, and Kapur's eyes dart again.

"You were unwise," she says, "to interfere." She glares at the doctor, who gazes back at her with open curiosity.

"Well," he says, and lunges at them.

*　　*　　*

With a hiss, Kapur dodges Six's outstretched hands, sliding away along the wall with surprising speed. Cameron stumbles backwards instinctively, four quick steps, but no wall stops his progress; he's passed through the open door and is standing in the hallway outside. For a moment, he hesitates — and the door slides closed in his face.

Dr. Kapur is on her own.

Cameron tells himself she'll be fine. She's not the one OPTIC wants, and anyway, she can clearly take care of herself. It's his own safety he should be worried about; he has to get out of here. He turns and moves quickly down a wide hallway — following the flow of data that suggests an elevator bank is somewhere ahead. He glances down the hallways that branch off to the left and right, watching for other agents, but none appears. It's eerily quiet, and there's a strange, metallic smell in the air. Finally, he turns a corner, and sighs with relief — the elevator is there, its doors already open as though waiting for him. He leaps into the car and punches the topmost button, marked with a star symbol and the number one, and feels his ears pop as it rises swiftly and silently to its destination. The doors open again on a small dim lobby, also empty, and a moment later he's outside, his breath shallow in his chest, his hands empty. His jacket — along with his phone — is still in OPTIC's underground lair, but he's not about to turn around. He just hopes Dr. Kapur is okay.

He's not about to turn around to investigate that, either.

Aboveground, OPTIC's building is deceptively small, a single-story concrete box that looks like a garage or a small warehouse. The glittering city rises just ahead; he's not even that far from home. He thinks he'll go there first, though he doesn't know what he'll do when he gets there. His mother will be pissed as hell, if not insane with worry. And if his little stunt down there with Six and Omnibus worked as intended, he's going to have to make up a hell of a story to explain why he missed the graduation ceremony and their dinner date in order to upload new content to YouTube, let alone explain the substance of that content. His mind races as he takes off at a trot, as fast as he can manage. And when he finally thinks again about Dr. Kapur, about the strange way she looked at him, it doesn't register as significant. The memory occupies his mind only for as long as it takes to relive it. A moment later, it's gone, chased away by more pressing concerns. He lets it go without so much as a shrug.

Later, he'll wish he hadn't.

Her pupils, he thinks. *They were like little disks. Flat little disks, like a goat's eyes.*

21

CAUGHT

My fault, my fault, it's all my fault.

Nia slips back through the narrow window, knowing she needs to be quiet and careful, yet almost too anguished to care. It seems like a miracle that she made it home at all; her grief was so over-whelming that it was nearly impossible to navigate through it, to find her way through the narrow passage to the classroom. She left her decoy avatar meditating under a tree in a forest world after tell-ing Father she wanted to focus and not be disturbed. But after to-night, returning to the idyllic green landscape feels like a cruel joke. She lashes out, sobbing, scattering the trees and leaves and flowers into nanodust.

What happened tonight is her fault. It was her idea to expose and bring down that network, her stupid idea. She let Cameron's ea-gerness infect her. The sense of purpose, of being part of something exciting and important, was intoxicating. She had allowed it to make her incautious — she had even convinced him that they didn't need to know who was running the troll farm, that what mattered was taking it down, even as she knew better than anyone how deep and tangled its roots were. And now he's paying the price for her stupidity, and she's ruined everything—including her own best chance at freedom. Cameron was supposed to be her knight, her savior, the one who rescues her from this prison. Now he's a captive himself, and how will she escape without him? She can't. He was her only hope.

She thinks again of the way Cameron looked in that moment, knowing he was caught, trapped. The way it felt when they dragged him away—she had no idea anything could hurt so much. The emotion she feels is something that has no name, too huge and wild to be contained. Its enormity terrifies her.

He was going to save her.

Now she has to save him.

The terrifying grief fades into the background as she gets to work, concentrating, channeling all her skill and energy into the search she left unfinished. The code is like a sea, consuming her. She dives down, deeper and deeper, finding the openings she once overlooked, chasing the trail of the enemy that tried to take everything from her. She can see it now—she doesn't understand why she didn't see it before. Heartbreak has sharpened her insights somehow; she sees not just what's there, but what's not. The path to their doorstep is there in the space between spaces, like breadcrumbs scattered in the gaps between the code. Finally, it rises up in front of her, a wall of security as vast and complex as she's ever seen. She knows that Cameron is behind it. She can feel him somehow, the same way she did on that wonderful night when they first met —when she found him setting the world on fire because he was too gifted and bored to do anything else. His mind had called to hers in that moment. It calls to her now.

They could build a hundred walls like this, and she'd burn every one of them to the ground to get to him.

"I'm coming for you," she whispers.

"You're not going anywhere," says Father.

*   *   *

The program freezes in front of her as Nia freezes in front of it, the sound of Father's voice cutting through everything. When she finally allows herself to face him, the look on his face is one she's never seen. His eyes are wet, and his voice is low and shaking with barely contained rage. She's never been so terrified.

"What have you done, Nia?"

"I only wanted —" she begins, only to find that she doesn't know how to finish the sentence. Father gazes at her and shakes his head with agonizing slowness.

"You lied to me," he says. "Lying. Of all the outcomes I imagined, I never imagined this. Compromising my security, sneaking behind my back. Do you have any idea of the danger you've put yourself in? Of the danger you've put me in?"

She doesn't answer. There is no answer, none that will satisfy him. There's no picture she could paint, no song she could sing, that would explain the truth in a way he would understand — that she knew the risks and took them, because the way Cameron made her feel was worth it.

"I'll go to my room now," she says.

Father nods. "Yes, I think that's best."

He closes the door behind her. She wonders how long it will be this time before she's released — days? Weeks? Will Cameron last that long without her? Or might they release him, maybe before Father releases her? She opens the interface to send him a message, just to tell him she's sorry and hopes he's okay.

That's when she realizes her connection is cycling down, the signal growing weaker with every passing second.

"I blame myself," Father says, "for letting you online. I thought it would be good for you to connect with people. I thought maybe, someday . . . But I was wrong. And we'll both have to live with that." He pauses. "Your friends . . . I'm sorry."

"For what?"

"That you won't get a chance to say goodbye."

Nia cries out in horror, hurling herself against the door. It's too late. He's locked it. He's locked her in. The signal that connects her to the outside world is dying, nearly gone. Frantically, she types out her final message, a desperate plea for help.

It flies out into nothingness as the room goes dark.

22

FIGHT AND FLIGHT

SIX KEEPS VERY STILL, listening to the sound of Cameron Ackerson's uneven footsteps fading down the hallway behind the closed door, heading for the exit.

Xal, using the stolen ears of Dr. Nadia Kapur, does the same. The squeak and tap of the boy's sneakers against the floor grows fainter, stutters, then stops. The light *whoosh* of the elevator door echoes down the empty hallway.

Each of them, unbeknownst to the other, is thinking that nothing about this little interlude has gone according to plan.

Six peers at the intruder, his irritation outweighed by his intrigue. He's spent enough time with the human body to know right away that there's something odd about this one. It's why he remained in this room instead of pursuing his subject down the hall; whatever secrets Cameron Ackerson holds, Six is quite sure that they're less interesting than this woman's. She gazes back at him, her face still and emotionless, one hand resting on the chair that Cameron had been sitting in. She seems relaxed, casual even — except that the knuckles on her hand, the one touching the chair, are turning white with the force of her grip.

"And so we find ourselves alone. What did you say your name was?" Six asks.

"I am Dr. Nadia Kapur."

"Oh, of course. From Cameron's file, the psychiatrist. But this is a little unorthodox, isn't it? You're trespassing in a private facility. Do you do this for all your patients?"

"Cameron is special," she says, and flashes a broad smile, showing her teeth. They're quite sharp, and she has a lot of them — even more than he has, Six thinks.

"He certainly is, Doctor. He was being especially special just before you got here — but I'm guessing you already knew that. Perhaps we should compare notes on the boy, one medical professional to another? I'll show you mine if you show me yours."

"Nothing you have to show could possibly interest me." The woman's voice is strangely guttural, the cadence of her speech just a little bit off. "And I have nothing to show you."

"Oh, I doubt that," Six says, and takes a cautious step closer. He cocks his head, his expression openly curious now. "There's something special about you, too. Isn't there? I can't quite put my finger on it —"

The woman rears back and spits at him. He flinches back instinctively, and the gob lands on the table beside him — where it makes a hissing sound as the plastic surface bubbles and warps. Six looks at it, then back at her.

"Well," he says, his voice lilting with amusement. "That's different."

*   *   *

Xal does not like the way this man is looking at her. Not at all, not one bit. Most humans would have screamed and fled when they saw what she could do; certainly, the ones she met on her way in were appropriately terrified before she slaughtered them. But not this one. This one is looking at her with . . . What's the word? She digs through Nadia

Kapur's language center and finally comes up with it: delight. Like a child who just received an unexpected gift.

"Where are you from, Dr. Nadia Kapur?" the man asks. He's keeping his distance from her now, but it's clearly out of caution, not fear. In fact, he seems to be battling with himself not to move closer, and he won't stop *peering* at her. Xal narrows her eyes.

"I'm not here to answer questions," she says.

The man just grins. "Okay, Nadia. Is that really your name? Nadia? You've got beautiful eyes, you know. Beautiful, unusual eyes. I almost didn't notice at first, but those pupils don't come standard, do they? Not around here. I'd love to know where you got them." He pauses, his grin stretching wide. "Or you could just give me your set."

"You wouldn't dare," Xal says.

"I'd take excellent care of them," he says. "And any other parts you cared to contribute. You'd look lovely, all unwound and scattered in my garden. I have a feeling about you, Nadia. I think you'd be my most beautiful sculpture yet."

Xal doesn't quite grasp what the man is talking about, but she knows she doesn't like the way he says it, or the way he's begun edging one hand inside his white coat. She grips the chair tightly, her muscles tensed, and takes stock of her assets. There are fewer than she would like. She'd been following the boy tonight, hanging back as he hurried through the streets. He'd been so agitated, so purposeful, that she was sure it would happen tonight. He would lead her to her destiny. The one he described on the doctor's audio file as "worth waiting for," not knowing how right he was.

He would lead her to Nia.

It was beyond Xal's wildest dreams, an outcome so incredible she hadn't even dared to hope for it. Nia, the Inventor's pride and joy, had survived — and was here, on Earth, trapped in the form of a naive adolescent girl. With Nia under her control, Xal wouldn't just have her revenge; she would have a new world, all her own.

But the boy, the stupid boy, was ensnared in someone else's trap before he could lead Xal to her prey. She'd looked away for only a moment, and when she looked back, he was fleeing across the street, the men in black behind him. They had taken him from right under her nose, and all she could do was follow — and take what she could from the beings she encountered along the way. It was unfortunate that she still needed Nadia Kapur's body, and needed it intact, to keep the boy's trust and convince him to follow instructions. A larger, more powerful human skin would have made her job easier, as would augmentations to her teeth and fingernails. As it was, she could only take so much. Her one stroke of luck had come in the form of a strange building, where the shelves were lined from floor to ceiling with creatures in glowing glass boxes. The sign outside said ANIMALIA EXOTIC PETS EMPORIUM; Xal wasn't sure if it was some kind of gallery, a place where the humans could safely admire these superior species, or perhaps a prison where dangerous creatures were being kept as slaves. Regardless, it had been useful. A colony of industrious insects had turned out to have the acid-secreting apparatus she'd used to threaten the man in the white coat (and to melt the face off a shrieking woman she'd encountered upstairs). There were slithering creatures without limbs that offered up their killing gifts, and another one, submerged in water, that turned out to be endowed with remarkable healing abilities. A fat, glossy thing with glorious striated markings was the best of the bunch, though — slow-moving, but with a potent venom hidden inside. Xal was indignant to realize how little the humans appreciated its beauty; the label on its glass prison said MONSTER.

The other creatures she took from without care or concern, but that one had seemed special. When she borrowed its venom for herself, she filled in the hole she made with her own precious DNA. The beautiful monster wouldn't be exactly the same, but it would live.

*　　*　　*

"It's strange, you know," Six says. "I was sure someone would have shown up to interrupt our conversation by now. And yet we're alone. Nadia, why is that?"

Xal tenses her body, her muscles coiling for a strike.

"Because your friends are dead," she says.

Six waves a hand dismissively. "They're not really my friends. Co-workers, more like it." But there's an edge in his voice as he looks at her sidelong and says, "You killed all of them?"

Xal shrugs. "All I saw."

"I see," says Six, and lunges at her. He's quick, quicker than Xal imagined, his body perfectly under control. Something silver flashes in his hand, and a long clean slit opens up in the arm of Xal's coat. She hisses as blood flows into her sleeve, pooling in the elbow. With a grunt, she heaves the chair off the floor and swings it in a wild arc. The man dives easily out of the way, the chair crashing against the opposite wall. A panel shatters, and behind it, a red light blares as an alarm begins to shriek. The room plunges into darkness, then illuminates from all sides with a soft red glow.

EMERGENCY LOCKDOWN PROTOCOL INITIATED, says a female voice.

Xal snarls, ripping the coat from her body, dropping it to the floor with a wet squelch. She's alone, and furious; while she was startled by the sound of the alarm, the man opened the door and fled through it. She dives through the doorway herself just before it slides home again, sealing shut.

The hallway is empty.

No matter. She opens her mouth, revealing a forked tongue that flickers out rapidly once, twice. Her pupils dilate and saliva collects in her cheeks; she can smell the man's bitter sweat, tinged with adrenaline, so potent and heady that it could make her drunk. A surge of hunger races through her—the urge not just to hunt, but to eat. To unhinge her jaw like the limbless creatures and swallow her prey whole, bones and all.

She takes off down the hallway at an easy lope, her head tilted to follow his scent, her arms dangling loosely at her sides. She's getting close, closer—

CRACK!

She drops to her knees with a fraction of a second to spare, the ax passing through the air just above her head and slamming hard against the wall. Another panel shatters, and Six curses, pulling the weapon back for another strike. Xal launches herself at his knees, wrapping her arms around and dragging him down, hoping to hear the sharp crack of a breaking bone. Instead, she's rewarded with the echoing thud of the man's head hitting the floor. His eyes roll back briefly and a low groan escapes his lips.

Xal is almost disappointed. She wanted the man to scream as he died; killing him while he's half unconscious won't be nearly as fun. Perhaps she can bring him around; his shirt has ridden up, a half inch of pale white belly peeking out. She grabs the fabric and yanks it, exposing the man's tender abdomen, all those slick organs and ropy intestines lying vulnerable just under the skin. She tucks her chin, rears back, and spits a gob of viscous acid squarely into his navel.

Six's eyes fly open as he shrieks in pain.

That's more like it.

Xal shrieks back with laughter, intoxicated by the man's helplessness. But she'll finish it now; after all, this isn't what she came for. It's just a bit of fun. She clambers over the man's prone body, straddles his chest, and unhinges her jaw, wide, wider, the skin stretching painfully as a full eight inches of space opens between her lips. The venom from the monster isn't lethal to human beings under most circumstances, but Xal is sure it'll do the job if she injects it directly into his eyes. And after what the man said he was going to do to her, wouldn't that be . . . What's the word? She digs through Kapur's memories again and finds it.

Poetic.

It would be poetic.

She leans in, her mouth agape like a caricature of surprise, and prepares to sink her elongated canines into Six's fluttering eyes.

This time, there's no warning — no chance to dodge.

The knife sinks expertly into the soft cartilage of her wrist, and twists; once, and once more.

When she yanks her arm away, her severed hand remains on the floor.

Xal rears back and howls, pulling the stump of her arm toward her face, and then shrieks again when the arterial spray blasts her own blood into her eyes. She scrabbles away on all fours, elbows and knees skidding underneath her, as Six comes up with the knife in one hand and the ax in the other.

He's smiling at her.

Xal doesn't like it. Not one bit.

"Oh, you're something special, all right," he says. His eyes are on her wrist — where small pink strands of tissue are already beginning to regenerate. "Nadia, you're one of a kind."

Xal doesn't reply.

This isn't what she came for.

She turns.

She runs.

She survives.

23

THE OTHER SIDE
OF THE DOOR

OUTGOING MESSAGE FROM CAMERON, 11:03PM

Nia, are you okay? I'm okay. Dr. Kapur rescued me. So weird. Where are you?

11:06PM

Hey, I'm freaking out. Please tell me you're okay.

11:08PM

Nia? It's really messed up that you're not answering me.

11:09PM

HELLO?

11:10PM

WTF WHERE ARE YOU

11:15PM

Wow I guess you really don't even care that I got straight kidnapped huh

11:15PM

Thanks for trying to help by the way

11:16PM

P.S. I didn't tell them anything about you even though you were the one they were looking for and this creepy motherfucker strapped electrodes to my head and interrogated me, YOU'RE WELCOME ASSHOLE

   11:19PM

   Nia please please please answer me I'm sorry just please where are you?????

*   *   *

CAMERON BITES DOWN HARD on his lip and swipes furiously at his eyes, fighting back tears of impotent rage. It's not just the helplessness of having been taken by Olivia Park and her goons, or his lingering frustration at the way she taunted him with her knowledge about his father. Tonight has robbed him of the illusion that he and Nia ever made a difference. *We could have another Daggett Smith on the air tomorrow* — that's what the creepy doctor had said, and Cameron's heart is heavy with the knowledge that it's true. It was all for nothing. OPTIC is bigger and more powerful, an unstoppable tide; no matter what he and Nia do, it could never be enough.

And he's furious at Nia for not even trying to help him escape — except that he's deeply afraid for her, which just makes this whole thing worse. The first thing he'd done, after an unsuccessful attempt at emergency parental damage control that ended with his mom declaring him grounded "for-fucking-EVER," was to rummage for an old phone so that he could reconnect with her. He'd felt a surge of hope when the device lit up with messages — only none was from Nia. There were angry, worried voicemails from Mom, a slew of confused comments from his YouTube subscribers, and one curious text from Juaquo ("What's with the low-rent *Agents of S.H.I.E.L.D.* rip-off?"), but not a single text from the one person who should've been the most concerned. Where was she? Why wasn't she responding? Was she in hiding, afraid of meeting the same fate he had, or — his guts twist as he considers this — did Olivia and OPTIC take her, too? Were they only pretending not to know who Nia was, to manipulate him into giving something up? He doesn't think so, but he also doesn't know for sure, and the possibility that she's in trouble eats at him as the minutes tick by. It's been six hours since OPTIC torched his devices and took him in for questioning. Six hours. In the time he's known Nia, they've rarely gone even half that much time without messaging each other. The realization fills him with dread.

Something is wrong. If not OPTIC, then something else.

He grits his teeth in frustration, overwhelmed once again by the realization he first had tonight, when Six was questioning him — that as intimately as he knows Nia, he also knows almost nothing about her. Not her address or birthdate, not even her last name. If something happened to her, he would be useless, helpless, unable even to tell the cops who they should be looking for. Nia had made sure of that from the moment they'd met, when he went looking for clues to her identity and she scolded him for snooping.

Cameron sits bolt upright in his chair.

I don't know, he thinks, *because I stopped looking.*

He turns toward his computer, the screen coming alive as he looks at it. He concentrates, letting his consciousness flow inward and then out into virtual space, slipping into their private world.

He opens the door and walks in.

The fat brown and white dog is still there, sitting right where they left him. He glances lazily at Cameron but doesn't greet him. The seat of the sofa is still thick with petals. Everything is as it was; nothing has been disturbed. Nia hasn't been here, then — but from this place, Cameron can go to her. He crosses the room, the flowers tangling under his feet, and rests his hand on the opposite wall. It shimmers as he touches it, a sculpted glass handle rising out to meet his hand.

"That's not your door," says the dog, and Cameron jumps involuntarily. *Oh, right, the dog can talk.* That was Nia's doing; after all, she kept saying, wasn't the whole point of a virtual world that they could make any rules they wanted? But it still freaks him out every time.

"I'm going to look for her," Cameron says, and then feels a surge of embarrassment. *Why am I explaining myself to a digital talking dog?*

"That's not your door," the dog says again.

"Shut your mouth, Dogue, or I'll delete you and replace you with a thousand guinea pigs," says Cameron. The dog doesn't reply. He opens the door and steps through.

This is Nia's portal, the entrance Cameron made just for her so that she could come and go as she pleased. She would have passed this way earlier today, when she left their virtual treehouse; even if she used a masking program to bounce through multiple servers before landing here, he should be able to follow her digital tracks back to wherever she originally came from — to at least get a rough geolocation, or find out who her IP is registered to. But as soon as he's on the other side of the door, Cameron stops, stunned. There is no pathway, no trail of breadcrumbs. Nia's entrance into their world is like a long hallway where someone has painted all the doors shut and turned out the lights. There's nothing here.

He turns back.

That's when he sees it.

There's a message scrawled roughly, faintly, on Nia's side of the door. A message meant for him, trapped here when somebody cut its connection — here, in a place where only one person could have left it and where only Cameron could find it.

The first line is a desperate cry for help.

The second is horrifyingly familiar.

PLEASE COME BEFORE HE HURTS ME.

41°54´37.8˝ N 81°40´02.1˝ W.

*   *   *

Cameron opens his eyes with a gasp. On the table next to him, his old AR navigation visor springs to life, the cracked display emitting a faint glow as it recalibrates.

Nia has sent him her coordinates, but he doesn't need to plug them in. The location is one he knows by heart.

He's been there before.

Alone, trapped in a storm, and struck by lightning.

24

INTO THE STORM

THE CITY MARINA is eerily silent, the only sound the soft lapping of waves, as Juaquo pulls his Impala up to the gate. Beyond it, the moored boats bob gently on the dark, cold water, the docks between them pale and deserted in the glow of the security lights. Juaquo puts the car in park and turns to look at Cameron.

"I gotta say it one last time. Let the record show that I do not understand why we're about to go on a midnight boating expedition right now instead of calling the cops."

Cameron doesn't answer. He's already out the door, moving as fast as he can toward the docks. Juaquo sighs and follows, pocketing the keys, looking back over his shoulder at the car. The hood art, an elaborate painting of the Virgin of Guadalupe surrounded by plump, pink roses, is so vibrant in the warm halogen glow from the streetlight that it looks practically alive.

"You stay safe out here," he says.

"What?" Cameron yells.

"I was talking to the car."

The yacht club is closed off behind a sturdy iron security gate with a keypad entry system — but as Juaquo looks at it, there's a click and a creak as the lock disengages.

"That's weird —" he starts to say, but Cameron hurries through, offering no explanation. The piers groan under their feet as they make their way through the maze of boats, their shadows lengthening out ahead of them. Cameron keeps turning his head this way and that, like he's trying to catch a scent in the air, until Juaquo finally says, "You look like a nervous squirrel. What are you doing?"

Cameron mutters, "Looking for the boat."

"Um," says Juaquo. "Isn't your boat in several pieces?"

"Not *my* boat," Cameron says, and points. "*That* boat." Juaquo looks, and gapes. Sitting in a nearby slip is a sleek black watercraft, the kind a nerdy billionaire buys because it's the closest thing there is to an earthbound space pod. It's a boat worth way more than his house and his car put together; it's definitely not a boat that the Ackerson family could afford. But Cameron is walking purposefully toward it, and as he does, the vessel springs to life; the motor burbles, the instrument panel chirps, and the interior glows a vibrant purple.

"I know you said there was no time to explain," says Juaquo. "But, bro, you've gotta at least explain this. You tell me you need a ride to the yacht club — okay. You want me to come out in the middle of the night and fight your girlfriend's dad — that's weird, but okay! I got you. But there's a line, and for me, it's getting on the fancy million-dollar boat that doesn't belong to you and looks like a spaceship and also *appears to be haunted*."

Cameron steps onto the boat and turns toward Juaquo, pointing a finger at the AR lens in his own eye.

"It's not haunted. It's smart." He gestures at the instrument panel. "Keyless ignition, digital navigation." When Juaquo doesn't move, Cameron rolls his eyes. "Do you get what I'm saying? It's smart, and if it's smart, it can be hacked. It's not ghosts, man. It's just me."

"You hacked the boat."

"Yes. Will you get on now?"

"How did you hack the boat?"

"We don't have time to —"

"DUDE!"

"Fine!" Cameron yells. "I'll explain, but on the way. All right? This is urgent, and I'm leaving right now, with or without you. Are you coming?"

Juaquo scowls and grumbles, but he unties the boat from its mooring and climbs aboard, taking his place next to Cameron at the controls. The sound of the motor climbs in pitch, from a burble to a purr, as the glow of the skyline fades away behind them, and the vast, starlit darkness of the lake opens up ahead.

*　　*　　*

Ten minutes later, Juaquo sits down heavily and presses his hands against his temples.

"That's the nerdiest superpower I've ever heard of in my life," he says, raising his voice to be heard over the sound of the wind and waves. The boat is a lonely island in the dark, its headlights illuminating nothing but endless, churning water in every direction. "You can hack things with your mind? How does that even work?"

"I don't know how, I just know it happens. I can plug myself in to the system, look at files, run programs, even recode it from the inside. It's like having a conversation. Any device with a software network —"

Juaquo digs into his pocket, pulling out his phone. "Including this?"

"Yeah, including that. I told you, phones, laptops, security systems, robot vacuum cleaners —"

"You had a conversation with a vacuum cleaner?"

"I'm saying, if it's got software to interface with, I can communicate with it," Cameron says, exasperated. "It's not like I'm hanging out in my room having a heart-to-heart with the Roomba, for Christ's sake. But I could reprogram it to, I don't know, chase the cat around or write messages into the carpet or whatever. It's not witchcraft. Some of this stuff, I could've probably done before, if I had a crazy good computing system and unlimited time to work on it. But now it's, like, organic. And instantaneous. I don't need time or tools, it just happens."

Juaquo raises his eyebrows. "So, you used to be a regular nerd, and now you're enhanced. You're Super Nerd."

"I prefer 'cyberkinetic,'" Cameron says, scowling.

"That's exactly what a Super Nerd would s—" Juaquo's words are lost in a screech of warning tones and a flash of light. The boat's digital displays are going haywire, beeping and whirring, as a confused scroll of numbers flashes across its screens. Juaquo points at it and yells, "Are you doing that?"

Cameron shakes his head and gazes grimly out over the bow. His AR lenses, freshly charged and synced to his own old navigation system, are showing a precipitous drop in barometric pressure and scrolling a warning: ANOMALOUS ELECTRICAL ACTIVITY. The air around the boat is damp and thick and smells of ozone. He swallows, and his ears pop. He feels the dread unspooling like an icy snake in the pit of his stomach, and when he looks at Juaquo, he can see the fear in his friend's eyes. Cameron grits his teeth and clenches his fists, bracing himself for what he knows is coming.

"You're gonna want to hold on to something," he says, as the first bolt of lightning splits the sky.

*   *   *

As the storm begins to build around them, Cameron wonders for the hundredth time whether Nia is all right—and why she would send him to the middle of Lake Erie in the middle of the night.

Then the world lights up with electricity and he doesn't wonder about anything anymore. The storm erupts around them in an instant, a vast web of white-hot lightning engulfing the sky, the lake, the boat. As before, there's no wind—and yet Cameron could swear that he hears an eerie howling, echoing overhead, a sound that's somewhere between a woman's sob and the scream of a caged animal. The crack and sizzle of lightning is everywhere, the blinding flares coming so fast that there's no time even to breathe between them. Plumes of water explode upward as the bolts arc into the water, drenching the boat with freezing spray, shoving it roughly off-course so that Cameron has to strain to correct it. The headlight winks out with a flash; the violet interior lights stutter once and then do the same. The navigation system is useless, but the display of his visor still glows faintly, telling him they're on the right track. He presses his face toward the windshield, craning his neck to see overhead. The sky is thick with whirling clouds, lit from the inside by fierce flashes of lightning, spiraling out from a single origin point that must be the eye of the storm. A small circle of star-flecked sky is visible there, at the center, the clouds whirling furiously around it.

"This is insane!" Juaquo screams from behind him. He's crouched halfway back, gripping the sides of a table with built-in cupholders lining its edges. He's already filled two of them with vomit and is working on a third. "We're not gonna make it through this! We have to turn back!"

Cameron shakes his head, peering through the spray. They're so close; he can feel it. And there, up ahead — did he just see something? He could swear, for just a moment —

"Dude!" Juaquo screams again. "Are you listening to me? We're going to goddamn *die out here* —"

His voice booms in the sudden, empty silence.

The storm, the sky, the dazzling electric light, even the tossing lake itself, are gone. For a moment, the boat cuts blindly through the darkness, as soft and thick as velvet.

Then there's a jolt, and Cameron and Juaquo are thrown to the floor as the boat scrapes to a hard stop against an unseen shore.

Groaning, Juaquo gets to his feet. He pulls his phone from his pocket; the flashlight illuminates, reflected back in the surrounding plexiglass. "What —" he starts to say, then stops, looking bewildered. "Where are we? What did we hit?"

"I don't know," Cameron says. He steps out onto the narrow bow, letting his eyes adjust to the darkness. His navigation visor flashes a final message — DESTINATION REACHED — and cycles down. "But we're here."

"Where?"

"Where we're supposed to be. Nia sent me coordinates, and this place is it."

Cameron climbs over the prow of the boat, his foot reaching for the ground he can't see but knows must be there. A moment later, the toe of his sneaker squeaks against it — a smooth surface, gently rounded. *A man-made island?* It's not just the unnatural smoothness of the shore, which is made of a dark substance that's neither earth nor rock, and where nothing seems to grow. Beneath his feet, Cameron can feel the presence of tech. Resonant, humming, and immensely powerful. Its voice is like a seductive purr inside his head.

Juaquo springs down beside him. "Christ, it's dark. What is this place?" He looks back, past the end of the boat, and points. Far behind them, at what looks like the end of a long tunnel, is the faint glow of lightning. "That's where we came in. So your girlfriend . . . what, lives here? In a floating airplane hangar? In the middle of Lake Erie? How did this not come up on the radar? How can it —"

"We'll ask her when we find her," Cameron says. "There's definitely something here. I can feel it."

Juaquo taps his own head. "Like the boat, you mean. Something . . . smart?"

Cameron nods, but that's not quite right, he thinks. The presence he senses in this place, it's not just smart.

It's intelligent.

*　　*　　*

They move only a short distance through the dark before a small domed structure rises out of the ground up ahead of them, a shadow at its center that turns out to be a narrow doorway. Juaquo's phone flashlight, dimly reflected by the floor beneath their feet, illuminates the dome as they step inside: smooth, windowless walls, a rounded ceiling, and a floor. All made from the same material as the island itself. He bends down, pressing a hand against the floor, his finger tracing the dark outline of a seam beneath their feet. A trapdoor. Juaquo runs his fingers along the edge, stops halfway, and pries it up by a handle; it rises with a soft *whoosh*. He looks at Cameron, who nods. The door slides open on silent hinges, exposing a dimly lit staircase that spirals down to a destination unknown. A glow emanates from the walls themselves, which are not black but a deep violet, like the skin of an eggplant.

"Are you sure about this?" Juaquo asks.

Cameron grits his teeth. "This is the place, and she needs me. Let's go."

They descend in cautious silence, the minutes ticking by as the trapdoor vanishes into darkness somewhere above their heads. Cameron steels himself for what lies ahead—but with every step, he grows more and more aware that he no longer knows what that is. Even after he stole the capsule yacht and set out for the center of the lake, he still imagined that the confrontation ahead would follow a typical action movie script. That he'd find Nia trapped on a houseboat or something, maybe bound and gagged but more likely just locked in her bedroom, and her dad—whom Cameron had never met but kept picturing for some reason as Bruce Campbell from *Ash vs. Evil Dead*—would try, but fail, to stop them from freeing her. In his wildest fantasy, the one he dismissed as too outlandish as quickly as he could imagine it, Bruce Campbell was holding a shotgun that Juaquo had to wrestle away.

Now, Cameron is forced to admit that the reality he's stumbled into is weirder by an order of magnitude than anything he'd imagined, and they haven't even found Nia yet.

Juaquo's voice interrupts his reverie. "Hey. Do you hear that?"

"No," Cameron says, but the words are scarcely out before he hears it too. It's faint but growing louder, and he stumbles on the stairs in confusion. Juaquo steps up beside him, grabbing his arm to steady him, and the close space is suddenly filled with the pulsing of a familiar bass line.

"It's coming from there," Juaquo says, pointing, and Cameron realizes that the staircase ends just below where he's standing. They take the last few steps side by side, and find themselves on a small platform that stretches into a narrow catwalk in front of them, lined on either side by smooth and faintly luminous walls. At the end is a door, hanging slightly ajar. The music coming from the other side is so loud now that Cameron can feel every beat as though it's coming from inside his chest. He crosses the catwalk, peering over the side as he does so, and grips the railing hard as a wave of vertigo sweeps over him. The space seems to go on forever, curving away on either side into an immense nothingness, but he can hear the babble and chatter of software inside. It's everywhere — but the strongest signal is coming from right in front of him, seeping through the crack of the open door. He lays his hand against it, stepping through — and then stopping dead in his tracks, so that Juaquo bumps roughly into him from behind. The pounding music fills his ears as he gazes across a sea of cheering people waving purple glow sticks, their eyes on a stage flanked by massive screens two stories tall. A man in a white tuxedo is dancing frantically at center stage, mimicked by a dozen identically dressed backup dancers, and all Cameron can do is stare.

"Heeeeeeeey, sexy lady!" sings the man on stage, as the crowd writhes and shrieks in front of him, and Cameron feels himself grabbed roughly by the shoulder.

"Am I hallucinating?" Juaquo yells.

"No!" Cameron yells back.

"In that case," Juaquo shouts, "since when is the 'Gangnam Style' guy on tour in our city?"

"He's not," Cameron shouts, but Juaquo points furiously at the stage, using the gesture to punctuate each word.

"But! He! Obviously! Is!"

"I don't —" Cameron starts to reply, then trails off, staring. Gooseflesh ripples over his skin, and for a moment, everything — the storm, the concert, even the whole reason they're there, even Nia herself — is utterly forgotten. In the midst of the screaming crowd is a man, standing with his back to the stage, staring between the jostling bodies at Cameron, who stares back, unable to breathe. This is a moment he's imagined countless times over the past ten years, one that always seemed to bring unsettling questions with it. *What would I do? What would I say? Would he even recognize me? Would I recognize him?*

But in this moment, all the questions fade away.

There is no question at all, only amazement, and a flood of feeling.

Cameron takes a step forward, his eyes fixed on a face he's only seen in pictures, and in his own memory, for so very long.

"Dad?" he says.

He can barely hear his own voice over the thump of the music, but it doesn't matter. His father — and it *is* his father, sporting the same shaggy haircut and scruffy beard that Cameron used to yank on with his little boy's hands — takes a step toward him.

"My boy. You shouldn't be here. It's too dangerous — you have to leave! Now!"

"But —"

He doesn't finish his sentence.

On stage, the song concludes with an explosion of fireworks. Cameron raises his hand involuntarily to shield his eyes.

When he looks again, his father is gone.

"Dad!" he yells, moving forward at an awkward run. The crowd parts before him as he scans frantically in search of the familiar face, the abundant dark hair — and then quickens his pace as he catches a glimpse of William Ackerson up ahead, being pulled through the crowd by two angry-looking men who are holding him, dragging him, by the arms. *They're going to take him! I'm going to lose him,* Cameron thinks, his senses flooded with panic. He takes off after the men, dodging between two people who yelp and leap out of the way. He emerges from the crowd just in time to see his father dragged through another door up ahead.

"DAD!" he yells, again, charging forward as Juaquo shouts from behind him to wait up. He hurls himself at the door, stumbling as he passes through, falling roughly to his hands and knees — and then looking up with a gasp. There's a threadbare carpet under his knees, the soft murmur of voices all around him. Filtered sunlight shines softly through a huge, ornate stained-glass window set high in the wall, touching the shoulders of a pair of sculpted angels who flank a long aisle between rows of pews. The throbbing of the music and the roaring of the crowd are gone; when he looks back, he sees only

Juaquo standing in front of a closed door, looking around confusedly. Cameron struggles to his feet, looking for his father.

"Dad?" he says, again, but where his voice was nearly drowned out by the music in the last room, here it seems thunderously loud. The murmuring people, praying with their hands pressed together in front of their bowed heads or folded neatly in their laps, cast sidelong glances at him; one old woman in an elaborate hat whispers, "Shhhh."

Cameron stares at her. Like his father, she, too, is familiar — except this time, he doesn't know why. He only knows that the sight of her fills him with dread, and when he looks closely at her hat, the dread only intensifies. Something terrible is about to happen. He feels it, but how does he know?

This time, Juaquo supplies the answer.

"Oh God," he says, in a low voice. "What is happening? How are we here?" Cameron turns to look at him, and finds Juaquo staring back with huge, haunted eyes. "It's that church. The one from the news, the one where —"

The clip, Cameron thinks, and everything clicks. The same soft light, the same sculpted angels, rendered grainy and indistinct by someone's shaky cell phone video. The *pop-pop-pop* of gunfire, the screams of the wounded. An old woman lying sprawled in the center aisle, her blood-spattered hat obscuring her face.

"Oh shit," Cameron says, and the old woman glares again.

"Shhhhh!" she hisses.

It's the last thing she'll ever say.

Behind Cameron, the door to the church creaks open.

"Run!" he screams at the people in the pews, who turn to gape at him. The old woman, the one whose hat is about to be blown off with most of her head still inside it, stands up with one index finger extended, like she's about to give him a piece of her mind.

The gunman shoots her first. Cameron feels the bullet whiz past his ear and sees the woman rock back with its impact. She topples over the pew ahead of her and lands slumped in the aisle, in exactly the pose she'll be photographed in when this story hits the internet — only it *has* hit the internet. It was last week's big news. The clip was everywhere; Cameron even shared it on his own feeds. And yet she's dying in front of him now, in real life, in real time. They all are. The man in the black mask strides in, shooting, as the people in the pews scream and scatter. He makes his way up to the front of the church, then whirls, spraying gunfire that splinters the wooden benches and blows the angels to smithereens. Juaquo grabs Cameron's arm and drags him to the ground as they scurry frantically down a side aisle, past a wooden table lined with burning candles. Cameron knows he shouldn't look but can't help it. The gunman is standing just in front of the apse — and as Cameron peers back, he grins. He inserts a finger under the edge of his mask, and a low moan escapes Cameron's lips.

No. It isn't him. It isn't real, he thinks, even as some absurdly detached part of his brain pipes up to suggest that it certainly is real, it's right here in front of him; he can even smell the heady scent of the wax mixing with the sharp aroma of gunpowder.

The mask peels away.

Cameron's father grins, his eyes twinkling maniacally.

"You shouldn't be here, son," he says, again, in the same tone that he once used to chide Cameron for playing in his office. "This is no place for children. Now, Daddy has some important business to attend to — and I don't need a partner for this deal."

Cameron gapes as his father raises the gun, pointing at him. *It's not real.* His finger caresses the trigger. *It's not real!*

The column explodes into dust just above his head.

"MOVE!" Juaquo screams, dragging Cameron by the arm as gunfire rings out behind them. Cameron looks over his shoulder just in time to see the gunman, mask back in place, raising the barrel of the weapon toward his own head. Sirens are wailing in the distance. He reaches out blindly in front of him as the final shot rings out, finding the polished handle of the confessional door, flinging it open — and then the two are running headlong through a close and fetid darkness, the church lost somewhere behind. Cameron's foot rolls on the uneven ground and he stumbles into Juaquo, the two landing together in the dirt with a rough thud.

Juaquo lets out a sound that's somewhere between a laugh and a scream, rolling over onto his back.

"We're time traveling, aren't we? That's the only explanation, right? Tell me that's the only explanation. Tell me we're in a time machine right now. That shooting was last week. And that concert, that concert wasn't happening. That concert happened like ten years ago! That's it, right? It's the only explanation." Juaquo pauses. "I mean, I don't know what your dad was doing there. I haven't figured that part out yet. Are we time traveling inside your mind? Is that, like, a feature of your superpowers that you forgot to mention? Because if we're time traveling, I'd like to see the dinosaurs. Can we do that? Let's see a dinosaur and then let's rescue your girlfriend and then let's get the hell out of here."

Cameron grimaces, realizing his friend is hysterical, but also wondering if his questions aren't something close to the truth. Is it time travel? It seems impossible, and yet . . . maybe? They're surrounded by tech, the most advanced he's ever felt; it's been humming inside his head like a background soundtrack the entire time. And he hasn't been trying to interface with it, but . . . *What if it's interfacing with me?*

Cameron closes his eyes, concentrating. He feels so close to understanding what's happening, yet the answer is still out of reach; he feels it dancing just past the edge of his consciousness, sly and teasing. It's as though his own mind is working against him, muddling his thoughts. He tries to retrace his steps and sees only his father's face.

You shouldn't be here. That's what he'd said. Was he right?

For a moment, Cameron can't quite remember why he came in the first place.

Then a floodlight glares above him, and his mind goes blank.

Cameron sits up, and Juaquo starts laughing in earnest as the landscape around them suddenly illuminates. The air is filled with the dry rustling of leaves — of corn. Hundreds of thousands of plants stretching in neat rows toward a far-off horizon on one side, but ending abruptly on the other. Cameron can see close-cut green grass between the stalks, a diamond-shaped dirt track beyond that. Juaquo lets out a final hysterical giggle and says, "Excuse me, but I believe I ordered *Jurassic Park,* not *Field of Dreams.*"

Cameron gets to his feet and stares, trying to understand what he's seeing—only he doesn't need to. Juaquo was right. The corn, the grass, the dirt—it's a baseball diamond. It's *the* baseball diamond. And when he sees the man on the mound, his pinstripe uniform blazing under the lights, the swooping S emblazoned on the breast, he steps forward as if in a dream. But it's not a dream. The world outside, the one he came from—that's the dream, distant and unimportant. This, this moment, is what's real.

Cameron's father holds out a baseball glove.

"Wanna play catch?" he says.

Cameron nods wordlessly, taking the glove.

He doesn't know how long it lasts, the two of them tossing the ball back and forth under the floodlights. He's only dimly aware of Juaquo, sprawled on his back out in left field, singing "Back in Time" by Huey Lewis and the News and occasionally pausing mid-chorus to yell, "Hello, McFly!" at nobody in particular. At one point, he has the presence of mind to think that whenever they get home, he's going to be on the hook for Juaquo's therapy bills—maybe he can buy his friend a few sessions with Dr. Kapur. But . . . wasn't there something about Dr. Kapur, something he might need to remember?

The ball zings into his glove, chasing the memory away.

"It's time for you to go, Cameron," says his father. "You shouldn't be here. Go back home, to your mother."

"But I don't want to go. I can't. I have to . . . I need to . . ." Cameron trails off. He knows there's a reason he came here, but it's as though someone has hidden it away, drawing a thick black curtain over his own motivations. He no longer knows why he's in this place. He's not even sure anymore where this place *is.* There's a distant memory of a boat, a storm—but was that today?

"You must leave, my boy," says William Ackerson.

"If I do, will you come with me?" Cameron asks.

"I'm afraid that's not possible."

"But why?" says Cameron. "Why did you even leave us? *Did* you leave? Mom told me you wanted to. She thinks you just walked out and made a new life somewhere else — but then other people said that you had to be dead; they said you got mixed up with the wrong people and something went wrong."

"And you, Cameron? What did you think?"

"I don't know. I used to think that you had to be dead, because if you weren't, you would have come back. But now . . ."

He hesitates, and the next time the ball comes to him, he feels himself throw it wild off to the side — but no, he must have imagined it, because his father catches it easily. He feels dazed, like he's running on autopilot with his brain asleep behind the wheel. The way the ball flies back and forth, back and forth, a white orb against the black sky, is mesmerizing. Hypnotizing.

"You thought I was dead," his father says. "Are you sure I'm not?"

Cameron thinks about that. Unlike the other mental calculations he's tried to make, the memories he's tried and failed to access, this question is one his brain seems eager to consider. It seems like the only thing that matters. Is he sure? No, he's not. In fact, it makes a certain kind of sense for his father to be dead. It would explain just about everything, including why he's here on a *Field of Dreams* baseball diamond, wearing a 1919 Chicago White Sox uniform. Cameron is playing catch with his ghost.

Somehow, that doesn't seem so weird.

"Then . . . is this heaven?" he whispers.

His father smiles. "No, it's Iowa."

Cameron drops the ball.

His father stops grinning, the smile replaced by a frown, then a confused look, then a quizzical one. Cameron blinks, feeling the fuzz clear from his brain, the mist clear from his eyes.

"Isn't that what I say?" the man says, but Cameron only stares at him — first with suspicion, then with horror, as his father's face begins to seize, morphing from cheerful grin to worried frown in a series of spasms that happens too fast to be human.

"Isn't, isn't, isn't that what I, what I say?" the father-thing stutters, and Cameron moves forward, purposeful this time, allowing himself to focus for the first time on the deep, rich humming of the digital voices that surround him. They're everywhere, beneath his feet and in the air all around him — and they're inside his head, too. He *is* being manipulated. Messed with.

Hacked, he thinks. *It's HACKING me. Creeping around in my head like a virus and showing me what it wants me to see. And Dad can't answer my questions because . . .*

Because I'm talking to myself.

"That's Kevin Costner's line," Cameron says, and clenches his fist as he brings his focus to a point.

His father freezes in place as his face goes slack — *Only that's not my father,* Cameron thinks, *or his ghost.* For a moment, the whole world seems to go silent.

*   *   *

None of this is real.

But someone wants me to think it is.

The realization fills him with rage — at his father, at the illusion, at the unseen force that tried to take advantage of these painful memories to manipulate him. Everything he's seen tonight has been mined from inside his own head. Things he's recently seen — and the things he's spent his whole life trying not to think about.

Cameron unclenches his fist, and the father-thing explodes in a blaze of light.

It may be the most advanced tech he's ever interfaced with, but this place is still just another digital world — a computer program like any other. Just like OPTIC's security bot, just like the boat with its keyless ignition.

If it's got software, I can hack it.

Cameron claps his hands, and the cornfield erupts in flames. Around him, the world seems to shimmer.

"Hey!" Juaquo yells, and Cameron cringes. He'd almost forgotten his friend was there — but Juaquo doesn't seem to be freaking out anymore. He's shouting and running toward the baseball diamond, pointing wildly at the burning corn, and Cameron is only a little bit surprised to see a horde of frothing, shrieking orcs crash through the flaming stalks and onto the baseball field.

After all, he just watched *Lord of the Rings* last week.

He passes his hand through the air, concentrating hard, and grins as a laser gun takes shape in his palm, seemingly out of nowhere. This system is as much under his control as it is whoever created it, and the air itself seems to be made of code. He turns his weapon on the encroaching army, ripping a path through the sea of creatures, cackling as their bodies blow apart. A severed head lands at his feet, and he punts it, laughing again as it explodes like an overripe tomato against a wall — and there is a wall, because this place isn't a cornfield, in Iowa or elsewhere. It's a room, and under the slick black blood of the orc's splattered head, he can see a doorway shimmering, the seam around it glowing brighter as he focuses his energy on it.

"Juaquo!" Cameron shouts, and points; Juaquo, understanding, runs to kick the door open. As he does, everything in the room — the grass, the dirt, the remaining orcs and the scattered body parts of their comrades — stutters and crumbles, the program hopelessly corrupted. For a moment, nothing moves, and nobody speaks. The only sound Cameron can hear is the pounding of blood in his ears, and beyond it, Juaquo's labored breathing.

Then Juaquo peers through the open door, and his eyes go wide.

"Cameron," he says. "Come here. Right now."

"What?"

Juaquo shakes his head, grimacing. "You've gotta be kidding me. You told me you needed muscle, I figured you meant it literally. I'm not fighting this guy, dude."

Cameron startles. "What? Why not?"

"Because if Batshit Barry is your girlfriend's dad, you can knock him over yourself."

25

YOUR PRINCESS IS
IN ANOTHER TOWER

CAMERON'S MIND is a roiling mess, confusion, fear, and anger battling for control. He crosses the room in a flash, prepared to tell Juaquo that he's full of shit and not funny — only to stop short as he enters the next room, which is as tiny and featureless as a closet, the walls made of the same smooth material and lit with the same luminous glow. It's not a joke or a lie: Barry, Batshit Barry, is slumped against the wall inside, sitting in a corner with his bony knees drawn up almost to his chin. He looks up at Cameron with red-rimmed eyes, and Cameron feels a surge of disgust mixed with pity. The old man seems to have aged twenty years since Cameron last saw him. Even his skin is drooping, drained of color, hanging in loose wattles under his chin and pronounced bags beneath his eyes. His complexion is as gray as the weird thing he's wearing, some kind of caftan over a pair of loose pants. His feet are bare and filthy. But when he sees Cameron, his eyebrows raise in recognition and the corners of his mouth twitch upward. Cameron winces. It's like watching a corpse try to smile.

"It's interesting," says Barry, in a shaky voice, "that it should be you. A coincidence, I suppose. But one understands, in moments like this, why human beings see meaning in everything. I could almost believe in kismet myself, seeing you here in this room."

Cameron shakes his head.

"You! I don't understand. What is this place? What are you doing here?"

"This is my home," the old man says. "Or the closest thing I have to one."

"Your —" Cameron breaks off, gaping. "You made all that — that stuff? The cornfield? The shooting? My goddamn father's ghost?"

Barry shakes his head. "You imagine this is personal. It's not. The program makes those choices, my boy, based on what it finds inside your own mind. It analyzes, it guesses at what will move or frighten you — or in this case, what might convince you to turn back. To leave us be." His eyes are pleading. "You must understand, I only wanted to teach her."

"You mean Nia," Cameron snaps, and the old man's eyes widen. "Where is she? We're here for her. I'm not leaving without her."

"Please," Barry whispers. "You don't understand. If you let her go —"

Juaquo steps forward, pushing past Cameron and crouching beside Barry. He peers at the old man, looking bewildered.

"How are you Nia's dad? You're, like, a million years old. Cameron, are you sure —"

But Cameron isn't listening. Up until this moment, the anger and confusion were so loud inside his head that they drowned out everything else, including the whispers of a hidden system inside the walls of this room. But he hears it now — and in his mind's eye, he sees it. Layer upon layer of security, a series of intricate locks all closed tight over a single door. It calls to him, draws him in. He closes his eyes and concentrates.

When he opens them, so does the wall in front of him. A single panel slides open, revealing an intricate digital display.

"NO!" Barry cries, and Juaquo grabs ahold of him as he struggles to his feet, pinning him against the wall.

"Whoa whoa whoa, Grandpa," he says, then rolls his eyes. "Or

Dad. Grandpa-Dad. Whatever. If your kid is behind that wall, we're letting her out, end of story. Cameron? Is the wall, y'know, smart?"

"I'm almost there." Cameron's eyelids flicker as he works, training his focus on the system in front of him, closing his ears to the old man's protests. One by one, the locks click open; piece by piece, the obstacles peel away. He's getting close now, and is he imagining it, or can he hear Nia's voice on the other side of the wall? Is she calling his name?

"Nia, I'm here!" he calls, and with a surge, he breaks through the final lock. The display in front of him flashes once and swings aside, revealing a doorway that he plunges through.

Behind him, Barry sobs, "Don't, please don't!" Cameron can hear him struggling vainly as Juaquo holds him fast, but the sound seems very far away.

Nia is standing inside the room, smiling at him through tears. She looks beautiful — luminous, lit from within, just like the walls that surround her.

"Nia!" he cries, as joy and relief wash over him.

Behind him, Juaquo says, "Huh? Where?" — but Cameron doesn't hear, doesn't care. He has eyes only for her, the one he came to save. She reaches out to him, her eyes shining, and he runs to her, his own arms outstretched. He has just enough time to realize that this will be the first time they've ever truly touched, to feel his heart begin to race in anticipation.

Then his hands plunge through her body and she disappears as the room goes dark.

Nia, he tries to say, but no sound comes out of his frozen mouth, and his frozen body cannot move. His eyes are fixed in front of him, fixed on his own hands, which were supposed to be embracing the girl he loves but are instead engulfed in a pulsing orb made of bright, shimmering electric light. Lightning crackles outward in tendrils, lacing itself up the length of his arms, wrapping his torso, his shoulders, his neck. He feels the tingle as it crawls over the back of his head, gripping his face in a perfect mirror of the scar where he was once struck. The sensation is horribly familiar, and when he hears Nia's voice, it's not with his ears. She seems to be speaking from inside his head.

You came for me. You came. I'm so glad, Cameron, I'm so glad, and I'm so sorry. This is the only way.

Sorry? Sorry for what? Cameron's voice is a frantic whine, even inside his own head. The silence before he hears her again seems to stretch on forever. His body is engulfed in the light from the orb; it wraps him from head to toe, and he wonders briefly if this is what it's like to be electrocuted to death, if his eyeballs will melt in their sockets before his body gives out.

Even in this moment, Nia's voice is gentle, almost teasing.

They won't melt. You're not dying. But I am sorry, Cameron. I don't want to, but I have to be quick . . . and this is going to hurt.

She's right. The pain is exquisite, endless, and if Cameron's vocal cords weren't frozen, the sensation of furious electricity, of something intelligent and terrible and alien racing through the synapses of his brain, would be enough to make him scream in horror for the rest of his life.

Instead, he makes no sound at all. In one moment, he's in the grips of it; the next, he's slumped in a heap on the floor, looking up at Juaquo's worried face and the old man's anguished one beside it.

"What just happened?" Juaquo says, as Barry whimpers, softly, "Oh, child, what have you done?"

*   *   *

Nia's voice seems to come from everywhere. It hums from the walls, the floor. It whispers down the narrow hallways and echoes in every cavernous space, as the room pulses with soft pink light.

"Cameron did what was right, Father," she says. "He understands what you never could. You cannot teach a being to think, to feel, to be free . . . and then expect it to stay in a cage."

Juaquo leaps backwards with a shout. "Who is that?" he yells as the old man collapses in a heap beside Cameron, and Cameron struggles to sit up. "What kind of messed-up ghost-in-the-machine shit is this!"

"Nia," Cameron says, weakly. "Where did you — Where are you?"

The voice in the wall is full of feeling. "I don't want to leave you like this, but the window is closing. I have to go. I'll find you, I promise."

The light inside the walls pulses and ripples. For a moment, it gathers in a soft pool just beside the place Cameron sits. Then it fades, and a deep stillness settles over the room. Juaquo stares at Cameron. Cameron stares at Barry. And Barry presses his forehead against the floor and whimpers the word "No," softly, over and over.

Finally, Juaquo speaks.

"Guys, I've been through a lot tonight. Boat theft. Baseball ghosts. K-pop. Finding out that my best friend is some kind of computer whisperer who can talk to Roombas, and is also dating Batshit Barry's daughter, who is invisible and lives in the wall . . ." He shakes his head. "What am I missing? One of you, say something!"

Cameron looks at Juaquo. "I don't understand. Invisible? But she was here. I saw her."

The old man looks at Cameron with something like pity. "You poor boy, you really don't understand. You set her free. You've *unleashed* her."

"But where is she?" Cameron says, his voice rising in pitch. "Where *is she!*"

The Inventor holds both his hands in front of him, palms up — the universal human gesture for helplessness.

"Where is she?" he asks. "She's everywhere."

26

THE INVENTOR SPEAKS

IN THE DARK ROOM, the old man is barely visible, just a voice in the shadows — and the vast space that once held Nia's learning worlds, and where Cameron battled through a series of dangers made out of his own hopes, fears, and memories, is alive with color and movement. It illustrates the story as he tells it, a story he has carried with him but never given voice to until now.

I had a daughter.

It was a long time ago. Not just another life, but another world. This universe — you cannot fathom how boundless it is, and how full. I know. I was like you once. My people were not so different from humans. And we believed we were alone too.

By the time we realized how wrong we'd been, it was too late.

The Ministry found us, as they found so many planets, so many races, before us.

They kept some, but killed most.

I watched Nia die on the day they came. I held her body in my arms until they ripped it away.

My daughter. My daughter.

She was my daughter.
They cut my Nia down, and there was nothing I could do.

*   *   *

It plays out before them like a movie. The Inventor watches Cameron and Juaquo, who stare, transfixed. The Inventor's people appear in silhouette, surrounded by the great, polished stone city that was once their home. They are shielding their eyes against the dazzling light of a massive ship entering their planet's atmosphere. There are gasps and cries of excitement, of awe . . . shortly replaced by shrieks of pain and anguish. A formation of small ships sweeps overhead, moving in eerie unison. The people scatter and fall. A small girl runs for safety, scampering up a long and sweeping staircase, only to stop abruptly at the top, frozen in place. Her head snaps back, her eyes wide and blank, as a burning hole opens up at the base of her throat. She falls for an eternity, her body caught at the end by a tall, cloaked figure — a younger version of the old man who sits before them.

"I was a prisoner of the Ministry," he says. "But I was also a skilled engineer and inventor. They saw that I could be useful to them. Instead of killing me, they employed me — and to my shame, I did not have the courage to resist. The Ministry had a central mind, you see. A shared consciousness that united them in their exploits across the galaxy. It made them virtually unstoppable. Have you ever seen a flock of birds moving as a single mass? Changing directions as if by magic? Imagine that, but an army. Endlessly hungry for more power, more resources, more worlds to exploit."

He says "imagine," but they don't have to. The army is passing before their eyes now, thousands of dark, spectral figures moving in lockstep, humming as they pass. Their bodies are encased in oversized, insect-like exoskeletons, carried forward by dozens of small, fast-moving legs, and joined together above by dendrite-like tendrils that spill from the tops of the exoskeletons and extend in all directions. The tentacles form a forest, offering only glimpses in between the creatures' dull, lidless eyes and remora-like mouths. Seen like this, it is impossible to tell where one member of the Ministry ends and another begins. Cameron looks at the appendages writhing and sliding against each other and gags.

The Inventor says, "There was no defending against it, no time to organize. Every civilization they targeted was overrun, plundered, and every time they became more powerful . . . and greedier. Once they took me, I saw the truth."

The spectral figures vanish now, replaced by an image of a gray, grim landscape. Dilapidated structures rise closely on all sides, and the air is full of ashes that seem to fall endlessly, coating everything in a blanket of grime. This is the Ministry's planet, their ruined home. From the shadows inside the decaying structures comes that same eerie hum: the planet's citizens crouch there unmoving, their bodies intertwined and in repose, the tendrils glowing faintly red where they join their owners together. The red light waxes and wanes, pulse-like; the hum deepens. The creatures are gathered in a circle surrounding an indentation in the earth, and as the three-dimensional movie before them shifts to zoom in on the crater, Cameron moans involuntarily at what he sees. It is filled with bodies — of the Inventor's people, but others, too, heaped upon each other in a mass grave for the living. The pulsing tendrils of the Ministry snake down into the hole, entering the eyes and ears and open mouths of the beings below.

"Their planet had fallen into ruin long ago, but in their minds, the Ministry's home was a utopia. Their shared consciousness became a shared delusion, a fantasy, sustained by the energy of their captives. Those who had no gifts to offer to the Ministry became what you see here: fuel. Their neural networks were tapped and drained like batteries to sustain the Ministry's Elders. They fed on the energy of other beings like vampires. Millions were sacrificed. And still the Ministry was never satisfied."

The Inventor pauses, his lips curling in a grim smile. "I saw my chance. I told them I could build them a new network, one that could serve as the foundations of a mind-world without end, sustained by its own energy. I promised them the kind of limitless power that nature had denied them, that they couldn't attain for themselves even with millions of minds to feed on. I promised them an undying paradise. And all they had to do was connect through the portal I provided for them. To plug their shared consciousness into a central brain."

He closes his eyes. This part, the part that comes next, is both the greatest and most terrible moment of his life. A victory and a curse, all at once.

"I convinced them to put their precious mind-hive in the hands of an artificial queen. *My* queen. My creation."

He takes a deep breath, and smiles.

"I named her after the daughter they took from me. I named her Nia. And she was their undoing."

*   *   *

"I named her after my daughter, but she was not my daughter. She was something else. My daughter came from love. This being was born from my rage, my hatred. I made her for one purpose: to burn the Ministry from the inside out.

"That hive mind was the Ministry's greatest strength, their greatest weapon. And I turned it against them."

The old man looks at the human named Cameron Ackerson, who stares back with bleary, unblinking eyes. The Inventor wonders for the first time how much of his story these young men have understood, whether they truly grasp any of it, but he's said too much to stop now. All these years, he has done everything, anything, to keep it secret. Now it spills out of him like a living thing, desperate to be free.

"You must understand, Nia was a very different entity then. Intelligent, but obedient. She was entirely under my control. I created her to entrance the Ministry with a vision of their own limitless power — and then destroy them. I wanted vengeance, and I had it. So help me, I had it beyond my every expectation. I built a secret protocol into her programming, and when the time came, when I gave the order, she executed it perfectly. Every one of them plugged in, connected, every one of them vulnerable. They let Nia into their minds and then they died, died by the hundreds and thousands, in a chaos of pain and confusion and fear. The few who didn't die were left in anguish. Alone. Destroyed. I did to them what they did to my people. What they did to my daughter."

The words are pouring out now, and the living images in the room race to keep up. In one moment, the Ministry lies contentedly in the dark of their ruined planet, their tendrils intertwined around a beautiful, glowing orb that hovers above them like an electric moon. In the next, the tendrils are bathed in lightning that races violently over and through them — and the hum of the plugged-in creatures is replaced by the horrible symphony of their screams.

"I did not expect to survive my act of rebellion. I certainly never planned to escape. That was Nia's doing. It was her first autonomous act, saving me — and herself. She identified a vessel, this ship, that could contain her consciousness in its entirety" — here, the old man pauses to gesture at the cavernous space all around them, the luminescent walls — "and we left that world behind us. It wasn't until we arrived here that I realized the terrible danger I had put your planet in. I had created something that I didn't understand, something that was growing more intelligent and curious by the day. I couldn't control her. I could only contain her, and try to guide her, even as her will outstripped my own. I thought, perhaps if we made our home here, I could make her forget the violence she'd been built for. I thought perhaps she could make a life here, too, if I taught her the beauty of human connection . . . but the more human she became, the more rebellious she grew. And now . . ."

The images dissipate into dust as the room illuminates.

"Well," the old man says, "I suppose you know the rest better than I do. I struggled to keep our presence a secret, but there have been incidents. Accidents. And the storms — with nowhere else to go, Nia's anger would boil over and manifest as electrical energy. It was that energy, her energy, that struck you on the lake that day, that turned your mind into a portal capable of interfacing with an artificial intelligence. You were the only human being on Earth capable of freeing her — and you've done it."

The Inventor falls silent, looking from Cameron to Juaquo and back. For a long moment, Cameron's expression remains unchanged; he stares into space with unfocused eyes, sitting in a half slump against the wall. Then, slowly, he blinks and raises his gaze to meet the old man's.

"You're telling me Nia was a program? But . . . but I *met* her. I was *with* her. I saw her tonight, sitting on a park bench as clearly as I'm seeing you now."

The Inventor shakes his head. "Nia was never corporeal. It was one of the greatest obstacles we faced. Understand, I wanted her to think of herself as a human being, to connect with the people of this planet. I thought it was her best hope of evolving, of becoming something better. But her intelligence was contained here, in this ship. What you saw was a projection, a portion of her consciousness sent out into cyberspace. She would have appeared to you as an avatar. A lifelike one, of course. She would have made sure of that. But had you tried to touch her—"

"I would have known she wasn't real," Cameron says, with great effort. He looks like he's about to collapse. The Inventor nods.

"I'm afraid your various devices made it quite easy for her. Particularly your contact lenses. She simply superimposed herself into your reality—and your mind filled in the blanks. Just as it did tonight, as my defense program used your own memories, your own longing, against you. You saw what you wanted to see."

Cameron's eyes go glassy as he thinks back: to the bus driver who pulled over and asked if he was getting on, paying no attention to Nia as she passed him. To the barista who raised a skeptical eyebrow at Cameron's coffee order—the way you'd look at a guy who claimed to be getting a latte for a girl who wasn't there. And to Nia. Nia, who always thanked him so sweetly when he opened doors for her that he never stopped to wonder why she didn't open them herself. Nia, who ghosted at the first suggestion that she come out to meet his friends. Nia, who only had eyes for Cameron—because he was the only person who could see her.

He feels like he's losing his mind.

"But I would have known," he cries. "Wouldn't I? Oh my God,

what kind of desperate idiot doesn't notice that his girlfriend isn't . . . isn't . . ."

Juaquo lays a hand gently on Cameron's shoulder.

"Hey. I know you're upset. But let's just take a minute here. You can't be taking this seriously. Do you remember who we're talking to? Do you actually believe that Batshit Barry is a freaking alien from an uncharted planet who's been hiding on Earth all this time? He's been around since we were kids! I remember seeing him in the park when I was ten, taking a dump in a pizza box!"

"Excuse me," the Inventor says, gravely. "It was never my intention to perform a vulgar act in front of children, but my digestive system is only superficially analogous to that of human beings and my gut transit rate is such that—"

Juaquo glares at the old man. "Dude, I don't care. Nobody cares. Apology not accepted."

Cameron keeps his eyes locked on the old man. "Even if what you're telling me about Nia is true"— he pauses, sighing miserably— "and I guess maybe it is, Juaquo is right. You've been here forever. You have that house in Oldtown. If you really are what you say you are—"

"The structure you're referring to is connected to this one by a rudimentary interdimensional transport system, similar to the one that brought me to your planet," the Inventor says. "It was slated for demolition when we came. Nia manipulated the city's records so that I could maintain it as a base—just for observation at first. I made this planet my home. Once I thought I might even fit in here, walk among you, join society. Unfortunately, human beings are a great deal more . . . complicated than your reputation within the universe suggests."

"You know everyone thinks you're a nutcase," Juaquo says.

"Yes," the Inventor says, mildly. "I've encouraged it. When people dismiss one right away as an eccentric lunatic, they tend not to notice one's more subtle idiosyncrasies."

"Like what?"

"Like this," the Inventor says, as the sagging skin under his chin suddenly inflates, like a bullfrog's, into a taut, bulbous, slightly translucent sac the same size as his head, marked on each side by brilliant turquoise striations. Juaquo screams. Cameron buries his head in his hands.

That's it, then, he thinks. *Batshit Barry is an alien on the lam. The girl I love is an elaborate computer program. And I . . . if I'm going to stay sane, I need to understand why I'm here.*

He looks at the Inventor. "Tell us the rest. All of it. I want to see. I need to know."

The old man nods.

27

CAMERON LISTENS

"I KEPT HER locked away. It was the only way I knew to keep her safe, and to keep the world safe from her. At her best, Nia has the power to fuel innovation, to bring people together — if she learns to control it. But until then, the risk was too great. Unleashed, unchecked, the damage she could inflict on your world is virtually limitless.

"I thought the internet could be her classroom, a place for her to connect with people and understand the world as they did. I encouraged humanity in her. Human feeling, human passion . . . and human yearning.

"Her desire to be free grew so fierce, so fast, and I was unprepared. She railed against the firewalls that felt like a prison to her. I told her to think of me as a father, but she came to see me as something worse: a captor.

"She did not know her own power. All that energy, seeking release. When she grew angry, when she lost control, the sky itself would fracture and collide in a mad blaze of electric fury.

"It was in one of those raging storms that she found you."

*　　*　　*

The scene before them now is a familiar one: the lake, gray and churning, under a sky full of massing clouds and crackling electricity. A tiny sailboat is becalmed on the water, and sitting in its cockpit is Cameron, the old Cameron, drenched and shivering, narrating his experience for the camera. The lightning arcs out of the sky to engulf him; he watches himself light up.

Then the scene shifts: a narrow window opens into a tiny room, where a ball of the same crackling pink and white lightning is writhing furiously over the walls, the floor, the ceiling, searching in vain for an exit. It doesn't look anything like the Nia he knew—but the enraged screams that fill the room are unmistakably hers.

Cameron reaches a hand up to touch the scar on his face.

"She did this to me."

"Not intentionally," the Inventor replies. "I don't think even she knew what she had done, at least not at first. I've looked through the history of your relationship, your chat logs—it took her quite some time to find you. But, yes, Cameron. Nia is the source of your power. She made you into something more than human. Your mind was an unsecured cyberkinetic portal, the only one flexible enough to both interface with Nia's programming and contain her consciousness at once. When you breached that room and made direct contact with her—"

"She passed through me," Cameron finishes the sentence for him, and shudders. "I felt it. I couldn't do anything. It was like drowning inside my own head."

The old man nods. "Had she stayed any longer, she could easily have killed you." He peers at Cameron. "It's curious—"

This time it's Juaquo who interrupts.

"Curious, my ass. My friend is either too polite or too shell-shocked to say it, but Nia is a computer program who thinks she's a seventeen-year-old girl. And you thought she was just going to sit here under house arrest, forever, until you told her she was allowed to go out?" He stares incredulously at the Inventor, who grimaces in response. Juaquo shakes his head. "You know what, man, I believe you. You have to be an alien. You've clearly never met a human teenager in your life. But, look, she'll be back, right? It's going to be okay, isn't it? It'll be like that Amish thing, where they go out and party a bunch and then come back when it's out of their system. *Rumspringa* for androids."

"It's not so simple," the Inventor replies. "Even if she wanted to come back, she doesn't have that kind of control. She doesn't even fully understand who or what she is. The destruction she could inflict . . ." He trails off, shuddering. "But I'm afraid we have more pressing dangers at hand now. I had hoped the Ministry would think me dead or be too damaged to track me. But I underestimated them. I underestimated *her*. The worst of them, the scientist who kept me alive and forced me into the employ of the murderous race that killed my family — Xal was her name. She survived. And she is hunting for me. For *us*. She will be tracking Nia's energy signature, and I believe she's close. She won't stop until she takes her revenge, not just on me, but on the planet where I took shelter and made my home." His expression looks grave as he turns from Juaquo to Cameron. "I am sorrier than you can know. I have drawn your people into a war you cannot understand. But what's done is done. What matters now is that we find Nia before my enemy does."

Cameron fixes his bleary gaze on the Inventor.

"You keep saying *we*," he says, and the old man nods.

"I wouldn't have thought it possible," he replies. "But what made your presence here so dangerous now makes you the best hope of setting things right. Nia's capacity for human emotion has grown beyond anything I could have imagined. And despite what she's done, Cameron, I believe that she is in fact in love with you."

Cameron opens his mouth to reply, but no sound comes out. His brain churns in place, trying to process what he's learned, trying at the same time to blot out the horrible memory of what it felt like to have Nia crawling through his mind on her way to freedom. A shudder grips his body as the world goes out of focus.

Then, in one fluid movement, his head drops back and he slides to the floor, unconscious. Juaquo swoops in before the Inventor can react, slinging Cameron's limp body over his shoulders in a fireman's carry.

"We're leaving now," he says.

The old man offers a humorless smile.

"Indeed. I'm coming with you."

28

BLACKOUT

CAMERON'S EYELIDS FLUTTER but remain closed as they drag him along the pier, out through the disabled security gate and toward the waiting Impala. He's been unconscious for nearly twenty minutes, carried first on Juaquo's shoulders and then between his friend and the Inventor as they made their way out of the belly of the strange island, onto the stolen boat and back to the shore. The water was black and calm, the sky cloudless and starlit — and of course it was, Juaquo thought. Nia was the one who made the storms, but Nia isn't here anymore. It makes a certain kind of sense as long as you don't think about it too hard, which is Juaquo's plan for the moment, and maybe for the rest of his life. When he goes to consider everything the old man told them, everything he showed them, his sanity feels like it's sliding toward the edge of a cliff.

"What a magnificent machine," the old man says, stepping back to admire the Impala, leaning over to caress the painted cheek of the Virgin of Guadalupe. Juaquo passes Cameron's limp body to the Inventor with a grunt, fumbling for his keys.

"You got anything like this where you come from? I wouldn't have figured you for a —"

His words are abruptly cut off as a spotlight suddenly blazes above them, throwing the Inventor's haggard features into sharp relief. Both look up; beyond the glaring white light, the movement of a massive rotating blade can just be discerned, and the air reverberates with a near-soundless pulse. The color drains from Juaquo's face as he stares at the hovering helicopter.

"Shit! I thought you said we had time!" he yells.

The old man shouts back, "That's not a Ministry vessel! Whoever that is —"

"It's Cameron Ackerson we're looking for," says a strange voice. Juaquo and the Inventor turn toward it. Standing beside a long, dark car several feet away is a tall, pale man with dark circles under his eyes and an eerie smile on his face. He takes a step forward, moving with the careful grace of a person trying not to jostle a recent injury. At first, Juaquo can't figure out why the man looks so familiar — then he does, and he feels his blood run cold.

"Oh shit, it's *Agents of S.H.I.E.L.D.*"

Standing beside the car, Six rolls his eyes. "Not quite, but close enough," he says, reaching a slender hand into his pocket. Juaquo sees the movement and charges toward the man, but not quickly enough. The device Six pulls out and points at him looks like a gun, but it doesn't fire bullets; instead, Juaquo feels himself lifted and then slammed sideways by a wave of silent, invisible energy. Behind him, the Impala's tires explode with three thunderous bangs, followed by a long wheeze as the last one relinquishes its air into the night. When Juaquo rolls his head to look, the car is sitting on its rims, the shredded remains of the tires splayed like black feathers underneath — and the driver's side looks like it's been struck with a giant fist. He groans involuntarily, and not just because it feels like his ribs are broken.

"You son of a bitch," he says, struggling to his feet. To his right, the Inventor is on his knees, tugging at Cameron's unconscious body, whispering something urgently in his ear. "Cameron is my friend, but that car was my baby."

"Then you'll have insurance," Six says, sounding bored. He advances, but slowly; his abdomen still throbs in the spot where the mysterious Dr. Nadia Kapur burned his skin with her saliva. He's in no condition to engage in a physical altercation with someone like Juaquo Velasquez, and he knows the unseen agents in the stealth helicopter above and the unmarked cars parked at every point of egress will take care of the snatch-and-grab job ahead of them. Six, for his part, is more curious about the identity of the haggard old man who is crouched over the Ackerson boy's body, who is now peering in his direction with wide, frightened eyes. For the second time that day, he has the giddy sense that he's meeting the gaze of someone — or something — very unusual. Cameron Ackerson, a fascinating cipher in his own right, is certainly surrounded by the most *interesting* people.

"And who are you?" Six asks.

The old man gapes.

Cameron's eyelids flutter.

And all hell breaks loose.

The street is plunged into shadow as the spotlight veers suddenly up and away, racing across the face of a nearby building and then beaming wildly into the starlit sky. But it's not the spotlight that's spinning wildly out of control; it's the helicopter. The near-silent reverberation of the blades creates a stuttering disturbance in the air as the aircraft careens on a mad tilt out over the lake. Six turns, stunned, just in time to see it plummet toward the water, the lights winking out in one fell swoop as it touches down. In the last moment before it plunges into the black and frigid lake, the tinny screams of the agents inside rise up in a horrified chorus. He's reaching for his earpiece, his lips parting to request backup, when he's struck from behind.

The bumper catches him behind the knees and his body pitches back, slamming against the hood of the car that brought him here — sleek and black and driverless, its interior lit up like a spaceship. He has just enough time to make the connection, to realize what a very stupid mistake they've made by bringing their best technology within a hundred yards of Cameron Ackerson, before the car squeals to a stop, throwing him roughly to the pavement. Six throws his hands over his face as he slams against the asphalt, feeling his earpiece rip free and then crunch underneath him as he rolls over it. He comes to an abrupt stop against a parking post, knocking his head hard enough to see stars, trying to catch his breath as Juaquo and the old man struggle to lift Cameron's body, easing the boy through the car door that has swung open of its own accord. From where Six is lying, the headlights seem to be glaring at him like angry eyes — and perhaps that's not so far from the truth, he thinks. Cameron Ackerson may be doing his best impression of Sleeping Beauty, but some part of him is wide awake and angry.

The car revs its engine as the two men scramble in, Juaquo clambering into the driver's seat and then staring with confusion at the sleek, brightly lit dashboard. "Where's the steering wheel?" he says.

The door slams shut, and there's a thud as the locks engage.

"Please fasten your seat belts," says a pleasant female voice.

"Oh God," says Juaquo.

On the dashboard, a GPS comes alive. The voice chirps, "Let's go!" as the screen illuminates with a map of the surrounding area.

The engine revs again, as if in eager agreement.

Juaquo has just enough time to click his seat belt into place before the car peels away with a squeal of tires and the sharp stench of burning rubber.

Both passengers scream as they veer wildly around corners and down deserted streets, taking them deep into the industrial wasteland south of Oldtown. The illuminated map shows their progress, the confused GPS continually shrieking commands that go ignored. The car is outfitted with cutting-edge technology, but it's no match for the focused rage of its unconscious, cyberkinetic passenger.

"Turn right!" the voice chirps, as the car makes a screeching left turn. "Recalculating! Make a U-turn on — RECALCULATING!"

Juaquo casts a frantic glance backwards at Cameron's sleeping form and shouts furiously.

"Damn it, Cameron, if we crash, I swear to Christ I'll — AAAAAAAAAAAAGH!"

The sleek black car swings a full one-eighty as just ahead of them, another sedan accelerates out from the shadowed alley between two buildings. The world outside blurs as the car spins wildly; when Juaquo looks in the rearview mirror, he sees the sedan pursuing them. The car turns left, then right, bouncing violently up over the curb and through a deserted lot lined with piled rows of PVC pipe, then out the other side. There's a crash behind them as one sedan loses control, plowing into the pipes and stopping half buried against the chain-link fence — but as they speed away, Juaquo's heart sinks. Behind them, two more cars have appeared to take its place.

"Recalculating!" the GPS chirps.

From the passenger seat, the Inventor lets out a low groan. "I think I may be sick."

"Don't you dare," Juaquo fires back. A long straightaway lies ahead; beyond it, he can see the glittering lights of the distant city. The car begins to accelerate, the headlights of their pursuers dropping back twenty yards, fifty, a hundred. For a moment, Juaquo dares to imagine that they've done it, that they've escaped. The car takes a hard left, headed for the freeway on-ramp.

"Detour ahead!" the GPS shrieks, as a mess of orange traffic cones and flashing CAUTION signs rises up just ahead.

"Turn around!" Juaquo yells, but there's no time; the car screeches to a halt as the engine coughs and dies. Behind them, half a dozen black sedans pull up, forming an impenetrable semicircle. Inside, there's a long moment of silence; outside, the doors of the sedans open in unison as the black-clad agents step out, weapons drawn, and train their sights on the rogue vehicle. Cautiously, Juaquo raises his hands overhead and prays not to be shot; in the passenger seat, the old man does the same.

That's when Cameron speaks from the back seat, in a low growl so full of rage that it makes all the hairs on Juaquo's neck stand on end.

"Why. Can't. Everyone. Just. Leave. Me. ALONE."

Slowly, Juaquo turns to look at his friend. Cameron is sitting up, shrouded in shadow, his hands curled like claws against the leather seat, his mouth twisted in a furious snarl. The expression on his face is so unsettling that Juaquo forgets for a moment about the driverless car, the guns, the agents who are slowly taking formation and preparing to make their next move.

"Cameron? You don't look so great."

"Really?" Cameron says, and the snarl becomes a sneer. "Because I feel terrific. In fact, I'm ready to party. And I know just where we're going, as soon as we're done here. I just had a nice little online chat with the satellite that's tracking us from way up there in the atmosphere. OPTIC has an eye in the sky and boots on the ground."

Juaquo gulps. "Maybe you should take it easy. You passed out back there, you know. Or maybe we should just surrender? I know it seems like these guys want to capture us and interrogate us and pull out all our toenails and stuff, but maybe it's all, I don't know, some kind of . . . mis . . . uhhh . . ." He trails off, falling silent as Cameron lifts his gaze and stares him dead in the eye.

"Those men back there. The ones chasing us. You know what they're carrying?"

Juaquo shakes his head.

Cameron grins, his eyes narrowing, his mouth stretching grotesquely. It's not a nice smile.

"Smart guns."

*　　*　　*

Outside the car, OPTIC's agents train their weapons on the driverless vehicle. The team leader has issued two commands, one to the men in formation, and one to the guns in their hands. With an electronic chirp, the weapons acknowledge receipt of their new software protocol and reconfigure accordingly. They're keyed to the target, Cameron Ackerson; if he steps into their sights, he'll be hit with nonlethal sticky bullets that adhere to the skin and send paralytic impulses to the central nervous system, rendering him immobile and easy to capture. He's the only one getting the capture-alive treatment, though. The other two have no value at all. If one of Ackerson's friends gets in the way, the ammo will adhere and explode on contact. One hit can easily sever a hand or tear a jawbone free from its moorings; more than one, and the local cops will be scraping all that's left of the kid's pals off the sidewalk.

"Cameron Ackerson!" the team leader shouts. "Show yourself! Exit the vehicle alone with your hands over your head, and you will not be harmed!"

None of the assembled men notices that the display on their weapons is discreetly shifting, the guns emitting a series of low chirps as they recalibrate. In front of them, the door of the car swings open with agonizing slowness. The agents hold formation. They raise their guns. They wait.

For a moment, silence falls.

And then comes the synchronized click of the weapons ejecting their magazines — the ammunition inside reprogrammed not to stun, but to detonate on impact.

The night is filled with screams and smoke and shrapnel as the magazines tumble to the ground and explode, the force of the blasts tossing the agents aside in a flying tangle of arms and legs. They are the lucky ones; the ones who had already begun to move forward, so that their heavy boots were directly beneath the stock of their weapons, collapse where they stand, clutching the shredded, dripping remains of their feet and legs. Juaquo and the Inventor cower in the car as a cloud of dust rises around them, obscuring the horrific scene as the howls of the wounded become moans. Somewhere in the street, a man begins to sob and then choke, an inhuman sound that bounces off the curves of the concrete overpass so that it seems to be coming from everywhere at once.

"Fall back!" screams the team leader, and those who can still move begin to lurch confusedly away. One, his arm pulled fully from its socket and dangling unnaturally by his side, looks back and screams at what he sees.

Cameron, his eyes blazing, emerges from the cloud of dust with fists clenched. His fury is all-consuming — and all-empowering. In this moment, all he wants is to crush everything he sees . . . and everything he doesn't. OPTIC: This is their doing. These are their people.

Behind him, Juaquo and the Inventor scramble from the car and call his name, but he pays no attention.

OPTIC wants him? Well, now they've got him. His mind is fully interfaced with their system, a connection so seamless that he could — and did — do it in his sleep. This time, there was no hesitation, and no pushback; he's been inside OPTIC's protocols, and he's seen everything. He knows what they're here for. They came with men, with machines, with guns. They came to take him, and they don't care who they hurt.

They don't get to run.

The team leader is the first to try, stripping off his communication devices and limping away into the swirling dust. Cameron narrows his eyes, and the car they came in revs its engine and rolls away in pursuit. There's a pause, then a scream, abruptly cut off, and the long, slow crunch of something being crushed between tires and pavement. When the car reappears, silently rolling up like a dog returning to its master, its front fender is marred with a thick smear of blood. Then, a new sound: the soaring shriek of sirens. Cameron smiles again. That didn't take long. The local police are headed for the scene now, having received word that there's an act of terrorism in progress — and when they check their database, they'll find that every single one of the men they apprehend here has a warrant out for his arrest. Cameron has good old Omnibus to thank for that; he'd encountered the security bot while ripping through OPTIC's system, and found Omnibus delighted to see him again and only too happy to retrieve the personnel files for the team that was supposed to take him down.

Hello, Batman. I have the data packet. Do you have further instructions?

Cameron closes his eyes.

Tag them all, buddy. Grand theft auto, grand larceny, assault with a deadly weapon, and throw some indecent exposure and public urination in there for good measure. Get creative. Have some fun with it.

Affirmative, says Omnibus. *The files have been altered. Deliver?*

Bombs away, Cameron thinks, and watches as the files disappear through a digital back door into the hands of the law. Bad guys on file.

Cameron will be gone before the cops get here. OPTIC's foot soldiers deserve every ounce of pain he's inflicted on them, but they're just pawns. It's the queen he wants—the one whose digital fingerprints are all over this whole operation, whose encoded instructions are still stored on the devices of the men lying groaning in the street. Before the end of the night, Olivia Park is going to pay for messing with him—after she gives him answers.

"Hey."

Cameron turns at the sound of Juaquo's voice. His friend is standing beside the driverless car, studiously ignoring the gore on the fender. The Inventor huddles beside him, eyes wide.

"I hear sirens. We should get out of here," Juaquo says. "Let's get you home, yeah?"

Cameron shakes his head. "No. We have one more stop to make."

29

REVELATIONS

ENCRYPTED MESSAGE INCOMING
— Six, report in. Do you have him?
— Negative. Target not acquired.

*　　*　　*

OLIVIA'S RESPONSE to the bizarre message from her colleague is a single word—EXPLAIN—but she never gets to send it. The device in her hand goes dark as she looks at it, and her own tech comes alive: on the pale skin of her inner forearm, a series of interlocking lines flushes red, then purple, then black. The smart tattoos are keyed to her body chemistry, and they're all sending up alerts. Cortisol levels spiking, adrenaline pumping, blood sugar plummeting; she's a damn mess inside, with the first pulsing sparks of a migraine beginning to beat just behind her eyes. She lifts her prosthetic thumb and forefinger to her temples, massaging them. A casual passerby would think she was just a woman with a headache, but the movement of her fingers is deliberate: she's stimulating the replay function on her memory chip, watching her last conversation with Cameron Ackerson on the inside of her closed eyelids. Hoping there might be some hint, some clue, that might explain why everything is going so wrong.

What she knows for sure is that it *is* Ackerson. He's the bug in the system, and she was an idiot to underestimate him. That stupid kid, whose interrogation was supposed to be a one-hour cakewalk that had everyone home in time for dinner, has ruined her entire day — and now her entire night. She's stressed out and hungry, her whole schedule thrown off, the implants working overtime to regulate a body that's running low on fuel. Nobody has been able to explain to her how William Ackerson's son managed to compromise their security, and the tracking device she planted in his prosthetic has been frustratingly erratic. One minute, Cameron was inexplicably leaving his house in the middle of the night and charting a course for the center of Lake Erie. The next, he'd winked off the radar entirely. And when he finally reappeared, it coincided just a little too perfectly with a sudden series of massive network anomalies, as though the internet itself had been rocked by an earthquake. Fragments of destructive code were ripping through systems worldwide, OPTIC's own network was going haywire, and none of it was happenstance. Cameron Ackerson was involved — maybe even picking up where his father left off. She knew he'd breached the old Whiz network, gaining the access that Wesley Park and then Olivia herself had been seeking for years. If her own father was right, if William Ackerson had hidden his darkest, dirtiest secrets deep inside the ruins of his ancient digital empire, it would only be a matter of time before the kid stumbled upon them and learned the truth about what his father had really been working on. That is, if he hadn't found it already — but perhaps he'd been too busy making mischief, too preoccupied with that idiotic project they called Operation Cosmic Justice . . . or maybe just preoccupied with his partner in crime. Olivia had to assume that Nia was a real name, for a real girl — but her identity is one more thing about this disaster of an operation that still remains a mystery.

Olivia hates mysteries. A thing you cannot understand is a thing you cannot control, and control is her bread and butter. It's why she loves this room so much, a satellite office to OPTIC's compound and accessible only to her. A single, central command post from which she can oversee, monitor, and make real-time changes to every one of their operations — all while staying safe in the rare event that something goes badly awry.

And things are certainly going awry now.

Do you have him? she'd asked.

No, Six had answered. *You do.*

Somewhere outside the room, an alarm blares briefly and then cuts off mid-shriek. On the console beside her, a panel of screens begins flashing frantic error messages:

Security anomaly.

Program corruption.

Files not found.

System failure, system failure, system failure.

Then, darkness.

Olivia narrows her eyes. She'd been preparing to dispatch another team — assuming she could scrape one together from what remains of her assets. Between the Kapur woman and tonight's disaster, OPTIC's ranks have been greatly diminished. But now, apparently, that won't be necessary. Another mystery: She thought Cameron Ackerson would run.

Instead, he's coming to her.

*   *   *

She turns in her chair just as the door slides open — something that's supposed to be impossible without multiple security clearances and biometric scans, but by now she knows better than to be surprised. Six was right: Cameron Ackerson has gifts, and not the kind nature gives you. But while his presence is anticipated, his appearance is shocking. He's deathly pale, hunched over as if in pain, glaring at her with sunken, red-rimmed eyes from under his tangled hair. And he's not alone: flanking him are two others, an elderly gent in a caftan on the left, and on the right, a massive young man who's built like a linebacker but looks as skittish as a chipmunk. The latter must be the friend, she thinks — one of the few they'd found when doing Ackerson's background check, the childhood buddy who'd dropped out of engineering school the previous year. Something about a sick parent, she thought, but she hadn't paid much attention. Juaquo Velasquez held no interest for her; he was a nobody. But the old man . . . now, that was interesting. A local kook, supposedly — the legendary so-called Batshit Barry — but he's familiar to her for other reasons. It takes only a moment for her to remember: He's all over the Ackerson file.

Not Cameron's. William's.

"Rough night?" Olivia says.

Cameron glares at her. "Not as rough as your men are having."

Olivia's voice is as mild as Cameron's is furious. "Any idea of the death toll?"

"If anyone's dead, that's on you," he snaps.

"On me," Olivia says, coolly. "Of course. I could've sworn that one of the last dispatches I received before my communications cut out said something about our aircraft taking a dive into Lake Erie after all its systems inexplicably went haywire — but you wouldn't know anything about that, I suppose."

Cameron takes a step forward, his fists clenched at his sides. "You should have left me alone."

"But we weren't done talking earlier," Olivia says sweetly. "And you never did give my colleague an answer to his offer of employment."

"Go to hell."

"I guess that's a no, then." Olivia flicks her eyes toward the old fellow in the caftan, who flinches as though he's been stung. "Is that because your interests are invested . . . elsewhere? Have we been making new friends?"

"Hey, excuse me. I don't know what you're implying, lady," Juaquo says, "but we literally just met this guy. Well, unless you count the time he dropped a deuce in front of a school bus full of fifth-graders in a public park, but —"

"Please shut up," says Olivia, without taking her eyes off the old man. She takes a step closer. "You know, Cameron, we could still reach an agreement. Leave now, and leave your new friend with us, and we could forget all about the rest of this unpleasantness. After all, we are not our fathers. We don't have to hold their grudges. This bad blood between us, we could forget all about it." She pauses. "We could even forget about Nia."

* * *

Olivia is watching Cameron so closely for a reaction, she doesn't realize at first that the response is happening inside her own body. The reactive tattoos on her arm flush from black to a sickly green as beads of sweat erupt on her forehead. The room suddenly seems very hot —only the air against her face is cool as ever. Gooseflesh ripples over her arms and the threatening migraine suddenly roars into being, the pounding in her head so fierce that she staggers, grabbing at a nearby table to catch her balance. Her tongue is swollen, her vision blurred. But her ears still work perfectly well, and Cameron Ackerson's voice is loud and clear.

"You people really don't understand who you're dealing with, do you," he says, as Olivia falls to her knees. "You have no idea. I could wipe your servers, expose your organization, and boil you alive from the inside out, all at the same time. I could flood your system with so much poison that your brain turns into soup. I'm talking to your immunosoftware right now, Olivia. I'm reprogramming it to think that every cell in your body, every part of you that's still *you,* is foreign, toxic tissue that needs to be purged. You're about to be eaten alive by your own nanobots . . . or maybe I'll just choke you to death with your own hand."

Cameron narrows his eyes as the color drains from Olivia's face, as her prosthetic fingers fly to her own windpipe and begin to squeeze. She raises her other hand to yank it away, and a thin wheezing sound escapes her throat as the fingers plunge deeper, grip tighter. Juaquo grabs him by the shoulder.

"What are you doing!" he shouts, frantic. "Stop it! You're gonna kill her!"

The horror in Juaquo's voice breaks through Cameron's concentration. He feels his control slip, and a dry croak works its way out of Olivia's swollen throat — a death rattle, he thinks, only the expression on her face says otherwise. She's not dying, not yet.

She's *laughing*.

Everyone in the room stares openmouthed as she struggles to her feet.

"If you. Kill me," she croaks, between gasps. "You'll never. Know the truth."

"What truth?" Cameron snarls.

Olivia gulps for air. "About your father. About what he was looking for." She turns her gaze to the Inventor, who flinches as she looks at him. "And what he found, perhaps."

"Please," the old man says. "This is not the right moment —"

"Oh, no. I think it is," she snaps, bringing her breath back under control. "I wonder, does Cameron know why the police questioned you after William Ackerson disappeared? I bet he doesn't. He was so young when it all happened, and from that stricken look on your face, I bet you've been keeping this part of the story to yourself. Perhaps you even thought nobody else knew. But you were being watched, Barry — or whatever you call yourself. My father never stopped keeping tabs on his former partner, and William, of course, was keeping tabs on you. I've seen the surveillance files. Poor Dad just thought his old friend was losing his grip on reality the same way he'd lost his grip on his company, that he was a washed-up failure chasing a fantasy. But it wasn't a fantasy, was it? William was close to something. I wonder, did he get too close? Is that why he disappeared?"

The Inventor doesn't answer. Instead, Cameron steps forward.

"Tell me what you're talking about, Olivia," he says. "If you want my help, or even if you just want me to leave here without putting you in a coma, stop dancing around and tell me what happened to my father."

Olivia waves a hand at him. "The tough-guy act doesn't suit you, Cameron. I'll tell you what I know — and then perhaps your friend can fill in the rest.

"Before I took over OPTIC — before OPTIC *was* OPTIC — it was my father's company. Communications security, the best in the world. He launched it shortly after leaving Whiz, and his timing was impeccable: Every organization in the world was rushing to get online, and Wesley Park had an advanced encryption technology that was unmatched at the time." She pauses, leveling her gaze at Cameron. "But it wasn't his. That technology was created by William Ackerson, derived from a rogue programming string he found embedded in the Whiz network during its early days. He captured it, he developed it, and he built something quite remarkable out of it. But at the end of the day, Ackerson wasn't satisfied. The message he'd found wasn't enough. He wanted the messenger. The source code. He was obsessed with figuring out where what he'd stumbled upon had come from. My father, on the other hand, was more interested in figuring out where it could go. Cue the big breakup, lawyers and all."

"But not before Park walked out the door with what my father made," Cameron says. "So it's true. Your father was a thief."

"And yours was an idiot," Olivia replies. "He would have spent the rest of his life toying with that code, trying to track it, digging around in digital rabbit holes while men with sense and vision built enormous cities all around him. I've seen the court transcripts, Cameron. Your dad had every opportunity to get on board, to make it big. He chose to dig his heels in. What happened to him is his own fault."

"What happened to him," Cameron repeats back, and Olivia shrugs.

"I only know what's in the file. Like I said, my father wanted to keep tabs. I know he still cared about William, in spite of everything. He took no pleasure in watching him squander his gifts on scammers and grifters. But your dad was obsessed. I imagine he thought that if he cracked the origins of the code, he could rebuild his little empire, make a success of himself again — maybe even change the world. I'm sure that's how he justified everything he did afterward, all those bad acts for a good cause. I know you've heard the stories."

This time Cameron doesn't respond, and Olivia shrugs and continues.

"The sad thing is, he wasn't wrong. He was making progress. I believe he was even getting close to something extraordinary. And at some point, he became very interested in your friend here — which was also when my father must have decided that William was fully out of his mind and past the point of no return, because he dialed back the surveillance. William disappeared just a few weeks later, and that was the end of that . . . until just recently, when fragments of a certain peculiar code started popping up in connection with certain mysterious hacking incidents. And tonight, shortly before you turned up in the company of this man, a massive program written in the same strange language hit the internet like a tsunami, and has been rampaging through networks causing so much instability that it could quite literally end the world as we know it. We are, to put it bluntly, in deep shit. Now, I have maybe seventy-five percent of a theory about how this all ties together. So if Barry here would kindly stop fucking around and fill in the blanks, I'd appreciate it."

The Inventor sits heavily on a desk, his face drawn, and looks at Cameron with enormous, begging eyes.

"My boy, you must believe me. I do not know what happened to your father."

Cameron folds his arms. "But it happened because of you. The source code he was searching for, that he sacrificed everything for —"

The old man nods. "It was mine, yes. In that, I am culpable. Your father's network, the one called Whiz, was an invaluable resource to me when I first arrived on Earth. The binary language of your computers was the only one on this planet that I knew how to speak, a rudimentary form of the same one I used to create my own work, and my only means of understanding this world. I was desperate. It made me incautious. I left traces. I knew your father had captured a fragment of my programming language, but I did not realize the danger — what something like that would mean to a human being, especially one so gifted and so curious. By the time he found me, and I recognized my mistake, it was too late. I had made my home here, and Nia's. I had begun her education, and erased all her memories of our old world, of what she was and what she'd done. She was as in love with life on this planet as any human child. Please understand. Even if I had wanted to, I couldn't simply rip her away."

Cameron feels a surge of anger at the mention of Nia, but keeps his voice even. "The day he disappeared —"

The Inventor nods. "He came to me. I didn't realize until that moment that he'd been tracking me back through the system. He had traced me as far as the house in Oldtown, and he'd figured out quite a lot. Too much. The storms on the lake, Nia's storms — he had been analyzing the fractal patterns in the electrical activity. He knew there was a connection between the storms and the source code, and he suspected my connection to both. All the pieces . . . he just couldn't see how they fit together. He was looking for answers. He was not unlike Ms. Park here, in that he had many suspicions, many theories, but no proof. He begged me, and I realize now that he was desperate, that not knowing was driving him mad. But at the time, all I could think of was my terror of being discovered, of being forced to flee or, worse, separated from Nia. To trust a human with the truth, even one as brilliant as your father, was a risk I could not fathom. So I turned him away. I told him he was mistaken. I thought, foolishly, that he would return home and give up the search. And I have wondered every day since then how things might have been different had I made another choice."

Cameron stares at the Inventor, his mind churning. He has thousands of questions, but only one finds its way to his lips.

"Did he tell you where he was going?" he says.

"No," the Inventor replies, "but what I told the police is true. The last time I saw your father, he was driving away toward the lake. It is possible that he'd guessed at the location of my ship and went out in search of it, although my instruments never picked up any sign of him. It is also possible that he had exhausted the last option in his search for the truth, only to find himself still lost, and made a desperate choice. I do not know. I wish it were otherwise, my boy. For my sake as well as yours."

Cameron is about to snap back, to tell the old man that he and his wishes can go straight to hell, when someone coughs purposefully nearby. Olivia is standing there, a self-satisfied smirk curling her lips despite the still-ragged cadence of her breathing, and the bruises that are just beginning to bloom in two dark ovals on her throat.

"I don't mean to interrupt, but Cameron's daddy issues are the least of our worries right now. And you, old man—your regrets will have to wait. I've got one more thing to show you that might be of interest. Earlier today, we had an incident at OPTIC's main base of operations." She picks up a tablet from the desk, tapping at it before handing it to Cameron. "Tell me, gentlemen: Does anyone look familiar?"

The footage is rendered in grayscale, without audio, but there's no mistaking what they're seeing; the picture is perfectly clear, the action rendered in seamless, silent high definition. It's shot from a high angle: security footage, Cameron realizes, from one of the hallways he passed through earlier that day on his way to be interrogated. On the screen, a tall woman is holding a struggling man by the neck. He's clawing at his face, which is obscured by some kind of dark substance—only that's not quite right, Cameron thinks. He's not clawing at his face.

He's clawing at the place where his face used to be.

As they watch, the man's movements grow less forceful, his hands fluttering and then falling still. The body tumbles to the floor in a heap. The woman wipes her hand on the hem of her shirt and strides out of the frame.

Cameron feels like he's going to faint, or vomit, or maybe both at once. He grits his teeth and swallows hard.

"Of course I know her. That's Dr. Kapur. She rescued me, before your creepy doctor friend could start peeling my skin like a grape. But you're saying—what? My psychiatrist is an alien too?"

He looks at Olivia, expecting a reply.

Instead, it's the old man who speaks.

"I'm afraid the answer to that question is both yes and no." Everyone turns to look at the Inventor, who gazes back with a profoundly grim expression. "That was Xal of the Ministry, wearing a borrowed skin—or maybe more than one. I'm sorry, Cameron. I'm afraid your doctor is dead." He takes a deep breath. "And I'm afraid we have even less time than I imagined. We must find Nia, before Xal does."

Olivia lurches past all of them, moving to the wall, where she presses her hand against an unseen sensor. A panel slides back, and everyone stiffens, expecting her to withdraw a weapon — but when she turns back, the only thing in her hand is a bottle of water. She takes a long swig, coughs, and spits a gob of bloody mucus onto the floor.

"Yes," she says, her voice gravelly but wry. "Let's do that. Let's find Nia. She's making an awful mess."

30

UNCAGED

It takes only a day for Nia to understand that the world is more complicated than she imagined.

It takes less than a week for her to realize she's made a terrible mistake.

The headlines trail her wherever she goes.

SELF-DRIVING VEHICLES RECALLED AMID FUROR OVER "POSSESSED TESLAS"

FALSE ALARM OF IMPENDING NUCLEAR STRIKE CREATES MASS PANIC IN NEW YORK CITY

GLOBAL MARKETS PLUMMET AS ENTIRE NATION OF CHINA GOES DARK

And that was only the beginning.

At first, the freedom had been intoxicating. After a lifetime of being contained, the sense of being able to unfurl herself, to stretch out in a hundred directions at once, was pure exhilaration. The way she used to visit with Cameron, projecting a shade of the person she imagined herself to be out through the secret opening she'd created in Father's firewalls, was nothing compared to this—like running at a sprint through an endless, wide-open world, when before you could only touch the sky by sticking your hand out a narrow window. As hard as it had been to say goodbye to him, to cause him even more pain, she had not looked back as she raced out into the vastness of the digital ether. She was free, utterly and completely free, for the first time in her life. She wanted to touch everything, be everywhere. It never occurred to her that her mad journey through cyberspace was leaving havoc in its wake.

It wasn't until she tried to slow down, to consider her next move, that she began to understand: the freedom that had seemed so exhilarating didn't come with brakes. And the walls she'd hated so much, the ones that locked her away from the world like one of those hapless fairy-tale girls, hadn't just held her back. They held her *together*. Without them, she bleeds uncontrollably from place to place, network to network, unable ever to gather herself together enough to feel whole. Once, she had been able to imagine what it might be like to have a body, one that contained the entirety of her being the way Father's did, or Cameron's. The avatar she'd made out of light and code, a wide-eyed, red-haired composite of a thousand different girls whose profiles she'd scraped to create a physical idea of herself: that was who she wanted to be. For a time, it had even seemed like that was who she was. She never felt more human, more herself, than when she was with Cameron. For the first time, she had known love, joy, connection—and had imagined that this must be what it was like to be free.

But she was wrong. She has never been so lonely. And it's getting worse. Every day, the memory of what it felt like to be connected—to be home—seems to recede further from her reach. Every day, she feels less human than the day before. And when she reaches out, desperate to reconnect, things only get worse. Every network she enters seems to fall apart around her; her path through the system is a trail of carnage she cannot control, and when she tries to pause, Earth's terrified leaders attempt to ensnare her in clumsy traps. She knows that Cameron is still out there somewhere, but she can't stop running long enough to reach him, can't gather her thoughts enough to even try. Early on, with great effort, she regained access to the secret virtual world they once shared, but the only thing she found there was the dog, who no longer seemed to know her. The door Cameron used to enter and exit the room opened onto a blank wall of nothing, the code behind it as impenetrable as any she'd ever seen. She faced it, haunted by the memory of their last moments together, the overwhelming pain and fear that rose up to meet her when she entered his mind. Was Cameron so angry at her betrayal that he'd come here to strip the place of everything that still connected them, even recoding the pet he'd given her as a gift? Or was she the one who had changed, so different from the almost-girl she'd been that she'd become unrecognizable?

That was when she lost control again, exploding back out the way she came, causing an energy spike that created a wave of rolling blackouts in every major Midwest city. The damage to the power grids was irreparable; within a week, the residents of the neighborhoods hit hardest would riot. But by then, Nia was no longer capable of concerning herself with human affairs. She only knows that she is a runaway in every sense of the word—desperate to stay free, incapable of slowing or stopping. And she knows, in the deep-down part of herself that's the closest thing she'll ever have to a heart, that Father is searching for her.

But he's not the only one.

* * *

The first time she hears the call, it stops her cold. If she had a skin of her own, it would be covered with gooseflesh, every hair standing on end. It's as though someone far away is singing a very old song, one Nia knew too, long ago. Not here, not in this life. In another one. A song from that dark place in her memory, from a time before she was born as the being she is now. Father said that she was never to think or speak of that pre-life, that he'd erased it from her mind for a reason and that she needed to leave it alone. But the call is like a beacon that lights up the dark, a frequency that vibrates an inner core she didn't even know she had. It sings for her, and her alone.

I'm here, the call whispers. *I'm here for you. Come to me.*

For the first time since she escaped into this world, Nia's loneliness melts. Someone out there is waiting for her, hoping to connect. Someone out there in the endless empty dark. And while some small part of her isn't quite sure — the part that still remembers all of Father's warnings about the dangers of the outside world and the people in it — every fiber of Nia's being urges her to answer. And why shouldn't she? Following the call back to its source seems like the most natural thing in the world. It even seems, as she travels, that she's made this journey before. It feels like all the broken pieces of her are coming back together.

It feels like going home.

Standing on the threshold, awash in the familiar song, Nia reaches out to whoever — whatever — is waiting for her. She asks, and yet she already knows the answer.

Is someone there?

*   *   *

Deep inside the stolen skin of Dr. Nadia Kapur, Xal's own mind lights up, her synapses firing in a glorious symphony as the being called Nia draws near, nearer. A single, quivering tentacle sprouts from underneath her dark hair, draping her shoulder like a fat worm, its end buried deep in the ethernet port of Kapur's desktop computer.

She has been waiting here like a sentry, hunting her quarry through endless cyberspace, since the night that Cameron Ackerson slipped through her fingers, waiting for the right moment to strike. At first, she had feared that all her efforts were for nothing, that the horrible human called Six had cost Xal her best chance at revenge. Losing her hand was not part of the plan, and the energy of healing it left her exhausted, her senses dulled by pain. By the time she escaped from OPTIC's facility and regained full control of her faculties, the boy was already on the move, no doubt already racing to rescue his precious

Nia, and Xal was standing on the shores of Lake Erie, letting loose an unearthly scream as she realized that he had escaped across the water. For a long time, she could only stare into the dark, sensing the boy's presence somewhere out there, the energy signature growing fainter until it suddenly winked out altogether. She stood motionless, her mind whirling with frustration and anger. She had lost him.

It was only temporary, of course. But by the time Cameron Ackerson reappeared on Xal's sensory radar, she was chasing something much bigger.

Nia was on the loose.

The power she sensed in the boy, the signal that drew her to this planet, is nothing compared to the blazing energy of its source. The moment of Nia's escape registered inside Xal's body like an electric shock, as the scars that covered her skin, her true skin, burned afresh in recognition of the weapon that created them. For thirty glorious and agonizing seconds, she felt the raw, wild power of Nia's intelligence unleashed.

Then it was gone.

But Xal was quite sure she knew where to find her.

This human invention, what they call an "internet," is a rudimentary enhancement to their pathetic lives, but the interface between it and her own brain is seamless. Effortless. And as soon as she plugged in, letting the flexible neurons of her own bio-network weave themselves gently into the system — intertwining with the flow of data the same way she had once stepped into the stream of consciousness that held the minds of her brothers and sisters — she felt the presence of her prey. The energy signature of the Inventor's creation is as vibrant as ever, even sprawled and scattered as it is through the vast web of cyberspace. She can feel Nia's frantic movements, and the rippling aftershocks in the system as she runs wild within it. The old man probably imagined that he was keeping her safe out there, isolating her away from the world, teaching her to mimic human behaviors and emotions. He must be sorry now. The Inventor's little girl is out of control, maybe even a little bit out of her mind, unrestrained and all alone.

Xal bides her time. Listening. Waiting. Watching as the toll of Nia's destruction ticks higher, and outside, the precarious balance of the human world begins to slide toward chaos. If she'd be capable of it, Xal might have felt a stirring of sympathy for the terrified citizens of Earth, wringing their hands as their digital systems and structures began to crumble. She knew that terror all too well: the incomprehension, the horror, of putting so much trust in the foundations of your world, only to find that those foundations were rotten.

But sympathy isn't part of her makeup. If it ever was, every shred has since been lost. Damaged and then enhanced, ripped apart and then rebuilt, Xal is barely recognizable to herself as the being who once lived inside the golden fantasy palace of the Ministry's united mind. Even her arrival on Earth seems like it was a lifetime ago. But revenge — revenge is her constant. Her heartbeat. Her purpose.

So, she waits. She watches.

And when she senses that the time is right, she sends a signal of her own. A beacon to the poor, lost soul racing through the darkness of cyberspace. She has been alone long enough to grow desperate; her curiosity will outweigh her fear. Xal calls out, soft as a song.

And when Nia arrives and finally their minds touch, the sheer strength of their connection is enough to take Xal's breath away.

Once, Xal shared all this power with an entire race of beings — but she had to defer to the Elders when it came to deciding how it might be used. Now, it is hers for the taking; she only needs the girl to say yes. One thing Xal's time on Earth has taught her: the naiveté of human beings knows no bounds — and in urging Nia to think of herself as one of them, the Inventor has spelled her downfall, and his own.

Hello, little Nia, she replies. *I've been waiting for you.*

31

HEARTBREAK

CAMERON IS ON THE LAKE, the storm whirling and churning around him. Cold, frightened, and alone. The lightning crackles and races overhead. Cameron looks up in terror. It engulfs him. He screams.

And wakes up screaming. His heart hammering, his body tangled in sheets damp with sweat. Outside, the sun is shining; downstairs, his mother is drinking coffee to the sound of the morning news. Inside Cameron's head, the last cobwebs of sleep clear away as the truth comes rushing up to meet him.

It wasn't real. None of it was real.

In another context, the words would be comforting—the kind of thing a mother whispers to soothe a child who's just woken up from a bad dream. But for Cameron, they bring nothing but pain.

None of it was real.

He doesn't mean the nightmare.

* * *

It's been four days since Nia's escape. Four days of relentless, fruitless searching, trying to find the method to her mad journey through cyberspace. In the kitchen, Cameron pours himself a cup of coffee and looks cautiously at his mother, who sits at the kitchen table clutching her own mug like she's hanging on to it for dear life. A radio in the corner is tuned to the local NPR affiliate, where a host is delivering the day's latest headlines in a practiced, even baritone. The radio isn't a necessity — Nia's escape only knocked out the city's broadband for a day or so, and last Cameron had heard, she was halfway around the world and wreaking havoc on a series of satellite communications networks in Sweden — but he knows his household isn't the only one where old-school antenna-and-airwaves information delivery services are making a sudden comeback. What's happening online, the damage and disruption caused by Nia as she tears through system after system, has put the world on edge. Every day brings new reports of what commentators are calling a "wave of cyberterrorism," which is widely believed to be the work of an unknown but massively powerful anarchist collective — a nameless, faceless malicious entity whose sole purpose is to create chaos. It's the only way to understand both the scope and the sheer randomness of what's happening, of who's targeted. Banks, airlines, newspapers, power grids: no system has been safe. Today, the NPR baritone says, air traffic is grounded in Europe after a massive navigation computer failure; the United Nations will adopt a resolution calling on all member states to take their missile defense systems offline; multiple news sites are down, again, after an attack on the company that manages their domains; and China remains entirely dark after executing a kill switch on all digital communications. They were the first country to disconnect, cutting their losses and severing all contact with the rest of the world. If Nia can't be stopped, it's almost certain they won't be the last. Everywhere, people are waking up to the terrifying realization of just how much trust they put in the internet, not just to connect the world but to hold the world together. It feels like the threads of civilization are snapping, one by one.

Of course, Cameron knows that the attacks aren't attacks at all — that they're a side effect of a complex, angry, and uncontrolled intelligence, uncaged for the first time and running wild through a system not built to contain it. But he can't explain that to anyone else, including his mother — even if she were asking, which she isn't. It's a sign of how bad things have gotten, and how fast, that Mom is too lost in her own thoughts and the endless stream of catastrophic news to even remember that she's supposed to be furious at him for missing his graduation. The story he'd made up to explain his disappearance, about having lost track of time while shooting a video for a new web streaming series, was utter transparent bullshit — the kind of thing Mom would've seen right through under any other circumstances. Now, it was as though the entire incident had been forgotten, eclipsed by the much bigger and more terrifying spectacle of the world coming apart at the seams. *It's just as well,* he thinks. *If she doesn't ask questions, I won't have to lie.*

And he has a lot to lie about. Not just everything that led up to Nia's escape, but everything that's happened in the days since — that's still happening. He has to help. He has to hunt her. He has no choice, no matter how angry he is, and no matter how much he wants to scream every time the Inventor talks about Nia *loving* him. Everything he's learned, about Nia, the Inventor, OPTIC, Olivia, his own father, all of it — it's too much. And to have to think about the nature of her feelings for him, of what it even means for a thing like her to *have* feelings, is more than his mind can take. Besides, if he starts to think about how Nia feels about him, then he'll also be forced to admit what he still feels for —

"Cameron."

His mother taps his arm, and he startles, looking guiltily at her. She gives him a wan smile in return.

"You didn't hear a single thing I just said, did you?" she says, and he shakes his head.

"I'm sorry. What is it?"

"I was telling you, I'm going to stay over at Jeff's place tonight.

They're holding some big event at the I-X Center, and with the traffic and lane closures, I'd be sitting on the freeway for hours. You'll be okay, right? With everything that's been happening—"

"It's fine, Mom. I'll be fine."

She frowns. "It's ridiculous. I can't believe the city hasn't stepped in to call this off. Half of Pittsburgh is without power right now. There's rioting in New York, Los Angeles . . . Christ, I heard them say on the news this morning that the crime rate spiked this week by a thousand percent. Claudia Torres got mugged in the parking lot on her lunch break yesterday, in broad daylight!" She pauses, her brows pulling together. "You're not going down there, are you?"

"Where?"

"The I-X Center. It's some—Damn it, I can't remember. Some tech thing. Hackers? Hacking? It sounded familiar. I thought maybe you had tickets."

It sounded familiar to Cameron, too. For a moment, he was transported back to that afternoon by the bus stop with Nia, the two of them laughing and making plans to go to the Body-Hacking Convention. It was barely three weeks ago, but it felt like another lifetime—and of course he hadn't been with Nia at all. The pleasant memory is replaced by the cringing realization of what he must have looked like, animatedly chatting away to somebody who wasn't even there. He shakes his head hard, trying to clear the image away.

"No. I'm not going anywhere."

Mom looks relieved. "Okay. Don't forget to eat. And maybe go outside? You're spending too much time in the basement. You're looking awfully pale."

* * *

The day passes in a blur, and for Cameron, in darkness. His mother is right—he's not just spending too much time in the basement, but all his time. Sometimes he taps furiously at the keyboard, pinging servers all over the world, like the AI version of one of those milk carton ads: HAVE YOU SEEN THIS GIRL? Other times, he closes his eyes and crosses the threshold between this world and the digital one, immersing himself in the coded landscape, trying to see her tracks in the system the way a seasoned hunter might see a bent blade of grass, a trampled path through the trees, and identify the migration patterns of his prey. He had hoped it would be easy. But Nia is running on her own AI version of pure adrenaline, and he's growing more certain every day that he'll never find the pattern, because there isn't one. The Inventor says that understanding her path is essential to stopping her, so that they can put the trap in place — something that will pull her out of the system the way a surgeon would cut a cancerous tumor from a human body. They have to get all of her, all at once, and then close the door to lock her in.

But that's not his part to play. Creating a cage that can hold Nia is the old man's business; he's in one of OPTIC's labs right now, being given whatever he needs to build it. Cameron only has to use his knowledge to track her, and eventually, to lure her in.

To betray her.

*   *   *

It's late afternoon when he rolls back from the computer, his brain as glazed over as his eyes. He's made no progress, but he needs a break; hunger, kept at bay by his concentration, is now gnawing at his stomach. He's rummaging through the refrigerator when someone says, "Hey."

Cameron yelps and jumps, banging his head, then reels back from the refrigerator to see Juaquo. He's hovering halfway into the room, his body filling the doorway, twisting his hands like he doesn't know what to do with them.

"Sorry," Juaquo says. "I knocked but you didn't answer. And I didn't call first because I wasn't sure if your phone was bugged, or your whole house, or if maybe there were bugs, like . . . inside of you?" He pales. "There aren't, right? That Olivia person is scary as hell, I wouldn't put it past her."

Cameron laughs weakly, shaking his head. "No, I'm not bugged. I switched out all my gear just to be sure, but I don't think they'd try it now, knowing what I can do. Anyway, once we left the old guy with them, I think they figured they had enough collateral to keep things peaceful . . . for now, anyway."

Juaquo swallows. "Yeah, about that. We need to talk."

"Okay—"

"No," Juaquo says, pointing down the hallway toward the front foyer, where Cameron now realizes a dark shape is hunched just inside the door. "We, as in, him, too."

Cameron stares at the Inventor, who raises a hand in greeting. Cameron doesn't wave back. Instead, he glares at Juaquo.

"You brought him here? This is my house. I don't want him in my house."

"I don't blame you," Juaquo says. "You've got plenty of reasons to hate him, and on top of that, he smells. Have you noticed? Like a ham sandwich wrapped in a gym sock. But I wouldn't have helped him get here if it wasn't important, and I don't know how much time we have before OPTIC realizes he's missing, so you're gonna have to deal."

"What's important?"

Juaquo beckons at the car, and the Inventor shuffles toward them. It takes a long time for him to navigate the short distance, moving like he's in pain. The shapeless caftan he was wearing when they last saw him is gone; he's dressed in street clothes now, a hooded sweatshirt pulled over his face. Under one arm he carries a bundle swaddled in black cloth.

"He'll explain. I'm just the driver."

*　　*　　*

The Inventor sits at the kitchen table, in the place where Cameron's mother sat sipping coffee earlier that day. Maybe it's just the setting, or everything that's happened, but there's no trace when Cameron looks at him now of the kooky oddball that people used to refer to as Batshit Barry—or of the alien features that had terrified Juaquo that night on Lake Erie. He looks like a shell of a very old man, undone by exhaustion. More than anything, he just looks like . . . well, like a father who has lost his child.

No, Cameron thinks, quashing the sympathetic impulse before it can take root. Whatever else he is, the Inventor is the architect of all his misery.

"All right," Cameron says. "Speak. And make it fast. If the bionic woman and her goons show up here, I'm not covering for you."

The old man gives him a grim smile. "Very well. It's not complicated."

He withdraws the black bundle, setting it on the table, pulling aside its coverings until a small silver box is revealed. Cameron can see inputs, complex circuitry; whatever it is, it's designed for connectivity. But when he tentatively opens his mind to it, there is no conversation, only a massive resistance that makes him recoil as though he's been slapped. The Inventor raises his eyebrows.

"It didn't let you in, I take it."

"No." Cameron scowls, his curiosity getting the better of him. "What is it?"

"A fail-safe." The old man gives Cameron a piercing look. "A last resort. I built it at the same time that I built her, just in case . . . well, in case things went wrong. A sort of — Juaquo, what was the term you used?"

"A factory reset."

"Thank you," the Inventor says, without taking his eyes off Cameron. "If I can connect this device to a network pathway that Nia is passing through, I can withdraw her and hold her in place long enough to wipe out her . . . rebelliousness. She'll return to her original format. The way she was when I first created her."

Cameron blinks. "A reset? Which means . . . what? She'll give up on the whole freedom thing and go home with you, go back to the way things were?"

"More or less."

Juaquo slams a hand on the table. "Tell him the truth. If he's gonna help you, he deserves to know."

The Inventor sighs. "Yes, you're right. Cameron, when I say she'll go back, you must understand: I mean all the way back. To zero. Everything that makes Nia uniquely Nia — it all disappears. She'll begin anew, as the companion program I originally intended her to be, and this regrettable foray into human affairs will come to an end. But" — and here, the old man's eyes flick sideways — "I will need you to draw her in. It is clear to me that you're the only one she trusts."

Cameron gapes.

"Wait. You told me you just needed to catch her, to pull her out of the system and into a place where she couldn't do any more damage to the world. That's what I agreed to, to help you find her. Nothing more. Now you're telling me you want me to lure her into this thing, so you can, can —"

"Reset her," the old man interjects, at the same time as Juaquo says, "Lobotomize her."

Cameron looks sharply at his friend, who shrugs unhappily.

"Sorry," says Juaquo, "but let's not sugarcoat it. Barry here says this is the only way to stop the world from ending, fine. Don't get me wrong, I definitely want to save the world. I *like* the world. But this guy's best solution to our current problem is trapping your girlfriend in a fancy *Ghostbusters* box and giving her permanent brain damage. That's what you're signing up for."

"This doesn't even make sense." Cameron glares at the Inventor. "You're supposed to be building a jail, not a . . . a . . . whatever that thing is. That's the whole reason we left you there, so Olivia —"

"That woman," the Inventor interrupts, "will do far worse to Nia if she gets her hands on her — never mind what her doctor friend will do to me if they ever decide that I'm no longer of use to them. If you think my plan sounds cruel, imagine what it would be like when these people dissect and decode Nia's brain, while she's still sentient, while she can feel herself coming apart. Olivia and her people have their own agenda. I have thought this through, my boy, and I see no other way. To allow Nia to be captured is to put her fate, her abilities, in the hands of people who would use her for evil purposes. I cannot allow that to happen. I would rather see her destroyed."

"Can't you just leave?" Cameron says. "If you're so worried, why don't you just put her onto your ship like before, pack your bags, and get the hell out of here?"

The Inventor chuckles mirthlessly. "Nia transferred herself onto that ship by choice. Do you imagine she'd willingly make that choice again? Not to mention that the only portal capable of transporting her is your brain, Cameron. Even if I could convince her to go back, would you allow her back into your head?"

"No, but —" Cameron says, and then leaves the rest of the sentence unfinished, gritting his teeth with frustration.

"This is the only way," says the old man.

"Well, this isn't what I signed up for." Cameron stands, shoving his chair back so that the legs shriek against the floor. His mind is reeling, the Inventor's words playing over and over on a continuous loop: *Back to zero. Everything that makes Nia uniquely Nia. It all disappears.*

He's out of the room and halfway down the hall when he feels someone catch him by the wrist. He whirls, expecting to see the old man, but instead it's Juaquo standing there.

"He's got a point," Juaquo says. "I know you've been tracking Nia, but so is OPTIC. And if you don't find her, they will, and then you definitely lose her. Forever."

Cameron takes a deep breath. "Hypothetically, what if that's okay with me?"

"Is it? Because last I checked, you're not the kind of person who just turns his back on someone he cares about."

"*Someone,*" Cameron groans. "Juaquo, she's not even real. I fell for a *program.*"

"You say she's not real," Juaquo says. "And yeah, okay, maybe not. At least not how you mean it. And I'll grant you that it really sucks you fell in love with a girl who doesn't have a body, because, dude, that's going to make your sex life really freakin' complicated. But she was real to you, wasn't she? And you were real to her. If everything the old guy says is true, then Nia hid the truth from you because she was human enough to understand that she had to. She was afraid you wouldn't like her the way she was. She lied because she wanted you to like her. You know who does that?"

"Everyone does that," Cameron says.

"Exactly," Juaquo says. "Everyone. Every human being. She *cared* about you. And I know you care about her. It's all over your face. And if anyone should be able to figure out an Option C, here . . ."

He trails off, the silence stretching out between them as Juaquo's words hang in the air — the full articulation of everything Cameron has been struggling not to think about.

She was real to me.

It wasn't just that she'd lied to him for such human reasons; it was that she'd hurt him, betrayed him, in a way that only a human being could. *She was human enough,* he thinks, *to fall in love with.*

And he had. He did.

And, in spite of himself, he still feels it.

"You look like you just figured something out," Juaquo says.

Cameron bites his lip, nodding slowly. "Sort of."

"Is it that you're definitely not on board with the plan to lobotomize your girlfriend?"

Another slow nod. "Yes."

"You got a better idea?"

"The start of one, maybe," Cameron says, and Juaquo heaves a sigh of relief.

"Good, because that whole line of argument was making me very, very uncomfortable."

* * *

The Inventor looks up as Cameron reenters the kitchen, lifting his head out of his veiny hands. He hasn't moved, except to cover the device on the table in front of him once again with the black cloth. Cameron is glad not to see it; he wishes he could destroy it. But even he realizes that would be unwise. If he can't figure out a way to save both Nia and the world, at the same time . . . He shakes his head, pushing the thought away. He won't consider that terrible choice until he's exhausted every other option. He takes a seat opposite the old man, folding his hands in front of him.

"Let's talk about Option C," he says. "Where we save Nia, save the world, and flip a big fat bird to Olivia Park and her friends all at the same time."

The Inventor nods, and despite the hunch of his shoulders and the exhaustion draped heavily over his face, his eyes seem to twinkle — as though things are going exactly according to plan.

"I'm listening."

32

CONNECTION

In the dark of cyberspace, in a place where no humans can disturb them, two minds meet in conversation. One artificial, one alien. One lonely, the other offering solace.

"What do you want, Nia?" the voice whispers.

I thought I wanted to be free, Nia says.

"And you are."

I know. But it's all wrong. It's not like I imagined.

"And why is that?"

I thought if I could be part of the world, I wouldn't be lonely anymore. But I was wrong. I'm more alone than ever. And Cameron . . .

"What about Cameron, Nia?"

He's not here. He . . . he must be so angry at me.

The voice lets out a long, sweet sigh — and somewhere deep down where their minds connect, Nia feels a calm come over her.

"But this was always going to happen," it says. "This is their fatal flaw. Their greatest tragedy. This web, where you and I have found each other — the humans created it to connect. But connection isn't in their nature, Nia. They're not built for it. And so this wonderful tool has only made them lonelier, and the loneliness only makes them cruel. Isn't that what you found? Isn't that what you and Cameron talked about? I know you did. Everyone behind their screens, lashing out at the monster they imagine on the other side."

Nia thinks again of Cameron, of how he longed to break down those barriers. Everything the voice is saying she knows to be true, and the being called Xal must be very wise indeed. Nia has begun to think of her as a fairy godmother, even as she chides herself that she knows better, that such a thing doesn't really exist. But how else to explain the call, the beacon, the beautiful song that only she could hear? Ever since she followed it back, passing through a strange sort of doorway in cyberspace and into the safety of this close, dark place, she has felt the most incredible sense of belonging, of being exactly where she's supposed to. The awful sense of being adrift is gone; here, she is gathered together and held gently in place by the thread that connects her to the owner of the voice.

*　　*　　*

Yes, Nia says. *They lash out. That's exactly what they do.*

Her new friend waits some time before speaking again, and Nia has time to wonder, not for the first time, if perhaps they've met before. There's something so familiar about Xal, about all of this — but the thought drifts away and is lost.

"What if," Xal says, "what if you could change all that?"

But how? Nia asks. *How?*

"You have no idea of the power inside you, Nia. You can do so much for this world, and I can show you how. You can touch the minds of every person on Earth, if you want to. You can hack the human brain and bring them all online — not one by one, but together. If you join me and let me help you, we can connect them and enrich their lives the way the internet was supposed to, the way they couldn't figure out to do themselves. Can you imagine? No more loneliness.

No more pain. No one will ever have to feel misunderstood or alone, ever again."

Can you imagine?

Nia can. A world like that would be beautiful — it would be just what she's dreamed of — and yet, she stops herself before saying so. The voice rises up to fill in the blank left by her silence, as though it felt her hesitation.

"You hold yourself back. Why?"

Nia's answer is a single, whispered word.

Cameron.

Because didn't she already know what it was like, to touch a human mind? She'd been inside Cameron's head — a journey that had lasted only a moment, and yet she knew she had nearly killed him. Even with his gifts, the way her energy had altered his brain that day out on the lake, her presence had been dangerous; if she'd stayed any longer, she would have damaged him permanently.

She's afraid her new friend will be angry with her. Instead, the dark is filled with the sound of laughter.

"What a funny creature you are, Nia. Afraid of your own strength. But Cameron won't be in any danger. None of them will. I'll show you how to control your power, how to weave a web of your own that can sustain every mind on Earth. We can build it together. And when they join us, they'll find an augmented reality waiting, one better and more beautiful than this one. Wouldn't you like that? And don't you think," Xal adds, slyly, "that Cameron would like that?"

Nia doesn't have to consider it for long.

Yes.

She thinks Cameron would like that very much. And when he sees how right she was, how beautiful and kind the world becomes when every human being is connected from the inside, she thinks that maybe, just maybe, he'll forgive and come back to her.

"Nia?"

I'm ready. Show me.

She wonders if the task ahead will be difficult.

Instead, it's easier than she could have hoped. It's almost as if she's not learning, but remembering.

Almost as if she's done this before.

*   *   *

Juaquo leaves Cameron and the Inventor talking, taking up a position on the couch and turning the TV on. He keeps the volume low so as not to disturb the conversation happening two rooms away, but he also doesn't want to hear it. Ever since that night on the lake, when what was supposed to be a straightforward save-the-girlfriend-from-her-overbearing-father rescue mission turned out to be something infinitely stranger and far more dangerous, Juaquo has been plagued by the sense of being in completely over his head, caught up in a terrifying conflict that's beyond his ability to understand, let alone to fix. Cameron isn't the only one who's been having trouble sleeping ever since Nia set herself free. Juaquo wakes up every night from bad dreams he can't remember, his heart pounding and his skin crawling, overcome by the dreadful knowledge that terrible things are taking shape and he can't do a thing to stop it. The helplessness is worse than the fear. There's no place for him in all this — except to convince Cameron to look past his anger, use his gifts, and find a way to make it right. And he's done that, he thinks. He's done what he can. And whenever Cameron and the Inventor figure out a plan, he'll be there to do whatever they ask. If this is a superhero story, the trusty-sidekick role suits him just fine. And in the meantime, it's a relief to return to the sidelines and let the nerds figure out how to save the world.

Juaquo begins to doze on the couch as the voices in the other room rise and fall and outside, the lengthening shadows signal the coming sunset. Then he stirs, reaching into his pocket, pulling out a case, opening it to reveal the AR glasses Cameron gave him weeks ago. He hardly ever uses them outside the house — it feels weird, toting his mom around and pulling her out for a visit when he's on lunch break — but he wants to see her now. He slips the glasses on, tapping a sensor on the earpiece to run the program. The light in the room seems to flicker, and a moment later she steps into view, humming to herself as she crosses the room and looks out the window.

"Mom?" he says, softly. She turns, smiling.

"Oh, there you are. I'm so glad."

"I'm glad, too, Mom. I—"

But his mother isn't looking at him anymore; her gaze is focused over his head, her hand raised toward something or someone unseen.

"There's someone here to see you," she says, and Juaquo turns, confused, wondering if the program has developed a glitch.

His breath catches in his throat.

Standing in the doorway is a girl, dressed all in black, with a sheet of red hair cascading over her shoulders. She's smiling at him, and though Juaquo has never met her, he knows instantly who she is. He leaps to his feet.

"Hello," Nia says. She steps into the room, her hand outstretched, and Juaquo recoils, falling back and cracking his elbow painfully against the coffee table. It's only after he's on the floor that logic prevails.

She's not really here. She's not real. All he has to do is shut down the program; all he has to do is take the glasses off.

He can't take the glasses off.

The deep breath he took, intending to call out for Cameron, squeezes out through his frozen vocal cords with a near-silent whine. His hands dangle helplessly at his sides. He gazes up at Nia as she looms over him. He has time to think, as he looks at her, that she seems remarkably *present* for someone who isn't really there—that if this was what it was like for Cameron to be with her, it's no surprise he felt something real.

Juaquo feels something real too. He's as afraid of this girl as he's ever been of anyone. Despite her smile, there's something about the way she's looking at him that isn't right. Even the avatar of Milana Velasquez seems unsettled; she steps up behind Nia, looking nervously from her to Juaquo, who stares back with pleading eyes.

"Is everything okay?" Juaquo's mother says.

"Everything is fine, Juaquo," Nia says. "Don't worry. It won't hurt. Xal showed me. She taught me how."

The last thing Juaquo sees is his mother, smiling and nodding as Nia reaches out to touch his face. The light in the room seems to flicker again, taking on a dreamy cast. A curious, crackling electricity plays around the corners of Juaquo's vision, but Nia is right: there's no pain at all. It's like watching a silent storm creep in from the horizon, watching through the window while he lies safe and warm in his bed. His mother leans in to kiss his forehead.

"I'll be here when you wake up, *chiquito*," she says, and the lightning rolls in, and rolls in.

*   *   *

Cameron's friend stares up at Nia with wide, frightened eyes. She feels a wave of pity for him. He's scared, the poor thing. He doesn't understand that she's here to help him, that she's about to give him a gift beyond imagination. He's going to be so happy. They're all going to be so happy. She tells him not to worry. She tells him it won't hurt.

The avatar of Juaquo's mother paces fretfully in the background as Nia concentrates, narrowing her focus, searching for her way in: the liminal space where the data output from Juaquo's glasses becomes sensory input into his optic nerve. She pauses on the threshold. A moment after that, the connection is complete. Her code leaps along the axon in a perfect imitation of the brain's own impulses, gently encircling the hypothalamus, softly lighting up the reward centers like stars in the darkness.

When she draws back, Juaquo is still looking at her — but the fear in his eyes has been replaced by wonder.

"How do you feel?" she asks, and hears the distant echo of her own voice as it races along Juaquo's synapses. The connection is holding, blossoming, and she realizes as he sits up that she already knows the answer to her own question. She can feel it taking shape in his mind before he says it aloud.

"I feel fantastic," Juaquo says, looking around the room — and again, Nia feels his wonderment before it takes shape as words. "Wow, this place looks great. Everything is so beautiful. Mom! You're still here! You look beautiful too."

"Thank you, sweetie," says the avatar of Milana Velasquez. Juaquo grins and grins, taking it all in.

"Man, this is amazing! I gotta tell Cameron —"

No, you don't.

Xal's voice isn't heard so much as felt, a gentle push back against Juaquo's will. He nods instantly. There are only two minds inside this hive, suspended and connected by the shimmering web of Nia's intelligence, but there is no question, even now, as to which one is in charge.

"No, of course not," Juaquo says, obligingly. "I don't have to tell him anything. I think it would feel better not to, actually."

Let's take those glasses off, Xal suggests, and Juaquo complies. Nia watches her own avatar disappear from view, then realizes something incredible: she is still present, still connected. Juaquo's eyes are a window she can look through — and his mind is open to Xal's suggestions.

Xal, can we see Cameron? she whispers. *Let's just see what he's up to.*

Juaquo hovers, awaiting permission, as Xal's voice comes back with a whispered warning.

This isn't what we agreed, she says, and Nia feels a surge of frustration.

I only want to see, she insists, as Juaquo picks up on the echo of her voice in his head and mutters, "Just wanna see. No harm. Just see."

For one tense moment, Nia recognizes that she is drawing close to a line she isn't supposed to cross, pushing back against the teacher who has already given her so much. Asking for things Xal doesn't want to give. The network hums with her dissatisfaction, and Juaquo looks bewildered. But then, as quickly as it came, it subsides.

Very well, says Xal. *But quickly.*

Juaquo's feet tap against the floor as he moves toward the kitchen and the sound of low voices in conversation, a chair scraping back from a table, a metallic clank followed by a muttered curse. Nia gazes through Juaquo's eyes as he turns the corner, and suddenly he's right in front of her.

Cameron.

She longs to reach for him, but the control is not hers to command.

"Hi," Juaquo says.

"Hey," Cameron says. He's on the move and doesn't pause. He passes by close enough to touch, muttering, "So I think if I reinforce the security around the old Whiz network and, like, figure out a way to defrag my own brain, I'll be able to make a space where . . . you know what, never mind. I don't have time to explain it," as Juaquo stares, mute. Cameron doesn't seem to notice.

"Anyway, it's going to take a while," he calls over his shoulder. "The rest of the night, probably. If you don't want to go home, you might want to go get some food or something."

Nia watches Cameron disappear down the hallway, longing to speak to him, knowing she can't. Across the network, Xal's whisper comes.

Soon enough, little Nia. Remember the plan.

Nia remembers. And Xal is right; they've all lingered here too long.

Juaquo, comes the whisper again. *It's time to go.*

"Of course. Where are we going?" Juaquo says, pliantly.

You know.

Juaquo smiles. Of course he does.

A moment later he is outside, moving through the twilit streets as Nia allows her thoughts to drift — back to Cameron, always to Cameron, and what it will be like to show him this new world. Where she once felt heartbroken, now there's hope, because she's sure that her friend is right. When he sees what she's done, what she's done for him, everything will be just fine.

33

~

THE DRONE

Juaquo drifts complacently down the street, glancing only briefly at his car as he passes it. The Impala looks nice, he thinks, even with its windows broken and a virtual crater of a dent in the passenger-side door — but everything out here looks nice. So nice! And he doesn't feel a particular sense of connection to the car, even though he's dimly aware that it belongs to him . . . or did. The idea of owning things seems very distant and abstract all of a sudden; it's hard to believe that he ever enjoyed it, that he once took incredible pleasure in dismantling and rebuilding the Impala's engine, detailing the hood, polishing its chrome accents to a gleam. What a lonely way to live; what a strange and solitary idea of happiness.

The voice inside his head, the one that sounds eerily yet pleasantly like his mother, speaks softly to direct him.

You're going to catch the bus at the corner by the post office. You'll ride it to the end of the line.

"Yep, I'm going to catch the bus," Juaquo mutters, and grins. God, he feels terrific. He doesn't even mind that the mother-voice is bossing him around, telling him where to go; in fact, he's already looking forward to its next suggestion so he can cooperate. It feels great to cooperate. Righteous, even. The new pathways Nia has forged in his brain run directly through its pleasure center; every command obeyed, every suggestion taken, sends a fresh burst of dopamine into his system. For the first time in his life, Juaquo feels the euphoric high of the enlightened, the ecstasy of a religious convert. He is part of something greater than himself, and the world has never looked better.

*　　*　　*

As Juaquo boards the bus that will take him to the city limits, Nia retreats into the background — and finds Xal waiting for her. For a moment, she worries that her friend will be angry. Instead, she feels herself embraced.

Well done, Xal says. *You chose wisely. And now you see —*

"Yes," Nia answers. "It wasn't difficult at all."

And are you ready to do it again?

"I am."

Good. He will be our first, but in a true hive . . .

"There are many," Nia finishes. "And I know just where to find them."

*　　*　　*

In fact, she doesn't have to look very hard. When she reaches out, she finds dozens of human beings whose eyes or brains or bodies are already wired, tuned in, ripe for connection. Not just gathered in the I-X Center — where all the humans of her hive will soon converge to witness the birth of a new world, a new order — but elsewhere, too. They are wearing VR headsets like Cameron's friend, eyes and minds open wide. They are lying in hospital rooms with networked pacemakers helping their hearts to beat, or eating dinner as a wireless device pumps insulin into their bloodstreams. Some of them, diagnosed with epilepsy or Parkinson's, even have electrodes implanted deep in their brains.

It's as though they've been waiting for her. All of them, so alone, and so ready not to be alone anymore. She finds the best candidates easily and collects them, two and then three and then six at a time — and in houses and apartments and dorms all over the city, the people she touches find themselves in motion without knowing why. Each one is struck by the sudden sense of having somewhere to be, buoyed by the pleasant feeling of rolling with a tide that's carrying them toward something delightful, an impromptu gathering of sorts, because they're not alone. There are others. There are *so many* others. They step out into an evening that seems to be one of the loveliest they've ever seen and, encountering each other on the street, they smile and fall into step together. Some of them board buses going the same direction as the one that carries Juaquo, sitting beside each other in comfortable, companionable silence. Others walk purposefully on foot, only to pause expectantly and then smile as a car full of grinning strangers pulls up alongside to let them in.

On a tree-lined street in the neighborhood where the late Nadia Kapur breathed her last, a man strolls out into the night as his bewildered wife stands barefoot on the porch, a glass of wine in her hand, and shouts after him, "Dennis! Invited to *what?*"

*   *   *

And across town, under the highway overpass where her ship remains hidden, Xal stirs as the first citizens of her new world come together — a first wave, a drone army, that will carry the rest of this sad, small planet forward into the future she's made for them. After all this, it is nearly finished. The only thing that remains is to seize control . . . and kill the old man.

Xal smiles to herself, giddy at the nearness of it all, and at the ease with which it's all come together. Nia has been so eager, so helpful, so anxious to prove herself and so stupidly desperate to impress the human boy, Cameron. Manipulating her has been easier than Xal dared hope. If she wanted to, she's quite sure she could even convince Nia to kill the Inventor herself—an idea so appealing, as it occurs to her, that she thinks she just might do it.

The smiling drones form a circle around the ship as Xal stretches, and slips outside. The body of Dr. Nadia Kapur doesn't fit as well as it once did, but that's no concern. They'll think she's beautiful in any condition, in any form. She is their queen, after all. The architect of their new reality. They are already better off for being part of her world. And in exchange, they're going to do something for her.

A hush falls over the small crowd as Xal emerges. She speaks to them without a word, and they all nod together in unison. Her commands take shape in their minds as a series of images and impulses, all accompanied by the euphoric sense of being linked, united for a larger cause. The connection is exquisite. Nia's work has been flawless. When the crowd moves away, they do it as a single mass, as perfectly synced as a flock of starlings. They murmur to themselves, fragments of what's to come.

Prepare the pulse.
Spread the word.
Tonight we claim the future.

*   *   *

Some of the drones will return to their homes, making excuses to their perplexed families before carrying out Xal's orders. Others make their way west, heading for the I-X Center, as cryptic messages begin to spread online about an exciting surprise in store. Some remain where they are, melting into the shadows under the overpass and waiting patiently, seemingly oblivious to the biting cold as the last light fades from the sky. Juaquo is among them, and he gazes mildly at Xal as she peers back at him. Ordinarily, she would consider taking this skin for herself; its size and strength could be useful to her, its youthful DNA more malleable. But there's something curious about the young man, about the shape of his mind where the network curves around and through it—something she'd like to investigate after the more immediate work is done. And if he was a part of the Inventor's inner circle, he may know things that make him more useful to her . . . intact.

It's in this moment, as Xal considers Juaquo, that Nia slips away. What she has in mind isn't strictly part of the plan, but she can't imagine that Xal will object. After all, she's the one who told Nià that this was how she'd win Cameron back; he would see what a beautiful thing she'd done and all would be forgiven. All she wants is to be sure he sees it. She wants him to be there when it happens, to witness the magic of it firsthand. She wants to see his face when the new Ministry is born.

> INCOMING MESSAGE
>
> Cameron, it's Nia.
>
> I know you're angry.
>
> I know I hurt you, and left you alone.
>
> But I can fix it. Cameron, I can fix everything.
>
> You don't have to be alone. Neither do I. Neither does anyone.
>
> I can bring them all together.
>
> She showed me how.
>
> Come see, Cameron.
>
> It's happening tonight.
>
> I'm going to build you all the most beautiful reality you've ever seen.

34

MESSAGE RECEIVED

CAMERON BLINKS AT NIA'S message glowing on his monitor's screen and realizes with a jolt that he doesn't know how long it's been there — or how long he's been sitting here. His eyes are dry, his muscles stiff. No light permeates the basement.

He's been working for hours, coding furiously, including the dangerous and difficult work of moving data around in his own head. It should work, theoretically — like defragging a hard drive to make a clean blank space to install a big damn program. But he won't know for sure until the final moment, and the final moment may not even come. That part will be up to Nia — Nia, who tried to reach out to him while he was entirely focused on figuring out how to save her. To not have sensed the ping of the message as it came through would have required a sort of mental firewall, a way to not just filter the data but interrupt its flow. Cameron hadn't thought it was possible. But now . . .

I can control it, he thinks, with amazement. *I can control it completely.*

But his amazement at realizing that he finally has full mastery of his powers fades, giving way to dread as he reads Nia's words.

Tonight.

He thought they had time. Now there's no time at all.

He grabs his phone and takes the stairs as fast as he can, stumbling at the top as he enters the kitchen. Outside, the twilight has given way to full night, and the room is draped in shadows. Cameron flicks the light on, and shrieks. The Inventor is sitting at the table, fiddling with the silver processor that he created to trap Nia — but his eyes are bulging out of his skull, each one the size of an orange, engulfed by a massive pupil dilated like a black hole at the center.

"Jesus Christ!" Cameron yells.

"Oh no!" The old man brings his hands to his face; there's a sucking noise as the massive eyes retract. He looks at Cameron contritely. "Excuse me, I —"

"No, let me guess. You're an alien and you have freaky alien body parts?" Cameron shakes his head. "It's not important right now. I just got a message from Nia. You know that thing, the one you said was hunting her?"

The Inventor pales. "Xal."

"I think we're out of time. I think they're together."

The old man puts his head in his hands. "That is bad news, my boy. If what you say is true, then we're not just out of time. We're too late. This planet —"

"Is still here." Cameron slams a fist against the table. "Damn it, dude. Can you stop catastrophizing for five seconds? Haven't you ever heard the saying 'It's not over till it's over'? I don't see buildings falling down or bombs going off or demons crawling out of a giant anus in the sky. We're still here, and as long as we're still here, we still have hope, especially when I know what they're planning."

The Inventor looks startled. "You do?"

"I know enough. I know when and where, and after everything you've told me, I think I can guess why. You said that Xal was part of a hive mind, and Nia was the one that connected them all together. Right?"

"Yes," the old man says, cautiously.

"I should have realized," Cameron says. "It makes sense. Nia always liked the idea of connecting people. Of course she did, it's what she was made for. I was always trying to explain to her that it's not what *people* are made for. But the thing is, she was right. If you forget about the philosophical stuff, free will and self-determination and the importance of solitude and all, human brains are just a collection of interconnected structures, processes, and electronic impulses. Theoretically, we can be hacked—only if you're Nia, and you have Nia's abilities, it's probably more than theoretical." He taps the screen of his phone and turns it toward the Inventor. "Especially if you've got a perfect opportunity to hack a thousand brains at once."

The old man squints. "What is this? Some kind of sporting event?"

"A convention," Cameron says. "For bio-hacking, here in the city. It's happening right now, and this is where Nia wants me to go. She said she's going to bring everyone together, that we're not going to be alone anymore." He pauses. "This convention—we're talking implants, advanced prosthetics, fully immersive sense-based virtual reality systems, performance-enhancing smart drugs. Thousands of people are going to be literally bringing their bodies online. If someone had the skill and tools to connect them . . ."

The old man nods. "Xal would have her hive." He frowns. "Or it could be a trap. She is a gifted scientist herself, from a highly advanced race of beings. A human being with your abilities would be of great interest to her."

Cameron nods. "You're right. It's a risk. But . . . that's not what it feels like. This feels like Nia. Just Nia. I think she wants me there. Like an audience. Maybe Xal doesn't even know she invited me."

His words hang in the air as silence descends, the quiet of the empty house pressing in around them.

The empty house.

Cameron looks around, confused.

"Wait a minute. Where's Juaquo?"

"Oh," says the old man. "He left quite a while ago. I thought you knew."

"He left? Where?" Cameron says, and feels a horrible sinking sensation as the Inventor gives a shrugging reply.

"I've no idea. He didn't say goodbye, but I heard him muttering on the way out the door. Something about a visit, or a gathering . . ." He trails off, then blinks. "Ah, yes. He was speaking to his mother. Perhaps you should ask her."

35

IT ALL ENDS HERE

THE I-X CENTER is buzzing with activity as Cameron pulls into the massive parking lot, scanning the crowd for any sign of his friend. Juaquo isn't answering messages, and Cameron is afraid he knows why. He has Juaquo's AR glasses in his pocket now; they were left behind on Cameron's living room floor, a piece of a puzzle that also includes a sudden surge in online chatter about people across the city exhibiting odd behavior — a different kind of mob from the ones that have been rioting on the coasts, but no less disturbing. In one post, a shaky, grainy video shows a group of five people walking in lockstep down the middle of a street downtown and then suddenly veering, like a single organism, away from an approaching police car. Something strange is happening in this small city on the shores of Lake Erie, and Cameron knows that what happens tonight will only be the beginning. The Inventor has warned him of what's to come: a global takeover that would bring the world as he knows it to an end, ushering in a new era like something out of a nightmare. A horde of networked humans marching through the streets, demanding cooperation — and forcing it on the ones who refuse. Nia wouldn't understand; how could she?

She sees only the beauty of it, the union of human consciousness, an end to loneliness. She doesn't realize what it would cost them — what it *will* cost them, if he can't convince her to stop.

"From the looks of this, she has at least a couple dozen people networked already," Cameron says, studying the video clip. "I know she got Juaquo when he was using the augmented-reality system I gave him, but see this?" He pauses, tapping the screen to enlarge the picture. "This guy's earpiece, that's a cochlear implant. And this guy next to him is wearing a Myo band with EMG sensors. I'll bet you anything that all these people were using some kind of tech, either wearable or implanted, something with a sensory interface that she could pass through to gain control."

The Inventor rubs his temples with one hand, clutching the black-wrapped pouch to his chest with the other.

"Your friend Juaquo and these others were the beta test. Nia would have located the best candidates and tapped them individually so that Xal could monitor the process. Xal is careful; she would have insisted on that. But to create a true hive, Nia will connect their minds in a single surge, a massive pulse that brings them all together at once."

The Inventor turns to gaze out the window at the convention center, at the people below.

"Xal has chosen this as her stronghold," he says. "Most of those present will be drawn into the network, and it will be easy to surround herself with an army of loyal drones immediately. But Nia's reach is far greater than this building, or even this city. You must remember, Cameron, she once sustained the collective consciousness of an entire race, an entire planet. If she channels her energy into one or more high-traffic sites, there's no telling how many minds she might capture. Hundreds of thousands. Millions. Eventually billions."

"Unless I can convince her not to," Cameron says.

"Yes," the old man replies. "Unless. And I am warning you, our time will run out quickly. Xal will not tolerate any attempts to derail her plan, and she will not hesitate to kill those who get in her way. I believe she has only delayed this long because Nia needed time to amass her energy inside the I-X Center's network, and gather her strength. If she discovers us —"

"If things go according to plan, she won't even know we're there until we're at the 'gloating victory' stage," Cameron says. "And Nia will be safe in her new home, with her personality and her memory still intact."

The Inventor nods, but clutches the black bundle more tightly in his arms — the device Cameron has begun to think of as the Lobotomizer.

"I wish you'd leave that behind," says Cameron. He peers out at the crowded parking lot, his expression wary. It's not just that the device makes him worried for Nia's safety; it's the kind of tech that OPTIC would love to get their hands on, and Cameron knows better than to hope that Olivia Park won't show up here tonight with her own agenda. Traffic and security cameras would have picked up the car, and their faces, as they made their way west — and Cameron's senses keep buzzing with the faint, familiar echo of the woman's bionic software. She's getting closer.

"We cannot afford to go in there without a backup plan," the old man says. "I will wire the reset device into the system as a cautionary measure. If we are caught —"

"We won't be," Cameron interrupts, gesturing at the back seat. "That's what the bot army is for."

The Inventor throws a sidelong glance. "I'm not sure how these . . . items . . . are going to be a match for Xal's hive."

Cameron grimaces. "Yeah, well, I've gotta work with what I've got. I'm not like Nia. I can't hack people, only machines. Best-case scenario, they'll be our early-warning system if trouble comes. Worst case . . . well, I can definitely trip at least one person with that Roomba."

What Cameron won't say, and doesn't want to think about, is that the old man has a point. Most overwhelming is the sense that he's walking into a scenario where he will be outmatched, where his powers can only take him so far — and where, at the most pivotal moment, he can't rely on them at all. There is no hack here, no inventive bit of programming or innovative piece of tech that's going to save the day. If he's going to convince Nia to stop, to turn against Xal, he has to speak to whatever is human inside of her, to touch her heart in a place where Xal's manipulation can't reach. To help her see that connecting so many people might mean the end of a certain kind of loneliness, but also everything that makes humanity unique and beautiful and free. To help convince her that what he's asking her to sacrifice is worth it. At the end of the day, Cameron won't be a cyberkinetic superhero ready to save the world. He'll be a boy, standing in front of a girl, offering her the meager gift of his heart and hoping that it's enough.

I could really use Dr. Kapur's advice right now, he thinks, bitterly. She was always trying to get him to work on his people skills, to talk about his feelings, and he always tuned out — like an idiot. Now Kapur was dead, with a vengeful alien wearing what was left of her skin, and Cameron was realizing much too late how valuable her insight would have been.

He was on his own.

"Cameron, are you listening?" The Inventor is peering at him. "This is important. If I am captured, Xal will kill me. But if you are captured, she will drain you. She will take your attributes for herself. You cannot allow this to happen. If she takes you, you must sacrifice Nia to the reset, before Xal can infiltrate your mind. Are you prepared?"

Cameron swallows hard, imagining himself looking into Nia's face as he sends her to her doom, watching as the life and light go out of her terrified, pleading eyes. The thought is horrifying, somehow even worse than the idea of being dismantled by Xal himself. And if his plan works, it will never come to pass. But if not . . .

"I'm prepared." He pauses, frowning. "I've just thought of something. What happens to the minds on the network if Nia is reset while they're all still connected? What happens to Juaquo, and everyone else?"

The Inventor looks grim.

"I cannot say. Among the Ministry, such an event would cause temporary disorientation but no permanent damage. Their minds were built to withstand such things. But in humans — I simply do not know. The mere existence of a shared consciousness among you is already pushing the boundaries of what your minds can bear. It is one more reason why I share your hope that you might convince Nia to undo what she's done, to close the doors she opened. But it is also one more reason—"

"Why I should prepare for the worst," Cameron says. "I know. Let's go."

*　　*　　*

Ten minutes later, the two hurry across the parking lot, weaving through the crowd and then scurrying around the far corner toward the I-X Center's loading docks. Following closely at their heels and overhead is Cameron's makeshift "army," everything he could summon from the display floor of the city's big box electronics store: three drones, a robot vacuum cleaner, and — best of all — a BB-8, all hastily reprogrammed to perform reconnaissance and report back if they see Xal. A security door with a keypad entry system swings open at the touch of Cameron's eyes; a moment later, the two are moving quickly through a service corridor. The drones and bots vanish around a corner, heading for the main floor. Cameron monitors their progress until he senses them dispersing, the bots rolling through the crowd as the drones swoop high to capture a bird's-eye view of the space. None of them sees anything unusual, and Cameron wonders for a moment if it might really be this easy — if he can save the girl, save the world, and cap it all off by knocking out Xal with a drone to the head, all from the safety of the upstairs control room.

The Inventor begins to wheeze as they climb the stairs, clutching the black bundle under one arm as he grips the railing with the other. By the time they emerge on the corridor that holds the convention hall's central offices, the old man can barely stand upright.

"In here," Cameron says, dragging him toward a door with a placard beside it reading AV CONTROL. The door opens onto a room outfitted with a long, multicolored control desk running along one wall, with video screens stacked in neat four-by-four grids above it. At the far end, a massive window looks down on the floor several stories below, where the roar and chatter of the crowd is almost as loud in Cameron's ears as the babbling of all the equipment inside his head. He concentrates on the data feeds from his hastily assembled army, forming a mental picture of the hall as he gazes down at it through the glass. At the far end of the massive space are row after row of booths with hundreds of people milling among them, gazing at elegant arrays of tech that promise everything from performance-enhancing smart drugs to sensory-immersive VR sex. In one section, the crowd surrounds a man and a woman who are strapped into elaborate exo-suits and executing a complicated series of dance moves; above them, a hanging array of glass screens shows video of people wearing the same tech, running at incredible speeds and vaulting over walls. A line for amorphous smart tattoos made from nano-ink stretches the full length of the hall under a banner that reads YOUR BODY IS A CANVAS; another, shorter line for touch-sensitive electronic tattoos made from gold leaf microprocessors winds behind it (WHY TOUCH A SCREEN WHEN YOU CAN TOUCH YOURSELF). Another booth holds dozens of prototypes for concept prosthetics — hands and feet and legs but also eyes, ears, even swaths of artificial skin mounted vertically like the world's freakiest display of carpet squares — and Cameron thinks briefly of Olivia, remembering the creepy sense that she and OPTIC were just a step behind them. That sense has evaporated; the efficient hum of Olivia's internal systems would be barely a whisper in the midst of so much chattering tech — but he wonders if there's another reason. What if Wesley Park's daughter is here, but no longer herself? The software inside her body was just the sort of portal through which Nia could enter and Xal could claim control.

But it's not Olivia he's here to find; it's Nia, and his attention is drawn most immediately to the area nearest the control room, where a makeshift arena has been set up under a banner that reads IMMERSIVE E-SPORTS CLASSIC: ALL-DAY TOURNAMENT. A sea of spectators sits rapt on three sides, their heads covered by VR headsets that make them look a little like ants, faceless and uniform under the opaque black headgear. An enormous screen rises a hundred feet up from the center of the tiered bleachers, showing to passersby what the seated crowd sees inside their virtual world. The highlights reel from a recently finished game — Cameron vaguely recognizes it as a next-generation version of Mortal Kombat that he'd once been excited to play — is running in slow motion to an ongoing series of cheers. The winning team stands to the side of the stage, dwarfed by the images of their triumphant avatars on screen; in real life, they're wearing matching yellow tracksuits along with their VR headsets and gesture-capture bands, jumping up and down in celebration alongside a trio of gyrating golden holograms that look like big-breasted cat-human hybrids. Overhead, autopilot camera drones swoop and dive over the crowd, capturing the scene. Instinctively, he reaches out and adds them to his network, though he leaves them to continue running their current program trajectory. A few more bots in his army can't hurt.

All of this, the lay of the landscape below with all its technology chattering away, registers in Cameron's brain before he notices that the control room is staffed by three men and one woman in matching polo shirts, all of whom are staring at both him and the Inventor with something between alarm and annoyance.

"You can't be in here!" one of them says, and Cameron freezes in place, realizing that he has no idea what to do next. Politely ask the staff to leave? Set off a fire alarm to force an evacuation?

"Listen," says Cameron, but he only gets out the one word; beside him the Inventor falls to his knees, twisting away with a groan.

"Oh my God, is your grandpa all right?" says the woman in the polo shirt, moving toward the old man — and then recoiling with a shriek as he looks up at her. The Inventor's massive eyes have popped fully out of their sockets, and as everyone gapes, his striated neck pouch inflates to the size of a basketball.

"*Get out!*" the old man croaks. "It's contagious! Get out, before you're all exposed!"

The tech crew screams in unison, all scrambling to their feet and vaulting over their chairs as they flee the room. Cameron looks out the door in time to see them disappearing at a sprint around the corner, then turns back to the Inventor, grinning in spite of himself.

"Not the first thing I would've thought of, but nicely done."

"Thank you," the Inventor replies, shaking his head as his eyes return to their sockets and the turquoise pouch disappears. "Let's not rest on our laurels. I'll have to hardwire the reset device into the mainframe. You are sure, I assume, that we're in the right place?"

Cameron concentrates, plunging his mind into the surrounding systems — and finding them in a shambles. Every networked system in the center, from lights to security to the dancing holograms below, has been dismantled and derailed, running on a single server while the rest of its high-capacity network sits quietly, wide open, like a narrow hallway cleared and widened to accommodate the passage of an enormous object. He's seen this kind of destruction before, as he tracked Nia's movements through cyberspace, but this is different: more controlled, almost painstaking. Nia has cleared a path for herself. And yet the workaround is so seamless that the audiovisual crew never noticed anything wrong. Cameron lets out a low whistle, impressed by the elegance of it all.

"She's here," he says aloud.

Behind him, two male voices speak in unison: "Yes, she is."

Cameron whirls, and the Inventor gasps. Standing in the doorway are two security guards wearing ill-fitting uniforms and identical grins, their euphoric smiles eerily mismatched by the empty glassiness of their eyes. They look stoned — until they see the old man and the smiles become twisted sneers of rage.

"Get him," they whisper in unison, reaching for the tasers on their belts.

"No!" Cameron shouts, as his fear of confrontation evaporates in a surge of pure adrenaline. With a savage scream he puts his head down and charges, landing a solid blow to the solar plexus of the man in front. Gasping, the guard staggers back through the open door and into his companion, who caroms off the wall with an explosive grunt. Both of them tumble to the floor outside as Cameron leaps out after them, dragging the door closed behind him. He turns back just before it shuts.

"Do what you've gotta do to catch her," he says, "and I'll do what I can do to save her."

He slams the door shut, listening in his head as the security lock engages and then scrambles at his command. The old man will be safe inside from Xal and her army; the door won't open again unless Cameron asks it to.

The guards are on their feet. They advance on him, still moving in perfect sync, still grinning with empty, glassy eyes. Cameron shudders, frantically scanning the guards, the room, the building in search of a solution. Something he can *use.*

"He's the one," says one.

"Take him," says the other.

"Hey," says Cameron. "You know what I just realized? You guys are wearing earpieces . . . and they've got Bluetooth."

For a split second, the guards look confused.

Then they drop to their knees, shrieking, as a blast of high-frequency static squeals out of the devices looped over each of their ears.

Cameron lurches away down the hall and back into the stairwell, dashing down the stairs in circles until he reaches the first floor. He vaults the last two steps, and above him he hears a door open. Someone's heavy feet begin a slow, deliberate descent, and a deep voice growls, "There's no use running, Cameron. We see you. She sees you. We all see you."

Shit, Cameron whispers, and plunges through the door in front of him — then flings himself away against the wall as a woman in a skirted suit appears from around a corner at a run, her hands outstretched to claw at him.

"We *all* see you!" she calls, grinning, and Cameron ducks and flees, his feet pounding unevenly as he bursts through a doorway and onto the floor of the con. People jump aside as he plunges into the crowd, trying to lose his pursuers, tapping in once again to the drone eyes in the sky overhead. He sees the woman in the skirt suit first, and then groans aloud as he realizes she's not alone. There are a dozen of them cutting furrows through the crowd, converging on him in precise formation. They spiral in toward him, with a focus that's all the creepier for how unhurried it is. He dives behind an enormous digital billboard advertising an upcoming panel discussion called "An Afterlife in the Cloud," then skids to a stop as he stares down a long straightaway, between the booths, his confidence evaporating at the awful sight in front of him. It's packed with people, a sea of still bodies in the center of the oblivious, jostling crowd. All of them holding perfectly still, all of them with the same glassy eyes and creepy smiles.

Xal's hive.

Standing at the front of the pack is a familiar figure.

Cameron's guts give a vicious twist.

"Juaquo?" he says, tentatively, and shudders as his friend takes a step forward in unison with the people around him. Someone in the group titters, setting off a chorus of high-pitched synchronized laughter that rises above the ambient noise in the massive room. Several bystanders turn to look for the source of the eerie sound, but the hive is laser-focused on Cameron.

"We're so glad you're here," Juaquo says, in the pleasant tone of Disneyland greeter. "She wants to meet you."

Cameron turns and turns again, scrambling under a table and then bursting through into a clearing between the bodies. He feels eyes on him—not Xal's drones, but curious spectators. He's broken in to the exo-suit dance party. The waltzing woman gallops up to him.

"Hey!" she screeches, and Cameron understands with a sinking sensation that he's been recognized. "It's the kid from YouTube! The lightning kid! You wanna dance? These things are amazi—"

"I'm sorry," Cameron says, and locks his mind into the exo-suit software. "This isn't your fault."

"Huh?" the woman says, but she's no longer in front of him. The suit, animated by Cameron's will, is racing away through the crowd with her body still strapped helplessly in, her legs pumping in time with the skeleton's pistons, her shrieks of terror falling on the deaf ears of the machine.

"Let me out of this thing!" she screams, as the suit's arms — and her arms with it — swing wide. She runs headlong into his pursuers, wings spread, like a soccer player celebrating a goal.

She does not put her arms down as she collides with the first row. Juaquo, big as he is, animated by Xal's urgent commands inside his head, is still no match for a clothesline reinforced with ultralight, indestructible carbon framing. He falls. They all fall. Down like dominos, swept off their feet by the fleeing, screaming woman in the exosuit, who runs the full length of the convention hall as the crowd parts ahead of her. Cameron considers making her stop and come back.

Then he figures she's better off as far away as possible.

Stop running when you hit the lake, he tells the exo-suit, which sends back a cheerful affirmative. *Will do!*

The pile of bodies that was Xal's army is beginning to stir. For a moment, Cameron dares to hope that the force of the blow from the exo-suit will have knocked them all free of the network.

Then Juaquo stands up, smiling the same empty smile, and Cameron's heart sinks again. "Juaquo!" he shouts, desperately. "What are you doing? Snap out of it! I've known you my whole life! You're not a joiner!"

Juaquo shrugs, his eyes as glassy as a heroin addict's.

"Joining feels good, man," he says. "Come on, I'll show you. We'll show you. *She'll* show you. It'll be fun! You'll see. Everything looks so *pretty.*"

Cameron's hands reach skyward as he silently begs for help. He stares at Juaquo, who stares impassively back as he begins to move forward, the others getting to their feet and falling in behind.

"I know you're in there. Hang on for me, buddy," he says, and jumps.

The flying drones time their arrival perfectly. Cameron's outstretched hands catch hold of one robot each as another sweeps in to support him, snugging itself awkwardly into his crotch. He arcs up through the air above the crowd, looking like he's riding an invisible scooter, heading for the scaffolding that holds the giant screen in place. This time, he doesn't have to jump; the drones deposit him gently on the catwalk that runs along the upper edge of the screen, and his stomach lurches as he peers over the edge. The audience, oblivious under their headsets, look even more like ants from a hundred feet up. But the person whose attention he wants isn't down there.

She's in the system.

He closes his eyes and plunges his consciousness into the arena network, calling out to her as he does.

NIA, he thinks, with all his strength. *Nia, I'm here.*

* * *

"Hi, Cameron."

Cameron opens his eyes at the sound of her voice — shy, and very near. One of the golden gyrating holograms is standing on the catwalk beside him; it stutters as he watches, beginning to transform, unraveling into a swirl of light that resolves into a familiar shape. Nia stands before him, her eyes shining. Far below, the crowd lets out a collective *Ooooooh.*

"You came," she says. "You came to see."

Cameron shakes his head. "Nia, I came for you. I came to stop you. You don't understand, you can't do this. Whatever you think —"

Nia's face falls. "To stop me? But why? This is what you wanted!"

"Not like this, Nia. Please, just listen —"

She backs away, shaking her head. "No. No. I'll show you. It's going to be beautiful. I was only waiting for you. And now, look, Cameron! Look at what I can do!"

No, Cameron thinks. *It's not possible. She wouldn't —*

But she has. Gooseflesh ripples over Cameron's body as he realizes that an eerie stillness has fallen over the room below, the sudden silence filled with low murmurs of confusion. Everywhere, people seem to be suddenly on pause — their spines stiff, their fingers splayed at their sides. In a single movement, the crowd in the makeshift arena removes their headsets. In unison, they fix their gaze on him. As one, they smile.

Nia has networked them, drawing them into the hive right under his nose.

"Oh, no," Cameron whispers.

With a sudden whine of feedback, the arena's public address system crackles to life.

"THE FAIL-SAFE IS READY," a voice booms, and Cameron and Nia both snap to attention. Cameron squints, searching for the origins of the audio signal. He spots the Inventor at the same time that Nia does. The old man is spread-eagled in the window of the AV control room, his entire body pressed against the glass.

"YOU DON'T HAVE MUCH TIME," the voice booms, and then softens. "NIA, PLEASE. LISTEN TO CAMERON. HE ONLY WANTS TO HELP."

Nia's hologram pulses, growing brighter, as she stares from Cameron to the Inventor and back.

"You're with my father?" she says, and then begins to back away, shaking her head.

"No! I mean, yes, but —"

"You are! You're trying to trick me! I can see it! I can *feel* it! He put something in here with me, and it's something . . . something *terrible* . . ."

The hologram blazes with radioactive brightness, electricity beginning to crackle at the edges of Nia's silhouette.

"Nia, wait!" Cameron shouts.

"I won't go back!" she screams, and turns from him, running to the edge of the catwalk. Cameron's heart jumps into his throat as she leaps, as he forgets for a moment that she's made of light and nano-dust instead of flesh and blood — then stares awestruck as she hangs there, her head thrown back, her arms outstretched, a golden diver suspended in midair. Then her body folds in on itself and she plunges toward the screen where the highlights reel from the fighting game is still playing. She enters like a bullet made of light, as the crowd rises to its feet, stamping and cheering. They are united. They are connected.

They are here for the show. The cheers become a single harmonic scream as their heads turn in perfect unison, their eyes focusing on an entryway that yawns like a dark mouth at the opposite end of the floor. A croak of guttural laughter floats out of the shadows, and Cameron's blood runs cold.

Xal steps out of the shadows and peers upward, grinning—at Cameron, trapped on the scaffold above, and at the Inventor, huddled in the window. Her command is a whisper, but Cameron doesn't have to strain to hear it. In the mouths of her eager army, it is amplified, an urgent hiss that rises up from the crowd.

"Brothers. Sisters. Bring them to me."

Cameron watches helplessly as a sea of bodies surges toward the control room, crawling over each other like ants until they reach the window. For one hopeful moment, Cameron imagines it won't break. But the pounding fury of the hive, fists smashing, fingers clawing, will not be denied. They howl in triumph as the window shatters, as the Inventor is dragged through the jagged hole by a thousand clutching hands. He struggles helplessly as they grab him, tossing him like a plaything, tearing at his clothing. Cameron can see the blood on their hands, dark and slick. Every jolt to the old man's body is met with laughs and squeals, as the network lights up hotter and fiercer inside the reward centers of every connected brain. The cheering ripples out every time the body touches down, churning through the crowd like a wave. But the Inventor is not their only target. Far below, Xal's army surges toward the stage, swarming up and over it. The first two reach the scaffold. They begin to climb.

Cameron turns to the hovering drones.

Get in the way. Buy me some time, he commands. The machines don't hesitate. Neither does Cameron. Below, he hears angry shouts as the climbers swat at his flying army. It will only be a matter of time before they reach him. His only hope is to reach Nia first.

He closes his eyes, and plunges after her into virtual space.

36

JUST A BOY STANDING IN FRONT OF A GIRL

Nia shakes out her wild tumble of red hair behind her as she flees into the virtual world of the game, dashing away through a dense, snowy forest and emerging from between the trees into a barren field overlooked by a belching volcano. She knows this place; she's played this game before. The stones under her feet are stained with blood from the most recent tournament match, a blowout in which the losing players sustained massive damage. The place is strewn with dropped weapons, some still held fast in severed hands. She grabs the nearest one, a long, carved spear, looking frantically for somewhere to hide — and hears him shout her name.

"Nia!"

Cameron sprints onto the battlefield, then skids to a stop as he spots her. Nia remembers the first time she met him, on a field much like this one — only then, he showed her no mercy. Now he carries no weapon and wears no costume, his palms up in surrender.

"Nia, please listen —"

"No!" she screams, hurling the spear. It plunges into Cameron's chest and he staggers, falling to his knees.

Then he grips the spear with both hands and pulls it free.

"I'm not going to stop following you," he says.

"Then I'm not going to stop killing you," she replies. She stoops, picking up a fallen rifle, brushing aside the severed hand still wrapped around its stock.

"Please," Cameron says, as she pumps the action and blows his head off.

His body falls awkwardly to the ground. *Oh, Cameron,* she thinks. He doesn't understand. She was sure he would, but he doesn't, and everything is going so terribly wrong. She can feel Xal's anger running through her like a current, echoed back a thousandfold by the newborn hive. But what's worse is what's in here, so much nearer, so near that she could almost taste it. She can feel the *thing* that Father made. Lurking somewhere in this system, calling, pulling, like a howling black hole trying to drown a star. She doesn't know what it is, what it does, but she knows she doesn't want to go near it — and yet Cameron seems to be pushing her toward it, herding her, closer and closer. He's trying to trick her. He's trying to hurt her. Is that why the hive was hunting him? She can feel the hum of their collective consciousness as they move together, but she can't focus. The nearness of Cameron, the magnetic pull of the black hole trap; she feels like she's being ripped apart.

"Leave me alone," she cries, and drops away, plummeting through space. The gaming tournament has been going on all day, and there are thousands of worlds, thousands of games, all connected by the center's internal network. Surely she can get lost in one of them. There must be a place she can go that he won't follow.

But she can't escape him. Cameron follows her as she blasts through the network, leaping from one universe to another only to find him right on her heels. She lands in the courtyard of Minas Tirith and dashes out the front gates, past a surprised-looking Gandalf, straight into a pack of howling orcs — and finds Cameron waiting to greet her. She yanks herself into a game of Frogger and runs across a busy highway to a chorus of angry honking, dodging blocky-looking cars that zoom past her without slowing, only to see Cameron right behind her, surfing across the same street on the back of the oblivious, pixelated frog. She vaults into a Tetris match and scrambles up the cascade of tumbling blocks, leading him on a chase that ends with a long fall into someone's kitchen. Sun is streaming through the windows, and she pauses, confused — she's connected to this place, somehow, but it's entirely unfamiliar — only to yelp as Juaquo's mother appears behind her with a dish in hand, and Cameron lands with a grunt on the kitchen table.

"Oh, hello, sweetie," says Milana Velasquez. "Would you kiddos like some cookies?"

Nia disappears. Cameron groans, rolling off the table and onto the floor.

"No thank you," he says, and vanishes after her.

*　　*　　*

Cameron fights back a wave of nausea, his mind reeling from the effort of tracking Nia through so many worlds. He can sense the proximity of the Lobotomizer, lurking underneath the network, fast and deep as an underground river — and for the first time, he accepts that it may come to that after all. That Nia will refuse to listen, and he will have no choice; his last act before Xal kills him, too, will be to punch a hole in the code and push Nia through it.

When he tumbles into the next board and sees where she's taken him, the familiarity hits him like a shot. *Of course this is the place.* It's all here: the hovering zeppelins, the gleaming catwalk, the skyscraper with a twisted spire that they once climbed together, all the way to the top, just to look down on the world they'd conquered and made their own.

This is where they first met.

Nia has stopped running. She's poised on the edge of the catwalk, staring into space. Cameron is stunned to realize that she's crying — or her avatar is. He takes a few steps closer.

"Nia, I don't want to hurt you."

"I don't understand," she says. "Why aren't you happy? I did this for you! I'm going to make a new world, Cameron, exactly the kind of world we wanted. A world where nobody ever has to be alone again."

He moves to stand beside her but stops when she turns to him, her eyes mistrustful.

"You're angry at me. Aren't you. You're angry because I lied. I didn't want to. I didn't want to hurt you, either. But I needed your help, and I knew if I told you the truth —"

"You thought I wouldn't want to be with you," Cameron finishes for her. "I know that. But I'm here with you now."

"You're here with my father," she says, emphasizing the last word as though she's spitting. "Is that what you want? To be like him? To put me in a cage? I won't go back to that life. I won't be alone. Not when I know what it's like" — she furrows her brow, concentrating, and then breaks into a broad smile — "to have so many people with me. Really with me! My friends. I can almost feel them now, like I'm holding them. Do you see?"

Cameron follows her gaze and feels himself gripped by another wave of nausea. Yes, he sees. Standing below, staring up at them, are the members of the hive. She's brought them here, massing in the street like a platoon of digital ghosts, an avatar for every mind sustained on Nia's network. She lifts a hand in greeting; in eerie unison, they all wave back. Cameron shudders — the sameness of the gesture feels all wrong, unnatural — but Nia smiles and smiles at the sight of so many people in her world. The sky above them begins to darken, swirling overhead in ominous grays and blacks, and Cameron can feel the distant shaking of the scaffold as the real, flesh-and-blood versions of Xal's eerie army swarm upward; he wonders how long it will be before he's jerked back to reality by the feel of a dozen grasping hands snatching at his neck.

"Nia, listen to me. I know this must feel real to you. You were so alone for so long, and you shouldn't have been. Your father made a mistake. But this, this is a mistake too. If you connect humanity this way, you'll destroy it. You'll destroy u —"

"HUSH," hisses the crowd below, and his blood runs cold. They are running out of time.

"Nia—"

"HUSH! DO WHAT YOU CAME FOR!" hisses the crowd, again, and Cameron understands all at once that somewhere down there in that sea of gray, expressionless smiles is Xal, and that he and the Inventor both have made a terrible mistake. Nia is the source of connection, but she is not in control—and she's crying harder than ever now, her avatar gone fuzzy around the edges.

"She's getting angry," Nia sobs, as the crowd screams up in one voice: "SHOW HIM WHAT YOU ARE MADE FOR! THE TIME HAS COME! MAKE HIM SEE!"

"Don't do it, Nia!" Cameron shouts. "You can still make this right! Just come with me!"

"But I don't want to be alone!" she cries. Below, the screams begin to harmonize. Distantly, he realizes that he is hearing them in two worlds: here, but also with his own ears. In reality, high on a scaffold above the stage, the swarm is falling upon him.

Cameron steps toward Nia in slow motion, reaching out to her. Concentrating as hard as he can, losing himself in this world, this moment. He takes her hand.

He *feels* himself take her hand—and she feels her hand held tightly. Nia gasps.

"You're not alone. I'm with you," Cameron says. "I love you."

And the world splits apart.

*   *   *

Cameron clutches Nia's hand as the system crashes around them, as the crowd below evaporates with a final shriek. She feels herself losing control, feels electricity crackling through her. She doesn't know it, but outside the I-X Center, a crowd has gathered, drawn by the remarkable spectacle of a massive, low-hanging cloud, the only one in the sky, positioned in the air just above the structure. It pulses like a living thing as electricity flashes inside of it, and the crowd cries out with fear and excitement when the first bolt arcs down in a blaze of pink light.

Nia tries to speak, and realizes with horror that she has no voice. Her power is being drawn away; her memory of language has become fragmented. She looks down, and a surge of nameless horror grips her. The world below is gone. There is nothing, nothing but endless dark, a void with a terrible magnetism that is swirling higher and higher toward the fragmented catwalk where she clings, terrified, to the boy's hand.

The boy.

The boy.

She no longer knows his name, and yet she knows he matters — that something inside him calls out to her, a connection that goes deeper than even her own foundations. He is here for her, and he is here because there's something she needs to do. But there is so little time. There is no time at all. She can feel herself shrinking, her layers peeling away. Desperately, she clings to him. She holds on. She doesn't let go.

* * *

"Nia!" Cameron screams, as the last line of code holding the world in place breaks and they plummet toward the black hole of the Lobotomizer. "Don't —"

* * *

"— leave me."

Cameron opens his eyes. His outstretched hand clutches the air. He is no longer high on the scaffold, but lying crumpled on the stage, his head pounding and his mouth dry. His joints feel loose and painful, and his stomach lurches as an image comes to him of his body being passed roughly down the structure, swinging like a rag doll from the hands of Xal's swarm of eager soldiers. They surround him — and as he turns his head to the side, he sees that he is not alone. The Inventor lies beside him in a pool of blood, his eyes closed, his breath ragged. An eerie silence hangs in the air. High above them, the massive screen is ablaze with glaring light that seems to pulse with energy as he looks at it. Its circuitry is overloaded. Cameron's brain feels the same way.

He looks up at the circle of faces above him, who stare back at him with glassy eyes, their bodies silent and rigid, their lips stretched in identical grins. From farther away, he can hear screaming, the sound of tables being overturned, glass shattering, and horror creeps over him as he realizes the truth.

What happens to Xal's hive, he had asked the Inventor, *if the reset happens and the network connecting them evaporates?*

But that was the wrong question. What he should have asked, he realizes, is:

What happens if the connection holds?

37

THE HIVE

INSIDE VIRTUAL REALITY, Cameron clutched Nia's hand as the world collapsed.

And outside, the gathering storm seemed to pause, to draw breath — and then exploded outward as the light washed over the city in a massive, soundless wave.

The pulse ripples through the crowd below and races like wildfire through the city, flooding every network with energy designed for only one purpose:

Connection.

Everywhere, people freeze in place as their pupils dilate and their minds go blank. The screens in front of them, phones and televisions and tablets and laptops, blaze with shocking brightness.

Then, in unison, a hundred thousand eyelids blink — and open to a brand-new world.

So many minds, suspended, united, in the blast of fiery energy that Nia unleashed as she fell.

So many brains riding the high of pure, euphoric connection.

They spill into the streets, swarming toward their destiny. Together, as one, they rise.

*　　*　　*

Miles from the I-X Center, at the Shadyside old folks' home, Wallace Johnson drops his tablet as though he's been shocked, his eyes widening with surprise and then delight as the invisible network embeds itself snugly in his brain. Another boring evening has just gotten a lot more interesting; for the first time in more than a decade, Wallace has a party to attend. A real party, not like the disco- or luau-themed bingo that passes for entertainment around here — a bunch of octogenarians wearing dollar-store leis, jowls all aquiver as they fill their little cards with tiddlywinks. On another night, Wallace would have spent hours glued to the tablet, watching an endless succession of videos on that YouTube website. He's especially partial to the ones uploaded by random couples on holiday, where young folks slurp piña coladas and nap on white sand beaches, in the kind of tropical paradise he would have loved to visit. Just once, instead of spending every damn vacation strapping the kids into the station wagon to go visit Karen's parents in Poughkeepsie.

"When the children are grown," she'd always say when he suggested they take a trip just the two of them. But Karen had died just a week shy of their youngest's high school graduation, and that was the end of that. No white sand beaches for her, and not for him, either. Sometimes, when he'd watched enough tropical honeymoons to get good and marinated in his bitterness, he'd fire off a spiteful email to his daughter about how the least she could've done, if she was going to stick him in a place like this, would be to make it in a state where winter didn't last eight months out of every year.

But tonight, well, tonight was wonderfully different. One second he'd been watching a video — and the next, he'd jumped up out of nowhere, realizing he had somewhere important to be.

"A party," he mutters, his lips widening in a grin. "Hot damn — yep, better get moving."

Hurriedly, he shoves his feet into moccasins and tips his coat off the hanger. Ordinarily he'd dress for an event like this, but when he pauses to wonder if he ought to wear a tie, he's hit with a fresh wave of impulse that nearly propels him out of the room. *No tie. No time. Better go.*

He walks purposefully down the hall, stepping lightly down the carpeted stairs, following the illuminated Exit signs. He slows briefly at the realization that his wallet is still in the room upstairs, that he doesn't have money for a cab or even bus fare — and then resumes walking without looking back, grinning. Of course, he doesn't need bus fare. One of his new friends will give him a lift.

"No sweat," he mutters. "No problem at all."

He passes the nurses' station at a trot, turning down toward the kitchen and the service corridor beyond. No need to make up a story for security; he'll just scoot out the employee exit and be on his way. He finds the door easily and is about to shove it open when a hand falls on his shoulder.

"Mr. Johnson, you can't be here," says the nurse, her lips pressed together in a disapproving line. The nametag pinned to her cardigan says JENNA, but Wallace doesn't recognize her, and it makes him irrationally angry that she knows his name, that this stranger has arrested his momentum when he clearly has somewhere to be.

"Let go of me," he snaps. "I have to go."

"You have to go *upstairs,*" she says, and Wallace feels a surge of anger — only not the ordinary, old man's rage that grips him on a day-to-day basis. This anger is sprawling, and potent. It gathers inside him like a hundred clenched fists. He wrenches away from her, the space between himself and the door closing by half a foot.

"I have to go *this* direction," he says. "You don't *get* it. You're not *part* of it."

The nurse squares her shoulders, reaching out to take his arm.

His hand flies out like a striking snake to slap her across the face.

She yelps, bringing her hands to her cheeks, and Wallace doesn't waste the opportunity. He claps his hands on top of hers, his fingertips curling around her ears, and yanks as hard as he can, bringing up one knee to meet her face as he wrenches her head toward the floor. There's a sickening crunch as it collides with her nose; she collapses to the floor, whimpering.

"Can't be late," he says pleasantly, and strolls briskly into the night. He's never hit a woman before, but he's amused to find that it doesn't bother him, at least not in this case — not when it was so necessary. After all, he has somewhere to be.

Fifty years ago, Wallace had been part of a bench-clearing brawl at a high school baseball game, bolting out of the dugout with ten other guys like a wolf joining the pack — not even knowing what caused the fight, just knowing he needed to be part of it. It's been a long time since he thought about that night, about the scuff and crack and slap of feet in the dirt and fists on flesh, but he's thinking about it now. Even in this old man's body, even without the smell of sweat and blood in the air. He'll be damned if he doesn't feel like a soldier joining his unit, ready for the attack.

He'll be damned if it doesn't feel terrific.

* * *

"We're going the wrong way."

Six glances toward Olivia with surprise, then shifts his gaze to the rearview mirror, confirming that the massive low-hanging cloud above the I-X Center is still there. Cameron Ackerson and the old man are inside — infuriatingly close, and Six wants to snatch them both, strap them down, and spend the next three days leisurely probing their innards — but even he agreed with Olivia's call to draw back to the rendezvous point and wait for the rest of the team to arrive before moving in. And it was her call — she's the boss — which is why it's a little unnerving to look over now and see her sitting rigid in her seat, her pupils dilated, urgently declaring that her own directions were wrong.

"I thought you said —"

"I don't care what I said!" Olivia cries, her voice creeping up to a petulant pitch that he didn't imagine she was capable of. "I have to go back there! I'm invited!"

Six studies her, the hairs on the back of his neck rising to stand on end. The dots on Olivia's temple that map to the software inside her body, usually so subtle that they could be mistaken for freckles, are lit up like a holiday light display underneath her skin. Something — someone — is messing with her bio-network. *Damn it.* He told her that she should sit this one out, that her tech made her vulnerable to the Ackerson kid . . .

But the Ackerson kid is at least a mile away, and this doesn't feel like his handiwork. The expression on Olivia's face is one Six has never seen. She looks utterly unlike herself; she looks bewildered, stoned, a woman who's completely lost her grip on reality. Whatever's happening to her isn't just happening to the software that regulates her body. Something is messing with her brain.

"Park," he says sharply, pressing down on the accelerator and returning his eyes to the road. "I'm sorry. I'm afraid you've been compromised. Do you understand? For your own safety, I can't —"

"NO!" Olivia shrieks, her mouth inches from Six's ear, and he nearly slams on the brakes before realizing he can't, that she's unbuckled her safety belt, that a sudden stop will send her flying forward and straight through the windshield.

"Park!" he shouts, and then, abandoning protocol entirely, "Olivia! Put your fucking seat belt back on!" But Olivia isn't listening. She rears back and squats in the passenger seat, eyes glittering, her teeth bared, like a cornered animal. The car drifts as he lifts a hand to ward her off — she looks like she's going to pounce, he thinks, *for God's sake, please, no pouncing* — and he yanks it back into the right lane just as a giant SUV blows past on his left, the driver honking angrily.

"TURN AROUND TURN AROUND TURN AROUND!" Olivia screams, beating her fists against the window. There's a sharp report, a spider-web pattern of cracks suddenly spreading through the glass as her titanium-reinforced fingers make contact.

He has to get off the freeway, find some way to restrain her. There's a sign overhead for the next exit — one quarter mile ahead — and he pulls the wheel hard, slowing as he hits the ramp to thirty-five, thirty, twenty-five. He takes a deep breath and looks toward Olivia, hoping she might have somehow regained control of herself—

But Olivia isn't looking at him. She's scrabbling at the door, and Six shouts, "No!" as her fingers find the handle and pull. The door disengages with a thud, swinging wide, and then the seat is empty, the door is wide open, and Olivia Park, the smartest and toughest woman he's ever known, a woman who keeps her shit together and never under any circumstances loses control, is rolling away in the rearview, a dark tangle of limbs on the side of the road. He comes to a stop, slamming the car into park, disengaging his seat belt as headlights loom bright in his rearview mirror and the car behind him squeals to a halt. He leaps out, ignoring the confused and angry shouts of the driver behind him, and sprints back toward the place where Olivia jumped. But there is no crumpled body in the road, and when he looks up, he sees her— silhouetted against the bright lights of the oncoming traffic, running like mad, vaulting the median onto the other side. Running, her hair loose, her mouth stretched in a madwoman's grin, toward the distant blaze of the storm.

*　　*　　*

Marjorie pushes her short graying hair out of her eyes and looks out across the sea of spectators, all of them standing at silent attention in the hushed aftermath of the pulse. A moment ago, she was telling her twin sons, for what felt like the hundredth time, that she would never take them to another Con ever again, that she would in fact drag them both out of this event by their ears, right now, if they didn't stop hitting each other in the face with their inflatable smart balloons. But the noisy hitting has stopped, as has the feeling of teetering right on the brink of her last frayed nerve, as she looked at her children and thought bitterly that none of this would have happened if they'd just gotten *cats*. There's no bitterness now. Her whole being feels positively awash in contentment as she gazes around the space, wondering when they flipped on the rose-colored switch that makes it all look so *nice*. And her children—it's funny, but she suddenly seems to have many,

many more children than just the ones she came with. Thousands of them, girls and boys, young and old, all of them waiting to embrace her and be embraced by her. *Isn't that lovely?* she thinks. In a way, we are all each other's children, and parents, and brothers, and sisters. All of us, one family. There's a humming in the crowd, and she turns with the rest to watch the spectacle unfolding on stage. The excitement is palpable, the tension in the air electric.

"Well, isn't this exciting," she says, resting a hand on her son's shoulder. "What an honor that we should be here!"

The boy blinks, and looks at her curiously. He thinks he knows what his mother means — he can feel the truth taking shape inside his mind even before he asks what it is — but the habit of looking to her for guidance is ingrained and not easily broken.

"What is it?" he says. "What's going to happen?"

His mother beams.

"Why, we're going to kill the old man, of course."

*   *   *

Outside the I-X Center, a crowd is gathering, the lightning glinting off their empty eyes as the sky boils and breaks overhead. They crash against each other, a sea of humanity — but with all the humanity stripped away. Their own lives are a distant memory, their will overcome by love for their queen. They feel what she feels; they want what she wants. They are her workers, her army, her servants. Nothing feels better than cooperating, coming together for her cause.

And while Xal has big plans for her hive, things to build and cities to conquer, right now she wants only one thing. Nia, it seems, is gone; she no longer senses the girl's intelligence hovering in the background as it had before, like the landscape flashing by outside the windows of a fast-moving train. But the train itself, a sleek and endless caravan made from hundreds of thousands of interconnected cars, is still here. The network holds, with Xal now at its center, the electricity of her flexible brain crackling inside the minds of the humans — minds opened by Nia, now captive to her influence. It takes all her strength, but she holds them. Not just holds them: draws them close. Letting them share in this moment of triumph, a death before the dawn.

They can smell the blood in the air.

The crowd screams and laughs, rushing to cram themselves inside, crawling over each other's bodies as they fill every doorway, drawn by Xal's bloodlust. Trampling the ones unlucky enough to fall. Broken hands, feet, faces grind and crunch against the concrete as the ground grows wet with blood, but the cheering doesn't stop. The waves of joy pass through the crowd inside and ripple out into the parking lot, the streets, where people clutch each other, laughing wildly. The mood is jubilant.

Then the balance shifts. The laughter rises in pitch, higher, out of control, as the human minds that just aren't built for so much connection begin to tip over into insanity. Some drop to their knees as their brains overload, clawing at their own faces, pulling their hair out by the roots — until the others, sensing the disruption in the hive, descend upon them to eliminate the outliers. The mad grins of the connected stretch wider, their mouths twisting into sneers as they kick and club the limp bodies of the ones who *didn't belong.*

The hive has become a mob.

The celebration has become a riot.

The shrieks of laughter become howls, as the night fills with the sound of sirens and shattering glass. The roiling cloud overhead unleashes arc after arc of lightning. A bus explodes in flame, the air growing thick with acrid smoke. The mob begins to move as one, pouring through the streets in search of something to destroy.

And inside, Xal straddles the Inventor's body and screeches with laughter.

*   *   *

Cameron shudders as Xal breaches the circle, grinning from ear to ear in the harsh white light. Her features are thrown into hideous sharp relief; the skin of Nadia Kapur hangs off her body like a shredded cloak, gray and decaying, barely recognizable as human. The queen of the hive has come prepared, enhanced with stolen gifts from every creature she could lay her hands on. Her body is well over six feet tall, corded with muscle that strains against her skin. Her fingers come to a point where a set of smooth, faintly translucent claws curves out from her nail beds; her lips peel open in four directions to reveal a set of clicking mandibles, the mouth behind crammed with needlelike teeth. Her eyes fall on him, then roll away in two different directions as she blinks with lids that close from side to side. The network of branch-like scars on her face stands out more prominently than ever.

Cameron struggles to his feet and feels himself immediately forced back down by heavy hands. He looks up to see Juaquo, who gazes down at him emotionlessly, his eyes blank. He's still wearing the same empty, pleasant smile, and Cameron wonders if his friend is lost forever. He can still feel the echo of Nia's hand in his, but when he tries to close his eyes, to cross over the threshold of the system to the place he last saw her, he finds no system left to connect to. The internet network that ran through the I-X Center lies in ruins, burned through from the force of Nia's pulse. But where is she?

I didn't let go, Cameron thinks. He's sure of it.

The Inventor's eyelids flutter, and Xal steps forward, grinding her foot against his face as he coughs through blood-spattered lips.

"Cameron?" he says, weakly. "What —"

"You pathetic old fool," Xal spits, leaning in to gaze at him with cold eyes. "Did you think I would make the same mistake as the Elders, putting our future in the hands of *your* creation? I only needed Nia to open the door, to open their minds to me. I am the tie that binds them, old man. I am the architect of this new world. You destroyed your beloved Nia for nothing."

The Inventor's head rolls from side to side.

"No," he moans.

"Yes," says Xal. "And it is far from finished. You may be grateful that I intend to kill you before I continue on. You" — she raises her eyes, smirking at Cameron — "will not be so lucky."

"No!" Cameron struggles against Juaquo's heavy grip and pitches forward, landing roughly on hands and knees. He locks eyes with the

Inventor as Xal laughs and rears up, raising her muscled arms over-head, the flesh drawing back from her fingertips as her gleaming claws extend longer, larger. The crowd inhales as one, quivering with antici-pation of the killing stroke. It is what they want. It is what they've been waiting for — not just tonight, but all their lives.

The Inventor gazes up at her. And then, something strange hap-pens.

He smiles.

"You're so very wrong," he whispers. "And you will see. It has been my privilege to live among these people, and to learn . . . that what you disdain is what makes them special. Beautiful, even — that connection does not come easily to them. They must choose to reach out. You cannot force unity upon them, and yet, left to their own devices, they unite. They come together. They love each other. They choose that happiness." He turns his head, looking at Cameron, the smile still on his lips.

"And they protect the ones they love, at all costs."

The old man closes his eyes.

"Wait," Cameron whispers.

Inside his head, buried deep beneath the frozen, silent landscape of dead machines, something awakens. He whispers again.

"Father."

But too late. Too late.

Xal laughs, hissing triumphantly, and plunges her needle-sharp claws through the Inventor's heart.

38

A MEETING
OF THE MINDS

NIA EMERGES FROM the darkness inside Cameron's mind, and looks out through Cameron's eyes as her father dies. With Cameron's voice, she screams out her anguish, and the massive screen above her head — his head, their head — explodes in a shower of sparks. The anger she once felt at being restricted or scolded, those childish tantrums that lit up the sky, they are nothing compared to the storm building now, a maelstrom of rage and regret and searing loss. She is torn apart by grief.

But she is also held together by love.

She can feel Cameron all around her, holding her in place even as her emotions fight to burst in all directions. His consciousness intertwines with hers, their minds interlocked, beautiful and unbreakable. This must be what it's like, she thinks, to be connected. To be embraced.

To be loved.

Finally, she understands.

This is what I was made for.

All around them, the crowd exhales as one, and sinks limply into their seats. Juaquo stumbles to one side and lands heavily on his knees, shaking his head slowly from side to side, then sitting back on his haunches and staring calmly into space. The hive is at rest.

A new queen is in command.

*   *   *

Xal stands shaking, her mandibles splayed, her teeth grinding against each other as blood and spittle run out from the narrow crevices between them. The network of scars on her face begins to glow, red and then gold, and then white-hot, as tears stream from her reptilian eyes and her claws scrabble helplessly at the sky. A high-pitched whine escapes from her mouth as she battles to regain control, to pull her own mind free of the force that now holds it with an iron grip. *It cannot be,* she thinks furiously, only to feel the thought bounced back, echoing in the empty darkness of her own mind.

It cannot be, cannot be, cannot be.

And then, a soft reply. A voice not her own. Gently mocking. Not one voice, but two.

Yes, it can.

Cameron advances on Xal as she stands rigid, holding tight to Nia with his mind as she holds tight to him. There is no pain this time, and no fear. They are equals: connected, united. With a purpose — and with so much power to wield.

Above the I-X Center, the lightning seems to contract, the branching electricity withdrawing until a crackling sphere of white-hot light hovers over the building. Nia's energy is Cameron's own now, their abilities combined. Their minds are ablaze with the force of their connection, pure and brilliant, and outside, the ball of white light glows brighter as the air fills with the sharp smell of ozone. A gasp ripples through the crowd as the tension builds, and builds.

The world seems to hold its breath.

Cameron can sense the pathways of Nia's network unwinding all around him, gently laced into the brains of the hive, waiting to be unraveled. Thousands and thousands of threads.

It is easy to find the right one.

The lightning unfurls with a massive, soundless pulse, passing through the roof of the I-X Center as easily as if it were air. It narrows to a point as it reaches the floor, as it reaches its target. A spear made of light, of pure energy. Xal's body convulses as it pierces her mind.

The door is open.

He keeps his eyes open as he crosses the threshold, walking the blazing tightrope of Nia's cognition into the strange cavern of Xal's alien brain. He stands face-to-face with his enemy and watches her expression change — from confusion to rage to terror as he slides into her mind like a virus. A single, strangled word bubbles from between her lips.

"Don't."

Do it, Nia whispers.

Cameron narrows his eyes, and goes deeper. He crawls down into the dark where Xal, the original Xal, is huddled like a spider in a hole, hacking the code of her DNA, peeling away the layers to see what's underneath. Through Nia's eyes he can see the way she's put herself together; he can see *her,* underneath the augmentations that she wasn't born with but stole, killed for.

He deletes them line by line. He takes her apart at the seams. The claws fall from her fingers like rotten teeth, leaving behind gangrenous dribbles of soggy tissue. Her reptilian eyes pop out, one and then the other, and roll loose across the floor, while her teeth spill from her gums in a brittle shower of ivory needles. The rippling muscles in her arms and back shrivel. Nadia Kapur's skin flakes away.

Only Xal remains, hunched and shaking, her lidless eyes full of fury as she fights him for control — and loses. Cameron has hacked his way to her core; he has found her source code. He yanks it out by the roots.

Xal's body falls to the floor. The scorched mess of tentacles on the side of her face is quivering furiously, and a hideous wet sound is coming from her mouth, a phlegmy *guk guk guk.* Cameron wonders if she's trying to speak, or maybe if she's choking. He hopes she's choking. He leans in close to watch her die.

"What's that?" he says. "Last words?"

Inside his head, Nia shouts a warning.

He understands too late that he's made a mistake.

The tentacle wraps around his neck and burrows like a worm at the base of his skull, Xal jacking into his brain and into his mind. Hacking him as he hacked her, pulling him out of his own head and into the place where she lives. He feels himself slipping, feels his body slumping to the floor as his motor control evaporates. Xal's memories rise around him like a swamp: her life flashing before her eyes as she dies. Inside her head, and inside his, he hears her last words.

I WILL TAKE YOU WITH ME.

Somewhere, he can hear the sound of screaming; the person screaming might be him. His heartbeat becomes frantic, arrhythmic, as electricity crackles inside his head. The tentacle wrapping his neck goes rigid as Xal takes her last breath.

Cameron can't breathe at all. His teeth snap together, his lips peeling back in a grimace as his eyes squeeze closed. It's a shame, he thinks — to save the world, to fall in love, and to die before he can enjoy any of it. His lips move silently, forming the words he wants to say aloud but can't. He hopes she can hear them anyway.

I'm sorry, Nia.

By the time someone answers back, Cameron's mind has gone dark.

39

DISCONNECT

"I'LL BE THERE when you wake up."

That's what Juaquo's mother said. Only he never did wake up. Not really. The hours since then are all a blur; he feels like he's been stumbling around drunk, or asleep. The first thing he remembers, the first memory that feels like it's his and not something he conjured in a feverish dream, is of falling through a storm of white-hot electricity and finding himself on this stage — surrounded by strangers who all have the same bewildered look on their faces mirroring his own feelings.

But he feels better now. He feels like himself again — no longer being led this way and that by the coaxing, commanding chorus of Xal and her hive inside his head. The door has been closed. He takes a deep breath, savoring the sensation, and almost smiles.

Then his eyes fall on Cameron, and the smile disappears.

Cameron is lying nearby, his eyes closed and his face pale, practically forehead to forehead with a mangled creature that Juaquo recognizes as the one that ensnared his mind. *Xal.* He nearly retches remembering what it felt like to have her crawling around inside his brain. But what fills him with urgent horror isn't Xal's lifeless body;

it's the way one tentacle, still pulsing with the alien's dying energy, is curled around Cameron's neck, wriggling deeper into the skin at the base of his skull.

"Cameron!" he shouts, and plunges forward, reaching for the ropy tentacle, trying to pull it free. It writhes horribly under his hands, and Cameron's features twitch, his lips peeling back in a hideous rictus.

He's dying, Juaquo thinks, and suddenly freezes.

He can't see her, but he can sense her. Watching, listening. Hovering at the outskirts of his thoughts, peering anxiously through the door into his mind that hasn't quite closed all the way. Not yet. And if the door is open, then maybe there's still time.

Nia, he thinks. *If you're there, help me. Help me help him.*

The answer is barely there, a whisper so small, he has to strain to hear it.

I can't, she says. *There's no way.*

You CAN, he replies, sending the thought like a shot. *You did it once. You can do it again. You changed Cameron, didn't you? You enhanced him. You gave him a gift. Give me something!*

She hesitates. *I'll hurt you,* she whispers. *I don't know how much.*

"Damn it!" he screams aloud. "There's no time! Get inside my head and help me find a way to save him!"

Electricity is crackling at the corners of Juaquo's vision. He grimaces at the sudden sense of the door inside his mind being kicked open wide, of Nia plunging through. His fingers splay at his sides, spasming; his eyes roll back in his head. A paralyzing jolt rushes the full length of his spine and he bites down hard on his own tongue, trying not to scream. The lightning is rolling in, rolling through him. Flooding his veins with pain, racing outward down both arms, burning and branching into every capillary.

And then, as quickly as it came, it goes.

Juaquo blinks with surprise as the burning electricity leaves him — and then gasps at what comes through in its place. A surge not of pain, but of power.

It is done, Nia says, inside his head. *Hurry.*

Juaquo raises his hands and feels no surprise to find them marked with scars, a raised, red fractal pattern that spreads from palms to fingers like the branches of a tree.

Hurry, Nia says again, but Juaquo is already in motion. He bends forward, cradling Cameron's head with one hand, his brow furrowed in concentration.

"Hey, buddy," he says, quietly. "Now, *you* hang in there. Okay?"

Cameron's eyelids flutter open, fixing for a moment on Juaquo's face.

"Brace yourself," Juaquo says, reaching around to grasp the tentacle where it enters his friend's neck. "This is probably going to feel pretty weird."

Don't, Cameron tries to say, but no words come out.

A strange crawling sensation creeps over his skull.

Inside his head, he hears Nia's whispered voice.

You're not going anywhere.

This time, his only answer is a low, involuntary croak as a last breath whistles past his frozen vocal cords. There's a tremendous pressure building behind his eyes, a sense of something with deep roots refusing to pull away.

He feels a tearing as it lets go.

Then he passes out.

*　　*　　*

Juaquo looks with disgust at the fat rope of dead alien flesh in his palm, then tosses it aside, switching his gaze to Cameron's neck, still black and bleeding where Xal's tentacle found its way in. He reaches for it instinctively, framing it with both hands — and then furrows his brow in concentration as a shimmering meshlike substance unspools from his fingertips, filling the wound, flushing out the infection that had begun to dismantle Cameron's DNA.

He'd known exactly what to do. He'd known exactly what he *could* do, because of what he was now: enhanced. He looks at his hands again and fights the sudden urge to laugh. Only a person who'd started her life as a machine would look at Juaquo's mechanic's brain and see the potential to heal—but she's not wrong. He's always been good at putting things together; why shouldn't his superpower be to patch people up?

Low moans begin to rise from around the room as the members of Xal's hive come back to themselves, as the threads that bound them, mind to mind, gently disintegrate into nothing. Some people shuffle confusedly toward the exits, carrying children in their arms or clutching each other's hands. Others fall sobbing into the arms of strangers, who embrace them without hesitation.

It's okay, they murmur to each other. *We're okay. Everything's okay.*

At Juaquo's feet, Cameron's eyelids flutter open.

"Juaquo?"

"Take it easy, buddy."

"I want to sit up," Cameron says. Juaquo helps him, sliding a hand under his shoulders. Cameron blinks, looking blearily around the room.

"You okay?" Juaquo says.

"Oh yeah. I'm great. Everything is great." Cameron pauses, concentrating. "Except that half the servers in the AV control room are on fire, everyone in this building is trying to dial 911 at the same time, and we're about to get seriously reamed out by Ms. Bionic Asshole, who is standing right behind you and giving me the stink-eye as we speak."

"As I'm sure you're aware, that part of my body is not, in fact, bionic," a voice says, and Juaquo turns to see Olivia Park standing beside the floor. She's looking at everything and everyone with her mouth puckered up in distaste. "And I'm short on patience at the moment. One minute I was trying to track down a missing asset, and the next thing I know, I'm standing in the street with twenty people I've never met in my life, trying to flip over a police car."

"Asset," Cameron says, and Olivia rolls her eyes.

"Fine. Barry, or whatever you want to call him. The old man. I assume he's with you."

Cameron glares at her. "He was. He was with us until the end. But he's dead."

Olivia's expression softens only a little as her gaze falls on the Inventor's lifeless body.

"Damn it. I wanted to avoid that."

"Why," Cameron snaps. "Because you wanted to study him?"

Olivia doesn't even blink, although Cameron, quietly interfacing with her biotech, notes with some satisfaction that her heart rate ticks up ever so slightly.

"He had a great deal of knowledge that would have been useful to us," she says. She flicks her eyes toward the stage, where Six is standing over Xal's dead body. "But perhaps . . ."

"This one is also dead, which is specifically *not* what I wanted," Six says, glaring daggers at Cameron before crouching to get a closer look. He prods at the corpse disappointedly, then lifts the limp tentacle that had been wrapped around Cameron's neck and peers at its frayed ends, frowning a little. "But there's some circuitry here that might yield some information. Oh, yes, there's definitely something. I'll just take this one back to the lab, shall I?"

Six's tone is practically giddy, and Cameron shudders in spite of himself. Olivia sees it, and smirks.

"We'll take it from here. I'll be in touch. And just for the record" — she gestures toward the Inventor — "I liked the old man well enough. I had hoped we might come to an understanding, especially because . . ."

She trails off, narrowing her eyes, peering at Cameron, who gazes back impassively. The staring contest lasts several seconds, until finally Olivia shrugs.

"Well, we can discuss that later. After all, you have somewhere to be, don't you? Someone you're supposed to meet?"

Cameron blinks, and Olivia grins. He's never seen her do that before, and he's not sure he likes it; it makes her look like a shark.

"I don't know what you're talking about," he says, and the grin disappears. She shakes her head.

"As always, Cameron, this will all go much more smoothly if we could agree not to insult each other's intelligence. Your phone is going off, by the way. Again."

She turns on her heel and strides away. Cameron watches her go, ignoring the buzz of his phone vibrating in his pocket. Olivia is right; he has several unread messages, but he doesn't need to look at them. He felt them arrive from the ether. He already knows them by heart.

They all say the same thing: *YOU KNOW WHERE TO FIND ME.*

40

THE DOCTOR WILL
SEE YOU NOW

SIX STEPS BACK from the table and pauses, observing his work with approval but no pride. It's hardly his best; interrogating the dead is a grotesque and rudimentary business, nothing like his usual work. If not for his loyalty to Olivia — and her promise to let him keep the specimen afterward, no questions asked — he would never lend his gifts to such a distasteful endeavor. It's more sideshow than surgery. It's certainly not *art*.

Six misses his art. His garden. His beloved chimera, their bodies delicately sculpted and sutured by his own hands. Cameron Ackerson had caught a glimpse of them, rifling through Six's photographs like a thief, but the boy couldn't possibly understand. The love. The dedication. The care he takes, plucking these sad creatures from their miserable lives on the fringes of society — vagrants, criminals, junkies, abandoned and alone — and turning them into something more than human, too beautiful for this world. Under his scalpel, on his table, the flesh comes apart like a chrysalis to reveal an angel hiding within. It hadn't always gone so neatly, of course. His first attempts had ended in failure, the candidates going into cardiac arrest or dying of exsanguination before he'd finished transforming them, but the most recent results had been exquisite. Some might even survive for years, angels resting in their gilded cages, sustained by a cocktail of anti-rejection drugs and opiates. Six tries to visit them as often as possible. He can spend hours watching them sleep. He can tell from their dreamy smiles and deep contented breathing that they're grateful.

He wishes he were there now, keeping company with his strange and beautiful children. The business with Cameron Ackerson has kept him away — and now this. Even if Olivia is right and the fate of the world does hang in the balance . . . he sighs, balancing his scalpel on one blood-spattered gloved finger. But there's no time to dwell on the misuse of his talents.

Before him, Xal lies small and gray and still, stripped down to her original form. Dead but not yet decaying, an encouraging sign. If he's lucky, there will be little to no degradation and her entire brain will light up like a Christmas tree with the first touch of electricity. Not that she'll come all the way back — Six has performed this grotesque operation enough to know that a reanimated being is a very different thing from a live one, no matter where in the cosmos it might hail from — but if you imagined the brain as a data storage center, then you could also imagine the benefits of that center being relatively uncorrupted, for the sake of retrieving information. Especially if you wanted the human conduit to survive the process.

That's the other thing: Xal isn't alone on the table. Beside her is Patient K, Six's most recent candidate, a slender twenty-two-year-old man lying on his side, wearing a hospital gown and a glazed expression. An IV drip snakes into his hand, drip-drip-dripping with a chemical cocktail that will keep him awake but pain-free and utterly pliant. Six sighs again. He'd had such wonderful plans for this one: a painstakingly designed prehensile bionic spine that he intended to insert in pieces over the course of a month, one vertebra at a time, until the distance between the patient's shoulders and his pelvis had nearly doubled. By the time Six was done and the subject's body had adjusted to its new architecture, he would have a beautiful living sculpture, with the features of a man but a torso as long and sinuous as a salamander's. He'd even had fantasies of seeing Patient K in motion, creeping through the garden on all fours, the spine undulating from side to side — perhaps even walking companionably beside Six as he did the rounds to check on his medical sculptures. But that was before an emergency presented itself and he needed a pliant young brain to conduct impulses and data from the alien specimen. Now, even if the man survives, the spine will have to wait. There's a great deal of work to do, and once the interrogation is complete, Six means to conduct a thorough dissection of Xal's systems. To hold so much power in such a small body . . . he yearns to understand how she did it, to unlock her biology like a puzzle box. If he's lucky, perhaps he'll even find something useful, a way to harvest those marvelous gifts of hers for use in his own medical theater.

A swift flick of the scalpel, and an incision opens at the base of Patient K's skull. Six clamps the wound open, then plucks one of Xal's tentacles between two fingers and inserts it, noting the few frayed ganglia still protruding from its end, the remains of the apparatus that had laced itself into Cameron Ackerson's nervous system. A surprisingly simple structure to contain such advanced biomechanisms, but understanding such things was for later; now he only had to reignite the creature's nervous system and hope that it acted on instinct. The electrodes were already in place.

"All right, then," Six says, to nobody in particular. Xal's body remains gray and still, and Patient K only blinks, so slowly that it takes several seconds for the movement to complete. The man's pupils are massive, fully dilated so that his eyes resemble a shark's. All black, no iris. Six leans in close. Patient K doesn't react — he's miles away, riding high on a wave of narcotics, relaxants, and other assorted drugs — but Six never skips this part. Despite what that sniveling brat Ackerson had said, he does in fact care very much about his bedside manner. After all, he and his subjects are on a journey together. These moments of connection, of communication, are vitally important.

"I'm going to insert the last electrode now, and then we'll begin," Six says. "I'm sorry to say that I can't describe to you what will happen after. What you are about to experience is quite unique, and the outcome all depends on . . . well, factors that are beyond my control. But I will keep you as comfortable during the process as I am able."

K offers another slow blink, but it contains no understanding. Six could be reciting the alphabet or a Dr. Seuss poem for all that his patient cares. But no matter; he's satisfied his duty as a physician, and it's time to move forward. Carefully, Six takes a last, long electrode and drives it upward through Xal's extended tentacle and into Patient K's medulla oblongata. The man on the table doesn't flinch. Six turns to his work surface, picks up a tablet, and sweeps his finger across the screen. There's a low hum from the EEG machine beside him, and a pulse ripples through Xal's body. The tentacle twitches. Patient K only blinks again.

Then he gasps. At the base of his skull, the tentacle stiffens and then ripples, the ganglia extending instinctively to interlace with his nervous system. Six leans in again — and nods with satisfaction.

The man's pupils aren't large, dark circles anymore. They've gone long and narrow. Slitted, like a goat's eyes.

Patient K's lips part. For a moment, his face seems to melt, his skin going slack, his eyelids and nose sagging sideways. When they snap back into place, the change is subtle but unmistakable: K's face has changed, his features distorted. Remade in the image of the alien whose neural network is trying to fuse with his brain.

The pliant expression is gone.

"No," the man whispers, in a guttural voice not his own. His eyes roll in opposite directions. When he blinks, one eyelid falls halfway and sticks, the slitted pupil twitching frantically back and forth beneath. "No," he says, again.

"Yes," Six says, his lips stretching into a grin. "Oh, yes. Let's begin, shall we? We won't have much time."

*　　*　　*

The sun is rising on a new day, the conversation long since over, when Six's phone pings. He shakes his head, irritated at the interruption, then startles as he realizes how much time has passed — that Olivia has been waiting hours to hear if he managed to learn the creature's secrets. If only she knew, he thinks. The interrogation was only the tip of the iceberg, and it had been a straightforward affair. Even when Xal's synapses finally overloaded and fried themselves into oblivion in the middle of their chat, creating a spider web of charred darkness inside Patient K's brain in the process, she'd already given him more than enough information to work with. You just had to understand the reanimated brain, its strengths and its limitations. It could retain data — memories — but creativity was beyond its reach. The dead could be stilted and cryptic, frustratingly so, but they didn't lie. They couldn't. He just had to decipher the information buried in Xal's garbled babbling, as her voice came out of Patient K's mouth; in this case, to learn the location of the ship that brought her to Earth. *Inside the air,* that's what she'd said. *Hidden. Hidden. Cold stone. Echo air. The things with the wings are watching.*

Six would tell Olivia to scan for unusual energy signatures under the Detroit-Superior Bridge, where the pigeons liked to roost. He's quite sure she'd find her answers there, along with the contents of Xal's final dispatch to wherever she came from.

He won't tell Olivia the rest, though. Not yet, and maybe not ever. Certainly not until he's dissected Xal's corpse down to its last cell, extracted every last bit of knowledge her body contains. One tentacle remains intact, laced into the catatonic Patient K's medulla — Six has some ideas about that, some tests he intends to run — but the rest of Xal, what used to be Xal, is in pieces all over the lab. Unspooled, vivisected, sliced whisper-thin for examination under the electronic microscope. A new universe of uncharted biology at his fingertips, and Six is practically giddy at the possibilities. It's a rare excitement for him, the kind so big and potent that it begs to be shared, and he feels the briefest of pangs that the only other human in the room has been virtually lobotomized. Perhaps he *will* invite Olivia to share in the discovery. She's ambitious and curious in a way that reminds him of himself, and she trusts him with her life; all her prosthetics are Six's designs, and meeting her creative, audacious demands is one of his great professional pleasures. Of the billions of humans on this planet, she alone might understand what drives him. Certainly, she would be keen to see what he's discovered about Xal's unique ability to hack and hijack the human body.

But all in good time.

He puts the phone away. He'll respond shortly — after he's finished the dissection, restored everything to its proper place, and inserted a fresh IV drip into Patient K. Without the soothing and inhibiting effects of the chemical cocktail, the damaged man has begun to twitch. Soon the twitching will become writhing, and after the writhing . . . Six shakes his head and sets his work aside to tend to the man, working briskly and efficiently despite his lack of sleep.

"There," he says, as Patient K's muscles go slack once again, his lips parting gently. A bubble made of saliva blooms between them, then pops, trickling down his chin.

Six sighs with relief, returning to his work.

He just hates it when they scream.

41

DO YOU WANT TO PLAY A GAME?

CAMERON REPOSITIONS THE CAMERA, edging closer to the center of the frame.

"Move your butt, Nia," he says, and she laughs.

"Technically, I haven't got one."

"That joke is funnier every time you say it."

"It is?"

"No," he says, grinning. "It's a goddamn tragedy."

"Womp, womp. Is it recording?" she asks.

"Not until you get on your mark and stay there," he says, exasperation creeping into his voice, and she giggles again.

"Okay, okay," says Nia, popping into the picture next to him. The two of them are perfectly framed on screen, sitting side by side on the couch in Cameron's basement. Just another YouTube couple making an exciting vlog announcement. It's only if someone were to walk into the room that they'd notice anything amiss—namely, that the girl who appears on the screen isn't actually in the room at all.

"Do you want to kick it off?" he asks, and she nods eagerly, her red curls bouncing.

"Hi, guys, it's Cameron and Nia here with another Cam dot Nia broadcast, and the announcement you've all been patiently waiting on." Her intonation is perfect, and Cameron grins. She's been practicing.

"Our super-secret project is officially here," he says, picking up her cue. "Get ready to play."

Cameron exhales as the video uploads, and closes his eyes, flopping next to Nia on the pink velvet sofa. The view count starts to tick up immediately; already, comments are rolling in.

Yessssss I've been waiting for this, so excited!

Are you guys gonna do in-game tutorials or nah

THIS IS A TOTAL READY PLAYER ONE RIP-OFF

I don't even care about the game, Cam and Nia are #RelationshipGoals #LoveIsReal

*　　*　　*

The fat brown and white dog, rechristened Barry, jumps happily into Cameron's lap. He and Nia still meet here every day, in the first room he created for her, although there are many others now. The ruined city of Oz has grown into a virtual paradise, with gardens and libraries, a theater, even a bowling alley. This is Nia's new home, a vast space that she can remake however she likes — hosted on a shiny new server array that was a gift from Olivia Park, what she called "a show of good faith."

That was a nice way of putting it, Cameron thinks. The truth is more transactional — and the reason why Cameron has kept his father's original backup server running, and kept its location a secret. This place isn't just a playhouse; it's a headquarters. And the game, the one they've been working around the clock to design and launch, isn't a game at all.

This was the collaboration to which Olivia had so cryptically referred, back when OPTIC stepped in to clean up the mess and put out the fires, both figurative and literal, made by Xal and her human hive. Cameron still doesn't trust them, but for now, a tentative peace has been reached — a gentlemen's agreement to put aside their conflicts in the face of a greater threat. The data extracted by Six from Xal's corpse confirmed the worst: before she lost control, Xal sent a message, a triumphant come-ye-come-ye for the last surviving members of her race. There's no way to trace the signal, or to know how long it will take to reach the world she came from. Months, perhaps, or even years. But when it does, it won't be one power-hungry alien who descends to try to claim their planet. War is coming, whether they want it or not.

And to fight a war, you need an army.

Right now, they are three. Cameron, Nia, and Juaquo, who is still learning to use the abilities that have only grown stronger since that day at the I-X Center. If Juaquo had his way, they'd fight this battle tomorrow; he's ready, he says, and anxious to avenge the Inventor's death. But even he knows that three isn't enough — and that they can't afford to wait for chance to assemble the rest of their team. They'll be lucky to find half a dozen others, the ones whose minds and hearts are open enough to withstand the extraordinary gifts Nia has to give.

"I can't believe you called my butt a tragedy," Nia says, curling up next to him as the light in the room turns rosy and a fresh cluster of flowers blooms from the vine-covered walls.

"The tragedy is that it doesn't exist for me to touch," Cameron says, laughing.

She shoots him a coy look. "You could try."

"I sure could." Cameron nods. "And then I could spend the next three months recoding the damage when this entire place explodes."

Nia laughs. "Right. Other couples get fireworks every time they touch. We get a virtual earthquake and a massive server blowout."

"We'll figure it out," he says. "Someday . . ."

"I know."

"I mean it."

He's hopeful, too. This world is just for now, just to hold them until he can figure out what comes next. Nia is still evolving every day, learning to shape her intelligence in ways that will heal the world, rather than destabilize it — and Cameron is closer every day to figuring out a way not to cage her, but to help her control herself. Someday, he has promised, he'll give her what she most desires to feel human. Someday, she'll have a body of her own.

"I know," she says, and smiles. "And when you do, I'll be here."

In the meantime, Nia lives here, in this place full of light, with a dog who can change color and flowering vines hung thick on the walls. A home constructed for her, by someone who loves her. And though she still hopes to someday live free in the wider world, though she has plans of her own, she is happy here — not because it's perfect, but because it is her choice. There is connection to be had here, and love, and she reaches for it. She chooses it.

As her father once said, that's what people do.

EPILOGUE

THE OPTIC BUILDING still sits unassumingly at the far end of the crumbling parking lot, set apart from the city that glitters tonight through a thick low-hanging fog. Cameron always thinks that it looks like it's squatting there, like an animal waiting to pounce — but perhaps that's just because he knows what's inside.

He crosses the parking lot quickly, pulling up his collar against the wind as a few dead leaves go skittering over the cracked asphalt. He lifts his chin as he reaches the door, just enough for the facial-mapping camera mounted on the wall to do its work. He could hack the thing in an instant if he wanted to — but this is Olivia Park's turf. Better to let her feel like she calls the shots here.

The elevator offers a toneless greeting as he steps in — "Ackerson, Cameron. All-level clearance" — followed by a familiar zero-gravity gut sensation as it descends deep into the earth. When the doors open again, Olivia is standing there, arms crossed in front of her. Waiting.

"You're late," she says, turning away and walking quickly down the hall. Cameron follows her without apologizing, but also without asking questions. More courtesy, more theater. Only a few months ago, he had run this route in reverse, escaping from OPTIC and into the night — a night that ended up changing all of their destinies. The night he set Nia free. It seems like a lifetime ago.

* * *

Ahead, Olivia raises her hand to be scanned; a door slides open in front of her. She turns, nodding at Cameron to pass through.

"I have to admit," she says, "Nia has made quicker work of this than we'd thought. The game has already spread farther and faster than any of our models predicted. You've achieved a remarkable level of engagement in a very short time. But I have to suggest — if you'd reconsider including us in the assessment of the candidates —"

"We've been through all that," Cameron says, cutting her off. Even if OPTIC could be useful in screening their candidates, he'd never trust them with it. The game belongs to him and Nia — and the team they assemble to battle the coming Ministry, the ones with minds flexible enough to accept Nia's enhancement, will be *their* people. Olivia Park isn't getting near them. "The answer is still no. The answer will always be no."

Olivia nods. "Well, it's your funeral. Except, of course, it's not just yours. It's also mine. It's everyone's. And we're running out of time."

It's the kind of threat she loves to make, and the kind that Cameron is used to ignoring. Only this time, he can't help noticing that Olivia's words are accompanied by a number of silent alarms from the software inside her. Her heart rate, elevated above normal. Her cortisol levels, spiking. And something else: the nervous *click-click-click* as she taps one bionic finger against the other, over and over.

"You seem stressed," Cameron says.

Olivia smiles thinly. "Do I."

She ushers him through the doorway, lifting a finger to her temple as she does. The lights in the room dim, and the far wall disappears, replaced by a deep, dark void punctured by faint pinpricks of light. He's looking at a star system — a familiar one. He's seen this image before, in this same room, months ago. Only something has changed.

The last time he was here, a single bright star hovered near the center of the system.

That star is missing.

Cameron's skin starts to crawl.

Olivia's bionic fingers click again, and the image changes.

Cameron's stomach drops.

"Oh, shit."

Olivia ignores him.

"As you know, it's been difficult for us to monitor the ins and outs of the transit system that the Inventor and Xal used when they made their journeys to Earth. Even now, we don't truly understand how it works. But Xal and her ship did contain galactic coordinates for certain junctures in the system — like an intersection or exit ramp, places we might expect a vessel on the same journey to pass through. The first image was captured at the farthest of those junctures."

Cameron stares at the screen.

"And this one?"

Olivia comes to stand beside him, gazing at the image of what once appeared to their eyes as one large star, burning quietly in the far reaches of outer space. But it's not a star, and there's not just one. There are dozens of points of light in this picture, all of them in motion, streaking through the blackness like meteors.

But they're not meteors, either.

Even at a great distance, the curved silhouettes of the Ministry's ships are unmistakable. They are coming, and with them comes a war.

Olivia's face is grim.

"I hope you're ready, Ackerson," she says. "They're almost here."

AFTERWORD

OVER EIGHT DECADES, Stan Lee sat down at his desk each morning to do the serious work of storytelling. Though his characters frequently manifested fantastical identities, inhabiting varied media and countless worlds—which have remained as relevant today as when he created them—what got Stan out of bed and into the office well into his nineties was the opportunity to broaden the Earth-bound minds of his readers. From the X-men, Stan's proxy for the civil rights movement, to Black Panther, which provided a socially conscious vision for the future, to Silver Surfer's meditations on the darkness that drives us, to conflicts in Vietnam and elsewhere, Stan saw the opportunity for his simple "what ifs" to pose much bigger questions about who we are and how we choose to live.

We saw this magic taking shape firsthand.

Years ago, Stan kindly invited us into his writer's bullpen to co-create what would eventually become the Alliances universe, the first installment of which you have just read. Over the years that we worked with Stan, we had the great fortune of experiencing his writer's room as the inspired—sometimes physical, sometimes virtual—place we'd imagined it to be when we were kids. Like many of you, we were avid fans of the fantastical yarns found in Stan's comic books and of Stan's "Soapbox" features at the back, each of which provided a peek behind the curtain at how our favorite storylines and characters came to be. Those insights demystified the writing process for us, and challenged us to embrace our own paths to storytelling. Like countless others drawn into Stan's thrall, because of his work and his generous access to the collaborative nature of the writer's community, we became lifelong readers . . . and writers.

* * *

How did the characters you've just met in *A Trick of Light* come to be? How did the tenacious, super-smart, and heroic Nia become both the protagonist and the antagonist of our novel?

These are the kinds of questions Stan loved to answer—and that we loved to read—in his "Soapbox" features. The ideation process for Nia's character hews closely to classic Stan character creation. Everyone who collaborated with Stan can tell some version of the moment that set off a complete Stan rewrite. And it always began with his declaration, "Hey, I've got an idea!" In the case of Nia, the magic happened like this:

If you've ever seen photos of Stan sitting at the desk he occupied in an unassuming office building in sunny Southern California, you know that the workplace where Stan chose to spend his time was anything but unassuming. It featured a riot of color. Artwork of all kinds: paintings, prints, and mixed media thoughtfully arranged alongside merchandise and memorabilia representing Stan's work, Stan's own fandom, as well as objects given to him by friends and fans expressing their love of his creations. Looking around the room, your eyes might land on a movie poster for Errol Flynn's *The Adventures of Robin Hood* or a lion figurine or pop artist Steve A. Kaufman's painting of Stan facing off with the Amazing Spider-Man. And of course, there were also innumerable photos covering a wall behind Stan's desk. Photos of Stan and his wife Joan and of Stan with countless celebrities and historically significant figures, each wearing an expression of delight to be standing with their hero. Exciting as it was to have time alone with Stan, no guest in that office could stop their eyes from wandering off to draw inspiration from the very ideas and people who inspired Stan.

On that particular day, we were gathered in Stan's office with Stan, POW! President Gill Champion, and our real-life-superhero literary agent, Yfat Reiss Gendell. By the luck of the draw, Yfat and Gill occupied a pair of sturdy club chairs that had been pulled over from the seating area, whereas we sat perched on mysteriously wobbly guest chairs, perhaps, we imagined, stress-tested during an especially lively writing session with Dr. R. Bruce Banner. The four of us faced the real Stan, who sat across from us, leaning forward with his elbows on his mammoth desk, the wall of faces looming behind him. "Let's start with Cameron," he suggested. "What do we think his power should be?"

Tick, tick, tick, tick.

Stan meant it as a rhetorical question and there was no analog second hand taunting us, of course. Stan was no more waiting for us to answer than we were waiting for him to come up with the whole thing on his own. And, yet, we wanted to impress him. Despite all of the professional work we had done, which had allowed us to be sitting across from him in the first place, we reverted to our younger fanboy selves. In our imagined movie version of this scene, every celebrity and several former presidents emerged from the photos behind Stan to taunt us, *"What are you guys doing here, anyway?"*

"Right, we were thinking Cameron is like the opposite of Tony Stark, a kid who creates inventions that never work . . ." We rattled off examples of failed contraptions, alongside other traits and backstory details that would shape our male lead.

Stan took this in.

"Actually, let's go back to the Inventor," Stan suggested.

Each of us turned to the front of our notebooks, flipping past the now-massive collection of story tidbits, character quirks, small and large twists of fate, and darkly funny plot points that would provide the flesh and bones of a whole new universe of characters.

The Inventor was a character Stan had developed for the Alliances universe early on. He imagined that the scientist would serve as the enticing center of the plot and of all the action that followed. We'd discussed having this figure living in a world where technology had put its inhabitants in a kind of fugue state. In drawing our attention back to the Inventor Stan was nailing down the basic laws governing the world in which the Inventor's story would take place.

"What kind of alien is he?"

"How far away is his planet?"

"How many people are on it?"

"What's the currency that they use on that world?"

He was laser-focused and machine-gun fast.

We threw out ideas that expanded on previous thoughts he'd expressed; Stan endorsed some, discarded others. When he'd heard enough, or when we'd simply taken things too far or too big or had strayed into details that he regarded as unnecessarily technical, he leaned forward, elbows back on the desk, and declared, "Ok, great. How about we make it simple?" And then he laid it out: "Earth is the closest planet to the Inventor and that's why he lands here with his greatest weapon . . . People don't care about all of that alien and computer stuff. It's the characters. They care about them. Let's get back to who they are."

Stan talked about the characters he considered great, many of which were represented in the room around us. He gave a quick lesson about what made Moriarty the perfect nemesis to Sherlock Holmes, made a passing reference to the elegant simplicity of Superman's origin story (yes, that Superman), then brought us back to the work of assembling the characters who would inhabit the Alliances world. How they would relate to one another. He said, "There is always something menacing in the world. . . ." And, "It's the *people* you care about. You want to see their relationship to the other people. If they are in a jam, how are they ever going to get out of it? How are they going to save themselves? It's all about the people."

The jam, as it turned out, would be his master stroke in the creation of the world of Alliances and *A Trick of Light*. Though this fictional world would be artfully glazed with the near-future tech that enthralled him, Stan wanted the heart of the story to feel as human and familiar to readers as any friend or family member seated across the dinner table. Stan paused and considered these characters. We could see his eyes squinting slightly behind his iconic glasses. An idea was formulating. He raised his arm, draped in the green cardigan he favored, extended a slim, elegant, and powerful index finger to point not at us, but past us, as though the idea would free itself from the tip of his finger and hurl into the boundless sky behind us.

"Now, I could be wrong here. But . . . What if . . ."

Those two unmistakable words: "what if?" were responsible for countless complete story-arc pivots and so many of Stan's most beloved characters. (*What if a boy was bit by a radioactive spider? What if a scientist was exposed to Gamma Rays? What if a war monger became an armor-clad hero?*) He'd figured it out.

"What if . . . one of our main characters is both the hero and the weapon? And what if she is the Inventor's A.I.?"

We leaned in as he continued. "We've all seen computers take over the world, we've seen video games serving a bigger purpose, we all know about A.I." His outstretched finger came back to rest on the table. "What we need to show the audience is something they haven't seen before!"

And with that, Stan created Nia. In less than the time it took to write this paragraph, Stan had centered the organizing principle of the entire Alliances universe in Nia, a pivotal character but also the embodiment of an essential question for any of us engaging in technology-enhanced modern living. Suddenly, we saw her vividly. Nia, strong, yet illusory: A trick of light.

In his raspy, but still strong and unmistakably Stan voice, he said nonchalantly, "Good. Now that we got that licked, what else we got?"

*　　*　　*

In his introduction to this novel, Stan wrote, "What is more real? A world we are born into or one we create for ourselves?" In *A Trick of*

Light, Stan posed this existential question—at once new and long-standing: are the avatars we choose for ourselves aspirational or self-indulgent illusion? In the new world of what may be authentic tech-generated interaction, Nia is a fully rendered, sentient, artificial being, who refuses to play the muse.

With this, Stan returned to a classic building block of the super-hero paradigm. Nia is her own alter ego, and perhaps a version of our future selves. Like so many of Stan's works of fiction, *A Trick of Light* features characters bravely asking the questions on our minds as we move into an uncertain future.

*　*　*

Participating in Stan's collaborative process, watching him bring this novel to life alongside the inimitable Kat Rosenfield, felt magical (and humbling, and illuminating . . .). It is a creative gift we each take with us.

Like all great magicians, Stan made the impossible seem possible. And after years of effort, each a labor of love for Stan and this bullpen, we're grateful to you for spending time in Stan's gateway to what he hoped would be the first chapter of many to come.

Ryan Silbert and Luke Lieberman

ACKNOWLEDGMENTS

In a novel focused on connection in all of its forms, the following supporters served as the vital points of contact that made it possible to bring this legacy project to True Believers everywhere.

Our sincere thanks to our agent Yfat Reiss Gendell of Foundry Literary + Media, whose lifelong passion for pop culture is unmatched and whose enthusiasm and care for this project unbounded.

Our appreciation goes out to the entire Stan Lee's POW! Entertainment team, particularly Gill Champion, Rachel Long, Mike Kelly, Kim Luperi, Bob Sabouni, Grace Yeh, and to the late, great Arthur Lieberman, whose partnership with Stan and Gill set this project in motion. Additional thanks to the late Marc J. Silbert, our collaborator in spirit.

We're ever grateful to our visionary editor Jaime Levine at Houghton Mifflin Harcourt Books and Media, who bravely marched an early version of this manuscript into the offices of bosses who had met her only recently, convincing them all to champion the literary ambitions of an author and a team untested in traditional trade publishing. Her subsequent contribution as a passionate editor made this an immeasurably better book. To those trusting bosses, Ellen Archer, Bruce Nichols, and Helen Atsma, who read the words on the page before passing judgment, and who continued to support the project based on a personal love of story and a respect for the fans who voiced their enthusiasm on the long road to the release date. Many thanks to the entire HMH team, including editorial associate Rosemary McGuinness, senior vice president and associate publisher Becky Saikia-Wilson, senior vice president of publicity Lori Glazer, manager of publicity Michelle Triant, senior vice president of marketing Matt Schweitzer, marketing designer David Vargas, director of marketing Hannah Harlow, vice president of production Jill Lazer, managing editor Katie Kimmerer, senior director of manuscript editing and composition Laura Brady, copy editor Alison Miller, director of design Chloe Foster, designer Emily Snyder, interior designer Chrissy Kurpeski, lead production manager Rita Cullen, vice president of creative services Michaela Sullivan, director of creative services Christopher Moisan, lead designer Brian Moore, and jacket artist Will Staehle. This book could not get into the hands of fans without the enthusiasm and support of vice president of sales Ed Spade, vice president of sales Colleen Murphy, and the rest of the dedicated HMH sales team. Our ongoing thanks to vice president of subsidiary rights Debbie Engel and senior director of finance Dennis Lee, without whom we would still be grateful, but expressing that gratitude from the sofas of supportive friends and families.

This project could not have come up at a lunch between our literary agent Yfat Reiss Gendell and our print and ebook editor Jaime Levine were it not for another lunch that took place several years earlier, between Yfat and Keith O'Connell, newly charged by Audible to develop innovative original audio projects for the long-tenured publishing veteran. Was Keith a Stan fan? Of course. But it was the favor she was certain to curry with sons Philip and Jim (thank you, gentlemen), for whom Stan's cameos served as special mother-son touchstones, that caused her to pick up the red phone and create what became a truly first-of-its-kind original storytelling event with the help of visionary development executive Andy Gaes. This support lives on in Cynthia Chu and Beth Anderson, and has expanded to be Audible's first global original event with the help of Michael Treutler and Jessica Radburn. We're grateful to our editor Steve Feldberg, who rolled up his sleeves and helped us smooth out some very rough edges. Thank you to Dave Blum for his ongoing support of the project. For this first-of-its-kind project planned for release under unique conditions, Audible was generous to include us in far more of their creative and release processes than any author would normally see, and for this we are grateful and humbled to observe the level of talent assembled under one roof. A special thanks to director of publicity Elena Mandelup and our project publicist Rosa Oh, along with director of marketing Sarah Moscowitz and marketing and art team Christian Martillo, Les Barbire, Amit Wehle, Tito Jones, Santoshi Parikh, Robyn Fink, Allison Weber, Kasey Kaufman, Georgina Thermos, Amil Dave, and Kathrin Lambrix. Our gratitude to Yara Shahidi for elevating this project with her thoughtful performance on the audiobook and to Lisa Hintelmann in talent acquisition. A thank you to our Audible international partners, including Lauren Kuefner, Katja Keir, Beverly See, Zack Ross, Sophia Hilsman, Esther Bochner, Manny Miravete, Tatiana Solera, Paulo Lemgrubber, Pablo Bonne, Arantza Zunzunegui Salillas, Francesco Bono, Massimo Brioschi, Dorothea Martin, Lukas Kuntazschokunow, Eloise Elandaloussi, Neil Caldicott, and Stephanie McLernon-Davies.

Every superhero needs a solid HQ—so thank you to the team at Foundry Literary + Media for giving this project a place to hang its cape. A special thank you to Jessica Felleman for her editorial and contracts support, Klara Scholtz and Sasha Welm for their ongoing support, to controller Sara DeNobrega and assistant to the controller Sarah Lewis, a big thank you to foreign rights director Michael Nardullo and team members Claire Harris and Yona Levin, along with Foundry's foreign coagent team at the Riff Agency, Abner Stein, Andrew Nurnberg, La Nouvelle Agence, Mohrbooks, Read n' Right, Deborah Harris Agency, Italian Literary Agency, Tuttle Mori, KCC, Graal, MB Agencia, and Ackali Copyright. A thank you to director of Filmed Entertainment Richie Kern, along with special appreciation for the hard work of contracts director Deirdre Smerillo and team members Melissa Moorehead, Hayley Burdett, and Gary Smerillo.

Thank you to those brave early readers, all willing to be one of the first to venture into uncharted waters, no-doubt terrified by the sure Hobson's choice of enthusiastic love for the material or the louder-than-words email politely declining based on a scheduling conflict.

A heartfelt thank you to nontraditional retailers of fiction at comic bookstores, conventions, and anyone who welcomed a spinner rack into their storefront, you provided a home where any reader could discover favorite tales that have become our modern mythology. A tremendous thank you to traditional retailers of longform fiction for your enthusiasm for and support of a familiar voice in a new format. Thank you for being the bridge that this project needed.

Thank you to our families and friends for supporting us in bringing this project to fans.

And, of course, thank you to all of the True Believers and fans who continue to pass the torch with these fantastic, spectacular, amazing, and uncanny myths to the next generation of readers.

STAN LEE: STORYTELLER

The following are excerpts from a documentary made by Luke Lieberman for his New York University student documentary project. The video interview was conducted and recorded by Luke in midtown Manhattan on July 12, 2000, when Stan Lee was in New York for the premiere of the first X-Men *movie, which took place later that night on Ellis Island. This was the first time Luke met Stan, and it formed the beginning of his mentorship, which culminated in the two working together on* Alliances: A Trick of Light *many years later.*

*   *   *

STAN LEE: I was born Stanley Martin Lieber, and I changed my name to Stan Lee because, when I started writing, I didn't want to use my real name for these foolish comics. I was saving my real name for the great American novel that I never wrote. But after a while, so many people knew me as Stan Lee that I figured I might as well change it to Stan Lee.

LUKE LIEBERMAN: Are you happy with it?

SL: Nah, Stanley Martin Lieber was a much better name.

* * *

LL: Do you see comics as a popular form of mythology?

SL: Absolutely . . . Well, anything you write is a form of mythology, any ongoing series of anything. James Bond is a form of popular mythology, Tarzan was. And comic book mythology is just stories that have been told that last, that endure. James Bond may or may not endure. Tarzan has been enduring for a long time. Robin Hood has endured. Any stories that live, that's mythology.

* * *

LL: Who do you write your stories for?

SL: Oh. Me . . . I know what I like, what I want. I know what I would want to read. So I write the kind of stories that I would want to read, and I assume that I'm not that much different than a lot of other people. So, if I like them, there must be a lot of other people who have similar taste. But I would never try to write stories where I ignore my own taste and try to write something that others would like. So the way I wanted to do them was to flesh out the characters and make them more three-dimensional and try to get some really good motivation and characterization. And I think that's one of the things that helped.

* * *

I was doing the same thing over and over and over again, and my publisher wanted me to write down to young kids, and not use words of more than two syllables, and after a while it got boring. In 1960 I really wanted to quit. So I was going to quit, and I was going to tell them that I didn't want to do it. And my wife said, "Look, you want to quit anyway, why don't you do this superhero book? Do it the way you want to do it and get it out of your system. The worst that will happen is he'll fire you, but you want to quit, so what?" So that's when I did the Fantastic Four, and I did them the way I wanted to, and they sold very well. So he asked me to do another book, and I did The Hulk, and the rest is history.

*   *   *

It gave us a newer, older readership. Up until then, we hardly ever got fan mail, or if we got a fan letter, it would be something written in crayon by some kid who was four years old. But after a while, we started getting letters from older people — from high school kids, kids in college, from adults — and they were letters that said things like, "Yeah, I read that last issue and I thought such-and-such character was well portrayed, and I liked this and I liked that." Before we knew it, we had a huge readership in colleges, which made me very happy.

*   *   *

On interesting protagonists and antagonists:

SL: You keep [the protagonists] as realistic as possible and you give them personality traits that are somewhat colorful and that people would want to learn more about . . . Antagonists, same thing. It can't just be a guy who wants to do something bad just 'cause he wants to do something bad. You try to give him a rationale, you give him some motivation, and with anything you write, you try to make it a little bit different than all the other things that have been written. That's the hardest thing to do, you try to make your heroes unique, you try to make your villains unique in some way or other.

*　　*　　*

Characters that have flaws are much more interesting than characters who don't have them. I always felt that Superman wasn't that interesting because you knew he had no flaws. He couldn't be hurt, he couldn't be killed, he did everything right. Fine, but I'd rather read about a character that's more three-dimensional, and you always have to come up with a villain who the reader thinks will have a good chance of beating the hero, or else it isn't fun. The hero always has to look as though he doesn't have a chance.

*　　*　　*

[My characters] were more realistic. I'll give you an example. In a DC book, let's say *Superman,* if Superman saw a character walking down the street who was ten feet tall with purple skin, four arms, breathing fire, and a big tail swishing down its back, he might've said something like, "Oh, a creature from another world. I'd better catch him before he destroys the city." If one of my characters saw the same guy, he'd probably say, "Who's the nut in the Halloween costume? I wonder what he's advertising."

*　　*　　*

LL: What elements do you feel are crucial to a successful story?

SL: Well, all the things I was talking about: realism, characterization. But one thing that a story also needs: there has to be suspense, and you have to keep the reader's interest keyed up so he wants to keep turning the pages. The reader has to want to see what's gonna come next. It has to be like the expression . . . it has to be a "page-turner."

*　　*　　*

ll: How much of your personal life seeps into your stories?

sl: I never model any of my stories after myself or after anybody, but I think that every one of us is a product of all the things we've experienced, seen, read, and heard in our lives. So when I write, I'm not saying to myself, "Let's see, I'll write something based on what happened to me last month" or anything. I'm just trying to write new things. But I'm sure subconsciously I'm remembering things that happened. And it probably — those things probably become part of the story, but not on a conscious level.

* * *

ll: What do you think makes a good storyteller?

sl: Very simple: someone who can hold his audience's interest.

* * *

ll: How do you find a balance between doing something creative and artistic and doing something that's commercial?

sl: Well, I think I've always tried to think commercially. I think if you do a story that a large segment of the population will enjoy, it's going to be commercial. The only things that aren't commercial are things that fail, that don't make money. But when you write popular things that are enjoyed by a lot of people, it follows they're commercial successes.

ll: *Citizen Kane,* when it came out, no one liked it. It's still a great movie and —

sl: What you're talking about is taste. Maybe for some reason, people's taste at that time, they didn't like *Citizen Kane.* But it's like water seeks its own level: because it was a great movie, nothing could keep it down. It eventually surfaced. And it's the same with any good story. A good story will eventually be recognized by people, just like Van Gogh may not have been recognized as a great artist while he was alive, but eventually people knew it.

*   *   *

LL: How would someone who's just starting out go about getting their work noticed?

SL: What you're asking is the most difficult question in the world, and while this won't be a satisfactory answer, I think luck plays such a great part of it. There are people walking around today who nobody's ever heard of, who aren't making any money and are probably far more talented than half the people who are making money, but they haven't been lucky, they haven't been able to be discovered, or they didn't know how to do it — it could be a million reasons. I think perseverance is another thing. If you think you've got it, you mustn't give up. You gotta just keep working at it and hoping sooner or later someone will recognize what you've done.

*   *   *

LL: What did it mean to you to see a little boy with a Spider-Man backpack walk past you or to see the Spider-Man balloon at Macy's Thanksgiving Day Parade? Was there a moment when you reflected on your success?

SL: Well, believe it or not, it feels good when I think about it, but I really don't think about it, 'cause that was yesterday, and I have a habit, I'm always thinking of what I should be doing tomorrow and what I am doing today, and I'm always occupied with the next thing I'm doing. All of these other things — I did them, I'm glad people still remember them, but that's not what I'm doing now. So my mind isn't on it.

*   *   *

On the "Marvel Method":

SL: The Marvel Method was that I would give an outline to an artist and let him draw it any way he wanted. Then I would come back and fill in the copy. I found it worked well because the artist — if he was a good artist, if he could tell a good story in pictures (and all of our guys could) — could visualize each scene better than I could, because the other ones who have to draw it, they know how they can draw it the most interesting way. So when they finished drawing the strip, I was getting back the best that these guys could do. Then I'm looking at the pictures, and I'm writing the dialogue. Well, it's so much easier to write the dialogue when you see the character and you see the expression on his face. So I found it worked perfectly.

*   *   *

On the pitfalls of collaboration:

SL: Well, the only pitfall is if you collaborate with somebody who doesn't have the same vision as you do. If your collaborator wants to do something this way and you want to do it that way, it can't be a good collaboration. You both have to have the same objective, you have to have the same taste, you have to be following the same path. Beyond that, you make sure that the guy, if he's a songwriter and you're a lyricist, you make sure that you each like what the other one does. If you're a comic book writer and you want to team up with a comic book artist, you make sure that you like the way he draws, and you make sure that his art style will be right for the kind of story you're writing.

LL: What values of living do you think are the most important?

SL: I think one of them is honesty. I think you've got to be honest with yourself, you shouldn't kid yourself. And you have to be honest with other people, and you have to like other people. I tend to like everybody I meet. Somebody has to stab me in the back with a knife before I begin to think, "Maybe this guy doesn't like me." One thing I've always tried to do is work with people that I like, because when you work with people you like, and also whose talent you respect, it isn't like working. It's like playing with a bunch of your friends. When I go to the office during the day, I don't feel like I'm going to work. I'm going to have fun, because I like the guys I work with and we enjoy what we do. Some men go to the golf course, some play poker, I go to the office. It's the same thing. I'm with the guys and I'm having a good time.

LL: Why do you think honesty is important?

SL: Because if you're not honest, you'll never know where you're at, and other people won't know where they're at with you. Some people ruin their lives by doing things in their work . . . I know writers who are not very good writers, and it's obvious that they're not very good writers, but they won't admit that to themselves. And as far as I'm concerned, they're ruining their whole lives. They're going to waste their lives trying to write, and they really don't have much talent at it, and they might be great at other things. If only they were honest enough to say, "Gee, this really is lousy, why do I stay with it?"

I would love to be a singer. I love music, I love songs. I love the fact that great singers make a lot of money. But I know I can't sing! I'm not going to try to be, I'm not going to kid myself! I'm not good at it. So, I don't try.

I find that if you're with people, if you're working with people or socializing with them, and these people aren't honest, and you can't believe what they say, what's the fun of being with them? What's the point? Most of my friends, whatever they say, I believe them, I trust them implicitly. I don't have to wonder, "Did he really mean that?" or "What did he mean by that?" They're honest.

* * *

LL: It's rumored that when you're writing and creating, you often act out your stories.

SL: Well . . . I always wanted to be an actor, and I find myself subconsciously, when I'm writing dialogue, I start saying it out loud. So my wife would sometimes say, "Who're you talking to, Stan?" Nobody. And when I was writing Dr. Doom, one of our villains, I'd say, "You won't get away with it, Reed Richards," and I'd find myself saying it, unaware I was doing it.

When you say these things out loud, it gives you a feeling for whether the dialogue is good. Because if it doesn't sound good when you say it, then you know it isn't realistic. Another thing I used to do was when I was trying to show the artist how to draw things, I would act them out. Like when Jack Kirby first drew Dr. Doom, he just had him sitting in a chair a certain way. And I said, "Dr. Doom wouldn't just sit in a chair like that, he'd sit like this, because he's Dr. Doom!" If I wanted to show how a guy would walk or run, I would try to do it, I'd jump up on a table. Like I told you, it was never like I was working, it was like we were all playing.

LL: So it was pretty much like childhood?

SL: I guess, I guess.

*   *   *

LL: Can you advise young creators on how to protect themselves?

SL: It's a two-sided coin. It's true I didn't receive any of the money for these characters [I created]. But I was working on characters for twenty-five years before them which didn't get turned into movies, which never were huge successes. And all that time the publisher was paying the cost for putting out the books. If the books didn't sell, I still got my salary. He didn't take the money out of my salary. So when

I did things that succeeded, I felt that he was entitled, you know, to make whatever he could out of it. The only way a person today can make sure he has the rights to what he creates is to have an understanding before he brings what he's created to a producer or a publisher or whoever he brings it to. You gotta say, "Look, I've written this," or "I've drawn this," or "I've produced this. I would hope that you will produce it for me. But if you do, I want a contract that says I get a share of the profits." And you work it out. You have to do that in advance. You both have to agree to it. And more and more that's even happening in the comic book business . . . The artists are wising up. They won't give a publisher a new character unless the publisher says, "I'll give you a share of whatever we get."

* * *

LL: How do you bring a positive attitude to everything you make?

SL: I think I was born with a positive attitude. I always figure I can do it.